THE SC[illegible]

Kimberley Chambers lives in Romford and has [illegible] at various times, a disc jockey and a street trader. She is now a full-time writer and is the author of six previous novels.

Also by Kimberley Chambers

Billie Jo
Born Evil
The Betrayer
The Feud
The Traitor
The Victim

KIMBERLEY CHAMBERS

The Schemer

HARPER

Harper
An imprint of HarperCollins*Publishers*
77–85 Fulham Palace Road,
Hammersmith, London W6 8JB

www.harpercollins.co.uk

A Paperback Original 2012
2

A catalogue record for this book
is available from the British Library

ISBN: 978-0-00-743501-2

Set in Sabon by Palimpsest Book Production Limited,
Falkirk, Stirlingshire

Printed and bound in Great Britain by
Clays Ltd, St Ives plc

MIX
Paper from
responsible sources
FSC™ C007454

FSC™ is a non-profit international organisation established to promote
the responsible management of the world's forests. Products carrying the
FSC label are independently certified to assure consumers that they come
from forests that are managed to meet the social, economic and
ecological needs of present and future generations,
and other controlled sources.

Find out more about HarperCollins and the environment at
www.harpercollins.co.uk/green

In loving memory of
Helena Ann Lewis
1970–2011

Acknowledgments

Firstly, a massive thank you to my editor, Sarah Ritherdon, and the team at HarperCollins for the fabulous opportunity that I have been given.

As always, love and gratitude to my agent, Tim Bates, my typist, Sue Cox, and Rosie de Courcy.

I would like to thank all the readers of my books for all your fantastic support, messages, reviews, etc.

And last but not least, a special thank you to my dear friend, Lady Heller. Thanks for the quote, sweetheart, with love from your posh pal, The Duchess!!

'Violence does, in truth, recoil upon the violent, and the schemer falls into the pit which he digs for another . . .'

Sir Arthur Conan Doyle,
'The Adventure of the Speckled Band'

Prologue

The woman sat on the deck sipping a glass of vintage champagne. The weather was glorious and the heavenly smell of the ocean always had a calming effect on her. As the man reappeared, the woman smiled at him lovingly. Usually when they sailed their boat, they brought friends along with them, but today the man had insisted they sail alone. 'I wanted it to be just the two of us for once; that's why I never told you we were going out on the boat until this morning. I wanted to surprise you and spoil you rotten.'

And surprised and spoilt rotten the woman had been. Mussels in garlic butter, salmon en croûte, strawberries and cream were all prepared and served up for her by her wonderful man. She had a surprise for him also and, as soon as he sat back down, she would tell him what she had been dying to tell him for weeks.

'Come over 'ere, babe, and look at this,' the man said, gesticulating for the woman to join him.

The woman walked over to the right-hand side of the boat and put her arms around the man's toned, suntanned waist. 'I can't see nothing. What am I meant to be looking at?' she asked, rather bemused.

Knowing it was now or never, the man forcefully grabbed

the woman by the shoulders, and swung her around so that her back was positioned against the gunwale. 'I'm sorry, but me and you are over. I don't love you any more and I'm going back to England.'

'Stop mucking about. You're not funny,' the woman said, with a hint of panic in her voice.

'I ain't fucking mucking about,' the man replied, as he put one hand around the woman's throat and used his other to lift her up by the crotch.

'Please God no! Why would you want to do this to me? Why?' the woman screamed, as her feet left the safety of the deck.

'Because you know too much about me,' the man replied, his face devoid of emotion. With one last movement, he threw her to the mercy of the sharks. The last words he heard her scream were, 'I'm pregnant.' Putting his hands over his ears so he didn't have to listen to anything else she might yell out, the man then calmly returned to the helm.

CHAPTER ONE

1983

Stephanie Crouch's stomach was full of butterflies as she marched up Dagenham Heathway hill towards the train station. It had taken her ages to decide what to wear, but she was happy with her choice of denim pedal-pushers, a *Flashdance*-inspired ripped grey sweatshirt and gold pump ballet shoes. Not only did she look trendy, but felt comfortable as well.

'Hurry up, Tam. You're walking as fast as a tortoise,' Stephanie complained to her best friend.

Tammy Andrews stopped dead in her tracks. The stereo system she was carrying on her shoulder had all but broken her back. 'Sod you, Steph. You can carry it the rest of the way yourself. I ain't one of them donkeys, you know.'

Laughing, Steph handed her pal the carrier bag of goodies they'd purchased earlier and relieved her of her burden.

'Why did you drag us up 'ere so early anyway? You know he don't get back till about six and it's only half four. We should have drank our cider in the park and then come up 'ere. My mum will kill me if anyone she knows catches me drinking and smoking.'

Ignoring her friend's concerns, Stephanie stood outside the station and planned her next move. She knew that Wayne Jackman went to every West Ham home game and she knew he arrived back at Dagenham Heathway at approximately six o'clock. 'I don't want him to think we're waiting for him, so I think we should sit opposite the station. He lives in Digby Gardens, so he's bound to cross the road,' Steph said, confidently.

Unlike Stephanie, Tammy was no fan of Wayne Jackman, the school heart-throb. Wayne, who was usually referred to as Jacko, was in the year above them at Dagenham Priory. Although Tammy had never spoken to him on a one-to-one basis, she'd seen and heard enough about him to know that he was bad news. He might be breathtakingly good looking with his blond hair and piercing blue eyes, but he was also flash, blatantly loved himself and had a reputation of being a bit of a bully.

Holding the stereo system between them, the girls strolled across the pedestrian crossing, sat down on the pavement outside a shop and delved into their bag of goodies. Neither came from wealthy families, so the three pounds they both received as pocket money every week was pooled together at the weekend to ensure they had a good time. Strongbow cider, twenty Embassy Number One, two packets of Hubba Bubba bubble gum, chips and magazines was all they ever treated themselves to.

Stephanie pressed the play button on the stereo and ignored the disapproving looks of passers-by as the music blared out of the speakers.

'I hate this shit music,' Tammy complained.

Stephanie laughed. Whereas she was deemed very attractive, Tammy was classed as the opposite. Fairly plump with reddish-gingery hair, most of the lads at school took the piss out of Tammy. Her nickname was Tampax or ginger minge, but Stephanie adored her best friend. In Steph's eyes, she was beautiful, loving and extremely funny.

Singing at the top of her voice to New Edition's 'Candy Girl' Steph handed her friend the fags and matches while she opened a bottle of cider.

'I bought a tape with me with "Baby Jane" on it. Can't we put that on, Steph?'

Stephanie shook her head vehemently. Wayne Jackman was a casual and was always dressed in designer tracksuits. He even owned a real Burberry jacket and he certainly wouldn't be impressed if he walked out of the station and heard the dulcet tones of Rod Stewart blaring out.

'You can put "Baby Jane" on when he's gone. Casuals like soul music, Tam, and I don't wanna put him off me.'

Tammy sighed. Ever since Wayne Jackman had last week wolf-whistled at Stephanie in the alleyway that led from the upper to the lower school, Steph had spoken of little else. 'Why don't you just ask him out? I'll do it for you if you like,' Tammy suggested.

Stephanie immediately shook her head. 'No! I'm gonna wait for him to ask me out.'

'Hide that cider, quick. One of my mum's mates is crossing the road,' Tammy hissed.

Stephanie put the cider back in the carrier bag, turned around and checked her hair in the reflection of the shop window. She'd recently grown her hair long and had begged her mum to let her have one of the shaggy perms that were currently all the rage. 'No. We can't afford it and you're far too young to be putting silly substances on your hair. Don't wanna go bald before you're twenty, do you?' her mum had told her yet again this morning.

Annoyed at not being allowed to have the perm she craved, Stephanie had created her own shaggy look. Instead of blow-drying her hair straight like she usually did, Steph had towel-dried it so it looked as if she'd just got out of bed, then plastered it with lacquer to make it stand on end.

'I hope Wayne likes my hair like this. Do you reckon he'll like it? Or do you think he'll prefer it the other way?'

Turning her head so that her mum's friend wouldn't stop for a chat, Tammy glared at her friend. 'You're really doing my head in now, Steph. Light me a snout and give me a bottle of that cider. If I don't chill out, I'm gonna scream.'

Pamela Crouch picked up the cloth, squeezed the excess water back into the bucket, then proudly set to work on cleaning her front door. Unlike some of her frowsy neighbours, Pam had been born and bred in the East End of London, where pride in the cleanliness of one's abode was of the utmost importance. Dagenham was different. People's standards here were lower than in good old Mile End.

Thinking of her dear old mum's strict values, Pam smiled sadly. It would be a year next week since the cancer had so cruelly taken her wonderful mother away from her, and Pam still thought about her each and every day.

'Pam, the old slapper's on her way home. Got a big black man with her today she has.'

Pam dropped her cloth and ran over to the garden fence to greet her next-door neighbour, Cathy. Like herself, Cathy was originally from the East End and, over the ten years they'd been neighbours, their friendship had grown from strength to strength. 'I can't see her,' she said, looking from left to right.

'She was in Sainsbury's. You should of seen the trolley-load of drink she had. The black man was definitely with her, I saw him put his hand on her arse. She must be on her way home with the booze. Where else would she take it?'

Pam shook her head in disgust. Ever since the old slapper had recently moved into the house opposite, she had been her and Cath's main topic of conversation. Marlene was her name, and the only other bit of information they could find out about her was that she'd lived in Bethnal Green before moving to Dagenham. It wasn't just the number of men Pam and Cath had seen visit the house that had earned Marlene her nickname. It was the over-the-top way she dressed, her snooty, up-her-own-arse attitude, her pregnant fifteen-year-old daughter, and the fact that she had old bits of sheet hanging in her windows rather than proper curtains.

'Ere she comes, look. I can't believe she's got the front to walk about dressed like a film star, yet she's got rotten old sheets for curtains. Talk about all fur coat and no knickers,' Cathy said, bluntly.

Pam surreptitiously glanced at Marlene and the black man. 'I bet he's a Ford worker. Probably got some poor unsuspecting wife tucked away somewhere,' she whispered.

Cathy's lip curled up. Her old man had got one of the barmaids in East Ham Working Man's Club pregnant, hence their messy divorce. Clocking the hatred towards Marlene on Cathy's face, Pam linked arms with her. 'Come on, let's go indoors and have a nice cuppa, shall we? I've got some cream cakes if you fancy one?'

'Let me pop in mine and sort my Michael's dinner out first. I'll give you a knock in about a half-hour or so,' Cath replied.

Pam shut the front door, made a pot of tea and plonked herself down on the armchair to rest her tired legs. She was only thirty-five, but life hadn't been kind to her and she sometimes felt twenty years older. At five foot one, Pam had always had an enormous appetite and had never been the slimmest of women, but since her husband had died, she'd gorged day and night just for comfort. Bringing up two daughters alone wasn't easy, and even though she now had a job in a bakery, money was still scarce. David's death had been a terrible shock at the time. He'd only been working as a steel erector for a month, when the police had knocked on Pam's door and informed her of his accident. She'd dashed straight up the hospital, but after falling from thirty foot of scaffolding, David had never regained consciousness. Her daughters Stephanie and Angela had both adored their father, and telling them the awful news was the most difficult thing Pam had ever had to do. Thankfully, at four and three years old respectively, the girls had been far too young to understand the enormity of what had happened and had just accepted the news of David's death as children that age tend to do.

Glancing at the picture of her mum on the mantelpiece, Pam sighed. Her wonderful mother, Ada, was the only person who had truly helped her cope after David's death. A matriarch East Ender, she had sort of taken over in her own way, and had been there for Pam and the kids whenever she'd been called upon. Losing her mum to cancer was horrendous for Pam. Her dad, Arnold, was still alive, but he was a simple man who had no idea how to cope with Linda's wants and needs. Linda was Pam's only sister and had sadly been born with dwarfism. Under the circumstances, Linda had led life to the full. She had attended mainstream schools, had always worked, and had much more of a social life than Pam had herself. However, her mum had always worried about Linda's welfare and had made Pam promise that if anything happened to her, she would look after her younger sister. A woman of her word, Pam had stuck to her promise. She had turfed Angela out of her bedroom and made her share with Steph, then Linda had moved into Angela's old room. Her daughters weren't happy about the sharing situation. They'd always got on fairly well as young children, but now they argued like cat and dog.

Pam was jolted back to reality by the arrival of her youngest daughter.

'Where's my shiny black leggings, Mum? Did you get 'em dry for me?'

Pam felt awful as she leapt out of the armchair. She had totally forgotten to wash the leggings and, unlike Steph who was little trouble at all, Angie was a demanding little cow at times. 'Oh, I'm so sorry, love. I've been so busy all day, it slipped my mind. Shall I rinse 'em through now for you?

Angela Crouch looked at her mother in complete and utter disbelief. One thing she had asked her to do, one small thing, and she couldn't even manage that. 'Don't bother! I'll have to wear them dirty. I bet if Steph had asked you to wash her leggings, you wouldn't have forgotten, would you?'

'Yes, I would have! Why don't you wear your white ones I bought you down the Sunday market?' Pam asked, with an apologetic tone to her voice.

'Because they ain't black and they ain't shiny Lycra. This is the most important night of my life, Mum, and thanks to you it's ruined now.' Angela stomped out the room. In her eyes, her Miss Goody Two Shoes of a sister was the apple of her mother's eye. Steph was the well-behaved, clever one who got great school reports. For years Angie had had to listen to her mum bigging Steph up to anyone who would care to listen, while the only mention she ever got was for underachieving or misbehaving.

Feeling second best did not suit Angela one little bit and it had made her harbour a secret hatred for her sister. She longed for Steph to slip up and dash her mother's dreams of grandeur. That would be hilarious.

Slamming her bedroom door, Angela walked over to her sister's bed. Unlike Angela, who had posters of her favourite popstars on the wall that her headboard rested against,

Stephanie had a photo of herself and their deceased father. Angie stared at it, then casually took her nail scissors out of her make-up bag. She snipped the string and smiled as she heard the sound of breaking glass.

Stephanie Crouch felt her body shaking with pure lust as Wayne Jackman stood outside Dagenham Heathway Station chatting to some pals. Dressed in a striking blue Fila tracksuit and white Adidas trainers, Wayne looked the absolute nuts, and Steph was aware of the glances he was attracting from other girls.

'Don't his hair look cool? I think he's got Brylcreem or something on it today. It don't look as blond as it does in school, does it? Do you reckon he's dyed it? Or, do you reckon it's the product he's used that's making it look darker?'

Bored shitless, and positive that Wayne didn't bathe and his hair was just greasy, Tammy Andrews ignored her friend's stupid questions and turned the volume on the stereo up.

'Quick, he's coming. Rewind it to Shalamar "A Night to Remember" while I light the snout up,' Steph said, with a hint of panic in her voice. She needed Wayne to see her drinking and smoking, otherwise he might just see her as some silly schoolgirl.

Tammy watched in amazement as Wayne and his two mates crossed the road and sauntered past her and Angela as though they didn't exist. 'Well, say something then. He ain't gonna notice you if you sit there like a tailor's dummy, is he?' she spat at Steph.

Overcome by nerves, Steph had all but lost her voice. 'I can't think of nothing to say,' she croaked, her mind completely blank.

Furious that they'd wasted hours dossing about up the Heathway when they could have been having a laugh with the lads over the park, Tammy stood up. 'Oi, Jacko,' she shouted out.

'Stop it! What you doing?' Steph squirmed, pulling at her friend's sleeve.

'Whaddya want?' Wayne asked, as he casually approached Tammy with his hands dug deep in his tracksuit pockets. His best pals, Mark Potter and Chris Cook, stood beside Wayne like two bodyguards.

'We wondered if yous wanted to meet us over the park tonight. There's a party over there and loads of us are going. We're all gonna get smashed, ain't we, Steph?' Tammy said, trying to sound cool.

'It all depends if you're gonna let us have a feel around that ginger minge of yours,' Mark Potter said, chuckling.

'You don't wanna feel round there. They don't call her Tampax for nothing, you know,' Chris Cook chipped in.

'You're such a wanker, Cooksie,' Wayne said, laughing. None of the lads called one another by their first names. Jacko, Potter and Cooksie sounded far more hip than Wayne, Mark and Chris.

When Wayne knelt down beside her, Stephanie's face reddened to a similar colour as Tammy's hair.

'Gonna offer me some of that cider, sexy?' he asked.

Hands shaking, Steph passed him the bottle she was holding.

'Gissa fag. Potter will have one an' all,' Cooksie said to Tammy.

Annoyed at the way the boys had taken the piss out of her, Tammy shook her head. 'We've only got six left and they've gotta last us all night,' she replied, haughtily.

'We've only got six left and they've got to last us all night,' Cooksie chanted, mimicking Tammy's voice.

Ignoring his pal's laughter, Wayne winked at Steph. He could tell how much she fancied him. He had the same effect on most girls, and he loved playing on his attractiveness and winding them up. 'So, why did you really call us over here? Did you wanna ask me something?' Wayne asked, staring at Steph intently with his piercing blue eyes.

Feeling as though she was about to faint, Steph shook her head frantically. Letting Wayne know that she fancied him was totally out of the question, so she had no option other than to lie. 'Tammy wanted to call you over. She fancies Potter,' Steph blurted out.

'You lying cow! I heard that and I do not fancy Potter. The reason we called you over is because Steph's got the hots for you, Jacko. Been doing my head in ever since you whistled at her in the alley. All I hear is Wayne this and Wayne that, so on Steph's behalf, will you go out with her?'

When Potter and Cooksie burst out laughing, Stephanie hung her head in shame. She'd experienced some embarrassing times in her life, none more so than when she'd fallen off the stage dressed as Rizzo out of *Grease* during her school play, but this beat that cringeworthy moment hands down.

Wayne chuckled. He could sense Stephanie's humiliation and was rather enjoying the enormous effect he was having on her. 'So, you wanna go out with me?' he asked, with a wicked twinkle in his eyes.

Stephanie shrugged. 'Yeah, I suppose so,' she replied, in almost a whisper.

Wayne grinned at Potter and Cooksie, then turned his attention back to Steph. 'Ask me properly and I'll see what I can do for you.'

Stephanie glanced at Tammy. This was all her bloody fault. 'Will you go out with me?' she mumbled, unable to look Wayne in the eye.

'Sorry, still can't hear you properly,' he replied, cockily.

Knowing it was shit-or-bust time, Steph decided to stand

up and brave it. Wayne must fancy her as much as she fancied him, else why would he want her to ask him out in the first place? 'Will you go out with me, Jacko?' she asked, boldly.

Wayne ran his hand through his trendy wedge haircut and smirked at his pals. 'I can't I'm afraid, darling. I've already got a bird and I've gotta dash now as I'm gonna be late meeting her. See you around, Steph.'

When Potter and Cooksie burst out laughing, Steph's eyes filled up with tears. Wayne Jackman had made her look a complete and utter idiot and she knew she'd be a laughing stock at school on Monday morning.

As the lads walked away in high spirits, Tammy tried to hug her best friend. 'Jacko's an arsehole, you're worth a hundred of him, Steph,' she said, truthfully.

Feeling both furious and degraded, Steph violently pushed Tammy away. 'This is all your fault. If you hadn't opened your big mouth, none of this would have happened. I hate you Tammy Andrews, and I never want to see you again.'

Bursting into a flood of uncontrollable tears, Stephanie picked up her purse and ran off as fast as she could.

With little money left every week out of their wages, Pam and Cathy did virtually all their socializing indoors. Neither women were big drinkers, but most Saturday nights they liked to share a bottle of Liebfraumilch between them. Sunday was the only day that neither woman worked, so it was nice to let their hair down a bit.

'How's the café been this week? Busy?' Pam asked her friend.

'Yeah, not bad. We keep attracting a crowd of school-kids though. The little sods are bunking off from the Priory, I think. Bleedin' nuisance they are.'

Pam chuckled. Cathy worked in a café in Broad Street

Market, which was only a spit's throw from their homes in Manning Road.

'What about you? How's the eating-in idea working out?' Cath asked, as she opened the bottle of wine.

Pam worked in a bakery in Dagenham East that had recently expanded and started an eating-in service.

'It's really begun to take off now. We've even started selling cooked breakfasts and jacket potatoes,' Pam said, excitedly. She was hoping the extra business would give her a much-needed pay rise.

'Quick, come 'ere. There's a blue van just pulled up outside the old slapper's with an old boy and a young fella in it,' Cath exclaimed.

'Someone's moving in by the looks of that mattress. I saw the black man leave about half an hour ago. Surely she ain't got another victim already?' Pam said, laughing.

'Well, it can't be the young one, he's younger than my Michael. She's gotta be moving the old boy in, surely?' Cath said, bemused.

'How is your Michael? I ain't seen him for ages. Still loved-up, is he?'

Unable to take her eyes away from the window in case she missed anything worth noting, Cath nodded her head. Her eldest son, Pete, had recently got married, and now it looked as though her youngest was about to fly the nest too.

'Only comes home to bring his washing back and stuff his face now. She's a nice girl, that Jane he's with, but I wish she didn't already have a kid. I reckon he'll move in with her soon, but I do worry about him, Pam. I mean, taking on another man's child ain't ideal, is it? And I've just found out the father of the kid is in prison. It's times like this I rue the day I moved to Dagenham, mate. If I had put me foot down with that philandering bastard of a husband of mine and insisted on staying in Poplar, my Michael wouldn't have even met this bleedin' bird.'

Pam nodded understandingly. Both her and Cathy's husbands had been born and bred in Barking, which was why they had ended up with council houses under Barking and Dagenham council. In Pam's case, her David had insisted Dagenham was a nicer area to raise children than the East End, but Pam had never been truly happy living there. She missed the old estate she had lived on and her frequent trips to Roman Road market. The pie-and-mash shops in Dagenham were rotten, in Pam's opinion, and not a patch on Kelly's up the Roman.

'Your Steph's home, looks upset she does,' Cathy warned her friend.

Pam ran out into the hallway to greet her eldest daughter. It was very unusual for Steph to arrive home before her weekend ten o'clock curfew, so she knew something must be wrong. 'Whatever's the matter?' she asked, clocking her daughter's tear-stained face.

'Nothing. Leave me alone,' Steph replied, trying to duck past her mother so she could run up the stairs.

Petrified that her daughter had been attacked, or even worse, Pam grabbed hold of Stephanie's shoulders. 'You ain't going nowhere, young lady, until you tell me what's happened. Has someone touched you?'

Collapsing into Pam's arms, Steph cried more tears than she'd ever cried before.

Unaware of the drama that was currently going on downstairs, Angela Crouch had got over her earlier sulk and was now thoroughly looking forward to her big night out. Unlike her sister, Steph, Angie had been into boys from a very young age. At ten, she'd had her very first French kiss and at twelve she had let Gary Ratcliffe tit her up, the Dagenham term for touching someone's breasts. However, even though she'd had plenty of boyfriends, Angie had never been in love before, not until now, anyway.

Turning the music up to Kool and the Gang's 'Get Down On It', Angela stood in front of the mirror singing into her hairbrush. Even though both she and her sister had always been called pretty, Angela knew she knocked spots off Steph in that department. Angie was twenty months younger than her sister and shorter in height, but knew she looked older. 'Get down on it, suck my helmet,' Angie sang, flicking her hair over her shoulders seductively. Her new boyfriend had taught her the rude lyrics to the song and Angie thought they were hilarious. Glancing at the Swatch watch her mum had recently bought her for her thirteenth birthday, Angie took the needle off the record. She'd arranged to meet her boyfriend at 7.30 outside the Princess Bowling Alley along the A13, and she didn't want to be late.

'What's a matter with you?' she asked, as her sister barged into the room and threw herself onto her bed face downwards.

'Don't ask! I ain't going a school Monday. I've asked Mum to find me a new school 'cause I ain't never going back to Priory again,' Steph wept.

Whereas she herself could turn on the waterworks on a regular basis just to get her own way, Angie had rarely seen Steph as upset before. She sat on the bed next to her, hoping that something bad had happened. 'What's up? I dunno what happened to your photo by the way. I was doing my make-up and it fell on the floor. I reckon the string must have snapped.'

'Sod the photo. I've fallen out with Tammy and I've made a complete fool of myself over a boy. I am such a fucking idiot, I hate myself.'

'Why have you fallen out with Tam?' Angie asked,

surprised. She knew how close her sister and Tammy Andrews were, and she had never known them to argue in all the years they'd known one another.

Needing to get the whole episode off her chest, Stephanie began at the beginning of the story and told her sister everything that had happened.

'But if you lied and said that Tammy fancied this boy's mate, then you can't blame her, Steph. It's you that's out of order. Who is the boy anyway? Why won't you tell me his name?'

'Because he goes to our school and I know what a big mouth you've got. Enough people are gonna find out what happened as it is, without you telling all your mates an' all,' Steph replied, truthfully.

'I won't say nothing, I promise. Tell me his name?' Angie asked, nosily. She was thoroughly enjoying her sister's despair and wanted to know more.

'Swear on Mum's life you won't tell anyone,' Steph said, solemnly.

When Angela crossed her heart with her right hand and repeated the oath, Steph sat up and squeezed her sister's hand. 'It was Wayne Jackman. He's in the fifth year, do you know him?'

The look on Angela's face immediately changed from a look of false concern to one of contorted rage. She snatched her hand away from her sister's and stood up. 'Wayne's my boyfriend, you slag!' she exclaimed.

Stephanie looked at her sister in pure amazement. Angela was only in the second year at Priory – she'd missed out on being in the year above because she had been born a week too late – so there was no way she could be dating Wayne, who was in the fifth year.

'You gotta be joking, Ange. Jacko wouldn't go out with a second-year girl. You sure you've got the right boy?'

With hatred in her bright green eyes, Angela glared at Stephanie. There was only one Wayne Jackman at Dagenham Priory, and not only was he gorgeous, but he belonged to her. 'I've told him I'm fifteen. I'm meeting him tonight, he's taking me to his mate's party in Beam Avenue. I swear, Steph, if you mess this up for me by telling him my real age, I'll never forgive you for it.'

'I won't say nothing, I promise, but he's gonna find out your age, Ange. How can he not? You go to the same school, you div.'

Putting her trendy beads on, Angela picked up her silver purse and pointed her forefinger nastily in her sister's face. 'That's for me to worry about, not you. I swear, Steph, if you ever say one word to him, I will fucking kill you.'

CHAPTER TWO

Stephanie spent all day Sunday moping about in her bedroom. Angela had flounced in and out a few times and, not wanting to face her sister, Steph had pretended she was asleep. Yesterday's heartbreak had now turned to rage, but Steph wasn't annoyed with her sister, she was angry with herself for acting like such an idiot. Wayne Jackman had humiliated her good and proper and, as Steph flicked through an old copy of *Jackie* Magazine, she vowed never to let another boy get the better of her again. If Wayne hadn't been dating her sister and had just let her down gently, she would probably still have been in love with him. Instead, she had managed to force herself to hate him overnight.

Refusing to eat her roast-lamb dinner by claiming she had a sore throat, Stephanie used the same lie on the Monday morning when her mum woke her up to go to school. Facing Wayne and his gloating pals was totally out of the question – she'd rather eat nails.

'Well, best you get that arse around that doctor's then and get yourself some antibiotics. You better not be trying to pull the wool over my eyes, young lady, because if I find out you're lying, I shall drag you into that school by your hair tomorrow,' Pam warned her daughter.

Stephanie waited until her mum had gone to work and her sister had gone to school before getting out of bed. She hadn't even had a wash or cleaned her teeth yesterday so, feeling filthy, she decided to run a bath. Turning the taps on, Steph went back into her bedroom and stared out of the window. The weather was dull and wet, just like her mood. Spotting a dark-haired boy leaning against Marlene's wall smoking a cigarette, Stephanie lifted the net curtain up slightly so she could get a better view of him. Steph was well aware that her mum and Cathy were obsessed with the coming and goings at Marlene's house, but surely this young boy wasn't her latest conquest?

Aware that the boy had spotted her staring at him, Stephanie let go of the curtain and quickly jumped back from the window. Boys were now vermin as far as she was concerned.

Tammy Andrews somehow got through her classes and, as the bell rang for home time, grabbed her schoolbag and ran through the corridors. Falling out with Steph had upset her greatly and she had to see her best friend to try and sort things out.

'Stop running, Andrews,' Tammy heard one of the teachers shout. She slowed down and, as she turned the corner, bumped straight into Wayne Jackman and his cronies.

'All right, Tampax. Where's your mate?' Mark Potter asked her.

'Can you get out of my way, please?' Tammy replied, glaring at the grinning buffoons.

'Tell Steph that I will go out with her, but only if she sucks me dick first,' Wayne said, laughing.

'Steph is worth a thousand of you, Jacko. Now get out my way before I grass you up to Mr Jones.'

Pushing past the lads, Tammy heard one of them refer to her as ginger minge. Furious that it was because of their idiocy that she and Steph had fallen out, Tammy turned around to face them again. 'You think you're so cool and hard, don't ya? Well you ain't. All three of you are complete knob-ends and you seriously need to grow up.'

Thrilled that she'd had the bottle to stand up to her and Steph's tormentors, Tammy ran towards her friend's house with a smile on her face.

'Steph, go round the shops and get me a carton of single cream. Lin'll be home soon and I'm cooking her her favourite,' Pam shouted up the stairs. She had rang the doctor's earlier to check that Steph had been to see him and, even though she had, Pam was still positive there was nothing physically wrong with her daughter.

Stephanie stomped down the stairs. 'But I thought Lin's favourite was chicken soup,' she said, sulkily.

'It is.'

'What do you need cream for then?'

Sick of the stroppy tone in her daughter's voice, Pam couldn't help but lose it as she handed her a fifty-pence piece. 'Because I put the cream in the bastard soup! I know there's sod all wrong with you, so get your arse round them shops before I really lose me rag. Oh, and tomorrow you're going back to school, like it or not, young lady.'

When Stephanie slammed the front door, Pam set to work on peeling the King Edwards. Her home-made soup was more like a chicken stew and Linda loved a big dollop of buttery mashed potato with it. Pam was pleased that Linda was now having an extremely fulfilling social life. In Pam's opinion her mother had always wrapped Linda in cotton wool and forbade her doing things that other women of her age liked to do. Since moving in with Pam, Linda's life had evolved somewhat. She now had a job working in the local Butterkist popcorn factory, had made plenty of friends there, and was always out with her workmates. This weekend was only Linda's second ever independent holiday. In April she had gone to a soul event in Caistor with her mates and this weekend had seen her trot off to Margate for a hen party.

'Hang on a minute,' Pam shouted, as she heard a loud banging on the door. She rinsed her hands under the tap, dried them on her apron and went to investigate.

'Is Steph there?' Tammy asked, nervously.

Unlike Angela's best friend, Chloe, who Pam had never really liked, Pam adored Tammy. 'Go and sit in the lounge, darling, and I'll make you a cuppa. She's only popped round the shop for me – she won't be long.'

Scuttling back into the kitchen to put the kettle on, Pam smiled. Her Stephanie was a strong kid, a chip off the old block, and Pam was positive that once Steph made things up with Tammy, she'd be back to her old jolly self again.

Walking down Broad Street, Stephanie had a strange feeling that she was being followed. She bent down to tie the lace of her trainer and furtively glanced behind her. She recognized the culprit immediately. It was the same lad she'd seen in Marlene's front garden earlier.

Grinning like a Cheshire cat, the boy broke into a jog and caught up with her. 'Hello. Barry Franklin's the name,' he said, holding out his right hand.

Stephanie felt her heart flutter as she stared into Barry's handsome face. He was tall and broad with big brown doleful eyes and a killer smile. 'I'm Steph. I've gotta go, me mum's asked me to get her some cream,' she mumbled, ignoring the handshake.

'I'll walk with you if you're going to the shop. I saw you come out your house. Just moved in opposite, I have, which makes us neighbours.'

Remembering her mum and Cath's conversations about

Marlene's hectic sex life, Steph decided to dig for gossip. 'Are you Marlene's new boyfriend?' she asked, seriously.

Barry Franklin burst out laughing. 'You're having a giraffe, ain't ya? Marlene's me muvver.'

'Tammy's here to see you, love. She's in the lounge,' Pam whispered, as she ran to the front door to greet her eldest daughter.

Stephanie handed her mum the carton of cream. She was secretly pleased that Tammy had made the effort to come round, but she didn't want to show it. 'Tell her to come up to me room,' she said, casually.

Thinking how much brighter her daughter looked since getting a bit of fresh air, Pam relayed the message.

Tammy cautiously opened her friend's bedroom door. She knew Angie wasn't at home as she'd dashed in, got changed, and shot out again about five minutes ago.

'I'm really sorry about the other day, Steph, but I swear I only told Jacko you wanted to go out with him because you lied and said it was me that fancied Potter.'

Stephanie smiled. 'And I'm sorry an' all. Are we mates again?'

Tammy hugged her friend and then told her how she had stood up for her and insulted Wayne and his mates.

'I wish I'd have seen their faces when you called them knob-ends,' Steph said, laughing.

'Their faces were a picture, mate. I mean, everyone's frightened of them 'cause they're meant to be the hardest fighters in the school, ain't they, but I showed 'em that we ain't scared.'

Steph nodded. 'I've got some major goss for you an' all. You know Wayne said he had a bird? You'll never guess who it is.'

Tammy reeled off half a dozen names then, sick of being

kept in suspense, begged Steph to tell her who the unlucky girl was.

'It's Angie,' Stephanie said.

'Angie who?'

'My sister, Angie.'

'No! Never! She's only just turned thirteen. Oh my God! What a pervert!' Tammy exclaimed.

'Apparently he don't know her age and he don't know she goes to our school. Can you imagine what a dickhead he'll feel when he finds out she's only in the second year?' Stephanie said.

'Where did she meet him? How long they been going out?' Tammy asked, excitedly. This was the juiciest bit of gossip she had heard in ages.

'I dunno. I felt a right div when she first told me, as you can imagine, but I'm over it now, so I'll find out more tonight.'

'I can't wait until the whole school finds out Jacko is some noncey cradle snatcher. Talk about spoil his street cred. He is gonna well get the piss taken out of him when everyone finds out,' Tammy said, grabbing Steph by the hands and forcing her to dance. 'Jacko is a pervert, Jacko is a pervert, la la la la, la la la la,' she sang to the tune of the Conga.

Stephanie reluctantly joined in. She would have laughed her head off if Wayne had been dating any other thirteen-year-old girl, but seeing as it was her own flesh and blood, she couldn't help but worry. Angela might be a stroppy little cow at times, but Steph would always love her dearly.

Cath let herself into Pam's house with her own key. Both women had front- and back-door keys to one another's houses, therefore never bothered to knock.

'And where's that dirty stop-out?' Cath shouted out.

'She ain't bleedin' home yet. Rang me from a callbox, she did. Her and the girls are having a couple of drinks in the Trades Hall apparently. All right for some, ain't it?'

Cathy laughed. She liked Linda immensely and admired her greatly for not letting dwarfism stand in her way. 'I treated us to a bottle of Liebfraumilch out me tips,' Cath said, handing the bottle to Pam.

'But it's only Monday. We won't get up for work tomorrow if we drink that,' Pam complained.

'You'll never guess what,' Cath said, excitedly.

'What?'

'I bumped into Lairy Mary up the Heathway today and she reckons the father of the old slapper's kids is some East End gangster called Smasher Franklin.'

Pam clapped her hands in delight. 'No! I always knew she looked like a gangster's moll. Oh sod it, let's open that bloody bottle of wine after all.'

Wayne Jackman put his hands on Angela Crouch's buttocks and thrust his erection against her midriff. He really did like Angie; she reminded him facially of a young Samantha Fox, but on the downside he found her very childish at times and her parents' strictness drove him bonkers. 'Don't go home yet, it's only seven,' he begged her.

'I've gotta go home. My aunt's coming round for dinner and my mum and dad will kill me if I'm late,' Angela lied. She'd had to pretend that her dad was a big thug and still alive because Wayne kept insisting on walking her home. She'd also conveniently forgotten to mention that her Auntie Linda lived with them and was also a dwarf.

Wayne sighed. He had been sexually active for over a year now and Angela's failure to participate in his favourite hobby was enough to send his frustration to another level.

'Look, I know you're frightened of your dad and you

can't stay out late, so what about me and you bunking off school tomorrow? I'll get us some booze and we can listen to records in my bedroom and stuff.'

'I can't. My mum will kill me if she finds out I ain't gone to school,' Angela replied nervously. She knew sitting in Wayne's bedroom would mean some serious kind of physical contact and she wasn't quite ready for anything like that yet.

Wayne moved his body away from Angela's and lit up a cigarette. 'I think me and you should finish,' he said, hoping his callous statement would have the desired effect.

'I don't wanna finish. Please don't pack me up, Jacko, please,' Angela begged, tears in her eyes.

'I'll be outside the Princess Bowl at half eight tomorrow morning. If you turn up, you're still me girlfriend, and if you don't, we're finished.'

Aware that Angela was now in floods of tears, Wayne smirked and walked away.

Back in Manning Road, Stephanie was telling Tammy about her encounter with Barry Franklin. 'He swears that he's starting our school tomorrow and he reckons he's gonna be in our class. I don't believe him though, Tam. He seemed a bit of a joker, so I bet he was just winding me up.'

'So what does he look like?' Tammy asked.

'He is quite good looking. I think you'd quite like him, Tam, but he definitely ain't my type. I'm off boys anyway. Just gonna concentrate on me school work from now on. I'll never get a good job in a bank or office in London if I don't pass me exams.'

Tammy nodded understandingly. She was also determined to do well in her exams as she wanted a better life for herself. Many a time she and Steph had discussed living in big houses in a posh area and having unlimited funds to shop for clothes and make-up.

Hearing a knock on her bedroom door, Stephanie turned off the dulcet tones of Kid Creole and the Coconuts. 'What?' she yelled.

'Lin's home now, we're gonna eat in a minute. Does Tammy want to stay for dinner?'

'Yes please, Mrs Crouch,' Tammy shouted out. Unlike her own mum, Stephanie's was a great cook.

'Best you come downstairs and ring your mother then,' Pam ordered.

Stephanie ran downstairs and gave her Auntie Linda a big hug. Unlike her sister, who was embarrassed over their aunt's lack of height, Steph adored having Lin living with them. At twenty-nine, Lin was six years younger than her mum. Steph loved her company and treated her more like an older sister than an aunt.

'How'd you get on, Lin? Didn't get drunk and flash at the men again, did ya?'

Linda chuckled. The last time she'd gone away with the girls to Caister they'd travelled by minibus, and on the way there Lin and two of her pals had flashed their bums at a coach-load full of blokes.

'No, I didn't do a moony. In fact I was the perfect lady,' Lin replied, with a naughty twinkle in her eye.

Cathy went out into the kitchen to help Pam bring the plates in. 'Where's Angie?' she asked.

'Christ knows! She promised she would be home by seven. I'm sure the little cow's got a new boyfriend. Been very secretive lately, she has, and I can read her like a bleedin' book.'

'Speak of the devil,' Cath whispered, as the front door opened.

'Where you been? You're over half hour late,' Pam yelled at her youngest daughter.

Visibly upset, Angela ignored her mother and ran straight up the stairs.

'Go and have a word with her, Steph. Find out what's wrong,' Pam shouted out.

'Come and stand outside the bedroom door,' Steph whispered to Tammy.

'What's up, sis?' Stephanie asked, entering their bedroom.

'What do you care?' Angie replied, wiping her eyes with her cuff.

'Of course I care. I am your sister.'

'It's Jacko. He's got the hump with me because I can never stay out that late. I think he might finish with me.'

When her sister let out a heartbroken sob, Stephanie actually felt very sorry for her. 'Where did you meet him, Ange?' she asked, hugging her little sister.

'In the bowling alley at the Chequers. I've told him so many lies, and if he finds out I know he'll pack me up.'

'What exactly have you told him, then?'

'I've told him I'm fifteen and I'm in the fifth year at Parsloes Manor. I've also told him that our dad's still alive and he beats me up if I'm late home or I date boys.'

'What!' Stephanie exclaimed incredulously. Angie lying about her age was understandable, but pretending their poor deceased father was still alive and darkening his name by calling him a violent bully was despicably low, even by Angela's standards.

'You know Dad was a decent man, so how can you say such bad things about him?'

'I only know what Mum's told me about him. I don't even remember the man. Anyway, Jacko thinks my surname is Marshall, so he ain't gonna know I'm talking about our dad, is he?' Angela replied, abruptly.

'You might as well just tell him the truth, Ange, because he's bound to spot you in school at some point.'

'No, he won't. All his lessons are in the upper school and mine are in the lower,' Angela said, confidently.

Stephanie shrugged. 'You coming down for some dinner? Lin's home.'

'No, I'm on a diet. Can you do me a favour, Steph? But I need you to swear you won't say nothing to Mum.'

'I promise I won't tell Mum.'

'I'm bunking off school tomorrow to spend the day with Jacko and I need you to write me a note and sign it with Mum's signature.'

'No way! Mum will kill both of us if she finds out,' Stephanie said, truthfully.

'But she won't find out, will she? Please Steph, you're the only one I know who can copy her handwriting – and I covered for you when you got caught at the fair.'

Stephanie debated what to do for the best. Angie was right about covering for her. Steph had sneaked off to the fair, got spotted by Lairy Mary, and Angela had sworn blind to their mum that they had been at the pictures together that day. Thankfully, their mother had believed Angie.

'OK, I'll do it, but only this once. Where you going with Jacko? You ain't going round his house, are you?'

'No, we're gonna get a bus into Romford and hang around the shops,' Angela lied.

'Just be careful,' Steph replied, as she left the room and shut the bedroom door.

'She is such a little bitch. How you suffer her I will never know,' Tammy whispered as the girls went back downstairs.

'She's only young,' Stephanie replied, protectively.

'Yeah, but she is such a nasty piece of work. Surely you must realize that?'

Not wanting to slag off her own flesh and blood, Stephanie shrugged. 'Whatever she is, Tam, Angie is still my sister and I will always love her no matter what.'

CHAPTER THREE

Angela Crouch was unsure if she felt excited or petrified as she stuffed some clothes and make-up into her schoolbag. Dagenham Priory had only just introduced a uniform policy for the younger pupils, and while Steph was still allowed to attend school in her own clothes, Angela unfortunately wasn't.

'What am I gonna do if Jacko looks in my bag and sees my uniform, Steph?' she asked, with panic in her voice.

'Don't put your bag down. You've no need to if you're walking round Romford, have you?' Stephanie replied, suspiciously. She had a gut feeling her sister was lying about where she and Wayne were supposedly going to.

'Please walk to the Heathway with me, Steph. I'll quickly get changed in the bogs, then you can take my bag to school with you.'

'I ain't lugging your poxy bag about with me all day. It's bad enough I've gotta forge you a note from Mum,' Stephanie said, angrily.

Angela had a habit of being nice to her sister when she wanted a favour in return. 'Please Steph, I beg you. I'd do it for you. What about that time I stole that lipstick out of Boots for you because you were too frightened to nick it yourself? I'd do anything for you, you know I would.'

Staring at the look of innocence in her younger sister's eyes, Stephanie smiled at her. 'All right, I'll take the poxy bag, but get your arse in gear 'cause I don't wanna be late for school. Your lies will get you into big trouble one day, Ange, you mark my words.'

Wayne Jackman shuddered as he got into the tide-marked, stained bath. His nan had obviously forgotten to put the immersion heater on again and the water felt like ice.

Wayne had been brought up in Bonner Street, Bethnal Green. He was the only son of his parents, Jill and Lenny, and had two younger sisters, Lucy and Samantha. Wayne's childhood was anything but perfect. His dad was always in and out of prison, and money was scarce, but he'd been happy in his own little way. One day in 1978, life had changed dramatically for Wayne when he'd arrived home one evening to find his house cordoned off. His dad had recently been released from Pentonville after serving a three-year sentence for GBH and, seeing as how the police had raided his house in the past, Wayne's first thought was that his dad had done something bad again.

'I live here. Let me see my mum,' Wayne had screamed on the evening in question, trying to barge his way through the crowd of coppers.

It had been Jean, his next-door neighbour who had tearfully broken the news to him. His mother had been stabbed to death by his own father. Months later, Wayne learned the reason behind his father's actions: his mother had been having an affair while he'd been in prison, and had got pregnant by the man he knew as Uncle Darren.

After spending a month in care, Wayne was sent to live with his dad's parents, Doris and Bill. His sisters had already been given a home in Leicester by his mum's sister, Kim, but she already had a son and didn't want him. At first, Wayne had missed his sisters immensely, but over the years he'd taken his grandparents' advice and all but forgotten about them. He had written to them twice, but they had never replied, and if they couldn't be bothered with him, why should he worry about them?

'Evil little whores. They'll turn out just like their mother,' his nan had convinced him.

Wayne was fairly happy living with his grandparents. They adored the ground he walked on, gave him plenty of money and a free rein to do whatever he wanted. The house was a total shithole and his nan and grandad were heavy drinkers, but neither of these things particularly bothered Wayne. As long as he was clean and wore nice clothes, how they lived their lives was none of his business.

'All right, boy? Whaddya want for breakfast?' Doris asked her grandson as he sauntered down the stairs.

'Just toast. I've gotta go and meet me bird. You're still going out, ain't ya?'

Rolling an Old Holborn cigarette, Bill chuckled. 'Don't worry, me and your grandmother won't stop you from sowing your wild oats, will we, Doll?'

'You just make sure you don't fall head over heels for her, Wayne. You don't want to end up in the same situation as your father, do you now?' Doris warned her grandson.

Not for one minute did Doris or Bill even think that their beloved son was in the wrong for stabbing his wife twenty-six times with a bread knife. In their eyes, the slag he'd married deserved her grizzly ending for betraying their Lenny in the way that she had.

'Roll us a snout, Grandad, I ain't got none till I go out.'

Doris handed her grandson two pieces of burnt toast, then fished through her purse for some money. Neither she nor Bill had worked for years, but they had all their Lenny's money hidden under the floorboards upstairs and he had told them to help themselves to it. What with their pensions and their regular wins on the horses, Doris and Bill lived their lives to the full.

'Get her a bit drunk, have your wicked way, then fucking well dump her,' Doris cackled, as she put a five-pound note in the palm of her grandson's hand.

Wayne chuckled, stood up and grabbed his jacket. He'd always found it funny that his nan had tits and a fanny herself yet harboured a hatred towards other women. Apart from her mate, Big Brenda, who she drank with in the Millhouse, all of his nan's friends were male.

'And don't forget to use a dunky. You don't wanna get the little tart up the spout,' Bill yelled, as Wayne opened the front door.

'I won't forget,' Wayne shouted back. Then, with a grin of expectation on his face, he headed off to meet Angie.

Due to her vain younger sister taking forever to do her make-up in the public toilets at the Heathway, Stephanie Crouch was ten minutes late for school. 'I'm so sorry, Miss,' she said, as she barged breathless into the classroom.

'Is that him?' Tammy whispered in Steph's ear, as she sat down at her desk.

'Is what who?' Steph replied, perplexed.

When Tammy pointed to the right-hand side of the classroom, Steph looked around and felt her heart start to beat nineteen to the dozen. It was Barry Franklin and he was grinning at her.

'Well?' Tammy asked, excitedly.

'Shut up,' Stephanie hissed.

Aware that Steph's face had turned a bright shade of red, Tammy smirked knowingly.

'Now we are all here, I would like to introduce you to our new classmate. Would you like to come to the front?' Miss Pratt said, gesticulating to Barry.

'I'm quite capable of introducing meself, if that's OK?' Barry said, as he strolled to the front of the classroom, full of confidence.

As he caught her eye and winked at her, Stephanie immediately looked away. Barry Franklin seemed to be having a worse effect on her than Wayne Jackman had and she would not allow herself to be humiliated again. Not now, not ever.

Angela Crouch was a bag of nerves as she sat gingerly on the edge of Wayne Jackman's bed. Wayne looked absolutely gorgeous today. He was wearing a pure white Sergio Tacchini tracksuit which seemed to make his blonde wedge haircut and piercing blue eyes stand out even more than usual.

'Cider? Lager? Or Scotch?' Wayne asked his girlfriend.

Unlike her sister, who drank regularly at weekends, Angela had barely ever touched the stuff but, not wanting to act like a kid, she opted for Scotch.

'Are you OK?' Wayne asked, as she took a sip and promptly started to choke. 'Yeah, I'm cool. Went down the wrong hole,' Angela gasped.

'You sure you don't want lager or cider instead?'

'No, I always drink Scotch,' Angela lied, taking another sip.

'What do you wanna listen to? How about the Fatback Band?' Wayne suggested.

'Yeah, I love that,' Angela lied. She actually had no idea who the Fatback Band were. She was more into Kajagoogoo and Culture Club herself.

Singing the words to 'I Found Loving', Wayne sat down next to Angela and pushed her into a backwards position on the bed. 'You make me feel really horny, do you know that?' he panted, as he fondled her breasts.

Still feeling extremely edgy, Angela pushed him off her and sat up. 'Can we have some more drink and play some music before we get off with one another? We've got all day, ain't we?' she asked, fearfully.

Sensing her anxiety, but also sensing that there was a good chance he was going to get his end away later, Wayne sat up and smiled at Angela. 'Your wish is my command, babe.'

At lunchtimes, Stephanie and Tammy had a regular routine. Firstly, they would walk to the little tuck shop which was a spit's throw from the school. The nice man in there would sell cigarettes singly to the schoolchildren for ten pence each and Steph and Tammy took full advantage of his kindness. From there, the girls would walk round to Broad Street where there was a parade of shops and a small indoor market. The girls' lunch usually consisted of a bag of chips from the local chippy, but occasionally, if they were feeling flush, they would buy a burger in the café and sit in there and eat it.

'Look, Barry Franklin's standing outside the chippy on his own. Let's go and talk to him, shall we? It must be horrible starting a new school when you don't know anyone, and he said when he introduced himself that he came from Bethnal Green,' Tammy said.

Lighting up the Player's Number One that she'd just purchased in the tuck shop, Stephanie felt hot and flustered but did her utmost to look and sound cool. 'Just walk past him. I can't be arsed talking to boys no more.'

'You like him. I can tell,' Tammy said, teasingly.

'No I fucking don't! Now shut up, and if you say anything to him, I'll never forgive you,' Steph replied, angrily.

'All right, ladies. Mind if I tag along with you? I don't really know anyone yet and I feel a right plonker standing 'ere on me own,' Barry asked, staring at Steph.

Unable to hold his gaze, Stephanie looked down at her feet. 'We've gotta go somewhere, ain't we, Tam?' she mumbled.

Tammy ignored her friend's awkwardness and smiled at Barry. Unlike Wayne Jackman, Barry seemed like a decent lad and there was no way she was going to leave him standing outside the chip shop on his own. 'We're only going to the café in Broad Street market. You can come with us if you like.'

Barry grinned. 'Cheers, girls, and to repay you for your kindness, lunch is on me.'

Over in Digby Gardens, Angela's earlier nerves had now disappeared and she felt both woozy and extremely confident. 'Can I have another Scotch?' she asked Wayne. At first, Angie had found the drink tasted horrendous, but after a couple of glasses, she'd sort of got used to the taste and she enjoyed the floating feeling that came with drinking it.

'Gissa kiss now, babe,' Wayne urged, as he handed Angela her drink.

Giggling, Angie pushed him away. She knocked her drink back in one gulp, then stood up. 'If you let me choose some music, then you can have more than a kiss,' she said, seductively.

Wayne grinned broadly. 'Tell me what records you want on, and if I've got 'em, I'll play 'em for you.'

'You got any Kajagoogoo or Culture Club?' Angie asked.

Wayne burst out laughing. 'No I ain't! That's little kids' music.'

Feeling her face redden as she remembered her own age,

Angela thought of the bands her elder sister liked. 'What about Duran Duran or Soft Cell?' she asked, composing herself once more.

'I've got Soft Cell. "Tainted Love" is one of my favourite songs ever. What's yours?' Wayne asked.

'"Tainted Love" is my favourite song an' all,' Angela replied. Steph used to play it all the time in their room and it had sort of grown on Angie over the past year or so.

Wayne put the seven-inch single onto his record player and set the arm so it would automatically repeat itself.

'I love you Jacko,' Angela said childishly, as Wayne positioned his body on top of hers.

'Take your top and knickers off,' Wayne ordered, his voice husky with lust.

'You're fucking beautiful, babe,' he whispered truthfully, when Angela stood completely naked in front of him. Her breasts weren't as big as some of the girls he'd slept with, but other than that, she was perfect.

Angela stared at Wayne as he took off his tracksuit top. His torso was fit and firm and he had one of them six-packs like she'd seen on some of the pop stars whose images were pinned up on her bedroom wall. When he took off his bottoms and put a rubber thing on his penis, Angela felt her nerves momentarily return. She had never seen a willy in real life before, and Wayne's was not only bigger than she had expected, but it was also sticking up in the air like a flagpole.

'I want you so much,' Wayne mumbled, as he pushed her back onto the bed and got on top of her.

'You're hurting me,' Angela cried, as Wayne tried to ram his penis inside her.

'Ain't you done this before?' Wayne asked, surprised.

'Tell me if you've done it before and then I'll tell you if I have,' Angie replied, showing her true age once more.

'Yeah, I've done it loads of times,' Wayne bragged.

'And me,' Angela lied.

Now he knew she wasn't a virgin, Wayne roughly thrust himself inside her.

Angela bit her lip to stop herself from screaming out in pain. A minute or so later, Wayne let out a funny groan and rolled onto his back. 'That was fucking amazing! Did you enjoy it, babe?' he asked, with a big smile on his face.

Angela nodded and tried to block the awful experience from her mind by concentrating on Marc Almond's voice. Angela had expected having sex for the first time would be pleasurable and romantic, but Wayne hadn't even kissed her during it. All he had done was get on top of her and then hurt her by shoving his big thingy up her.

'Do you want to do it again?' Wayne asked, putting a comforting arm around Angela. He had just noticed the blood on the end of his penis, so now guessed she had lied and it was her first time.

'Not yet. Let's have another drink first and listen to the music for a bit,' Angie replied, miserably.

As a happy Wayne leapt off the bed to pour the drinks, he sang at the top of his voice to the chorus of the song.

Wanting to cry, Angela shut her eyes. If what she had just experienced was meant to be love, then the words in the song must be right: it was bloody tainted.

Tammy Andrews lived in the opposite direction to Stephanie, so they arranged to meet that evening and said goodbye outside the school gates. Carrying her own schoolbag on one shoulder and her sister's bag on the other, Steph set off to meet Angie outside the public toilets at the bottom of the Heathway Hill.

''Ere, let me carry your bags for you. I'm walking your way,' Barry said, as he caught up with Steph.

'Nah, it's all right. I ain't going straight home. Gotta meet my sister at the Heathway. One of these bags belongs to her.'

'Well I'll walk to the Heathway with you then. Give us that bigger bag 'ere, I can see you're struggling.'

'Thanks,' Steph said, as she handed him her sister's sports bag. Barry had been such a gentleman in the café earlier. He had insisted on paying for her and Tammy's cheeseburger and chips, and had even bought them a packet of ten Benson to share. When Steph had first laid eyes on Barry, she had known he reminded her of someone famous, and while sitting in the café it came to her who it was. She had recently seen the film *The Outsiders* and Barry Franklin was the spitting image of the boy she'd fancied in that. Tammy had told her when they'd left the café that the actor in the film who looked like Barry was called Matt Dillon.

'So how old's your sister then? And why you got her bag?' Barry asked, breaking the silence.

'Angie's thirteen and I've got her bag 'cause the little cow bunked off school today. Does my head in, she does, but I do love her. You won't tell your mum she bunked off, will you? If mine finds out, she'll kill her.'

Barry chuckled. 'I might be a lot of things but I ain't a grass, girl. Where I come from, grasses get shot.'

'Why did you buy me and Tam fags and lunch? It was a nice thing to do, but why did you do it?' Stephanie asked, suspiciously. Her mum had drummed it into her from an early age never to let a boy buy her anything because they would always expect something in return.

'I bought you fags and lunch 'cause I like you. Where I come from, that's what boys do when they like a girl.'

Feeling her stomach start to somersault, Stephanie looked away from Barry's intense gaze. 'I can take the bag from 'ere. I'll see you tomorrow at school,' she said, annoyed with herself for feeling the way she did.

Barry handed her the bag and at the same time grasped her hand. 'Let me take you out, Steph? I work, so I can afford to take you anywhere you wanna go. You choose and I'll pay.'

Feeling her hand start to shake, Stephanie snatched it away from Barry's and stared at the pavement. Wayne had humiliated her beyond belief and she didn't fancy a repeat performance of that. 'I dunno,' she replied, with an ill-at-ease tone to her voice. She felt confused. Wayne was the first boy she had ever really liked, and now she felt the same about Barry. Did all fourteen year olds fall in and out of love so quickly? Tammy had never had a real boyfriend, so she would have to ask some of her other school friends if her feelings were normal.

Barry grinned. He knew that Steph liked him and would eventually say yes, so he decided to give her some space. 'Look, I'm gonna shoot off now. Why don't you give me your answer tomorrow lunchtime? I won't ask you in class, I'll meet you and Tam down the café again and you can tell me there.'

'OK,' Steph replied, not knowing what else to say.

Pecking her on the cheek, Barry Franklin ran off while Steph stood rooted to the spot.

Angela Crouch stood outside the public toilets feeling like a woman rather than a child. Her and Wayne had done it four times and each fresh attempt had been more pleasurable for Angie than the previous. The bit she'd enjoyed the most was when Wayne had put his finger between the lips of her vagina and moved it up and down. That had felt really good, and at one point she had felt really weird, like she wanted to scream out with joy. Unfortunately, though, Wayne had then stopped.

Seeing Stephanie approaching the pedestrian crossing, Angela ran across the road towards her. 'Thanks, sis, I owe you one,' she said, as she took her bag off her.

'How was your day? Did you and Jacko have a laugh in Romford?' Steph asked, chirpily.

'Yeah, we had a brill time. Why you looking so happy? Has something happened?' Angela asked, suspiciously.

Desperate to tell someone her wonderful news, Stephanie made her sister promise not to tell their mum.

'Cross my heart and hope to die,' Angie swore.

Stephanie explained all about Barry, without leaving out any detail. 'He paid for our lunches, bought us some snout and he says he'll take me anywhere I want to go. He works at weekends as what's called a fly pitcher – like a market trader – and he's the image of that famous actor, Matt Dillon. Oh Ange, he is gorgeous, and he only lives across the road to us. I can even stare at him through our bedroom window.'

Angela was baffled. To her knowledge there was no handsome boy living across the road to them, and she fleetingly wondered if her sister was making the whole story up. 'I dunno who you mean, Steph. The only boy anywhere near our age living over the road is four-eyed Timmy, and he certainly don't look like Matt Dillon. You ain't making it up 'cause you're jealous of me and Jacko, are you?'

Stephanie laughed and shook her head in disbelief. Her sister was so self-centred, everything was always about her, her, her. 'Barry's only just moved in. He's Marlene's son.'

'Oh my God! Mum will go mad if she finds out you're going out with the old slapper's boy,' Angie exclaimed.

'Well, she ain't gonna find out, is she? Don't you dare tell her, Ange, 'cause if you do, I shall tell her about you and Jacko and I'll tell her you bunked off school as well.'

Angela shot her sister a disdainful look. 'I swear I won't say anything, OK? But, I'm telling you now, when Mum does find out, she will go mental.'

CHAPTER FOUR

Dressed in faded Levi jeans, a navy Lacoste jumper and white Nike trainers, Barry Franklin put on his grey flat cap and grinned at his reflection in the mirror. He was very aware of how cheeky and good looking he was, but he wasn't big headed about it.

'Why ain't you at work?' his mother asked accusingly, as she crept up behind him. Even though Barry was only fourteen, now he was living with her again, Marlene expected him to pay his way by bunging her the odd fiver or tenner here and there.

'I took the day off. I'm taking a bird out instead,' Barry replied, truthfully. He had always had a difficult relationship with his mother, and had only moved back in with her because his dad was up in court again next week and was guaranteed to get another little holiday at Her Majesty's Pleasure.

'If you've got money to spend on some little tart, then you can pay me some housekeeping,' Marlene spat, holding out her right hand.

Barry handed his mother a tenner. 'Where you off to today, Mum? You look well smart,' Barry said, politely.

'I'm going out with Marge. She's found a proper little

boozer over in South London. Reckons it's full of villains and they don't let the women buy a drink in there. I need to find meself a decent man who will look after me. I don't like this bleedin' Dagenham. A woman such as I deserves to live somewhere better, Barry.'

Even though he didn't think his mother deserved sod all, Barry nodded in agreement. His dad said leaving his mum was the best move he had ever made, and he had been furious that she had kept his surname after their divorce. 'Fucking old rotter she is. Only kept my name to give herself some undeserved street cred,' his dad ranted on a regular basis.

'So where you taking this bird and who is she?' Marlene asked, nosily.

Stephanie had told him that her mum was very strict about her dating boys, so knowing what a loud-mouth his mother could be, Barry decided to lie about her identity. 'Her name's Sue and she's in my class at school,' he said. 'I'm taking her up Roman Road, then I might show her around our old stamping ground.'

Marlene sneered. 'If you see that wanker of a father of yours, remind him he has an ex-wife and a pregnant daughter who are both skint.'

Barry nodded. His dad, Smasher, had been appalled when he had found out his sister Chantelle was pregnant by an Indian drug dealer from Ilford. 'Dirty little whore she is. Like mother like daughter. I want no more to do with her, son, and I ain't having no Paki kid calling me grandad,' Smasher had screamed on learning the news.

Pecking his mother politely on the cheek, Barry picked up his fags, lighter and door key. He wasn't due to meet Stephanie for another hour but, as always, his mother was doing his head in and he couldn't wait to get away from her.

* * *

Due to enduring a mild bout of gastroenteritis, Pam and Cathy had both been off work for the past two days.

'How you feeling, girl? I'm on the mend, I think,' Cathy shouted, as she let herself into Pam's house.

'I've still got the shits, but I feel a lot better than I did,' Pam replied.

'Ere, wanna hear the latest?' Cathy asked.

'Yeah.'

'Lairy Mary popped round yesterday. She reckons that the old slapper's daughter is pregnant by some Indian fella who's inside for possessing heroin. He comes out next week, so Mary reckons.'

Pam put her hand over her mouth in shock. 'What a scumbag family they are! That young boy we saw moving his stuff in last week is the old slapper's son, apparently. Edna next-door-but-one reckons he's started at Priory. I hope they don't put him in either of my girls' classes. He looks more Steph's age than my Angie's.'

'Yous two talking about us?' Angela shouted as she galloped down the stairs, followed by her sister.

For the second time in minutes, Pam stood with her jaw wide open. Both her daughters had lipstick and mascara on and Angela had gone one step further by plastering her eyelids with bright green eyeshadow.

'Where're yous two off to, all done up to the nines?'

'Just out,' Angela replied, stroppily.

'Out where? Yous pair got boyfriends or something?' Pam replied, knowingly.

'No! We're just meeting some friends over the park,' Stephanie lied.

Knowing that turning the tables was always the best way out of a difficult situation, Angela immediately turned them. 'Me and Steph wanna know why you were talking about us? What we done wrong now?' she asked, accusingly.

'We weren't saying anything detrimental against you girls, were we, Cath?'

'No. We was talking about the old slapper's son across the road. He's started your school by all accounts, and your mother said she hoped he weren't in any of your classes.'

Unable to stop herself, Angie started to giggle.

'Come on, let's go,' Stephanie said, grabbing her sister roughly by the arm.

'I weren't born yesterday, you know. In your opinion I might be past me sell-by date, but I ain't bleedin' simple. I know you've got boyfriends and I shall find out who they are,' Pam shouted angrily as the front door slammed.

Cathy raised her eyebrows. 'Girls, eh! Who'd have 'em?'

Bill Jackman was quite pleased that his grandson was stuffing a bit of fluff, but his wife had her concerns about the situation and had insisted on hanging around to meet the girl.

Wayne agreed to the introduction. As long as his grandparents didn't cramp his style, he didn't care what they did. He knew he was lucky to be allowed to have the house to himself to bed a girl, none of his friends were, and he couldn't wait to have sex with Angela again. He had seen her every evening this week, but she'd flatly refused to let him have his wicked way with her over the park, even though he'd begged her. When the doorbell rang, Wayne bolted into the hallway. 'All right, babe? Come and say hello to me nan and grandad,' he said, dragging Angela into the lounge.

'Hello,' Angela said, awkwardly staring at her feet. If they sussed her real age, she was dead meat.

'Nice to meet you, love. Our Wayne says you live with your mum and dad near the Heathway. Is that right?' Doris probed, nosily.

'Yeah,' Angela replied.

'What's your mum and dad's names? I'm always up that Heathway.'

'Pam and David Marshall,' Angela lied.

'Come on, Doll. Let's leave the kids to play records and stuff,' Bill urged, gently shoving his wife out of the room.

'Well? Pretty little thing, wasn't she?' Bill asked as he shut the front door.

'Horrible little cunt! Couldn't even look me in the eye – and if she's fifteen like our Wayne says she is, then I'm fucking Doris Day.'

Barry and Stephanie took the District Line train to Bow Road Station and then had a ten-minute walk to get to the market. 'Have you been up 'ere before?' Barry asked.

'Yeah. My mum comes from Bow and my grandad still lives here. We ain't been to visit him for ages though. I was only about twelve last time I came to the market, I think.'

'Do you wanna pop in and see your grandad while we're up this way? I'll wait for you outside if you like,' Barry asked, thoughtfully.

'Nah. He'll probably be in the pub anyway,' Stephanie replied, truthfully.

Stephanie felt her heart flip as Barry held her hand. Her nerves hadn't embarrassed her so far today, but the feel of Barry's warm hand pressing against her own felt like an electric shock entering her system. 'Let's have a fag,' she said, snatching her hand away and riffling through her small silver shoulder bag.

'What time you gotta be back later?'

'Ten. Are we hanging about up here all day or going back to the Heathway later?'

'Firstly, I'm gonna introduce you to the geezer I work for. Then, I'll treat you to lunch. We can have a mooch up and down the market, then I'm gonna take you up to Bethnal

Green to show you where I come from. Our last stop will be the Bishop Bonner pub. It's where my dad drinks and I really want you to meet him.'

'I can't meet your dad, Bal. Say he tells your mum and then my mum finds out?' Stephanie replied, horrified.

Tilting Stephanie's chin upwards so that she made eye contact with him, Barry treated her to his killer smile. 'Look, babe, I know you don't want your mum to know that we've been out together and I can understand why. No one wants their daughter associated with a muvver like mine, but my dad's a good geezer. He's gotta go away for a while next week and, seeing as you're the first girl I've ever really liked, I'd be well chuffed if you'd meet him. He'll adore you, I know he will.'

Stephanie's heart was pounding at twice its normal rate. Did Barry just say that she was the first girl he had ever really liked, or had her ears deceived her? 'OK, I'll meet him then,' she croaked.

Wayne and Angela spent the whole afternoon at it like rabbits. After her initial painful experience, Angela had taken to sex like a duck takes to water and had even learnt the art of giving a blow job.

'Suck it again for me, Ange. It's your fault it keeps getting hard,' Wayne said, bluntly.

Angela smiled. Wayne had told her earlier that she gave him the best sex he'd ever had and Angie liked to feel indispensable.

'Do you love me, Jacko?' she asked him coyly.

Desperate to feel her plump warm lips around his penis again, Wayne nodded. 'Yeah, of course I love you, babe.'

Stephanie Crouch shook hands with Barry's boss, Steve. Most Indian people Steph had met before, including the two boys in her class at school, were very reserved, kept themselves to themselves and spoke in weird accents, but Steve was entirely different. He was loud, funny and sounded more cockney than she did. When Barry had first told her he was a fly pitcher, Steph hadn't quite understood the occupation. She hadn't wanted to ask in case she made herself look silly, but now she knew exactly what Barry did. A fly pitcher was someone who hadn't been given a pitch by the council so stood on a street corner selling their wares. Steve and Barry sold kingsize bath towels, and Barry would act as a look-out for the police and market inspectors while Steve used his witty sales patter to charm the public.

'Do you ever get caught?' Steph asked, as they said goodbye to Steve.

'Nah, and even if we do we only get a slap on the wrists. Got eyes in the back of me head, me,' Barry replied, laughing.

Stephanie smiled broadly as Barry held her hand again. Everybody knew him down Roman Road market and she could sense how popular he was with the other traders. 'That's a nice top, ain't it?' she said, pointing at an off-the-shoulder baggy red sweatshirt.

Barry dragged her over to the stall she was pointing at. 'Bag me up one of them red sweatshirts please, Joanie,' he ordered the lady who was serving.

'I can't let you buy that for me,' Stephanie said, amazed by Barry's generosity.

Handing Steph the sweatshirt in a carrier bag, Barry turned towards her. 'I really do like you, Steph. Please say you'll be my girl?'

Barely able to believe her luck, a completely besotted Stephanie nodded her head with glee.

* * *

Marlene Franklin was sitting opposite her friend Marge in the Albion pub in Woolwich. Marge's real name was Karen, but she had earned her nickname because her legs tended to spread quicker then Stork margarine. The name didn't bother Marge at all. She loved sex, always had done, and if people were jealous of her success rate with the male gender, then that was their bloody problem.

'Does this dress look all right? You can't see me knickers when I walk, can you?' Marlene asked her pal as she returned from the Ladies.

'No, you look stunning, mate, and them blokes in the corner can't take their eyes off you,' Marge replied, truthfully.

Pouting her lips just like the models did, Marlene sat down and crossed one leg seductively over the other. At thirty years old, Marlene still looked rather youthful for her age, and with her bright red lipstick, false black eyelashes, and thick blonde hair that she curled herself with heated rollers, Marlene considered herself to be the spitting image of Marilyn Monroe. Today, she had made a special effort and had worn the short, leopard-skin dress that she had stolen from a designer boutique in Hornchurch. Marlene was an expert at shoplifting. She would always wear bulky clothes to go out shopping, would try lots of items on in the fitting room, then would walk out with her favourite underneath her own outfit.

Marlene smiled coyly as an elderly man in a tan Crombie-style coat winked at her. She knew he couldn't take his eyes off her fishnet stockings and high-heeled black suede shoes, and who could blame him?

'So have you finished with that Winston now?' Marge asked her friend.

Marlene took a sip of her gin and tonic. If the men didn't start buying them drinks soon, they would have to start ordering halves of lager just to make their money last out. 'Yep. I made him buy me a load of shopping at Sainsbury's last weekend, then told him I couldn't see him no more as I felt guilty he had a wife. Gutted he was, even rang me up on Monday crying, but I warned him if he contacts me again I was gonna go round his house and tell his wife everything.'

'I thought he was quite handsome. He had a fit body,' Marge said. She had a thing about black men and had been quite jealous when she had first laid eyes on Winston.

'He had a big black cock, I know that much. Made my bleedin' eyes water, it did,' Marlene said, laughing.

'You must be mad finishing with him.'

'Didn't have enough money for me, mate. A Ford worker is hardly gonna keep me in a life of luxury, is he? Especially a married one with three poxy brats.'

'Don't look now, but I think that old bloke's coming over,' Marge said, nudging her pal.

'Good afternoon, ladies. I was wondering if you'd allow me the honour of buying you both a drink,' the man asked, resting his gaze firmly on Marlene.

Marlene smiled. The man was old, short and was certainly no looker, but he reeked of money from his Rolex watch to his shiny leather shoes. Marge had never been backwards in coming forwards. 'Yes please, mate, we'll have two large gin and tonics.'

When the man pulled an enormous wad of fifty-pound notes out of his pocket, Marlene's eyes lit up like beacons. She waited until he walked up to the bar and then turned to her friend. 'I'm gonna snare this cunt, Marge. Watch and learn, girl.'

Stephanie Crouch was enjoying one of the best days out she had ever had in her life. After Barry had bought her the red sweatshirt, he had insisted on buying her pie and mash for lunch. He'd then bought her a red rose off the flower stall, two drinks in the Needle Gun pub, and UB40's new single 'Red Red Wine', which Stephanie absolutely adored.

'I've had such a fab day, Barry, thanks ever so much,' she said, joyfully. She had never had a proper boyfriend before, and walking along Roman Road holding Barry's arm felt that good, she thought she might burst with happiness.

'The day ain't over yet, babe. We're going to meet me old man now.'

'Is his real name Smasher?' Stephanie asked, seriously.

Barry laughed. Steph's naivety was one of the things that endeared her to him so much. 'Nah. His real name is Barry. I was obviously named after him, but everyone calls him Smasher as he used to be a fighter years ago. He used to smash everyone's lights out, he did – hence his nickname.'

'Really?' Steph exclaimed.

'Yeah, back in the day he used to fight for money. They were illegal bouts, but he's proper hard my dad. Only ever lost twice in his life, he did.'

'So, where's he going on holiday then?'

'What you on about?' Barry asked, bemused.

'You said he was going away next week,' Stephanie reminded him.

'He's going to prison, Steph, not Butlins. He got caught with a lorry-load of knocked-off TVs,' Barry said, chuckling.

Feeling a bit stupid, Steph quickly changed the subject. 'Whaddya wanna do when you leave school, Bal?'

'I wanna be just like me dad. He's always wheeled and dealed and he's loaded. I don't mind the markets, but I ain't never gonna work nine to five for some mug who orders me about. I'm clued up enough to get by without all that. What do you wanna do, girl?'

'I want to get a good job in a bank or an office up town.

My typing teacher, Mrs Belson, reckons I'd make a brilliant secretary. I think one day I'd like to run my own business, but not until I'm much older.'

'A girl with ambition, eh? That's what I love about you, Steph.'

At the mention of the word love, Stephanie felt her face turn beetroot red and she quickly changed the subject once again. 'I bet it's horrible for you starting at a school where you don't know no one, ain't it? Have you made friends with any of the boys yet?'

'Don't you worry about me. Get on with most people, I do. Anyway, I've got a good pal in the year above us. He used to live across the road from me in Bethnal Green and we used to hang around together as kids. Saved me life once, he did, when I was a nipper. I couldn't swim and I fell into a river. He jumped in and dragged me out.

'Aah, that's nice. What's his name? I might know him.'

'His name's Wayne, babe. Wayne Jackman.'

CHAPTER FIVE

Cath had just unscrewed the lid on her and Pam's Saturday treat, when there was a tap-tap at the front door. Busy cutting up a giant-sized pork and egg pie, Pam turned to her friend. 'Answer that for me, Cath.'

Cath did as she was told and ran back into the kitchen. 'It's the police, Pam. They wanna speak to you, mate.'

Pam immediately thought that one of her girls had had an accident and, ashen-faced, ran to the door with the big knife still in her hand.

'Whatever's wrong? Is it my daughter?' she gabbled, near to tears. The police had turned up on her doorstep like this on the day that her wonderful husband had been killed, and just the sight of the PC brought back terrible memories for her.

'Do you mind putting that knife down, Mrs Crouch?' the officer said in a jovial tone.

'Is it my Steph? Or is it my Angie?' Pam cried, handing the knife to Cathy who was now standing by her side.

Realizing that Mrs Crouch was becoming very distraught, the young PC held his hands up, palms facing her. 'Calm down. It's nothing too serious. Can you just confirm that you have a sister called Linda Tate? And if so, we need confirmation that she lives here with you.'

'Yeah, Linda lives here. She's my younger sister. Is she OK? What's wrong with her?' Pam asked, in a panic-stricken tone.

The young PC smirked. 'Nothing, unless you count being extremely drunk. There was a minor incident earlier in the Trades Hall Social Club, Mrs Crouch, and when our officers arrived at the scene, your sister tried to attack the female PC. We had to arrest her, and she will receive a caution for being drunk and disorderly. No charges will be brought against her for the attack on the policewoman, as there was no real harm done.'

Pam gasped. She was mortified. 'I am so sorry, officer, and I can assure you nothing like this will ever happen again. As you are probably aware, Linda suffers from dwarfism, and because of this she gets drunk very quickly. I shall be having a serious chat with her later, don't you worry about that. Is she on her way home now?'

'No. We thought it best to let her sober up a bit first, and then we'll either get an officer to drive her home or call her a cab. I wouldn't be too hard on her. Linda has been rather amusing back at the station. She originally gave us her name and address as the Queen Mother who lived at Buckingham Palace.'

Pam was fuming. 'I'll give her the Queen Mother when she gets home here, officer. Thank you for being so understanding. Linda's condition makes life difficult for her at times, if you know what I mean?'

When the officer nodded understandingly and walked back to his colleague who was waiting in the car, Cathy burst out laughing.

'Don't laugh, it ain't funny,' Pam said, cursing her younger sister under her breath.

'I'm sorry, mate, but she is a fucking case, your Linda. The

Queen Mother, Buckingham Palace. What must the Old Bill have thought of her? And she's tried to beat up one of 'em.'

Unable to see the humorous side of her sister's outrageous behaviour, Pam shook her head in despair.

Stephanie Crouch was as quiet as a mouse as she sat down at a table in the Bishop Bonner pub. The knowledge that Barry and Wayne Jackman were pals had left her with a feeling of uneasiness and she didn't quite know how to handle the situation. She was positive that if Barry found out that she had recently asked Wayne out, he would then finish with her himself.

'You all right, babe? You've gone ever so quiet on me. What's up?' Barry asked, handing Steph half a cider and sitting down next to her.

'Nothing. I'm just a bit tired, that's all,' Stephanie fibbed.

Barry could smell a lie a mile off. 'Is it me dad? I know he comes across as a bit intimidating, but he's such a top geezer when you get to know him, Steph. He was only winding you up when he took the piss out of your ripped jeans. He didn't mean it nastily.'

Glancing over at the bar where Smasher Franklin was standing with his pals, Stephanie managed a weak smile. Barry's dad had looked daunting to begin with. He was tall, had enormous muscles, a squashed nose and three scars plastered across his weather-beaten face, but he'd won Steph over immediately with his wit and charm.

'I really liked your dad. He is so funny, Barry, and I wish I had a dad like him. Mine died when I was little and I never really knew him at all.'

Chuffed to bits that the introduction had gone so well, Barry leant towards Steph and kissed her on the cheek. 'Now we're together, he'll sort of be your dad an' all, won't he? You're always gonna be my girl, Steph.'

Looking at the intensity in Barry's eyes, Stephanie's heart was filled with happiness, but also dread. Asking Wayne Jackman out could prove to be the biggest mistake of her life, and if it ruined her relationship with Barry, she would never forgive herself for being such an idiot.

After spending most of the day entwined in a variety of sexual positions, Wayne and Angela were now sitting at the entrance to The Mall on Heathway Hill, drinking a bottle of cider.

'This is boring sitting 'ere, I feel like a kid. Let's go down the Princess Bowl, eh?' Wayne suggested.

The Princess Bowl was where Angela had first met Wayne, but because so many kids from their school hung about there, now she and Wayne were actually together, Angie was worried about being seen there with him. One day, when she was older, she would tell Wayne that she had lied about her age, but she didn't want it coming out just yet.

'I like it when it's just me and you, Jacko. All your mates will be down the bowling alley and I'll be bored if you're talking to them.'

Wayne sighed. He liked Angie, but her childishness did his head in at times. If she wasn't such a good shag, he would have probably dumped her by now.

Over in South London, Marlene Franklin was sitting in a Chinese restaurant in Bermondsey, having a whale of a time with the gentleman she had met in the pub earlier.

'So why do people call you Jake the Snake then?' Marlene asked, giggling. She rarely had the opportunity to drink herself senseless on expensive champagne, so had been indulging herself in the stuff, big time.

Jake Chaplin was a short, unattractive, pointy-nosed, fifty-two-year old South London villain. He was an extremely clever fraudster and had made plenty of money over the years by selling gullible people properties and timeshares that had ceased to exist. Clicking his fingers to indicate to the waiter that he required yet another bottle of champagne, Jake grinned at Marlene.

'People call me Jake the Snake because I'm as slippery as a boa constrictor. Slithered out of many a difficult situation over the years, I have, Marlene. I'm a very clever man, darling.' When Jake laughed out loud and lit up yet another cigarette, Marlene ignored his awful yellow teeth, his weaselly looking face, and his spindly, nicotine-stained hands. All she saw was money and a ticket out of Dagenham.

'Do you think Marge will be all right with your mate?' Marlene asked, pretending to be concerned. She knew Marge would be all right if she spent the night with the entire England rugby squad.

Jake chuckled. 'They don't call my mate Donkey Dave for nothing, you know. I'm sure he'll show your friend Marge a good time, if you know what I mean?'

Fluttering her eyelashes and pouting seductively at Jake, Marlene squeezed his bony hand. 'And what about you? Do you know how to treat a lady?'

Jake the Snake licked his thin lips in pure anticipation. He'd never struggled pulling women, because of who he was, but it had been a good few years since he had pulled one as pretty and young as Marlene. Looking lovingly into her eyes, Jake grinned. 'Tomorrow, my dear, you and I are going shopping. I will spoil you something rotten, and if you treat me kindly in return, I can guarantee that you will never want for anything ever again in your entire life.'

Leaning forward, Marlene locked lips with Jake. When his tongue entered her mouth, for a split second she felt physically sick, but instead of showing her repulsion, Marlene responded by kissing Jake passionately. Shutting her eyes, Marlene pretended she was kissing her screen idol, Mel Gibson – that's what she always did when she got intimate with a man she didn't fancy.

'You are so beautiful, Marlene,' Jake said, as their kiss came to an end.

Marlene grinned. Jake was in her clutches already and this was one snake that she was not going to let slither out of her grasp.

Back in Dagenham, Angela was trying to find out more about Wayne's life. 'So, what's it like going to a football match? When are West Ham playing at home next?' she asked, genuinely interested. Angie knew nothing about football whatsoever, but decided because Wayne was so passionate about it, if they were going to be together forever, perhaps she should start learning.

'It's wicked, babe. Me, Potter and Cooksie are in a firm called the ICF. We've had many a scrap, especially when we go to away games. Well hard, we are,' Wayne bragged.

'Do you fight people?'

'Yeah, we fight the supporters of other teams. The firm's run by some older geezers and they're all casuals, like us. Well cool they are, and proper organized. We wanted to hang about with 'em ages ago, but I think they thought we were too young. They've accepted us now, though – they call us the young ICF.'

Angela was perplexed. She'd always thought football was about kicking a ball around a pitch, not brawling. 'Can I come to the next game with you, Jacko?'

Wayne burst out laughing. In his opinion, birds and football were as unsuited as a dog shagging a cat. About to answer Angela's awkward request as diplomatically as he could, Wayne heard someone call his name.

Spotting his two best pals jogging towards him, Wayne

quickly stood up and brushed any dirt off his turquoise Lacoste tracksuit.

'What you doin' hanging about here, you wanker?' Cooksie asked him, laughing.

Leaning against the wall, Wayne grabbed hold of his groin area, nodded towards Angela and chuckled. 'She's worn me out, lads. Had a bit of a marathon sesh earlier, and I'm shattered. Where yous two been?'

Potter showed Wayne the inside of his carrier bag. 'Dalston, got meself a new pair of Kickers in red.'

'Sweet,' Wayne replied, studying the boots.

'Do you wanna come round Danno's with us? He's got a free house for the weekend and is having a bit of a piss-up,' Cooksie suggested.

'Yeah, why not. You coming Ange? We're going round Danno's.'

Thrilled that Wayne had invited her, Angela stood up. 'Who's Danno?' she asked, casually.

'Danno's in our year at school. You won't know him, he goes Priory.'

Relieved that Danno didn't go to Parsloes Manor, the school that she had pretended to go to, Angela grinned. She knew none of the lads in the fifth year at Priory, so knew her secret would be safe. 'Come on then. What we waiting for?' she said.

Barry Franklin waited until they got off at Dagenham Heathway before confronting Stephanie. 'Look, babe, you've hardly said a word to me all the way home and I know something's up. You might as well just tell me what's wrong. Don't you wanna go out with me any more or something? 'Cause if you don't I'd rather you just be honest with me.'

Barry's words made Stephanie feel all emotional inside and she knew she had no choice other than to come clean.

Surely it was better to tell Barry the truth herself than let him hear it from Wayne Jackman's sarcastic mouth.

'I do wanna be with you, Bal, it's not that. You're gonna finish with me when I tell you what it is, I know you will.'

Aware that his girlfriend was seconds away from bursting into tears, Barry held her in his arms. 'No matter what it is, I will never finish with you, babe. I like you far too much to do that, so just tell me what's bothering you.'

'It's Wayne Jackman. I asked him out just before I met you and I made myself look a right div an' all. I didn't really like him, not like I like you, I swear I didn't,' Stephanie said, fearfully.

Barry Franklin burst out laughing. 'I know you asked Jacko out, he told me what happened. Is that it? I ain't bothered about that. I'm just glad he knocked you back, 'cause you wouldn't be with me otherwise, would you?'

Stephanie was astonished by Barry's calmness over her confession. 'What, so you don't mind? I thought you would dump me when you found out. That's why I've been so quiet since you said you were friends with him.'

Tilting Stephanie's chin towards him, Barry wiped the tears from her eyes with the cuff of his jumper. 'Jacko's OK, you don't know him like I do. It's all about us now, girl. Sod anyone else and the past. It's only me and you that matters.'

As Barry leant towards her and kissed her properly for the very first time, Stephanie Crouch truly felt that she was the luckiest girl in the world.

Angela Crouch was thoroughly enjoying herself around at Danno's house. Apart from the host and Wayne and his pals, there were eight other boys there, and Angela was extremely aware that at least six of them couldn't take their eyes off her beauty. There were only two other girls at the house and Angela was relieved that they were both overweight and also quite ugly. From a very early age, Angela had always craved to be the centre of attention, and tonight she most certainly was.

'Sit down. You're making a show of yourself,' Wayne said, grabbing Angela's arm to stop her from dancing seductively to Culture Club's 'Karma Chameleon'.

'No I'm not! I'm just enjoying meself and you're only jealous because you know all your mates fancy me,' Angela said, confidently. Seconds later, the self-satisfied smirk was wiped off Angela's face as Tanya MacKenzie, a girl she had always disliked immensely, and who was in the same year as her at school, walked into the room.

'Let's go home. I need some fresh air,' Angela said, grabbing Wayne by the arm.

'But it's only nine o'clock. I thought you didn't have to be in till ten?'

'I feel a bit sick,' Angela lied, turning her back on Tanya. She was desperate for Tanya not to spot her.

'What you doing 'ere, Crouchy? This house belongs to my family and you ain't welcome.'

'Come on, Jacko, let's go,' Angela pleaded, her voice now frantic.

Tanya MacKenzie was Danno's cousin, and ever since the day she had first set foot inside Dagenham Priory, she had hated Angela Crouch with a passion. Tanya and Angie were both blessed with pretty faces, and Tanya knew if it wasn't for Angela being around, she would be the best-looking girl in her year by a mile. Not only that, but Angela was also a bitch and a liar, which had made Tanya despise her all the more.

'What's going on? And who's Crouchy?' Wayne asked, in bewilderment. Angie had told him her surname was Marshall, so why the bloody hell was Tanya calling his girlfriend Crouchy?

Realizing that Wayne and Angela were an item, Tanya burst out laughing. Ever since Angela had grassed her up to a teacher for writing graffiti on the toilet walls last term, Tanya had yearned for her revenge, and now she was about to get it. She turned to Wayne. 'I'm calling her Crouchy 'cause that's her surname. You ain't going out with her, are you, Jacko? She's a slag and a liar and I bet she ain't told you how old she really is, has she?'

As Spandau Ballet's 'True' blasted out of the speakers, humiliation drove Angela to tears. 'Please, Jacko, let's go now,' she begged.

Aware that all his mates were watching the embarrassing confrontation, Wayne was fuming. He grabbed Angela's shoulders and slammed her against the lounge wall. 'What's your real name and how fucking old are you, Ange? Don't lie to me, 'cause I will kill you if you do.'

When somebody turned the volume on the stereo down, Tanya nudged her mate and walked over to where Wayne and Angela were arguing. 'Her name's Angela Crouch and she's in the second year at Priory. I should know, she's made my life hell.'

'Is this fucking true?' Wayne screamed.

'I'm so sorry. I was gonna tell you, but I thought you'd pack me up,' Angela sobbed as she ran from the room.

Desperate to save face in front of all of his mates, Wayne chased after Angela, grabbed her roughly by the arm, and slapped her around the face. 'You lying fucking bitch. Now, get away from me. I don't ever wanna see your face again, got it?' he yelled.

Crushed beyond belief, Angela let out a wounded howl, and ran as fast as she could down the street.

Unaware that another drama was just about to kick off, Pamela Crouch was busy dealing with the one that already had. The police had kindly dropped her sister home half an hour ago and, instead of being apologetic over her unruly behaviour, Linda seemed to think it was all one big joke.

'It ain't fucking funny, Linda. Mum must be turning in her grave if she's looking down and knows you got yourself arrested. It's ever since you've been knocking about with them factory girls, you've been acting like a bloody hooligan. I think you should look for another job. You need to find one where you mix with normal women. Bad influence, that mob from the Butterkist are.'

'No they ain't! For the first time ever, sis, I've actually met people who accept me for being me – and let me tell you, I'm having the time of me bleedin' life. My friends are blinding and I love each and every one of 'em dearly, so don't you dare try and spoil things for me. I will never forgive you if you do, and I mean that. And if you keep nagging on at me like Muvver did, I'll go up that council first thing Monday morning and get meself a place of me own,' Linda replied.

Huffing and puffing, Pam stood up. 'Who wants a brew?' she asked.

'Yes please,' Linda said, winking at Cath as Pam left the room. Linda might have a height impediment, but her brain was as good as Margaret Thatcher's and she certainly knew which buttons to press when it came to her elder sister. Threatening to move out worked like a dream every time, and Linda just wished she had learnt the art of being so cunning when she'd lived with her domineering bloody mother.

When the front door opened and slammed, Pam looked up from her tea-making duties. 'Angie, get your arse down here,' she shouted, as her sobbing daughter bolted straight up the stairs.

'What's wrong with Madam?' Linda asked, walking into

the kitchen and opening the fridge door to hunt for some chocolate.

'Christ knows! Go up and see if she's all right for me,' Pam replied. She'd had enough stress for one day to last her a lifetime.

'No chance,' Linda said, bluntly. She adored her eldest niece Stephanie, but in Lin's eyes, Angela was a petulant little mare, and there was no way she was getting involved in the child's latest fiasco.

About to plead with Linda, Pam was saved from doing so by Stephanie's arrival home. 'What's in that bleedin' carrier bag?' Pam asked suspiciously as she clocked her daughter trying to hide the bag behind her back.

'Just a sweatshirt,' Stephanie said, as casually as she could. She could hardly tell her mum that the old slapper's son who lived across the road had bought it for her. Her mother would have a fit.

'You ain't nicked it, have you? Where did you get it from?' Pam asked, bluntly.

'Romford Market and I bought it out me pocket money, if you must know,' Steph replied, stroppily.

Swallowing her daughter's lie, Pam raised her eyes towards the ceiling. 'Go upstairs and see what's wrong with your sister. She's just come in, breaking her heart, she was. You know what she's like, she won't tell me sod all – but I ain't silly, I bet it's to do with a boy.'

Relieved that her lie had been believed, Stephanie shot straight up the stairs. 'Whatever's the matter?' Angela had the covers over her head, but Steph could still hear her sobbing like a baby.

'Go away. Leave me alone,' Angela screamed.

The girls slept in single beds either end of the room, and Stephanie knew if she didn't sort this particular drama out now and Jacko had dumped Angie, her sister would make her life hell for weeks to come. Sitting down on the edge of Angela's bed, Steph comfortingly put an arm across her body. 'I knew he'd find out your age sooner or later, sis. It was only a matter of time,' she said in an understanding voice. 'I told you to tell him the truth before someone else did, didn't I?'

Angela was not only heartbroken, but also bloody seething. Not only had she lost the love of her life and been humiliated by Tanya MacKenzie, but she now had her know-it-all, patronizing sister to contend with as well. Unable to admit that she should have listened to Stephanie's advice about admitting her age, Angela leapt out of the bed like a banshee. 'Jacko never found out my age. It ain't what you think it is, OK?' she shrieked.

Stephanie was used to her younger sister being an actress – she'd grown up with her tantrums – but as Angie's body began to shake uncontrollably and her sobs echoed against the walls of the bedroom, Stephanie started to become seriously concerned. 'Whatever's happened? You can tell me, Ange,' she said, holding her distraught sister in her arms.

Rocking to and fro, Angela clung to Stephanie's chest. She was good at lying and needed some sympathy. Also, if Steph thought she was going to get her hands on Wayne now, she had another think coming.

'Has Jacko done something bad to you, Ange?' Stephanie asked. She had tears in her own eyes now, such was her sister's distress.

Angela was racking her brain for the perfect answer and, remembering the fantastic sex she and Wayne had experienced earlier, she could only think of one thing to say. 'If I tell you, you must promise never to tell Mum or anyone else.'

'I swear I won't tell a soul,' Stephanie promised.

'Jacko forced me to have sex with him. He raped me, Steph.'

CHAPTER SIX

After spending all day Sunday consoling and caring for her sexually abused younger sister, Stephanie headed off to school on the Monday morning like a bull in a china shop. She'd left an hour earlier for two reasons: one because she needed Tammy's advice, and secondly because she'd wanted to avoid Barry. Seeing Tammy standing outside the Church Elm fish bar, Stephanie ran towards her.

'Why the early meet? You ain't done it with him, have you? And why didn't you come round yesterday? We were meant to be going down Dagenham Sunday Market,' Tammy asked, slightly annoyed that her pal had let her down.

'Let's go to a café. We can't talk here,' Steph said, grabbing her pal's arm.

Five minutes later, the girls were sitting in the café on Heathway Hill nursing a mug of tea each.

'What's a matter, Steph? You look like you've got the weight of the world on your shoulders. Is it Barry? Did he do something to you when you went out with him the other day? If he's upset you, I'll have his guts for garters, mate.'

'It's not Barry. I had a fab day out with him, the best ever.'

'Well, what's wrong then?'

'It's Angie.'

Tammy had little time at all for her best friend's younger sister. In her eyes, Angela was an extremely nasty piece of work, but Tammy had learned to be diplomatic about her for Steph's sake. 'What's she done now?' she asked, raising her eyebrows.

Leaning forwards so that the workmen sitting on the next table couldn't hear what she had to say, Stephanie explained everything that Angela had told her.

Tammy listened intently, but couldn't help but be sceptical. 'You sure she's telling the truth, mate? I don't wanna slag your sister off, but you know what a liar she can be. What about when she told you that poor old man who lived across the road had touched her and it turned out she'd made it up 'cause he'd caught her nicking the milk off his doorstep and she knew he'd tell your muvver.'

Remembering the incident with the old man who used to live across the road, Stephanie shrugged. 'Yeah, but when my mum went to confront the old man, Angela admitted she was lying, didn't she? She was only about eight when she said that and I'm sure she ain't lying about Jacko. She was in a proper state yesterday, Tam. That's why I couldn't come to the market with you. She ain't even gone to school today. I begged her to let me tell Mum or ring the police, but that just made her even more hysterical. I've gotta say something to Jacko. He ain't getting away with this. At least if I let him know that I know, he won't go near Angie ever again. I'll threaten the bastard and tell him if he goes within fifty yards of her, I'll tell the police everything.'

'Jacko might be a flash wanker, Steph, but he don't look like no rapist to me. How do you know that Ange and him didn't just get drunk and have sex? I mean, she lied about her age to him, didn't she?'

Annoyed that her best friend was questioning Angela's morals instead of backing her, Stephanie gave her what for. 'If this happened to your sister, I wouldn't call her a liar. Wayne Jackman is gonna get a piece of my mind at lunchtime and if you don't wanna back me up, then I'll do it on my own.'

Adoring Stephanie more than anyone else in the world, Tammy squeezed her hand. 'I can't stand Jacko anyway, he's such an immature prick, and of course I'll back you up. What are mates for, eh?'

Barry Franklin couldn't concentrate on anything his history teacher, Mr Holst, was banging on about. Steph had been meant to meet him yesterday evening, yet she hadn't turned up and Barry was desperate to know why. Glancing across the classroom at her, Barry chucked his exercise book down on the desk in frustration. He thought their date on Saturday had gone really well, and he was sick of racking his brains trying to work out what he'd done so bloody wrong. He'd left for school early this morning and had hung about on the corner of the street for half an hour, smoking fag after fag and waiting for Steph. He knew she must have avoided him somehow. But he needed to know why.

Relieved when the bell rang to signal lunchtime, Barry flew out of his seat and grabbed Steph by the arm as she made for the corridor. 'What have I done wrong? Why you avoiding me?' he asked, accusingly.

'It's not you. Look, I can't talk now because there's something I've gotta do. Wait for me after school and I'll tell you about it then,' Steph replied.

Noticing the tears in Stephanie's eyes, Barry ignored the sniggers from some of his classmates and pulled his girlfriend into his arms. 'If someone's hurt you, I'll fucking kill 'em. Tell me what's wrong and let me deal with it.'

'No one's hurt her, Bal. She just needs to sort something out, that's all. She ain't doing it alone, I'm going with her,' Tammy said in an abrupt tone. Barry had only known Steph for what her mother would call 'five bloody minutes' and if he thought he was taking her best mate away from her by giving it Mr Macho, he had another think coming.

Not wanting to overstep his newfound boyfriend role, Barry held his hands up in a posture of surrender. 'OK. I'm off to grab some lunch and I'll catch up with you after school.'

Marlene Franklin was in her element as she showed her friend Marge the expensive clothes that Jake the Snake had bought her the previous day.

'Fucking hell, Mar! I love that fur jacket, how much was that?'

'Five an' a half – and see them shoes? They were over a oner. He took me to Harrods. Fuckin' Harrods, can you believe it? I think I'm in love.'

Marge burst out laughing. She knew that Marlene always put a pound note above good looks, but Jake the Snake was so vulgar, he actually abused the privilege of being ugly.

'Have you shagged him yet? Aw, Mar, I don't mean to laugh, but he is fucking ugly, ain't he? He reminds me of a bald version of that actor who played Fagin in *Oliver Twist*, what was his name?'

Ignoring Marge's nasty jibe, Marlene debated whether to tell her that she had sucked Jake the Snake's rather flaccid little penis the previous night, but she quickly decided against it. What was the point? Marge would only take the piss and Marlene knew only too well how ugly some of the men who Marge had slept with were.

'You do make me laugh, mate. Talk about the pot calling the kettle black. Anyway, enough about me. What happened with you and Donkey Dave?'

'Dirty bastard, he was. A right fucking pervert. Shagged me up the jacksie all night and then shoved a bottle up me fanny in the morning.'

Marlene laughed. Marge was pure filth in the bedroom department, so for her to call Donkey Dave a pervert was more than enough proof that he must have been bad. 'So, you seeing him again?' Marlene asked.

'No I ain't! Walking like John fucking Wayne I am. I'm sure he's done some internal damage to me. Sod that for a game of soldiers. What about you? I take it you're seeing Fagin again?'

Trying on her fur coat once more, Marlene turned to face her friend. She truly believed she was Marilyn reincarnated, which was why she was forever using her famous film quotes. This time she used the Sugar Cane one out of *Some Like It Hot*. '"Real diamonds. They must be worth their weight in gold",' she drawled, before reverting back to her cockney accent. 'Yes, Marge, of course I'm gonna bleedin' see Fagin again. Not only that, if he proposes, I shall marry the old bastard.'

Wayne Jackman was a creature of habit and Stephanie knew that he and his pals always spent their dinner times at the same chip shop where they would play on the fruit machine. 'He's not 'ere yet. Let's wait by the alley, so we can jump out and surprise him before he gets to the chippy. I don't want the whole world to hear what I've got to say. Ange will kill me if she finds out I've said something to Jacko. She made me promise on Mum's life that I wouldn't, but I crossed my fingers behind me back,' Stephanie said.

'He's coming now, Steph. Potter and Cooksie are with him. You ain't gonna say nothing in front of his mates, are you? Shall I call him over?' Tammy asked, feeling slightly edgy.

Staring at Wayne Jackman sauntering down the road like he owned it, Stephanie felt her blood start to boil. He was laughing and joking with his mates like he didn't have a care in the world, while her poor sister was sitting at home, distraught and scarred for life. Unable to control her temper for one moment longer, Stephanie ran towards him. 'Oi Jacko! I wanna word with you, you fucking pervert.'

Potter and Cooksie immediately started to laugh.

'You ain't still got the hump 'cause I knocked you back, have ya?' Wayne asked, cockily. He still hadn't put two and two together with the Crouch surname and had no idea that Stephanie and Angela were actually related.

'You fucking wanker! I know what you did to my sister, you scumbag. Do your friends know you're a rapist? Well, do they?' Steph shouted.

As realization crept in that Stephanie was Angela's sister, Wayne's face whitened and his usual brash persona wilted like a flower that had just been trampled on by hobnail boots. 'I never raped your sister. She was all over me like a rash and I would never have gone near her in the first place if she hadn't lied about her age.'

'You raped her! She told me you raped her,' Stephanie screamed.

Aware that a crowd had started to gather, Wayne grabbed Stephanie by the arm and dragged her towards the nearby alleyway. 'You stay there. This is between me and her,' he told Cooksie and Potter.

'You ain't taking my mate nowhere where I ain't going,' Tammy said, supportively.

'Well, best you listen to what I've gotta say an' all then, Tampax,' Wayne hissed. He pushed Stephanie against the stone wall, and with his eyes glinting dangerously, gave her a piece of his mind. 'If you weren't dating my old mate,

Bazza, I swear I would knock you out for embarrassing me like you just have. How dare you call me a rapist? Your sister told me she was fifteen and she was well up for it, if you know what I mean?'

'So why did she dump you then? Why did she come home in such a state on Saturday if you never did anything wrong?' Steph screamed, accusingly.

'Because I took her round Danny MacKenzie's house and his cousin Tanya was there. She's in the same year as your fucking sister and she told me who she was and her real age. If you don't believe me, you can ask Danno or Tanya what happened – or Potter and Cooksie, they were there an' all.'

Stephanie felt her face start to redden. 'I'm only going by what my sister told me and she swears you raped her.'

'Leave it now, mate. Let's go, eh?' Tammy urged her pal. She was positive Wayne was telling the truth.

Determined to have the last say, Stephanie pointed her forefinger into Wayne's smarmy face. 'If you ever go near my sister again, I'm gonna call the police and tell 'em what you did to her. Understand?'

Wayne grabbed Stephanie's finger and bent it backwards. 'You better shut your mouth, Crouchy, before I shut it for you. I never did anything to your lying slag of a sister that she didn't want me to do, got it? And if you ever call me, or tell anyone I'm a rapist ever again, I will fucking kill you and that sister of yours. I'm a member of the ICF so, if I was you, I'd watch your back.'

Aware that if she didn't drag Stephanie away, things were about to get very ugly indeed, Tammy grabbed her friend by the arm and virtually dragged her down the road.

'You think Angie's lying, don't you?' Steph asked, near to tears.

'Steph, you told me this morning in the café that Angie

had told you that Jacko still thought she was fifteen. He obviously doesn't, so someone's telling porkies, mate.'

Stephanie turned to her pal. 'I'm gonna check out Jacko's story, and if I find out that he's telling me the truth and Angie's lying, I swear I'm gonna rip her head off.'

Pamela Crouch scuttled home from work as fast as her heavy-sized frame would carry her. She hadn't been able to concentrate on her job in the bakery today, as she knew that there was something wrong with her daughters. All day yesterday, Stephanie and Angela had been holed up in their bedroom. They'd barely touched the nice roast-lamb dinner she'd cooked, and when she tried to enquire what was wrong, both girls had virtually bitten her head off. Pam wasn't stupid. She knew this latest drama was more to do with Angie than Steph, but she also knew it must be serious, as Angela had flatly refused to go to school this morning by feigning a migraine.

'Pam! Pam!'

Hearing her name called, Pam turned around and waved at her friend Cathy.

'Jesus wept! Been shouting your name for the past five minutes. You gone mutt and jeff or summink?'

'Sorry, mate. In a world of me own. Murders, I had with them girls of mine yesterday, and what with Lin being arrested an' all, I dunno if I'm coming or bleedin' going.'

'Have you seen Marlene's new man yet?' Cathy asked, excitedly.

'No. What's this one like?' Pam asked, nearly dropping her bag of leftovers from the bakery in shock. Pam always brought home any cakes, pasties, pies or sandwiches that were due to be thrown away. It helped her make ends meet.

'He turned up yesterday morning in a big flash silver

Jaguar. Old boy, he was, but he looked like he had a few bob. The old slapper was done up to the nines when she ran outside to greet him. Then they snogged in full view of the whole street. She's got no decorum whatsoever that woman. I mean, it weren't five minutes ago she had that black man round there.'

'Well I never!' Pam exclaimed. 'I feel sorry for that son of hers, you know. What an environment to bring a young boy up in.'

'Lairy Mary was telling me about that son of hers. She reckons he's a nice kid, but is a proper Arthur Daley in the making, just like his father was. A right little wide boy he is, by all accounts. Works as a look-out for a fly pitcher down Roman Road Market and is as cunning as a fox, Mary said.'

By the time she reached the front gate, Pam felt a whole lot better. Her girls might have their faults, but at least they were normal kids. Children like Marlene's stood no chance in life.

With the help of Barry, Stephanie managed to check Jacko's story out straight after school, and within seconds of confronting Danno and then his younger cousin, Tanya, Steph realized that not only had she made a right mug of herself, but that Jacko's version of events was actually true.

'No disrespect, but your sister is an out-and-out liar and a bitch. Everyone in our year hates her and she tells fibs about just everyone and everything,' Tanya informed Steph, bluntly.

Walking home with Barry by her side, Stephanie felt incredibly stupid. 'I don't like Jacko, Bal, and I probably never will, but I feel terrible about calling him a rapist. Will you apologize to him for me? I can't face saying sorry to him meself.'

Barry put a supportive arm around his girlfriend's shoulder. He hadn't yet set eyes on Steph's younger sister, Angela, but he already sensed that the girl was a wrong 'un. He'd met one or two similar girls when he'd lived in Bethnal Green, and he could sniff out a vindictive personality a mile off. To accuse somebody of rape when it was anything but, was appalling in Barry's eyes, and he knew if and when he met Angela, he would hate her on sight. 'I actually think you should apologize to Jacko yourself. Trust me, Steph, when you get to know him, he's proper and, seeing as he saved my life, I'd really like yous two to get along. I know he can be a mouthy prick at times, but he weren't like that when we lived in Bethnal Green. I think he larges it in front of them pricks, Potter and Cooksie. Give Jacko a chance, please – for my sake.'

'But I feel such a div. Not only have I accused him of being a nonce, but it weren't long ago that I asked him out meself. He must think I'm a right loony.'

Barry grinned. Jacko had told him what had happened between him and Steph at lunchtime and Barry was pleased that he'd managed to sort things out for his girlfriend so quickly. 'You and Jacko will get along just fine, trust me on that one, and the only reason you asked him out was because you hadn't then met me. Let's just say he was the next best thing, eh?'

Stephanie smiled. 'I'd better walk the rest of the way on me own now. We don't wanna get caught out, do we? Not only that, I've gotta get back and deal with Angie. I ain't letting her get away with this one, Bal. I've always been soft with her, but this time, she's gone one step too far.'

'Are you gonna tell your mum what she said about Jacko?' Barry asked.

'Nah. If I do that she'll probably grass me up about seeing you.'

Desperate to share a kiss with his girlfriend, Barry leant towards her.

'Don't! I'm frightened someone might see us,' Stephanie said, glancing up and down the road.

Barry sighed. He knew Steph was only concerned about being seen with him because of who his mother was, and already the situation had started to piss him off a bit. 'Look, I know my mum's a bit of a girl, but she's no Myra Hindley. Why don't you just tell your mum you're seeing me? It will make things so much easier in the long run,' he suggested.

'Look, I must go now, but I'll meet you in the morning on the corner of Ford Road and we'll walk to school together. I do really like you, Bal, so please don't think that I don't,' Steph said, avoiding his awkward question.

Unable to stop himself, Barry grabbed his girlfriend around the waist, pulled her towards him and kissed her passionately. Pulling away, he winked at Steph. 'And I like you, girl. Probably more than you'll ever know.'

Pamela Crouch was absolutely seething. For months her Angela had been harping on about dying her hair blond, and today, when she was supposed to be ill, Pam had arrived home to find that her daughter had disobeyed her orders and now had a mop of frizzy hair that resembled a low-class prostitute.

'Where did you get the money from, Angela? I know you had no pocket money left and I had two pound notes in my purse this morning and one has miraculously disappeared. If it ain't bad enough you've gone behind my back and done something I forbade you to do, you've been stealing off me as well, ain't ya?'

About to deny the accusation, Angela welcomed the distraction of her sister arriving home. 'Mum reckons I've stolen money out of her purse, Steph. Tell her I ain't. I borrowed a pound off you, didn't I?' she lied.

After the day she'd had at school, Stephanie couldn't help but lose it with her little sister. 'You're a liar, Ange. I never lent you a penny, and not only that, you lied about Jacko an' all, didn't you?'

'Who's Jacko?' Pam asked, perplexed.

Angela stared at her sister with a look of pure hatred on her face. Steph had promised not to divulge her secret to anyone and she had obviously been making herself busy. 'You bitch! I told you to keep your mouth shut,' Angela screamed, as she flew at Stephanie.

'Stop it! Stop it!' Pam yelled, as a full-scale argument began.

'She told me she'd been raped, Mum. She's an evil, wicked liar,' Stephanie shouted, as her sister tried to drag her around the room by her hair.

Pam knew that her girls had always bickered, but she had never seen them as bad as this before. 'I said, stop it,' she yelled, barging her way into the ruckus, while trying to pull them apart.

Angela took a deep breath when her mum made her sit on one side of the lounge and Stephanie on the other. If her humiliation over the Jacko episode hadn't been bad enough, her sister had made it a whole lot worse by opening her big mouth at school and snitching on her to her mum.

'Now, what's going on? And what's all this about a rape? Don't lie to me, the pair of you, because if you do, I'll have your guts for garters,' Pam shouted.

Angela knew that there was only one way to worm herself out of this difficult situation and that was to turn the tables.

'Can I just say something first please, Mum?' she asked, in a childlike, innocent-sounding voice.

'Go on, but don't you dare lie to me, Angela,' Pam replied, in a threatening tone.

Smirking at her sister, Angela turned back to her mother. 'You know that old slapper over the road, Mum. Stephanie's going out with her son.'

CHAPTER SEVEN

Angela's revelation left Pam temporarily dumbstruck, but suddenly she found her voice again. 'This had better not be true, young lady. If I find out you've been within one hundred yards of that old slapper's son, you're grounded for life.'

'It ain't me you wanna be worrying about, it's her. At least I ain't been having sex with boys and then accusing 'em of raping me,' Stephanie screamed. She was furious that her sister had betrayed her trust.

'You lying bitch! I ain't never had sex with anyone, Mum, I swear I ain't,' Angela yelled.

Pam felt physically sick. Angela had only just turned thirteen years old, and the idea of some boy taking advantage of her innocence was almost unthinkable. 'Who is this boy?' Pam asked Angela.

'He's no one. I just liked some boy, that was all, and pretended to Steph that I was going out with him. He's fifteen, Mum. As if he's gonna go out with some silly kid like me. I only told Steph 'cause I wanted to see if I could trust her not to tell you. It was a test and she's failed it.'

'You are such a wicked liar. I can prove it, Mum. Wayne Jackman thought Angie was fifteen 'cause that's what she told him and she pretended that she went to Parsloes Manor.

She also told him that Dad was still alive and he beats her up.'

When Angela leapt off her chair and flew at her sister again, Pam started to weep. 'Stop it! Just bloody stop it,' she screamed, grabbing Angela around the neck.

'I hate you,' Angela spat at Steph, as her mum bundled her into the hallway.

'Get up them stairs now. And you're going back to school in the morning, young lady. Taking no more of your crap, I ain't.'

When Angela ran up the stairs sobbing, Pam marched back into the lounge. 'So, have you been knocking about with that old slapper's son? And don't lie to me 'cause I'll find out the truth,' she told Steph.

Unlike her sister, Stephanie was not a good liar, so decided it would be in her best interest to come clean. 'Barry's lovely, Mum. He's nothing like Marlene. He's the complete opposite and he is so kind to me.'

Pam was furious. 'You are not seeing that boy again, do you understand me? I'll be the laughing stock of the street if anyone finds out you've been knocking about with Marlene's son. Ain't you got no respect for yourself? You silly little mare.'

'Me have respect for myself! What about Angie? At least I ain't done nothing with Barry. At least I don't have sex with boys.'

'Your sister has just turned bloody thirteen. She hasn't had sex with anyone yet. She makes these stories up to try and impress you. As for your behaviour, disgusted I am, Steph, and you're grounded until further notice. No more going out gallivanting until I know I can trust you again.'

'But I ain't done nothing wrong,' Stephanie cried out.

'That'll be for me to decide. Now get upstairs and say

sorry to your sister. I've got enough on me plate without yous two at one another's throats. I've given the pair of you far too much leeway and now it's all going to stop.'

When her mum walked into the kitchen, Stephanie let out a huge, racking sob.

Barry Franklin stood on the corner of Ford Road the following morning. Within seconds of spotting Steph walking towards him, he just knew that there was something wrong. 'What's up, babe?' he asked, genuinely concerned.

'Everything. I had a big row with Angie and then she grassed me up to Mum. She told her that me and you were going out together and me mum went mad. I'm grounded now. I ain't allowed out no more,' Steph explained, her eyes welling up with frustration.

'Don't worry. We'll still find a way to see one another. What about if I have a word with your mum? I'm sure if she meets me, and realizes I'm no monster, she'll change her tune.'

'No! That will just make things worse. I wouldn't mind but Angie ain't even been grounded. If she hadn't had sex with Jacko and then cried rape, none of this would have happened.'

Barry held his tearful girlfriend in his arms. 'I'm gonna jib school today and shoot up to Bethnal Green again. My dad's trial starts on Wednesday and he's having a going-away bash in the Bishop Bonner. Jacko's coming with me, I'm meeting him at the Heathway. He remembers me dad well and he ain't seen him for yonks.'

Stephanie looked at her boyfriend in dismay. The thought of being near Barry all day at school was the only thing that had got her out of bed this morning, and now he wasn't even going to be there. 'Can I come with you?'

'Course you can. But what about your mum? Say she

finds out you ain't gone to school. I don't want to get you into even more trouble.'

Furious with her mother for siding with her sister rather than her, Stephanie shrugged nonchalantly. 'Bollocks to my mum. I'm coming with you, Bal.'

Unaware that her sister had decided to play truant, Angela Crouch had to suffer the humiliation of facing Tanya MacKenzie again.

'Look, girls. The silly slag's dyed her hair blond so we don't recognize her. How's Jacko, Crouchie? Seen him lately, have ya?' Tanya asked, gloating.

Instead of retaliating like she usually would, Angela held her head high and, with her nose in the air, walked past Tanya and her childish mates. She was still gutted that she and Wayne weren't together, but after spending two days moping about and crying, Angie had now decided it was time to move on. Wayne Jackman might be as fit as a butcher's dog, but he wasn't the only fit boy in the world and, with her stunning beauty, Angie was confident that she could get virtually any boy she wanted.

'Why weren't you at school yesterday? Was it because of Jacko? I heard what happened. That slut Tanya's told half the school,' Chloe asked, catching up with her friend.

Angela smiled. Chloe was her only true mate, but even though they were close, Angela had no intention of admitting how devastated she'd been over the Jacko saga. 'I had a sore throat yesterday, so me mum told me to stay home,' she lied.

'So, has Jacko packed you up now? That's what Tanya's been telling everyone.'

'No one's packed no one up. I just don't wanna go out with Jacko no more. He's a bit boring, to be honest,' Angie replied, untruthfully.

Chloe linked arms with her pal. 'You'll never guess who's asked me out?'

'Who?'

'Darren O'Brien, and Dal reckons that his older brother Jason fancies you.'

Angela Crouch could barely believe her luck. Jason O'Brien was in the year above her and Chloe. Not only was he extremely hot, but Angie knew for a fact that Tanya MacKenzie had recently got one of her mates to ask him out for her, and he'd said no.

'I'll go out with Jason. Arrange it for me,' Angela said, her eyes shining with glee. Her mum had always said that when one door shuts, another one opens and Angie couldn't help but think what a wise mother she had.

The atmosphere between Stephanie and Wayne was somewhat icy on the train journey, but by the time they'd had a few drinks in the pub, the frostiness had all but thawed.

'I always knew yous two would get along just fine. Can't have me best mate and me bird hating one another, can I now?' Barry said, happily.

Stephanie looked at her boyfriend and raised her eyebrows. 'So how come this pub is open at ten o'clock in the morning then? I didn't think pubs opened till lunchtime,' she remarked, changing the subject. She had been ultra-polite to Wayne for Barry's sake, but she still wasn't sure of him.

'Pubs open whenever you want 'em to in this neck of the woods, especially if you're loaded like my dad is. This boozer's owned by a famous footballer, you know,' Barry informed her.

'Really! Where is he?' Stephanie asked, expecting to see the man in question serving behind the bar.

Wayne and Barry both chuckled. 'He don't bloody work

here. He plays for Tottenham and his family run the pub for him,' Barry explained.

'What's his name then?' Stephanie enquired. She didn't know the first thing about footballers, but was hoping it was Glenn Hoddle because she knew who he was and thought he was lush.

'His name's Steve Archibald. Look, I'm just gonna have a quiet word with me dad outside. Yous two will be all right for a bit on your own, won't ya?' Barry asked.

Glancing at one another, Wayne and Stephanie both nodded. When Barry walked away, Stephanie felt her earlier awkwardness suddenly return and, not knowing what to say, stared at her glass of cider.

Wanting to put things right between them, it was Wayne who decided to say something first. 'Listen, I'm sorry about what happened with your sister, Steph. I swear I wouldn't have gone out with her if I'd known her proper age. She told me she was fifteen, I swear she did.'

'That's OK,' Stephanie replied, meaning it. The way she felt at the moment, she hated her bloody sister, and any trouble Angie might have got herself into was all her own doing, nobody else's.

'I'm also sorry about the way I spoke to you an' all, and your mate, Tammy,' Wayne said, honestly.

'Don't worry about it. We all say silly things at times, me included. I'm sorry for calling you a rapist,' Stephanie said, feeling incredibly stupid.

Sensing that Steph felt a bit embarrassed, Wayne grinned at her. 'Don't worry about that either. I've been called a lot worse things in me time. I'll get us another drink, shall I? What do you want, another half of cider?'

Stephanie nodded and studied Wayne as he sauntered up to the bar. His bark seemed far worse than his bite all of a sudden.

'There you go,' Wayne said, handing Stephanie her drink. He sat back down opposite her and raised his pint glass. 'To new beginnings, eh?'

Stephanie smiled. 'To new beginnings.'

Angela Crouch spent the entire maths class doodling on the cover of her exercise book. *Angela loves Wayne* had now been scrubbed out completely and had been replaced by *Angela + Jason* with a love heart surrounding it. As the bell rang for lunchtime, Angie grabbed Chloe's arm. 'Where do Darren and Jason go at lunchtime?' she asked her friend.

'I don't think they hang about together at school. Darren goes to the tucky, I think, then goes round Gel Parker's house. He only lives in Ridgewell Close.'

'Well, let's go to the tucky. I want to ask him if Jason wants to go out with me myself.'

Chloe nodded then, arm in arm, the girls walked giggling towards the tuck shop.

'There's Jason. Look!' Angela squealed, excitedly. Unlike Wayne Jackman, who was blond, lean and tall, Jason O'Brien was dark-haired, stocky and short. He was quite handsome, though, and in Angela's eyes looked a bit like George Michael.

'Go and talk to him then,' Chloe urged her pal.

Jason was standing on the corner of School Road, smoking a cigarette. He had two pals with him, neither of whom Angela knew.

'I can't go over there while he's with his mates. You go and speak to him, Chloe. Tell him to meet me outside the tucky in five minutes and I'll talk to him there.'

Knowing how headstrong her friend could be, Chloe knew she would never hear the last of it if she didn't comply with Angela's orders.

‘Wait till I’m out of sight,’ Angela hissed, as Chloe went to march straight over to the boys.

As Angie half ran towards the tuck shop, she came face to face with Tanya MacKenzie and her smarmy-faced sidekicks.

‘Excuse me, please,’ Angela said politely, as they tried to block the pavement to stop her from getting past them.

‘If you’re looking for Jacko, don’t bother, ’cause he’s got a new girlfriend now. Really pretty, ain’t she, girls?’ Tanya hollered, urging the fellow members of her four-strong gang to join in with her torment.

‘Yeah, well pretty she is, and she’s sixteen,’ piped up Sharon Jones, Tanya’s best friend.

‘I ain’t bothered. I’ve got a new boyfriend myself,’ Angela replied, determined to wipe the self-satisfied smile off Tanya MacKenzie’s face.

‘You all right, mate?’ Chloe asked, appearing by Angela’s side.

‘No, she ain’t all right. She’s off her head if she thinks we believe she’s got a new boyfriend. We know what a liar she is,’ Tanya said, laughing.

‘Well, for your information, Angie ain’t lying. She’s going out with Jason O’Brien if you must know,’ Chloe replied.

Tanya MacKenzie stood open-mouthed. For the past eight months she had been besotted with Jason O’Brien’s dazzling good looks, and had recently plucked up the courage to ask him out. Jason had said no, and Tanya was sure he had only knocked her back because she was in the year lower than his, so how could he now be going out with Angela bloody Crouch?

‘You’re lying. You’re only saying that ’cause you’ve heard that I like Jason. You keep your hands off of him, Crouchie, do you hear me?’ Tanya spat.

Seconds later, as if by magic, Jason O’Brien walked around the corner and made a beeline for Angela.

'Do you fancy coming to the chippy with me?' he asked, grinning at her.

Clocking the look of jealousy on Tanya's face, Angela smirked. 'Yes, I'd love to, Jase.'

Stephanie Crouch had had such a brilliant day out with Barry and Wayne that she felt no guilt at all about bunking off school. Unlike her sister, Steph had never played hooky before, and she knew if she forged a letter in her mum's handwriting, none of the teachers would bat an eyelid.

'You enjoyed yourself today, babe?' Barry asked, as they stood on the platform at Mile End station waiting for the District Line train.

'Yeah, I've had a fab day. Why did Jacko shoot off?'

'Jacko wanted to see some old pals while he was in the manor,' Barry replied.

He waited for the commuters to get off, then led Stephanie over to two empty seats in the corner. 'Jacko and me are both cut from the same cloth, babe – that's why I have so much time for him. He's a go-getter, just like I am. I mean, one day me and you might have kids and stuff and you want the best for 'em, don't you? I dunno about you, but I don't wanna be stuck in Dagenham for the rest of my life, or Bethnal Green for that matter. I plan to buy a big house in a posh area and then, one day, when I do have kids, I wanna give them all the stuff that I never had.'

Sort of understanding what Barry meant, Stephanie beamed from ear to ear. Barry must obviously really like her if he was mentioning them having kids one day. 'That's what I want too,' she gushed.

Much to the disgust of the two old ladies sitting opposite, Barry kissed Steph passionately.

'Bloody disgusting! No wonder our birth-control rate is

going mad in this country,' one of the old ladies said to the other.

Totally besotted with one another, Barry and Stephanie carried on kissing as though they were the only two people on the train.

'Why don't we jib school tomorrow an' all? Me mum's going away for a week with her new bloke. She's going to Spain and is sodding off first thing in the morning. Me sister won't be about tomorrow either, 'cause her bloke's coming out of nick and they're having a do for him round at his brother's house. It might be the only day we can have the house all to ourselves. What do you say?'

Stephanie felt her stomach immediately tie itself up in knots. She liked Barry, really liked him, but she wouldn't be fifteen until another few months, and certainly wasn't ready to take their relationship to another level yet.

'What's up?' Barry asked, noticing her reluctance to answer his question.

'I dunno. I suppose I'm just worried if someone catches me coming in or out of your house and I'm worried about the other stuff. You know?'

'What other stuff? All we're gonna do is drink, smoke and play music. I'll never make you do anything you don't wanna do, babe.'

The two old women tutted and stared at one another. 'To think my Albert died in the war for kids like these,' the fatter lady whispered to the other.

'Well, if it's just for a beer, fags and some music, yeah why not?' Steph agreed, grinning.

Barry squeezed Stephanie's hand and stared intently into her eyes. 'That's my girl.'

CHAPTER EIGHT

Pamela Crouch was not in the best of moods. She had spent the whole of the previous night sitting up in Oldchurch Hospital's A&E department, and was so tired, she knew she wouldn't be able to go into work today.

'I'm sorry, Pam,' Linda said, as they finally left the hospital and got into a cab.

'I should hope you bloody well are! Six hours I've just sat up that poxy place. I mean, whatever possessed you to walk home alone, Lin? You know if you're pissed and you fall over, unless you're with someone you can't get back up again.'

'The cab firm I use only had two drivers on and the man on the phone said I'd have to wait an hour. Anyway, I weren't that pissed. I just tripped over on a bit of uneven pavement,' Linda fibbed.

'Don't you start lying to me an' all, Lin. I've got enough on me plate with them two deceitful daughters of mine forever telling me porkies, without you insulting my intelligence an' all. I ain't bloody stupid. Even the nurse told me you'd had a skinful. You'll have a pickled liver if you carry on at the rate you're going. I mean, you're out on the piss every night. It ain't normal.'

'I'm sure I only go out a lot now because I was stuck indoors for all them years with Mum. I'm just trying to make up for lost time, I suppose,' Linda explained.

Pam squeezed her younger sister's hand. 'Just promise me you'll either get a cab home or get one of your mates to walk back with you in future. If that man hadn't found you lying on the pavement, you could have bleedin' stayed there all night and died of hypothermia.'

'I won't do it again, I promise. So, how are the girls? Are they talking again yet?' she asked, sensibly changing the subject.

Pam shook her head sadly. Since their argument at the weekend, her daughters hadn't spoken a single word to one another, and the looks of hatred flying between them were breaking Pam's heart.

'What about that Marlene's boy? Has Steph seen him any more, do you think?'

Pam shrugged. 'I can't stop her seeing him at school, can I? All I can do is make her come straight home after school, not let her out at weekends, and hope it will just fizzle out. Cath knows, obviously, but apart from you I've told no one else, so make sure you don't tell anyone either. I know your mouth's as big as the Blackwall Tunnel when you're pissed.'

'Speak of the devil,' Linda said, as the cab driver turned into their street.

Pam stared out of the window. Marlene was wearing skintight black shiny Lycra leggings and an in-your-face zebra-print top. The new boyfriend was putting a suitcase in the back of his posh Jaguar and Marlene was hugging her pregnant daughter by the gate. Pam paid the cab driver, then urged her sister to get out of the taxi.

'Why don't you go and have a word with her? Just tell her to keep her son away from our Steph. I'll say something to her if you like?'

Pam shook her head. She had never been one for confrontation, especially in full view of the street. Seeing the boyfriend go back into the house and come out with another case, Pam pushed Linda up the path.

'Let's just hope that she's bought a one-way ticket to wherever she's going and is taking that bastard son of hers with her,' Pam said.

Hearing laughter and chatting outside in the street, Angela Crouch lifted the curtain up and stared out of the window. She smirked as she laid eyes on Barry Franklin for the very first time. He had a dark diamond-patterned Pringle jumper on, pale grey tracksuit bottoms and white trainers.

'He's proper horny and well out of your league. You have no chance of holding onto him,' Angie said to Steph, nastily.

Stephanie sighed. She hated falling out with her sister. 'Let's stop all this silliness and make up, shall we? Mum's worried about us and it's so not fair on her. Friends again?'

Ignoring Stephanie's outstretched hand, Angela smirked. 'Drop dead, you bitch.'

Relieved when his sister was picked up in a Datsun by her boyfriend's brother, Barry did his best to tidy up a bit. Both his mum and his sister hated housework and he didn't want Stephanie to think his family was frowsy. Satisfied that the lounge no longer resembled a bomb site, Barry made two trips upstairs to get his record player and records. He hadn't wanted to suggest to Steph that they sat in his bedroom, in case she got the wrong end of the stick. Glancing at the clock on the wall, he picked up his front-door key. Stephanie had been so petrified about being seen entering his house that he had arranged to meet her in the alleyway down Ford Road. Feeling a tingly feeling inside his stomach, Barry picked up his carrier bag and, grinning like a Cheshire cat, sprinted down the road.

Angela met her friend Chloe at their usual spot and, arm in arm, they walked to school discussing their love lives.

'So, do you really like Jason then? Or, do you just wanna go out with him to wind Tanya up?' Chloe enquired.

'Both! I love winding that bitch Tanya up, but I do really like Jase an' all. I was looking at pictures of Wham in *Smash Hits* last night and he so does look like George Michael.'

'Well, Darren wants us all to go on a double date on Saturday. He said we'll go to Romford, have a mooch round the shops, then go to the pictures. You up for it?'

Angie nodded her head excitedly, then immediately scowled as she saw her sister's best friend Tammy approaching. 'What do you want?' she asked, rudely.

'I just wanna know where your sister is. She weren't at school yesterday and I didn't wanna ring her at home in case your mum answered and I got her in trouble. Is she bunking it? Or is she ill? She never met me this morning, so I take it she ain't in today either? She did try and ring me late last night, but I was out with me mum.'

Angela grinned from ear to ear. This bit of information was priceless. 'I think you'll find she's bunking off to spend time with the old slapper's son – and thanks for telling me; I didn't know.'

'Don't say nothing to your mum, will you? Steph would never grass you up if this was the other way round,' Tammy said, alarmed that she'd just put her foot in it. She could tell by the vicious look of glee on Angela's face that she would try and use the information to get her sister into trouble.

'Don't worry. Cross my heart and hope to die, I won't

say nothing to me mum,' Angela said, smirking at Chloe and doing a cross sign across her chest with her right hand.

'You should grass the bitch up,' Chloe said as Tammy walked away.

'Oh, I'm gonna. My mum had a right go at me over me hair again this morning. She said if I don't dye it back to brown by next weekend then I ain't allowed to go out. Wait till she hears about her blue-eyed girl bunking off school to spend time with Barry. My hair will be the last of her problems. She'll go apeshit,' Angela cackled.

Chloe laughed. 'You gonna tell her as soon as you get in from school? Why don't we go down the baker's where your mum works at lunchtime and we can tell her together?'

'She ain't gone to work today. Anyway, I've got a better plan.'

'What?' Chloe asked, excitedly.

'I'm gonna go and see Mr Jones at lunchtime. I'll tell him that she's bunking off, then he can tell me mum. That way, Steph won't know that I've dobbed her in the shit.'

Chloe Martin stared at her best pal in awe. Angela Crouch was so clever and such a wicked schemer. 'That's brilliant, Ange! Totally brilliant.'

Oblivious to the fact that her sister was planning to grass her up, Steph was in a panic over something completely different.

'All right, babe? Sorry I'm a bit late. I wanted to tidy up a bit before you came round. My muvver would never win an award for cleaning and my sister is such a messy cow,' Barry explained.

'We can't go back to your house. We're gonna have to go somewhere else,' Stephanie said in an agitated voice.

'Why? I told you all we're gonna do is have a few bevvies, a smoke and play some records,' Barry replied, dismayed by Stephanie's sudden change of heart. Didn't she trust him or something?

'It's not that. My mum ain't gone to work today. Me aunt fell over pissed last night and my mum got a phone call at one o'clock this morning. There is no way I can chance coming back to yours while she's at home. If she catches me, she'll kill me and you both.'

'I've bought me mum's leopard-skin jacket with me and the black hat she wears for funerals. Surely she won't recognize you in those? She'll just think it's me old girl.'

Stephanie shook her head. 'My mum saw your mum going away this morning. She ain't stupid, Bal, and I can't take the chance of being caught out.'

Putting his thinking cap on, Barry came up with a plan. 'I'll tell you what we'll do. We'll climb over the fence on the corner of the road and get to mine via the back gardens. The back ain't locked, so we'll go in that way.'

'But say someone sees us in their back gardens?'

Barry laughed. 'I'll wear me muvver's coat and you wear her hat. No one will recognize us. Come on, where's your sense of adventure?'

Stephanie giggled and grabbed Barry by the hand. 'Come on then, let's do it.'

With Chloe by her side, Angela ran up the long alleyway that led from the lower to the upper school. She and Chloe had arranged to meet Jason and Darren outside the chip shop so they could eat lunch together and she hoped she could find Mr Jones quickly.

'Slow down. I've got a stitch,' Chloe complained, holding her side.

'You'll have to keep running else we'll be late to meet the boys. I hope I don't bump into bloody Jacko,' Angela mumbled, out of breath herself.

Once inside the upper school entrance, Angela slowed down as she spotted Mrs Belson, Stephanie's typing teacher. 'Excuse me, where's Mr Jones?' she panted.

'Probably in the staff room, my dear. Best not to disturb him while he's eating his lunch,' Mrs Belson replied sensibly.

Ignoring the teacher's advice, Angela grabbed Chloe's arm and headed towards the staff room. Mr Jones had a reputation amongst the older children for being rather unapproachable and a bit of an ogre, but Angela didn't really know him, therefore wasn't scared at all. As bold as brass, Angela knocked on the staff-room door.

'Is Mr Jones there, please?' she asked a male teacher she had never seen before.

'He's having his break at the moment. You'll have to come back after lunch,' the teacher told her.

'I can't come back after lunch and it's very important,' Angela replied, obstinately.

'Wait there,' the teacher said, shutting the door again.

Mr Jones was a rather tall man with a booming voice and a Basil Fawlty-esque walk and physique about him. 'Yes. Make it quick,' he snapped, as he closed the staff-room door behind him.

'Hello sir. My name is Angela Crouch and my sister Stephanie is in form 4P. Because I'm so worried about her, I didn't know who else to speak to apart from you, as I know you're her head of year,' Angela said, in a butter-wouldn't-melt voice.

'I know Stephanie. What is wrong with her?'

'There's a new boy in her class. His name is Barry Franklin and Steph has been bunking off school to spend time with him. I know how important these last two years at school are for her, and I would hate to see her mess her exams up because she has fallen for some stupid boy.'

Chloe wanted to burst out laughing, but instead joined

in the fun. 'Angela loves her sister dearly, Mr Jones, so she was wondering if you could speak to her mum. Ange don't wanna be seen to be a snitch, do you, Ange?'

'No, sir,' Angela replied, desperately trying to keep a straight face.

'OK, I will contact your mother this afternoon. And yes, you are right. Your sister is a bright girl, and she would be silly to throw all that away over some lad.'

'Thank you, Mr Jones, and can you keep my name out of it, please?'

Nodding his head, Mr Jones excused himself and went back inside the staff room.

Roaring with uncontrollable laughter, Angela and Chloe ran down the corridor and out through the school gates.

After her earlier reluctance to set foot inside Barry's house, Stephanie Crouch was now completely at ease and thoroughly enjoying herself.

'You look so pretty today, babe,' Barry stated, as he lit them both a cigarette and topped Steph's drink up.

Stephanie grinned. She had worn the red off-the-shoulder sweatshirt that Barry had bought her at Roman Road Market. Teamed with tight faded jeans, big hoop earrings and the make-up she'd applied in the alleyway earlier, Steph was quite happy with the finished result.

'Weren't it funny climbing over them fences earlier? What about when you got your foot caught?' she said, giggling.

Barry raised his eyebrows. He'd felt a right wilf when he had taken a tumble in front of his girlfriend, but could now see the funny side.

'So, why don't you like cider? Have you just never liked the taste?' Steph asked, when Barry cracked open another can of lager.

'I used to like it, but got pissed on it at a mate's party

when I first started drinking. Ill for days, I was, and the taste of it now just makes me feel sick,' Barry admitted.

'You big girl's blouse,' Steph said, chuckling.

'What did you call me?' Barry joked, clambering on top of Steph and pinning her arms to the dirt-stained carpet.

'Get off me,' Steph snapped, pretending to be angry.

Barry silenced her by snogging her passionately. This was the first time they had ever kissed where he had been lying on top of her, and he immediately felt himself becoming aroused.

Stephanie responded to the sweet taste of his gentle mouth but, as soon as she felt the hardness of his penis poking into her thigh, she froze. Stephanie had been quite a late starter with boys compared to her sister and some of the other girls in her year at school. Apart from Barry, she had only ever kissed two others properly, and she had never gone any further than that.

'You OK?' Barry asked.

'Yeah. Can I put some more music on now? The record's stopped,' Steph replied, desperate to get away from the feel of her boyfriend's rock-hard penis. Part of her wanted to see it and touch it, but she would be far too nervous to do so in case she did something wrong.

'I'm just going a toilet,' Barry said, as he bolted out of the room like a racehorse. His hard-on was sticking out like a flagpole in his loose-fitting tracksuit bottoms and he was embarrassed to let Stephanie see it in all its glory. He could tell how edgy and inexperienced she was, and even though he had been sexually active for the past year or so himself, he didn't want to put his new girlfriend under any pressure, or make her feel uncomfortable in any way.

Stephanie sorted through Barry's record collection. She had noticed the big bulge in his tracksuit bottoms when he had darted out of the room and was relieved to see it had disappeared on his return.

'Can I put some Spandau Ballet on?' she asked him.

Barry nodded and lit up another two cigarettes. 'Tell me more about your family, Steph. I've heard you mention your aunt lives with you, but I haven't seen her yet. Is she your mum's sister?'

Stephanie sat on the sofa next to Barry and felt contented as she snuggled up against his chest. She told him all about Linda and made him laugh over her love for alcohol and some of the hilarious stunts she had pulled. 'I think my mum worries about our Lin more than she does about me and me sister. No wonder she's started to find grey hairs on her head.'

Barry chuckled. 'She sounds a right case, your aunt. I'll have to meet her one day – you know, when me and you are out in the open.'

'I reckon my mum will still be wanting me to be single when I'm twenty-one. Does my head in, she does,' Steph joked.

'You shouldn't be too hard on your mum. She only worries because she cares about you and she loves you. My mum has never worried about me or my sister. She just tends to think about herself.'

'So, what's this new boyfriend of your mum's like, then? Whereabouts they gone on holiday?'

'His name's Jake and he's short, old and loaded. He's taken her to Spain, but I dunno whereabouts, she didn't say.'

'So, has she gone for a week? Or two?' Steph asked.

'Supposedly a week, but you never know with my muvver. About two years back she was seeing this geezer called Quiet John. They called him that 'cause he was a right loudmouth bastard. He took her to Spain an' all. She left me and me sister indoors in our old house on our own. She only left us a score for food and then didn't come back for a month. She fell in love with a waiter while she was out there, dumped Quiet John and stayed out there on her own for three weeks.'

'Oh my God! What did you and your sister do? Did you go and live with your dad, or what?' Steph asked, appalled. All of a sudden her own mother seemed like the best in the world.

'Me dad was in nick at the time, but me and Chantelle got by. We both had to go out thieving just to make ends meet and a few of our old neighbours cooked us dinners and stuff. We couldn't tell 'em where mum actually was, though. Me and Chantelle were worried that they'd tell the Old Bill and we'd get put in care. Mum weren't that popular in Bethnal Green either, you see. The neighbours would have loved to have seen her banged up for abandoning us. They all liked me and me sister, though. I think they felt sorry for the pair of us.'

'Poor you,' Stephanie said, wrapping her arms around her boyfriend's neck.

As Spandau Ballet's 'True' started to play, Barry stood up, grabbed Steph's hands and pulled her off the sofa. 'Let's have our first dance together, shall we?' he said, laughing.

Stephanie grinned when Barry began singing the words to her. 'You've got a great voice and I really love this record,' she whispered in his ear.

Barry stared intently into his girlfriend's eyes. 'And I really love you, Steph. One day, me and you will get married and, when we are, we'll dance to this as the first song at our wedding. Deal?'

Feeling a happiness inside her heart that she had never felt in her life before, Stephanie was stunned. Unable to answer Barry's question because her voice seemed to have deserted her, she smiled and nodded at the same time. For the first time in her young life, Stephanie Crouch was completely and hopelessly in love.

Pamela Crouch's right hand shook like she had a bad case of the DTs as she put the phone back on its receiver. 'Oh, Cath. I'm at my wits' end, I really am,' she shouted, as her friend let herself in the house.

'Whatever's the matter? Is it Lin? Have they taken her back into the hospital again?' Cath asked, alarmed.

'No, Lin's upstairs asleep. It's my Stephanie. She's been bunking off school to spend time with that old slapper's son. I've just had her head of year on the phone. She ain't been in today or yesterday. I'm gonna kill her, Cath. I will march her into that school of a morning and wait outside and walk home with her if I have to. Say she's in his house now? They could be up to anything. I'm going over there. I'll murder that little bastard if he's laid one finger on my baby, I swear I will.'

Cathy had never seen her best friend in such a distressed state. 'Calm down, and whatever you do, don't do nothing rash. Good job I treated us to a bottle of Liebfraumilch from the offie. I thought you might fancy a glass because of the performance you had with Lin last night. You go and sit in the lounge and keep an eye on the house while I pour us a glass. We can have a drink and discuss things properly.'

Pam walked over to the window and stared at Marlene's house. Marlene had recently replaced the sheets she'd had up at the windows with what looked like cheap heavy curtains, but they were always closed as she had no nets up. 'What am I gonna do, Cath?' she asked her friend.

Cathy handed her pal her drink, then sat down on the sofa and sipped her own. 'Do you want my honest opinion?'

Pam nodded.

'The more you try and stop Steph seeing that boy, the more she's gonna want to see him. If you hadn't forbade her to have contact with him, and grounded her, she wouldn't be bunking off school, would she?'

'So, what you trying to say? That it's my fault?' Pam asked, in a narky tone.

'I'm only being truthful with you, Pam, so don't get your knickers in a twist with me for trying to bleedin' help you. I know you don't want your Steph seeing that boy and I don't blame you, but they're only kids and it will soon fizzle out if you just let 'em get on with it.'

'What's going on? Can I have a glass of that wine?' Linda asked, walking into the lounge still half asleep, with her dressing gown on.

'No you bleedin' well can't! If you're thirsty go and make yourself a brew. You've only just woken up, for Christ's sake,' Pam said.

'I'll make one in a minute. What's up?' Lin enquired, raising her eyebrows at Cathy.

Cathy explained all that had happened and her opinion on the matter.

Linda listened intently, then turned to Pam. 'I think Cath's spot on. By stopping Steph from seeing this boy, you're just pushing her away. You need to just let it run its course. I bet you any money you like, if you allow them to see one another, it'll all be over within six weeks.'

'But how can I? I mean, didn't you say Lairy Mary said he was a right cocky little bastard?' Pam asked Cathy.

Cathy laughed. 'How can Mary call anyone cocky when her own nickname's Lairy? Means the same thing, don't it? Actually, Mary popped in the café again yesterday, and 'cause I knew you were worried about Steph, I asked her some more questions. She was actually quite complimentary about the boy. Said he was a rough diamond, but had a heart of gold. She said he was streets above that mother and sister of his. She reckons the sister is a complete wrong 'un, just like her mother.'

'What should I do then? I mean, I can't let Steph carry on seeing him if I haven't met him. I need to see and speak to the lad before I agree to anything.'

'Invite him over for tea or something?' Lin suggested.

'I'll make sure I'm here with you if you feel awkward. I mean, if the mother's pissed off on holiday and left the boy alone, you've got the perfect chance to get to know him without involving that old slapper, ain't you?' Cathy said.

Pam sighed. 'I suppose I'm just gonna have to take your advice, mate. I'll let Steph see the boy and hope and pray it's all over before it started. If it don't work, we'll have to think of a Plan B, 'cause as God's my judge I would rather commit murder than watch my daughter end up with Marlene as a mother-in-law. My life I would.'

CHAPTER NINE

Angela Crouch skipped home from school as happy as a dog with two tails. Getting revenge on her bitch of a sister felt like the best feeling in the world and she couldn't wait to experience first hand the repercussions of her little chat with Mr Jones. Another reason why Angela was feeling so ecstatic was because she had just had her first snog with Jason O'Brien. He was a much better kisser than Jacko had been, and she had felt Jason's rock-hard penis rubbing against her thigh. Having now experienced sex in the raw, Angela decided she was rather partial to it and she couldn't wait to have her wicked way with her new boyfriend. Wayne Jackman was history now, but he had been a learning curve in Angela's life and she was determined to use the skills he had taught her to keep Jason interested in her.

Angela let herself in with her key and was surprised to see her mum, aunt and neighbour Cathy, sitting in the lounge sipping wine. 'Bit early, ain't it? Turning into right alkies, yous lot are,' she said, giggling.

'Cheeky little mare,' Cathy mumbled under her breath. She was no big fan of Pam's youngest daughter.

'After the day I've had, I deserve a crate of bleedin' wine, I dunno about a glass,' Pam said, defending herself. Up until recently, she and Cath had only had a bottle of wine between them on a Saturday evening; now it seemed to be at least two or three nights a week because their lives seemed so bloody stressful at the moment. Cathy's son had moved in with his wayward girlfriend and Pam had never been so worried about her girls in all her life.

Angela smirked. If her mother had had a bad day, it obviously meant she had already spoken to Mr Jones. 'Where's Steph? She not home from school yet?' she asked, innocently.

'Your guess is as good as mine. Now go upstairs and get washed and changed. We're all eating dinner at the table this evening. Me, you and your sister need to have a nice little chat,' Pam replied in a stern tone.

'What am I meant to have done wrong now?' Angie asked, pretending to be annoyed.

'It ain't you, it's your sister. Now do as your mum says,' Linda urged her niece.

Cock-a-hoop that her vicious little plan had worked, Angela ran up the stairs with a big smile on her face.

Stephanie giggled as she and Barry climbed over the last fence. 'I can't believe we've trampled on everyone's gardens. I hope no one saw us,' she said to her boyfriend.

'I wish you didn't have to go home yet. Can't you sneak back over when it's dark again?'

Stephanie shook her head. 'I'm still grounded, I think. It's more than me life's worth to get caught tiptoeing over to your house.'

Barry put his arms around Stephanie. 'Why don't we skip school for the rest of the week? My sister will be out and about with her bloke, so we should have the place to ourselves. We might as well make the most of it while me mum's away and, if you're gonna forge a note, you might as well write one for being off for a whole week rather than just two days.'

Seeing a woman walking along the street with a bag of shopping, Stephanie ducked out of Barry's arms in case the woman knew her mum. She was truly tempted to have the rest of the week off school, but knew that by doing so, she was asking to get caught. 'I'd better not have no more time off, Bal. I ain't even spoken to Tammy yet – say she rings my house and puts her foot in it or something?'

'Ring her as soon as you get in. Please Steph, my old man's up in court tomorrow and I really don't wanna be sitting in a classroom worrying about him. I wanna be with you.'

Feeling desperately sorry for her boyfriend for having such a tough family life, Stephanie looked into his soulful eyes and melted. How could she say no when his dad was about to be banged up? 'OK. I'll meet you same time, same place.'

Hearing the front door slam, Angela Crouch bolted down the stairs like a whippet. She had no intention of missing one second of her stuck-up sister getting the scolding of her life.

'All right, sis? How was school?' she asked, chirpily.

Steph eyed her little sister suspiciously. Angela had never asked her how her day at school had gone before, even when they were on good terms. Steph could see by the evil glint in Angie's eyes that she knew that she had been playing truant. About to plead with her sister to keep her big mouth shut, Steph was stopped from doing so by her mother marching into the hallway.

'Get your arse up them stairs and freshen yourself up before dinner. You and I are gonna have a nice long chat, young lady. In fact, we're all gonna have a nice long chat, because I ain't having this family going off the rails.'

Feeling anxious, Stephanie ran up the stairs. Angela had obviously grassed her up, which would put paid to her spending the rest of the week with Barry, but at least nobody knew she had spent the day with him at the old slapper's house. Her mother would have strangled her as soon as she had walked through the front door if she'd known that.

Desperate to speak to Tammy, Steph kicked herself for not coming home a bit later and using a phone box. There was only one phone indoors. It was downstairs, and Steph knew she wouldn't be able to speak properly with her mum and sister earwigging. Taking a deep breath, Steph looked into the mirror and smiled. Barry Franklin had told her he loved her today, and nothing that her mother said to her could mar the happiness she currently felt inside.

Usually, Pam and the girls ate their dinner sitting in front of the TV with a tray on their laps, but wanting to eat and chat like a proper family for once, Pam set the dining table. Cathy was staying for dinner as well and Lin would be there, too – it was unusual for Linda to even be in at meal times, as she usually finished work and went straight to the pub.

Angela was the first to sit down at the table. 'What we got for dinner then, Mum?' she enquired. She couldn't wait to watch her sister squirm, and just knew she was going to enjoy this meal whatever old crap her mum decided to serve up.

Knowing what a fussy little mare her youngest daughter could be, Pam immediately went on the defensive. 'Minced beef hotpot and don't you dare start whinging and saying you want something else, 'cause I ain't in the bloody mood today, Angela.'

When the phone rang, Lin answered it immediately. 'Steph, Tammy's on the phone,' she shouted out.

Stephanie bounded down the stairs, snatched the phone out of her aunt's hand and dragged the lead into the hallway.

'Can you talk?' Tammy asked.

'Not really,' Steph replied. The kitchen and the lounge opened off the hallway and her mum was no more than ten feet away from her, serving the dinner up.

'I thought I'd better warn you, I think I might have put my foot in it with your sister today. I asked her why you hadn't been at school and I could tell by her reaction that she didn't know. I'm really sorry, Steph. I know what a bitch Angie can be, but I made her swear on her life that she wouldn't tell your mum.'

Stephanie was feeling more confused by the minute. Something was wrong. The house had had a strange kind of atmosphere about it when she'd first come home, but her mum had just smiled at her, so perhaps Angela hadn't opened her big gob after all. 'Don't worry about it, mate,' Steph whispered.

'Have you been spending time with Barry? Will you be in school tomorrow?' Tammy asked.

'Yes, and I dunno. Listen, I've gotta go, Tam, me dinner's ready I think.'

'If you ain't at school tomorrow, try and ring me from somewhere else. I'm dying to hear all the goss,' Tammy said. School just wasn't the same without her best pal by her side. She was beginning to wish that Steph had never met Barry bloody Franklin, as she felt she was losing her friend.

'Will do. Bye Tam,' Steph replied.

'So, why are we all sitting at the table, Mum? Is this a special occasion or something?' Angela asked innocently, when her sister sat down between Cathy and Linda.

'Eat your dinner first and then me and yous girls will have a nice little chat afterwards,' Pam replied, quite calmly.

Stephanie locked eyes with her sister, then stared at her plate. She wasn't at all hungry. She felt far too loved-up to eat, but knew if she didn't try and force her dinner down her gullet, her mum would go apeshit.

'I can't eat no more, but that was lovely, Mum,' Angela lied a few minutes later. She was a bit worried that her mum kept saying she wanted a chat with both her and Steph, and Angie really hoped Mr Jones hadn't dobbed her in the shit.

'I've had enough as well, Mum,' Stephanie mumbled. She wanted to know what was wrong, as the waiting to find out was doing her head in.

Seeing her mother leave her own dinner, Stephanie began to feel more nervous than ever. Her mother usually ate like a horse; if her appetite had deserted her, perhaps she was seriously ill or something. She might have that terrible disease, cancer. One of her friend's mums at school had just died from that. 'Are you ill, Mum? Please tell me what this is all about? Because you're really worrying me now.'

Pam took a gulp of her wine and stared at her deceitful eldest daughter. 'The only thing that is making me ill is the worry over you and that boy. I know you've been bunking off school to spend time with him, and I'm sure you were in his house today, as I kept seeing the curtains twitch. Now, don't lie to me, Steph. Were you in that house?'

'You cow!' Stephanie spat, glaring at her sister.

'Now don't you start blaming her. It was your head of year, Mr Jones, that told me, not Angela. Well, was you with that boy in that old slapper's house or not?'

'Just tell your mum the truth, sweetheart,' Lin urged, squeezing her favourite neice's hand.

'Yeah I was, but all we did was play some records. We've nowhere else to go, have we? I'm too frightened to be seen with him in case you go off your head, and I only bunked off 'cause you grounded me. I love him, Mum. Barry is the kindest, nicest boy I have ever met in my life and I won't let you stop me seeing him just because of who his mother is. It ain't fair,' Stephanie whinged.

Angela's smirk was completely wiped off her face as her mother stood up and urged Steph to give her a hug. 'I need you to promise me that you'll never play truant again. These last two years at school are your most important and I'll be so disappointed if you don't get good marks in your exams, Steph.'

Surprised by her mother being so understanding, Stephanie began to cry. 'But, what about Barry? How am I meant to concentrate on me school work if I ain't even allowed to see him? I promise I won't ever bunk off school again and I'll work really hard, if you just let me see him sometimes, Mum. Can I see him, please?'

Pam still hated the thought of her beautiful daughter being involved with Marlene's son, but seeing Cathy smile at her and remembering her friend's wise words, Pam bit her lip and nodded. 'I'll allow you to see him, but only if I can meet him first.'

Angela watched the scene unfolding in front of her in complete and utter disbelief. Her little chat with Mr Jones was meant to have spelt curtains for Steph's relationship with Barry. Instead, all it had done was enhance it.

'Can I go and tell Barry now, Mum? Shall I get him to pop over in a bit?' Steph said, overcome by excitement.

Pam looked at Linda and Cathy.

'Yeah, sod it. If this lad has you grinning like you are, girl, then we all wanna meet him, don't we?' Lin said, winking at Steph.

'Well, I don't wanna meet him. All yous lot have done for weeks is stare out the window and slag off the old slapper over the road, so why have we now suddenly gotta be nice to her son? I'm going out! You all make me sick,'

Angela spat venomously, pushing her chair so hard it almost toppled over.

Pam grabbed her youngest daughter's arm. Mr Jones had let on that Angela was extremely worried about Steph and had spoken to him, and Pam knew that the spoilt little cow had only done it out of spite. She had always been more lenient with Angela, just because she was the baby of the family, but from now on things were about to change. 'You ain't going out nowhere, young lady. You'll sit 'ere with us tonight and be polite to your sister's boyfriend, and then tomorrow me and you are going up the Heathway to get you a hair dye. As I told you the other day, you ain't going out to play at all until you dye that hair of yours back to its original colour. Look like a bloody child prostitute, you do.'

Absolutely livid that her mother seemed more bothered about the colour of her hair than Stephanie bunking off school, Angela burst out crying and ran up the stairs. 'I hate you. I hate you all,' she screamed.

Hearing the springs on the bed bouncing up and down once again, Barry Franklin turned up the volume on the TV to drown out his sister's cries of unbridled passion. He had once been really close to Chantelle when they were young, but just lately they seemed to argue like cat and dog. Chantelle despised the fact that he still had a good relationship with his father. She also treated her pregnancy as though she had a serious illness and, since Barry had moved back home, she had expected and screamed at him to wait on her hand and foot. Debating whether to go out and find Jacko, Barry heard the doorbell ring.

'What you doing 'ere? Get inside quick,' he urged.

'You'll never guess what! Mum wants you to come over to ours,' Steph said, with a big grin on her face.

'You winding me up or summink?' Barry replied, bemused.

Hearing terrible noises coming from up the stairs, Stephanie nodded towards them. 'What's going on up there?'

'It's me sister and her boyfriend. Doing my head in, the pair of 'em are. Did your mum really say I can come over?' Barry asked, conveniently changing the subject.

'Yep, but I've had to promise her I won't bunk off school no more, so I can't take the rest of the week off,' Steph explained, apologetically.

'I must get changed and put some aftershave on. I don't want your mum to think I'm some tramp. Why did she change her mind, Steph?'

'I think my bitch of a sister grassed on me, but Mum reckons Mr Jones, our head of year, rang her up. It don't really matter now. As long as we can be together, that's all I care about, don't you?'

Barry nodded. 'You shoot back home and I'll be over in about ten minutes, babe.'

Hearing laughter coming from downstairs, Angela Crouch lay on her bed, absolutely seething. She had seen Barry Franklin walk across the road half an hour ago. She had been spying through the curtains, and he looked even fitter close up than he had from a distance.

'Go away,' Angela yelled, as she heard a knock on her bedroom door.

Ignoring her daughter's order, Pam marched in and sat on the edge of Angela's bed. She stared at her daughter's pretty, tear-stained face, and her earlier annoyance with her immediately vanished. 'Don't sit up here on your own, love. Come downstairs and say hello to Barry, eh?'

Angela sat bolt upright. 'And why would I wanna say hello to him? What's next? Gonna invite the old slapper round for tea, are ya?'

Pam spotted a look of jealous hatred on her youngest daughter's face and, unable to stop herself, gave her a short, sharp slap around it. 'You, young lady, should be ashamed of yourself. I know it was you that spoke to Mr Jones. He actually believed that you were such a nice young girl, you were frantically worried about your sister. Well, I know differently, but I will never tell Stephanie, because she would be so bloody hurt. That girl has been a good sister to you, and it's about time you started appreciating all of your family a bit more. You're rude to Steph, me, and Lin, and its not bloody good enough. It's my fault, I know that. Since your father died, I've always babied you, but I can see now that it's not done you any favours at all, and things have to change, Angie.'

Angela threw herself into her mother's chest. 'I'm so sorry. I will try and be nicer to everyone, I promise I will.'

Pam held her tearful daughter in her arms. She knew deep down that her Angela was a good girl. 'Please don't cry. I love you so much, darling.'

'I promise I'll dye my hair back to its normal colour tomorrow, and I will say hello to Steph's boyfriend,' Angela sobbed.

Pam smiled. She had known that a few sharp words would be the thing to bring Angela back to her senses, and she had been absolutely right. Kissing Angie on the nose, Pam stood up. 'You dry your eyes, angel, and come downstairs when you're ready, eh?'

Angela nodded.

As soon as Pam shut the bedroom door, Angela walked over to the mirror, stared at her reflection and smirked. She needed to get back into her mother's good books; if that meant pretending to like her bitch of a sister, then pretend she would.

CHAPTER TEN

As summer came to an abrupt end and autumn kicked in, Stephanie and Barry's relationship seemed to go from strength to strength. Steph kept her promise to her mum by attending school regularly and working hard in her lessons, and Pam allowed Steph to spend time with Barry in return.

'Hurry up, Ange. I'm meant to be meeting Tammy in half hour,' Steph shouted, banging on the bathroom door. She and her sister were now on speaking terms, but were hardly best buddies.

'You're such an impatient cow. You ain't gonna be here later when Jase comes round, are you?' Angela shouted, flouncing out of the bathroom with a towel wrapped around her as though she were the Queen of Sheba. Angela had pestered her mum for weeks to allow her to bring Jason O'Brien home for dinner. 'It ain't fair! Barry's round 'ere all the time and I have to put up with that. How comes Steph's allowed to bring her boyfriend round and I ain't? You always side with Steph,' Angela had whinged only yesterday. Her drama-queen act had worked, and her mother had agreed that Jason O'Brien was now welcome at the house as well. Today he was coming for roast dinner, the first of many, Angela hoped.

'No. I won't be here later. Barry's taking me out for a meal,' Stephanie said, feeling extremely grown-up. Apart from a regular plate of chips in British Home Stores in Romford, or the odd sit-in at McDonald's, this would be the first proper meal that Steph had ever been out for without an adult being present.

'Where you going?' Angela asked, with a hint of jealousy in her voice. Not only did she think Barry Franklin was far too handsome and entertaining to be dating the likes of her plain, boring sister, the way he treated her also really got Angie's goat. Barry was forever buying Steph clothes and gifts. Even though Angela was happy with her Jason, she was still narked that her sister was being treated like she was some kind of bloody princess.

'He's taking me to Pizza Hut. It's well ace in there and they have this big posh salad bar,' Steph said, proudly.

'What's that in aid of then? Is it a special occasion?' Angela asked, desperately trying to keep the spite out of her voice.

Stephanie wasn't a very good liar, she never had been; so, red-faced, she came clean. 'It's Jacko's sixteenth birthday if you must know. Tammy's coming with us as well.'

'Jacko ain't going out with that pig now, is he?' Angela asked, bluntly.

'Tammy ain't no pig! She is lovely, and no, they are not going out together. Jacko is a much nicer person now he don't hang about with Potter and Cooksie all the time, and me and Tam get on really well with him now,' Steph explained.

'Well, bully for you,' Angela said, nastily.

Ignoring her sister's sarcasm, Stephanie wished her a nice day and took her turn in the bathroom.

Over in the East End of London, Barry Franklin was giving it all the spiel. 'Come on ladies and gentlemen, you can't beat my prices. Fifty quid in Harrods these little beauties sell for, hand on heart. Now, am I gonna charge you fifty today? No, I'm not. Nor will I charge you forty, or even thirty for that matter. Today, ladies and gentlemen, this state-of-the-art electronic toy is all yours for a tenner.'

'Be careful, son. The Old Bill are heading this way,' an old man shouted out.

'Bollocks,' Barry mumbled, as he packed the kiddies' toys into the big grey suitcase and rapidly made his way back to Aldgate East Station. It was just over three weeks now since his mum had disappeared off to Spain and, seeing as she had left him virtually no money, Barry had had to work fly pitching toys down Petticoat Lane Market on a Sunday just to get by. His boss, Steve, had said he could have the bath towels to sell but, because they were so heavy, Barry hadn't been able to take him up on his offer. Instead, he'd had a word with another pal of his and had been selling knocked-off plastic robots instead.

The train journey back to Dagenham from Aldgate took about thirty-five minutes and, as he usually did, Barry spent his time on the train thinking about Stephanie. Once or twice in the past, Barry had thought he had been in love, but he now knew that he hadn't. The way Steph made him feel was nothing he had ever experienced in his life before. They had yet to make love, but Barry was sure that she was the girl he wanted to spend the rest of his life with. Sex wasn't everything and, even though Barry was gagging to pop Stephanie's cherry, he was determined not to put pressure on her. He loved her that much, he would wait for years to do the deed if she wanted him to.

Barry's daydreaming nearly caused him to miss his stop, but he somehow managed to prise the doors open just in time. Suitcase in hand, he jogged home as fast as his heavy load would allow him. He hadn't had a magnificent day today like he had last Sunday, but he reckoned he'd cleared fifty quid, which was enough to take Steph out and see him through the next few days. Now his sister's bloke was out of nick, he didn't have to support her any more and, worse ways, he could always skip school on Thursday and work up Roman Road with Steve. Inserting his key inside the lock, Barry heard the phone ringing. He dashed to answer it in case it was Steph. It wasn't. It was his mother ringing from a callbox in Spain.

'How's my lovely boy?' Marlene asked when she finally worked out how to put the money in the slot.

Barry was immediately suspicious. He'd only heard from his mum once since she had gone to Spain, and that was to tell him that she had no idea when she would be home. As for calling him lovely, 'little bastard' was the nearest thing he'd ever had to a compliment off her in the past. Guessing his mum had split up with Jake the Snake and was now after money for the air fare home, Barry sighed. 'How much do you need?' he asked in a sarcastic tone.

'What do you mean?' Marlene asked.

'Money! How much money do you need, Mum? I ain't got a lot, but I suppose I can get hold of it for you somehow.'

'I don't need no money, Barry. And even if I did, I wouldn't ask you for it, would I? You're my favourite son, you are.'

About to remind his mum that he was her only son, Barry decided not to bother. The only other reason in the world she could be being nice to him was that she was drunk, so he decided to humour her instead. 'Nice to hear from you, Mum. I've gotta go now as I'm taking me girlfriend out and I'm running a bit late.'

'But you don't even know why I'm ringing you yet. What happened at your father's trial? Did they bang him up?' Marlene asked, hoping they had.

'No. The trial ain't finished yet. Look, what exactly do you want, Mum?' Barry asked, his patience wearing thin.

'Me and Jake are flying home tomorrow. Got a big surprise for you, boy, we have,' Marlene cackled.

'Don't tell me, you're getting married,' Barry replied, wearily.

'Nope. It's better than that. Gonna have to go now, got no more change on me. See you tomorrow afternoon. Love you.'

Barry put the phone down and stared at it in shock. His mum had been nice, too nice, and that worried him greatly. Convincing himself that Marlene was either pregnant or had had a personality transplant, Barry smiled at his own humour and dashed upstairs to have a bath. He couldn't wait to see Steph and, as soon as his mum arrived home, he would tell her his own big secret as well. He was in love with the girl across the road, and if his mother didn't like it, she would have to bloody well lump it.

Stephanie and Tammy giggled excitedly as they sat on the top deck of the 174 bus that took them to Romford. They had had a great morning mooching around the Dagenham Sunday Market and had both treated themselves to the latest number one record, Billy Joel's 'Uptown Girl'.

'I can't wait till we get posh jobs up London. We'll be uptown girls then, won't we?' Stephanie said, staring at the cover of the seven-inch vinyl.

Tammy lit up two cigarettes and handed one to her pal. 'I dunno if I wanna get a job in an office up town now. My sister's new boyfriend is a policeman and he's been telling me loads about his job. It sounds dead exciting, so I think I might be a copper.'

Stephanie burst out laughing. 'You are joking, ain't ya?'

Tammy shook her head. 'Nah, I ain't. I think I might get

bored being stuck in an office or bank from nine till five. Being a copper must be brill.'

'Well, don't be saying you wanna be a copper when we get to Pizza Hut, will you? Jacko's a member of that West Ham football hooligan gang and my Barry is an illegal fly pitcher,' Steph reminded her.

Seeing the funny side of her career choice, Tammy giggled. 'So, have you done anything with Barry yet or what?'

'No, nothing much.'

'What's nothing much mean? Have you let him tit you up or finger you yet? You ain't wanked him off, have you?' Tammy asked, excitedly.

'Ssh,' Steph replied, as she noticed a lady turn around from the seat in front and give them both a filthy look. She had let Barry fondle her breasts and put his hand inside her knickers, but she wasn't about to discuss that on the 174 bus.

'Tell me then?' Tammy whispered, impatiently.

'No, not on here. Tell me about you and Jacko. You seemed ever so cosy the other night. Do you like him, Tam?'

'Yeah, but only as a mate. I ain't Jacko's type, Steph, and even if I were I wouldn't want your bleedin' sister's leftovers. We do get on well though. He's more of a laugh and so much nicer than I ever thought he would be. I used to think he was so up his own arse, but he ain't when you really get to know him, is he?'

Stephanie nodded in agreement.

'So, when you gonna shag Barry then?' Tammy asked, in her usual none-too-quiet voice.

The woman who had looked around earlier stood up and glared at the girls. 'Charming!' she mumbled, as she moved seats.

Unable to stop themselves, both Stephanie and Tammy burst out laughing.

* * *

Pam had been not only surprised, but also delighted by how nice Angela's boyfriend was. She had been extremely reluctant to welcome Jason O'Brien into her home, as she felt Angie was too young to be having boyfriends, but Jason seemed rather shy, sweet, yet charming at the same time.

'So what does your mum do on a Sunday, Jason? Does she cook a roast as well?' Pam asked, trying to find out if the boy came from a decent home.

'Yes, Mrs Crouch. My mum and dad are both very religious. They go to mass every Sunday morning, but Mum always puts the meat on before they leave, so we all have a nice roast dinner when she gets home.'

Pam glanced at Cathy as if to mentally say: please don't swear. Linda was out on the lash again, all of them spoke like navvies at times, and now Angela – of all people – had brought home a boy who came from a godly family. 'So, what church do your parents attend, love?' Pam asked.

'My family are Irish Catholics. They go to St Peter's Church, near the Chequers.'

Pam was Church of England, but knew very little about her religion – or anyone else's, for that matter. 'Would you like some dessert now, Jason? I've got homemade apple crumble, or there's plenty of ice cream in the freezer, if you'd prefer that?'

'You're not still hungry, are you Jase?' Angela said, kicking her boyfriend under the table.

'No thank you, Mrs Crouch. I'm really full up,' Jason replied, politely.

'Can we please go upstairs and play some records now, Mum?' Angela asked, in her innocent, childlike voice.

Pam thought carefully before answering. She refused to let Stephanie and Barry sit in the bedroom together because she found it inappropriate. It was different with Angie though. She had not long turned thirteen, and seeing as her boyfriend came from a church-going family, she really couldn't see the harm in it. 'You can, but don't you dare tell your sister, as I don't want her sitting upstairs with that Barry,' Pam replied.

'Come on, Jase,' Angela said, grabbing her boyfriend by the hand.

'And make sure you behave yourselves. I shall be checking up on you regularly, you know,' Pam shouted out, as her daughter bolted up the stairs with Jason in tow.

Angela pushed Jason against the landing wall, snogged him passionately and smirked. 'We'll be on our best behaviour, I can promise you that, Mum.'

Wayne Jackman stared wistfully at Stephanie and Barry as they walked up to the salad bar laughing and joking. He wasn't jealous of their happiness. He was just annoyed with himself for not taking Steph up on her offer when she had asked him out in the first place.

'You OK, Jacko? Shall I order us all another drink?' Tammy asked. They'd been ordering glasses of Coke and sneakily pouring the vodka in from a bottle Barry had bought to the restaurant with him.

'Yeah, order some more up, girl,' Wayne replied, chirpily. He liked Tammy, thought she was great fun, but she was no ravishing beauty and he certainly didn't fancy her. Steph was the looker of the two. She had intelligence and an aura about her, and Wayne could kick himself for choosing her stupid sister over Steph. He must have been mad and blind, but it was too late to do anything about it now. When Barry and Steph returned to the table, Wayne smiled at them. 'Get the vodka out, Bazza.'

Making sure none of the waitresses were looking, Barry poured a generous amount in all four of their glasses, then screwed the lid back on the bottle. He lifted his glass aloft,

'To a top geezer who I owe my life to. Happy birthday, Jacko.'

With the washing-up out of the way, Pam flopped down in the armchair opposite Cathy.

'Shall I open that bottle of wine now?' Cathy asked, hopefully.

'No! We can't keep drinking the bloody stuff, Cath. We'll have problems before you know it and we'll have to join that Alcoholic's Anonymous group. We should just drink it on a Saturday night like we used to, or the odd special occasion.'

Cathy chuckled. Pam could be such an old fuddy-duddy at times. 'We're hardly bleedin' alkies are we? There's only a couple of poxy glasses each in a bottle. Anyway, it is a special occasion. It would have been my twenty-fifth wedding anniversary today.'

Pam looked at her pal in amazement. 'But you hated your old man, Cath.'

'Yeah, I know. Still a bloody special occasion though, ain't it?'

Pam burst out laughing. Sometimes she didn't know what she would do without having Cath to lighten up her day. 'Go on then, you pisshead.'

'Pot calling kettle,' Cathy joked.

Suddenly remembering her youngest daughter was up in her bedroom with a boy for the very first time, Pam leapt out of the chair. 'I'd better go up and check on 'em. They're a bit quiet up there, ain't they?'

'Stop worrying and sit back down. The top forty's just started and you know how your girls are addicted to listening to them bleedin' charts. You can guarantee Angie is making that poor boy listen to the rundown like she's made me and you listen to the shit in the past. She's only thirteen, Pam.'

'You reckon that's all they're doing, then?' Pam asked, feeling relieved.

Cathy grinned. 'Of course it is.'

With the top-forty chart on in the background, Angela released Jason's big, hard penis from the zip of his jeans and, without warning, shoved it inside her mouth.

'Oh, Ange. That feels great, but say your mum comes up?' Jason panted. He had only ever slept with one girl in the past and receiving a blow job was a completely new pleasure for him.

Flicking her tongue over the top of Jason's penis like Jacko had taught her to do, Angela opened her eyes, glanced at the look of ecstasy on her boyfriend's face, and sat up.

'Don't stop,' Jason groaned.

Smirking, Angela stood up, wedged her dressing-table chair under the door so that her mum couldn't get into the room, took her knickers off and lay on the bed. 'Fuck me,' she urged Jason.

'I can't! I ain't got no johnnies and it don't feel right with your mum sitting downstairs.'

'You don't need johnnies if you pull it out at the right time, and don't worry about my mum, she couldn't get in here even if she tried.'

With his hormones unable to look such a gift horse in the mouth, Jason held his penis in his right hand and rammed it inside Angela as hard as he could.

CHAPTER ELEVEN

Stephanie said goodbye to Tammy outside the school gates then, hand in hand, walked home with Barry. Some of the other kids would snigger or make snide remarks over their obvious affection for each other, but Steph and Barry were in their own little bubble and really didn't care what people said.

'So, why weren't Jacko at school today? Do you think he's still hung-over from yesterday?' Steph asked her boyfriend.

'Nah. He told me he weren't coming in. He's gone to visit his old man in prison. Wait there, while I use this phone box. I'm gonna ring one of me dad's mates. I wanna find out if he's been sentenced yet.'

Stephanie stared at Barry through the glass panels on the big red door. She couldn't work out by the expression on his face whether the news he was being told was good or bad. 'Well?' she asked, as he finally opened the door.

'Four years he got.'

'Oh, I'm sorry, Bal,' Stephanie said, putting her arms around her boyfriend to give him a comforting hug.

'It ain't as bad as it sounds. He'll be out in two if he behaves himself. I used to really like living with him though,

Steph. Don't get me wrong, I'm glad I moved to Dagenham else I would never have met you, but I hate living with me muvver and sister. They both treat me like I'm their slave. Me sister used to be all right years ago but, since she's been with her bloke, she's got even worse.'

'Surely the council should give your sister a place now she's pregnant? My mum reckons a lot of these young girls get pregnant on purpose these days, just so they can jump the housing queue,' Stephanie said.

'They ain't allowed to give her a place until she's sixteen, I don't think. Her birthday's the beginning of December, so hopefully she'll move out then. Oh shit, me muvver's home already,' Barry said as they turned the corner.

Stephanie immediately let go of Barry's hand as she spotted Marlene. She was wearing a short mauve skintight Lycra dress and had a big straw hat on her head. Her sandals were white and they had the biggest stiletto heel on them that Steph had ever seen.

'Barry!' Marlene exclaimed, opening her arms and running towards her son.

'I'd better get indoors,' Steph said, bluntly. She didn't want to face the wrath of her mother if she was caught talking to Marlene.

'I'll knock for you later,' Barry said understandingly, as his mum stumbled towards him in her high heels and fell into his arms.

'Gissa cuddle. I ain't 'arf missed you, boy. Me and Jake had a wonderful time. We bought you back some bottled sangria and I got you two hundred fags. That girl you were walking along with ain't your bit of fluff, is she? Can't stand her fat fucker of a mother. She always looks down her nose at me,' Marlene said as she clocked where Steph went.

Barry stared at his mother in utter disbelief. He could never remember her cuddling him before, not even when he was a small child – and her saying she had missed him, that was a first as well. As for her buying him presents, she never treated him to sod all and had even forgotten his birthday for the past two years running. Ignoring Marlene's question about Stephanie, Barry stared her straight in the eyes. 'I ain't no div, Mum. Something's going on, so best you tell me what. Are you getting married? Are you pregnant? Just spit it out, I'm a big boy now.'

Marlene burst out laughing. She hated children, didn't even like the two she'd given birth to very much. 'Don't be so silly. I'd rather sew me fanny up than have any more kids. Got enough on me plate with you and your bleedin' sister, ain't I? Where is Chantelle, by the way?'

'Out with Ajay somewhere. So, are you getting married or what?'

Marlene linked arms with her only son. 'No, it's much more exciting than that. Let's go and open that sangria. We'll discuss it indoors.'

Pam and Cathy were stuck to the living-room window like two tubes of superglue.

'Will yous two come away from that window. I don't want Barry to see you spying on him. It's embarrassing,' Stephanie said, annoyed.

Pam watched Marlene tottering up the path in her ridiculously high heels, then turned to face Steph. 'I really don't think it's a good idea that Barry comes over here now his mum's home, love. You can still see him and that, but don't bring him indoors and don't you dare go over there.'

Stephanie looked at her mother in total dismay. 'But why not? Barry enjoys coming over here. What am I meant to say to him, Mum?'

Pam shrugged. Barry had done nothing wrong, but there was no way he was stepping foot over her threshold now his mother was back home. Say Marlene saw him and came and knocked on the door? Or, even worse, say she expected an invite herself?

'Please don't stop Barry from coming round, Mum,' Stephanie begged.

'I'm sorry, Steph, but I told you when the boy first came round here that he was only allowed to have dinner and pop in until his mother came back. I will not have my name darkened by being involved with that old slapper, so I'm sorry but the answer's no. Now, that's the end of the matter.'

Devastated by her mother's callousness, Stephanie grabbed her school bag off the sofa and ran up the stairs, sobbing.

Barry pulled a face as he sipped the drink that his mother had given him. He had never drunk sangria before, and in his opinion it tasted vulgar – a bit like sweet vinegar.

'Don't you like it, boy? Wanna shot of JD with me instead?' Jake the Snake asked.

Barry nodded his head. Both his mother and Jake the Snake kept smiling at him and he was becoming more perplexed by the second at their sickly niceness towards him. 'So, what's this big news, then?'

Marlene grinned. 'Jake's bought a bar in a really posh part of Spain. It's beautiful, Bal, and it's gonna be called Marlene's.'

Barry was well chuffed. If his mother moved abroad and his sister moved out, he would have the whole house to himself. 'That's blinding news, Mum. So, when you going out there to live?'

'Next week. I ain't telling the authorities I'm living out there though, because I don't wanna lose me social money or this house, so if anyone asks you, just say we've bought a holiday home and we're flitting backwards and forwards. I can't wait for you to see it, Barry. It's top notch and we're gonna sell all posh food in there as well. Jake's hired a proper chef, ain't you, babe?' Marlene gushed, squeezing her sugar daddy's hand.

'Sounds ace. I'll have to come out there for a holiday one day,' Barry replied, chirpily.

Marlene burst out laughing. 'You dopey sod! You'll be moving out there with us. You're gonna love it, Bal, and you wanna see the girls out there. You'll have a field day, son.'

Barry looked at his mother in stupefied shock. 'I don't wanna move to Spain. I wanna stay 'ere. I don't mind having holidays out there, but I like it in England.'

'Don't be such a stick-in-the-mud. You'll love it in Spain. What boy your age wouldn't wanna be surrounded by the sun, sea and pretty girls. And you'll be loaded. Jake's gonna pay you well, ain't you, Jake?'

'How's a hundred sovs a week sound?' Jake asked, grinning.

'I couldn't give a shit if you were paying me a thousand sovs a week, I still wouldn't wanna go to Spain. I like living in Dagenham. I like my job on the market and I ain't leaving me girlfriend. I love her too much.'

'Love! You're fourteen years old, boy. You don't know what bleedin' love is at your age. Anyway, you'll easily find another bird out in Spain. Tell him how pretty the girls are out there, Jake.'

When Jake began to speak, Barry was so infuriated, he stood up. 'I ain't fucking going and you can't make me go if I don't wanna,' he screamed.

Marlene leapt off the sofa and grabbed her son by the shoulders. 'Oh yes I can! I'm your mother, and now your father ain't gonna be around to look after you, you have no choice but to live wherever I wanna live.'

'But what about school? Can't I finish me schooling and

then come out there if you still want me to? I can look after meself, you know that. And what about Chantelle? She'll be about to keep an eye on me, won't she?'

'Don't give me all that old bollocks about school. You might be clued up and streetwise, but you're hardly academically bright, are you? You've always said you couldn't wait to leave bloody school and work full time. Well, now's your fucking chance to make something of your life. Just think of how well off you're gonna be, earning a ton a week at your age.'

Barry sat back down in the armchair and put his head in his hands. If he hadn't already met Steph, he would have jumped at the chance of moving to Spain and earning a hundred quid a week, but he couldn't bear to be parted from her. 'I ain't going, Mum. I'm sorry, but I just can't leave me bird.'

'You can and you will, boy. Jake needs you to help him run this bar, we both do, so like it or not, that's what you'll be doing,' Marlene snapped back.

'Can't you just employ someone else to do it?'

Marlene's earlier façade of being nice had now all but disappeared and she was becoming more irate by the second at her ungrateful son's attitude. 'No, we fucking well can't! Now you listen to me, Barry. I don't want you with me in Spain any more than you wanna be there, but we need your help. There's a lot of heavy lifting and stuff to be done, and we need someone who can keep an eye on the place who we can trust. Jake ain't as young and fit as you are, so you can do all the donkey work, while me and him run the actual gaff. There is no way we are employing any of them Spaniards, 'cause we can't stand the greasy bastards, and if we employ a decent English bloke, he's gonna cost us big bucks. So, like it or lump it, boy, you're moving to Spain. Now, do yourself a favour and get that smacked-arse face of yours out of my sight before I give you what for, you selfish little fucker.'

Absolutely furious, Barry grabbed his door key and ran out of the house.

Stephanie was lying on her bed crying when Angela came into the room.

'What's up? Has Barry dumped you or something?' Angela asked, hopefully.

'No, it's Mum,' Steph replied, wiping her eyes with the cuff of her sleeve.

'What's she done?'

'She won't let Barry in the house no more because his mum's back. It's just so unfair when he ain't done nothing wrong.'

'Aah, that ain't right, sis. Shall I have a word with her for you? See if I can get her to change her mind.'

Surprised by her sister's unusual kindness, Stephanie nodded and hugged her. 'I'm really glad we're friends again. We musn't argue no more in future. How did you get on yesterday when you bought Jason round? Did Mum like him?'

'Yeah. Mum thought he was cool. His parents go to church and stuff and when Jase told her that she even let us sit up here in the bedroom.'

'Did she?' Stephanie asked, surprised. Her mother had forbidden her to sit upstairs with Barry. She had said it was unethical.

'You stay here and I'll go and have a chat with Mum now for you,' Angela said, kindly.

Pam was in the kitchen peeling potatoes when Angela bounded down the stairs. 'Don't start driving me mad saying you're hungry because dinner's gonna be a good hour or so yet,' Pam warned her daughter.

'I wasn't going to. Mum, you know that now Barry ain't allowed in here no more, I can still bring Jase round, can't I?'

'Yes, providing you both behave yourself, you can.'

Grinning, Angela ran back up the stairs.

'Well, what did she say?' Steph asked her sister expectantly.

Angela sat down on her sister's bed and squeezed her hand. 'I asked her to change her mind, Steph, but I'm sorry, she still said no.'

Barry Franklin's mind was all over the place as Wayne Jackman handed him another can of lager. 'They can't make you go if you don't wanna go, Bazza. Ain't you got an aunt and uncle you can live with or something? I would ask me nan and grandad if you could stop with us, but I know me nan will say we ain't got enough room. She's always moaning saying we need a bigger gaff as it is.'

'My dad's brother lives in Canvey Island, but he's got four kids of his own. Anyway, you don't know my mother as well as I do, Jacko. If she says I'm going to Spain, then I'm fucking going.'

'You can always run away,' Wayne suggested.

Barry rubbed his tired eyes. He could probably leave school and do some extra shifts with Steve, but he only got paid fifteen pound a day to keep look-out and that was hardly going to put a roof over his head and pay all the bills. 'I can't live on shirt buttons, Jacko. I think the only way out for me is to go to Spain, save the oner a week, then come back to Dagenham and get a place of me own.'

'How long will you be away for? And what about Steph?'

'There's no point me coming back before I'm sixteen, mate. My muvver is a cunt, and if I scarper before that she will only come back to England and find me. If I toe the line and work hard, perhaps she will let me come back for holidays and stuff. I mean, a ton a week ain't bad dosh, is it? I'll be cakeo by the time I'm sixteen, if I'm careful with me earnings. Steph is bound to be pissed off, but I know she loves me and I'm sure she'll wait for me. I'm fifteen next June, so she's only gotta wait just over a year and a half and I'll be back for good.'

'A ton a week is proper money, mate, and if someone offered me that, I'd bite their hand off. Course Steph will wait for you and, while you're gone, I'll keep an eye on her and make sure she's OK.'

Barry gave Wayne a manly hug. 'Cheers, Jacko, you're a diamond.'

Refusing to sit in the same room as her mother, Stephanie Crouch ate her plate of shepherd's pie leaning over the kitchen top.

'Why don't you come and sit in 'ere with us? You can't eat properly standing up,' Pam shouted out.

About to throw a sarcastic reply her mother's way, Stephanie was stopped from doing so by the shrill ring of the doorbell. Wondering if it might be Barry, she ran to answer it.

'What's a matter?' she asked, as she clocked her boyfriend's sad-eyed expression.

'I need to speak to you, Steph. Not 'ere though. Can you come out for a bit? We'll go for a walk somewhere quiet, where we can talk in private.'

Stephanie was immediately alarmed. Surely Barry wasn't going to dump her? 'Wait there while I get me key,' she said. She didn't want to have to tell him that her mother had barred him from setting foot across the threshold. He looked upset enough as it was.

'You'd better have eaten that dinner, young lady, and you

make sure you're back 'ere by nine at the latest. You ain't taking liberties like you did last week, coming in at half past on a bleedin' school night.'

Ignoring her mother's whingeing voice, Steph grabbed her door key and slammed the front door. She waited until she and Barry were a few minutes away from the house, then nervously asked the all-important question. 'So, what do you wanna talk about?'

Saying nothing, Barry led Steph towards the park and was relieved to find it was relatively empty. 'Do you wanna fag?' he asked, as he gesticulated to her to sit down next to him on a bench.

Annoyed that Barry was keeping her in limbo, Stephanie snatched the fag out of his hand and glared at him. 'Am I about to be dumped?' she asked, bluntly.

With emotion seeping into his voice, Barry explained everything.

'But you can't go, Bal. What am I meant to do without you?' Stephanie said, shocked to the core.

Barry held his distraught girlfriend tightly in his arms. This was even more heartbreaking than he thought it would be – he felt like blubbing himself. 'It won't be forever, babe. I promise you I will save every bit of dosh I earn and the day I turn sixteen I will fly straight back home. I can get a job then, on the market or something, and I'll be able to afford me own place. If you like, you can even move in with me. You'll be sixteen then an' all, won't ya?'

'But that's ages away. Please don't go, Barry. Can't you live back in Bethnal Green or with your sister and her bloke? I'm frightened if you go you'll meet someone else and I'll never see you again,' Steph sobbed.

'The only other option I've got is to run away, Steph, but apart from dossing on a mate's sofa round 'ere or in Bethnal Green, I ain't gonna be able to afford or get a proper place to live. My muvver can be a right bitch and I know she'll tell social services I've done a runner. Then, I'll get put in one of them fucking kids' homes with all the waifs and strays of the world. Trust me, babe, if there was any other way out of this, I'd have thought of it by now. There ain't, so I might as well save up the oner a week that Jake's gonna pay me for our future together. Eighteen months ain't the end of the world and I'll be back before you know it. Look on the bright side, at least you can concentrate on your exams while I'm gone, eh?' Barry said, kissing Steph lovingly on the forehead.

'So, when will you be going?'

'Next week, I think. I'll write to you every single day and I can ring you at weekends and stuff. If I work hard, me mum might even let me come home to visit you as well. I'm sure Jacko can sort it so I can stay at his for a week or whatever at a time.'

Stephanie felt as though her heart had just been sliced in two. Barry was her first true love and now, after an extremely short but happy romance, he was about to be cruelly snatched away from her.

Barry tilted Steph's chin towards him so he could look her in the eyes. 'I need to ask you something and you must be truthful with me.'

Biting her lip to stop it wobbling like a distressed child's, Stephanie nodded.

'Swear on your life that you'll wait for me, Steph.'

'Cross my heart and hope to die, but you must swear to me that you'll never go out with any other girls,' Steph croaked.

Barry wasn't the tearful type. His mother had brought him up to be tough; even from a very early age, he had forced himself not to cry because of the good hiding he received in return on the odd occasions he had. For once, though, Barry could not suppress his emotions. Staring at Steph, he wiped his tears away with the cuff of his jacket. 'I swear to you, Steph, that I will wait for you. I love you, girl, and I always will.'

CHAPTER TWELVE

The days leading up to Barry's departure were very emotional for Stephanie. Every spare second she had, she spent with her boyfriend, but even though they did some fun things together, there was always a tinge of sadness in the air.

'So, when's lover boy leaving? Has his flight been booked yet?' Angela asked.

'He's flying out on Monday morning. I dunno what I'm gonna do, Ange. I love him so much,' Steph replied, her eyes welling up, as they regularly seemed to lately.

Angela smirked. She was thrilled that Barry was emigrating. In her eyes, he was far too much of a catch to be with Steph. Even though she had Jason, Barry's generosity towards her sister, and the way he looked at her so adoringly, always made Angela want to vomit. 'You'll meet someone else, you know. There are plenty of good-looking boys out there.'

Stephanie looked at Angela in horror. She probably didn't mean to be so bloody infuriating, but she really was at times. 'I don't want no one else, Ange. I'm waiting for Barry and he's gonna wait for me.'

'Have you done it with him yet?' Angela asked, nosily.

'No. I really do fancy him, but I'm scared of doing it.'

'Don't be scared. I've done it with Jason and it's brill. He's better at it than Jacko was.'

'You shouldn't be sleeping with lots of boys at your age, Ange. You don't wanna get a bad name for yourself.'

'I haven't slept with lots. I've only done it with two. You should stop being a prude and try it, Steph. It's well good, but don't be surprised if you don't like it the first time, 'cause I didn't. It hurt.'

Stephanie digested her sister's words, but said no more on the subject. Unbeknown to her family, she had arranged to spend the night with Barry. His mum and Jake were holding a big leaving bash over in South London this evening, and they and Barry's sister were all staying in a hotel and wouldn't be home until tomorrow. As luck would have it, Tammy's parents were also away for the weekend. Steph had begged her mum to let her stay over at her friend's house, and had promised that Tammy's older sister would be there to keep an eye on them. Pam had been suspicious at first and had wanted to know the ins and outs of a duck's arse, but after learning that Tammy's sister's boyfriend was a policeman, and believing Steph's lie that Barry would be at the leaving party with his mother, Pam had allowed her to go ahead.

'Right, I'm off now,' Steph said to Angela, as she zipped up her overnight bag.

'You ain't really staying round Tam's, are you?'

Stephanie loved her little sister, but knew deep down she could never truly trust her. 'Yes I am! What makes you say that?'

'Because I saw Barry's mum and her boyfriend leave earlier. His sister and that Indian boyfriend of hers were with 'em an' all, but your Barry weren't.'

'Barry's been to work. He's meeting his mum at the party later,' Steph replied, producing the only viable excuse she could think of.

Angela laughed out loud. Steph was lying, she had it written all over her bright red face. 'You just enjoy yourself, and don't worry about Mum. She was still at work when they all went out earlier and I won't say nothing to her, I promise.'

'You'd better bloody not,' Steph said, glaring at her sister.

'I won't!' Angela said, honestly. Had circumstances been different, she would have been tempted to grass Stephanie up but, seeing as her sister's relationship was all but over anyway, there was little point in doing so.

Barry sighed wistfully as he put the two fillet steaks into his mother's battered-looking old frying pan. He'd worked his last shift at Roman Road Market today, and his boss had handed him a fifty-pound note as he'd left. 'You're a good lad, Bal. Definitely the most reliable I've ever had working for me. If and when you come back from Spain, they'll always be a job here waiting for you,' Steve had told him.

Barry checked that the steak was sizzling nicely, then washed the salad. He had quite a flair for cooking, due to his mother's inability to do so, and even though he would never admit it to anyone, in case it spoiled his street cred, he rather enjoyed it. He looked at his watch. He was meeting Steph at the corner of the road at seven and they would then do a bit of garden hopping for the very last time. He couldn't wait to hold her in his arms all night long, and had even changed his sheets so that the bed smelt nice and fresh. If tonight was the night when he and Steph made love for the very first time, he wanted everything to be as perfect as it possibly could be.

Pam and Cath were tucking into a plate of Scotch eggs when Linda walked into the lounge wearing an old tracksuit.

'Ain't you going out tonight?' Pam asked in surprise. It was unheard of for Lin to sit indoors on a Saturday evening, and Pam's first thought was that her sister must be ill.

'Nah, I don't fancy it. I thought I might just stay at home and have a drink with yous two.'

'Don't you feel well?' Pam asked, concerned.

'I feel fine. I'm just gonna shoot round the offie and get some lagers. Do yous two want anything?' Lin asked.

'Get us another bottle of Liebfraumilch and some of them Twiglets,' Cathy said, handing Lin a five-pound note.

'And get me one of them Double Decker bars,' Pam yelled out, as Lin shut the front door.

'Do you reckon she's ill?' Cathy asked her pal.

'Nah, she ain't ill, but I'll bet you a pound to a piece of shit she's done something wrong.'

Stephanie Crouch felt like the Queen as she wiped her mouth with the serviette Barry handed her. Her boyfriend had treated her to a slap-up three-course meal and had laid the table like they did in posh restaurants. They had eaten Heinz tomato soup with crusty rolls for starters, fillet steak and salad for main and chocolate mousse for their dessert. They had also shared a bottle of fizzy white wine and Stephanie felt extremely grown-up as Barry topped her glass up again.

'Ain't it romantic, Bal, sitting 'ere like this? The meal was so lovely. I ain't no good at cooking and wouldn't have a clue how to do the steak like you did it.'

Barry laughed. 'When we move in together, I'll teach you how to cook properly. Then we can take it in turns. You can cook one day and I'll cook the next.'

Stephanie smiled sadly. 'I so wish you weren't going to Spain, and it ain't eighteen months till you come back, it's eighteen months, three weeks and two days. I worked it out in bed last night.'

Barry stood up and urged his girlfriend to do the same thing. He kissed her passionately and let out a groan as his penis began to harden. 'Shall we go upstairs, have a lie-down on the bed and play some records?' he asked.

Stephanie stared into Barry's doleful brown eyes and ran her fingers through his thick dark hair. He looked irresistible today in his navy Sergio Tacchini tracksuit and she knew the girls would be all over him like a rash in Spain. Steph held Barry's hand and, without saying a word to him, she led him up the stairs.

As Pam had predicted earlier, Linda's tongue started to loosen by the time she had drunk beer number three. Christmas was less than eight weeks away, and as Pam and Cathy discussed who would cook what this year, Linda butted into the conversation. 'Had a bit of agg in the Trades last night, I did,' she said, cockily.

Giving Cathy an 'I told you so' glance, Pam turned towards her younger sister. 'You didn't get yourself nicked again, did you?'

Linda shook her head. 'Nah, nothing like that.'

'Spit it out then. What you done now?'

'I had a row with the treasurer. He said I was pissed, but I weren't, I swear I weren't. So I abused him and he barred me.'

'What? Barred you for good?' Pam asked, hopefully.

'I dunno if I'm barred for life yet. My mate Sue's brother is on the committee, so he's gonna have a word in the week, see if he can sort it out for me.'

'So, what did you say to upset the treasurer then?' Cathy asked Linda.

'I can't remember exactly, but I think I called him an old cunt.'

Pam looked at her sister in horror. She hated the C-word.

'You can't go round calling people terrible words like that, Lin. No wonder the poor man barred you.'

When Cathy burst out laughing, Pam glared at her friend. 'Don't encourage her, Cath. I mean it.'

Slurping her lager out of the can, Linda began to giggle. 'I only told the truth, he is an old cunt.'

Stephanie was incredibly nervous as Barry unclipped her bra under the quilt cover. He had touched her breasts before, but he had never actually seen them in the flesh. 'You're so beautiful, babe,' Barry groaned, as he put his mouth around her right nipple.

Stephanie winced. The last boy Tammy had got off with had sucked her nipples and she had said it was great. Steph disagreed. Barry seemed to be sucking hers too hard and, instead of feeling any pleasure, all she felt was pain.

Even though they had been going out for over a month now, nothing sexual had taken place between them, and as Barry wriggled out of his Y-fronts and put Steph's hand on his rock-hard penis, Stephanie felt her whole body freeze. She had never seen or touched a willy in her life before, and not knowing what she was meant to do with it, she decided to squeeze it and hope for the best.

'Nah, don't do that, babe,' Barry said, grabbing her hand. He threw the quilt to one side and began wanking himself off. 'Do it the way I'm doing it,' he urged her.

Looking at Barry's penis standing upright, Stephanie glanced at her naked breasts and began to freak out. This was all too much too soon. Not only did she feel stupid because she obviously didn't have a clue what she was doing, she also felt way out of her depth. When she pulled the quilt back over herself and burst into tears, Barry stopped masturbating and put a comforting arm around her. 'What's a matter, babe? We don't have to do nothing if you don't want to, you know.'

Not wanting to admit that all she knew about sex was what she had learned from idle schoolgirl gossip and graffiti on toilet walls, Stephanie thought of the best excuse she could. 'I can't do it, Barry. I would if you weren't going away to Spain, but I think if we do it, it's gonna make me miss you even more. You don't mind, do you? Can we just get dressed and have a cuddle?' Stephanie wept.

Barry had never felt so frustrated before in his life. He wanted Steph badly, but he would never force himself upon her, even though a small part of him wanted to. 'You get dressed, go downstairs and pour us both a drink, babe. There's beers and cider in the fridge,' he said, sensibly.

'Ain't you coming downstairs as well?' Stephanie was worried her naivety might have put him off her and that he might have second thoughts about their relationship continuing.

Not wanting to admit that he needed to finish off masturbating, Barry smiled. 'I'll be down in a minute and I've gotta nice surprise for you. You go pour the drinks and I'll see you down there in a tick.'

Stephanie felt incredibly stupid as she awkwardly chucked her clothes on and ran down the stairs. Her thirteen-year-old sister wasn't frightened of having sex, so why was she? Perhaps she had something wrong with her and she would die a bloody virgin.

Barry thought of Steph's breasts as he shut his eyes and brought himself to an orgasm. He really wanted to take the memory of their first sexual encounter to Spain with him to give him something to think about in the long dreary months ahead, but he knew that wasn't going to happen now. In a way he was quite pleased that Steph seemed so prudish, as if she had turned out to be a nymphomaniac, he would have had far more to worry about in his absence.

Wiping the evidence of his little activity off his sheets with a piece of toilet roll, Barry put his tracksuit back on and took the two little black velvet boxes out of his bedside drawer. He had spent forty out of the fifty pounds that Steve had given him on this little gesture, and he really hoped Steph liked it.

Stephanie was sitting on the sofa feeling guilty and dreadfully sorry for herself when Barry walked in the room. She took a large gulp of cider and handed Barry a can of lager. 'I'm really sorry, Bal. You ain't got the hump with me, have you?'

Barry knelt down in front of Steph and placed one of the velvet boxes into her right hand. 'I could never have the hump with you. Now open that.'

Stephanie gasped with glee. 'Oh it's lovely. What is it? Is it a locket?'

Barry shook his head and snapped open the other box he was holding. He took the gold pendant out and placed it next to Steph's. 'See what it is now?'

'It's a gold heart!' Stephanie exclaimed.

'It's a heart broken in two pieces, but when you join 'em up they fit together. I'm gonna wear mine every day in Spain to remind me of you, and I want you to do the same in England. It's like a broken heart, ain't it? And that's what ours will be while we're apart. But every time you feel sad, I want you to remember that when I get home, that heart will fit together again, forever.'

'Oh Barry, that's so romantic.'

Barry took the pendant from Stephanie's hands and did the clasp up around her neck. 'You'll never be able to forget about me now, babe, will you?'

Stephanie let out a tortured sob. 'I will never forget you, Barry, not ever.'

* * *

At six a.m. on the Monday morning, Stephanie was glued to the bedroom window as Barry helped Jake carry the suitcases out to the waiting taxi.

'Please come down and say goodbye properly,' Barry shouted up to her.

Totally distraught, Stephanie shook her head and sobbed like a baby. Her tortured breathing was steaming up the glass window and she rubbed it with the sleeve of her dressing gown just to get one last proper look at the boy she adored so very much.

'Pull yourself together and go down and say goodbye, Steph,' Angie urged her. She was rather enjoying her sister's heartbreak and wanted to watch Steph mug herself off in full view of the street.

'I can't make myself look a fool – and I've got my pyjamas on,' Stephanie cried.

Angela leapt out of bed and handed Stephanie her black Puffa jacket. 'Quick, you'll regret it if you don't.'

About to take her sister's advice, Stephanie saw Marlene walk out of the house dressed in a long fur coat. 'Get in the cab, you soppy little bastard,' she shouted at Barry.

Fingering the piece of gold heart around her neck, Steph opened the window. 'I love you, Bal,' she yelled.

Barry smiled at her. 'And I love you too. I'll write to you as soon as I get there, and I'll bell you at the weekend at the time we agreed.'

As Marlene clouted Barry around the head, then glared at her, Stephanie quickly shut the window. When the taxi driver started the engine, Barry glanced up one last time and waved. Holding her pendant tightly in her left hand, Steph waved back with her right. Seconds later, the love of her life was gone.

CHAPTER THIRTEEN

In the days that followed Barry's going away, Stephanie was in absolute pieces. She couldn't eat properly, was barely sleeping, kept bursting into tears in her classroom, and spent hours sitting on the stairs waiting for the postman to deliver his mail. She also turned fifteen and had the worst birthday ever.

'You've gotta snap out of this, Steph. You're making yourself ill and you're making me ill with worry at the same time,' Pam informed her daughter, as her face crumpled once again when the postman arrived and there was still no letter from Barry.

'I can't relax until I've heard from him, Mum. Say the plane crashed or something? He promised he'd write to me everyday, but I ain't heard a word yet. Say he's met another girl and forgotten all about me already?' Stephanie wept.

Pam took her daughter by the hand, led her into the lounge and sat down in the chair opposite her. Steph's erratic behaviour had worried her so much this week that she had rung up work this morning and told her boss that her daughter was ill and she would need to take a day or two off to care for her. 'Barry will write to you, I know he will, but I told you only yesterday that his letters will come by airmail and they take ages to arrive.'

'But he promised he'd write to me every day.'

'And he probably has! Once you've received the first one, you'll probably get letters off him most days after. You must remember, though, he is working, Steph, and he might not have the time to write to you every single day. Now, you've not eaten enough to keep a rabbit alive this week, so how about me and you shoot down to Broad Street where Cathy works and get ourselves a nice bit of scran in her café. You've gotta eat, angel. Barry ain't gonna want you if you're all skin and bones, is he?'

'I so wish he hadn't gone to Spain, Mum. I ain't got nothing to look forward to now. I hate his mother, she is such a bitch.'

Pam moved over to the sofa where Steph was sitting and held her in her arms. She knew her daughter was bound to be upset after Barry had left, but she hadn't expected her to be anywhere near this bad and she was beginning to wish that the old slapper hadn't emigrated after all. To make matters even worse, Marlene's daughter was still living at the house opposite and her Indian boyfriend had now moved in with her. Day and night they had music blaring out, and Pam was sure that they were serving up drugs from there as well, as they seemed to have more visitors than a whore-house handing out free prostitutes.

'Listen to me, Steph, and listen to me carefully. If that boy truly loves you and you love him, then you will end up together, no matter what. Your dad was in the army when I first met him. Away for months on end he was, and I barely saw him for the first year we were together, but we still ended up getting married, didn't we? I know that Barry going away is horrible for you, but instead of moping about, darling, you need to look at it as a small blip. Nothing will ever get in the way of true love, remember that. Now, I'm bleedin' Hank Marvin and so must you be, so let's go and put some food in our stomachs, shall we?'

For the first time in days, Stephanie managed a weak smile. 'OK, and thanks, Mum.'

Another person worried about Stephanie's mental state was her best friend Tammy, and as she explained the situation to Wayne Jackman, he seemed just as concerned as she was.

'Perhaps I should have made more of an effort to check that Steph was OK. I promised Bazza I would keep an eye on her for him and I sort of guessed she would be a bit down this week. Shall I talk to her and see if I can cheer her up a bit?' Wayne asked Tammy.

'I dunno. Nothing I've said or done seemed to help and she ain't even come into school today. What about if we go and knock for her tomorrow morning and take her out somewhere for the day? I think we should go for a drink. It'll do her good to let her hair down, and she might even have had a letter or phone call from Barry by then. He promised he was gonna ring her every Saturday morning at nine o'clock, English time, so if we knock for her about ten, she might have lightened up a bit if he's phoned her.'

'I'm meant to be going West Ham tomorrow, but I can meet yous early evening. Why don't you go round there in the morning, take her for a mooch round Romford or somewhere, and then meet me at Heathway Station at six o'clock. Then we can all get pissed together. My nan and grandad go up the Millhouse on Saturday nights, so we can sit round mine and play some music and stuff, if you like? It's better than hanging about on street corners in this cold weather, ain't it?'

Tammy grinned. 'That sounds like a fab idea, but you ain't bringing Cooksie and Potter with you, are you?'

'Nah. I still see 'em at football and in school and stuff, but I don't really hang about with them any more. I've been knocking about with Danno instead.'

'Who's Danno?'

'Danny MacKenzie. Top lad he is, but I think it's best if it's just the three of us tomorrow in case Steph's still upset and stuff. I shouldn't think she's gonna wanna spill her guts in front of strangers, and Danno's in my year, so she won't know him that well.'

Thinking what a nice chap Wayne Jackman had turned out to be, Tammy stood up. 'See you tomorrow at six then.'

Stephanie woke up feeling a lot better the following morning. Not only had getting some food inside her and the chat with her mother done her the world of good, but she was also extremely excited, as today was the day that Barry had promised to phone her.

Seeing her sister buzzing about like a blue-arsed fly, Angela sat up in bed. 'What you gonna do if he don't ring?' she asked.

'Of course he'll ring if he said he will. Why wouldn't he?' Steph replied, anxiously.

'Because he might have met another girl. Even if he ain't yet, I bet he does when the holiday season starts. That Spain is full of pretty birds in bikinis and stuff and Barry ain't exactly shy, is he?'

'How do you know what Spain's like, Ange? We've never been no further than Camber Sands.'

'Because I've seen it on the telly. All the girls walk about naked and stuff. If I was you, sis, I would forget all about Barry and find yourself another boyfriend who lives in England.'

With her sister's words dampening her sprightly mood, Stephanie sank onto her bed and put her head in her hands. 'I won't forget about him, Ange. Not ever.'

* * *

Pam sang away happily to a song on the radio as she put the sausages into the pan of lard. This was only the second Saturday she had taken off work in over a year, and when she had called in this morning to tell her boss that she would return on Monday, he had promised to pay her her full week's wages. 'Steph, Ange, breakfast is nearly ready,' she shouted out.

'I don't want mine yet. It's quarter to nine and Barry'll be ringing soon,' Steph replied, bounding down the stairs. Her stomach had butterflies and she knew that she would be unable to eat a morsel, let alone one of her mother's massive fry-ups.

'It won't be ready for another five minutes or so, and if Barry does ring, I'll keep it warm in the oven for you.'

'Why did you say it was ready now then?' Angela asked, appearing behind her sister.

'Because I wanted to know if you wanted beans or bloody spaghetti with it,' Pam yelled. Sometimes she wished she had given birth to two boys, as they couldn't be as much aggravation as girls, surely?

'I'll have spaghetti,' Angela said.

About to tell her mother she wanted neither beans nor spaghetti, the phone rang and Stephanie darted towards it. Angela grinned as an excited Stephanie answered it and then her voice deflated like a burst balloon. Angela had told her friend Chloe to ring at exactly this time and was thrilled she had remembered to do so.

'Can't you call her back? You know I'm waiting for Barry to ring,' Steph said, handing the phone to her sister.

'No, I can't,' Angela replied, snatching the phone out of her sister's hand.

Steph paced up and down the hallway listening to her sister waffling on about a load of old rubbish. It was five to nine now and she was so afraid that she would miss

Barry's call. Frustrated beyond belief, she started to cry. 'Please, Mum, tell her to get off the phone,' she begged.

Clocking her daughter's distressed manner, Pam marched into the hallway with the spatula in her hand. 'End the call now and tell Chloe you'll ring her back after you've eaten your breakfast,' she ordered Angela.

'No, why should I? You're only saying that 'cause she wants to use the phone,' Angela replied, nodding towards Stephanie.

Pam lifted the spatula above her head as if to hit her youngest daughter. 'Put the phone down now, else you're grounded all weekend.'

Angela did as she was told, with so much force that the phone very nearly broke in two. 'I hate you. You always stick up for her,' she screamed, as she ran up the stairs.

Seconds later, the phone rang again and Stephanie grabbed it. 'Barry, is that you?' she croaked emotionally.

'Of course it's me, babe. How you doing? Did you have a good birthday? I've sent you a card.'

'No. I had a rubbish birthday and I've missed you so much,' Stephanie said, tears rolling down her cheeks at the sound of his cockney voice.

'I've missed you an' all. I hate it out here, Steph. There's so much work to be done in the bar and all me muvver and Jake do is sit on their arses drinking and larging it. I've lost about half a stone in weight 'cos I don't stop grafting. It's awful.'

Relieved that Barry wasn't having a good time, Steph stopped crying. 'Is it hot out there? Have you seen loads of pretty girls in their bikinis yet?' she asked, remembering what her sister had told her earlier.

'You're having a laugh. The birds are pig ugly, it's bleedin' freezing, and it certainly ain't bikini weather. Have you got my letters yet? I sent the first one to you on Wednesday.'

'No, but me mum said they take ages to come. As soon as I get it, I'll write straight back to you.'

'Listen, the pips are going and me money's gonna run out soon. Just remember I love you. If you're missing me, look at that heart and remember what I told you.'

'I will, I love you too, Barry,' Steph replied tearfully, before the line went dead.

Angela, who had been earwigging at the top of the stairs, couldn't help but laugh. Her sister was such an unclued-up sap. 'Love you too, Barry,' she mimicked.

Tammy Andrews was in a world of her own as she walked towards Stephanie's house. She had a major crush on Wayne Jackman, was so looking forward to seeing him tonight, and even though she had a feeling that with her ginger hair and freckles, she didn't have a cat in hell's chance, she couldn't help the way she felt about him.

Tammy walked into a newsagent's, bought a can of Tizer and sat down on a nearby bench. When they had first got involved with Wayne Jackman, Tammy had thought he was the biggest dickhead ever to walk the earth. How wrong was I? Tammy mused, as she sipped her drink. Wayne was kind, thoughtful, funny, and with his ravishing good looks, possessed every quality Tammy wanted in a boyfriend. Debating whether or not to tell Steph about her crush on him, Tammy quickly decided against it. Not only would it be embarrassing if Steph mentioned it to Wayne and he was repulsed, but with Barry leaving as well, it just didn't seem like appropriate timing. Pleased with her sensible decision, Tammy threw her empty can under the park bench and ran the rest of the way to her friend's house.

'Barry rang. He hates it out there, Tam, says it's real boring, the girls are ugly, and all he does is work,' Stephanie exclaimed, as she opened the front door with a smile on her face.

'See, I told you so. What else did he say?' Tammy asked excitedly.

Stephanie led her friend into the lounge and repeated the conversation virtually word for word until she was interrupted by her little sister.

'He said I love you, Steph; then she said, I love you too, Bal,' Angela mocked.

'Go away. This is a private conversation,' Steph yelled.

'She is such a bitch that girl. If she was my sister I'd have throttled her by now,' Tammy said as Angie slammed the living-room door.

Stephanie shrugged. She had spent years sticking up for Angela, but just lately, even she felt that she was running out of excuses for her sister. 'I don't know what's wrong with her, Tam. I mean, this morning her mate Chloe rang up just as Barry was meant to ring. I begged her to get off the phone, but she wouldn't, not till me mum stepped in and sorted it.'

'I bet she told Chloe to ring her at that time on purpose,' Tammy said, knowingly.

'Nah, I don't think she'd do something as evil as that, but she can be a bitch at times. I don't understand why, though. She used to be so sweet and loving. I reckon she'll grow out of it when she's older, don't you? I mean, who's to say people never said the same about me and you when we were thirteen.'

Tammy gave a sarcastic smile, but said nothing. In her eyes, Angela was a vile piece of work and would never be any different, but she didn't want to upset her friend by saying so. They were sisters, after all.

Wayne Jackman sauntered out of Dagenham Heathway Station with a real spring in his step. West Ham had just won and he was in the mood for getting drunk to celebrate the rather rare occurrence of his team playing so well.

'All right Jacko? You look cool. Is that a new tracksuit?' Steph asked, punching his arm playfully.

'Yeah. Me mate's chored it in Holland for me,' Wayne replied, dusting the top of his new red Fila tracksuit down in case it had picked up any nasty bugs on the filthy District Line train he'd just got off.

'So, are we still gonna get some drink and go round yours?' Tammy asked, unable to look the object of her affection straight in the eyes.

'Yep, that's the plan. Or shall we really push the boat out and have a couple in the Church Elm first?' Wayne suggested, cheekily.

'Me and Tam couldn't get served in there last time we tried and we've only got our pocket money on us, Jacko. How much is half a cider in there?' Stephanie asked, opening her purse and counting the change she had.

Wayne grinned, put one arm around Steph, the other around Tammy, and led them down Heathway Hill. 'I can easily get served in there and I've got plenty of dosh on me.'

Half an hour later, Tammy and Steph were sitting in the corner of the pub, on their second half of cider, listening to the music pumping out of the jukebox. Both girls felt extremely grown-up and were enjoying themselves immensely.

'So what did Bazza have to say then?' Wayne asked Stephanie.

Stephanie repeated the conversation she'd had with her boyfriend and then showed Wayne her present. 'It's half a gold heart split down the middle with a jagged edge. Barry's wearing the other half and he says when he comes home, our hearts will fit together perfectly, forever.'

Wayne chuckled. 'He was always one for words and gestures, was our Bazza. When we were kids he had a crush on a girl called Rosie Smith. He used to write her little verses and leave her presents under her mother's plant pot. Trouble was, she was five years older than him and she was also his babysitter.'

Tammy laughed, but Stephanie didn't.

'I'll get us another beer. What is it, same again?' Wayne asked, standing up.

Tammy nodded, and as Wayne walked towards the bar, she lit up two cigarettes and handed one to Stephanie. 'Ain't he cool, Wayne? I mean, when we first got talking to him up the Heathway that time, who would have thought we would all be good pals like we are now?'

'Yeah, he's really nice,' Steph said, sadly.

'What's a matter with you? You've been on cloud nine all day and all of a sudden you look like someone's just died.'

Stephanie turned to Tammy and clutched at her arm. 'It's that story that Jacko just told us. I mean, if Barry has a history of buying presents and sweet-talking girls, how can I know that he can be trusted? My sister said that in Spain all the girls walk around half naked, and she reckons that Barry'll be off like a shot in the summer when all the holidaymakers arrive.'

'Don't take no notice of your bloody sister. Not only is she a bitch, but she's also jealous of you, Steph. She is envious of what you and Barry have, that's why she's saying stuff like that. I saw her face that day when Barry brought you that bunch of flowers when he came round your mum's for dinner. She was furious, mate, proper jealous, so don't you dare let her spoil things for you.'

'What's up?' Wayne asked, as he returned from the bar with the three drinks in his hands.

'Steph's worried about what you just said about Barry giving that girl the presents and stuff. Tell her she's got nothing to worry about, will you, Jacko? That cow of a sister of hers, your ex, has been sticking her oar in an' all trying to twist Steph's mind.'

Cringing at the mention of his underage ex, Wayne leaned across the table and held Stephanie's hands in his. 'Obviously, now Bazza's in Spain, things can change, but even if he does date other birds, I'm sure he will still come back on his sixteenth birthday. Anyway, whatever happens you've got nothing to worry about – I'll always be here to look after you. I'll never leave you like Bazza did, and that's a promise.'

When Steph began to cry, Tammy stared at Wayne with her mouth wide open. Thank God she hadn't told anyone how she felt about him. The look in his eyes, what he had just said, the way he was holding Stephanie's hands so tenderly. It all added up now. Barry Franklin wasn't the only person in love with her best friend, Wayne Jackman was as well.

CHAPTER FOURTEEN

As Christmas approached, Stephanie became more and more concerned about whether her and Barry's relationship could survive the distance between them. He still rang every Saturday morning, but was only ever on the phone for a couple of minutes, and his letter writing had dwindled to just one or two per week. Steph knew she still loved Barry, and whenever he rang her he told her the same, but Steph couldn't help but wonder if her sister and Wayne, who had warned her not to build her hopes up too high, were actually right.

In his last few letters, Barry had mentioned a girl called Sally who he had become good pals with. Apparently, they were both in the same boat, which is why they had clicked. Sally's father was a villain from Manchester and had fled to Spain because of an armed robbery that went wrong. Sally was very much in love with her boyfriend, Johnny, and had had to leave him behind in England. That's why they got on so well, Barry had explained in his latest letter. Barry had also told Steph that Sally was plain, dumpy, and not his type at all, but Stephanie only had his word for that. Reading Barry's letter again, Stephanie debated whether to wake Angela up and ask her opinion. Angela had really changed over the past couple of weeks. Not only had she started being incredibly nice to Steph, but she also seemed very quiet and tearful. Stephanie guessed that things weren't going so well with Jason, but knowing how volatile her sister could be at times, she decided not to pry too much.

'Oh, you are awake,' she said, as Angela turned around to face her.

'I've been awake for ages. I was just lying here thinking about stuff,' Angela replied.

'Look, tell me to mind my own business if you want, but I know something's wrong, Ange. Is it Jason? Has he finished with you?'

Angela's lip began to tremble. She shook her head, then burst into uncontrollable tears.

'Whatever is the matter?' Stephanie asked, as she leapt off her own bed to comfort her little sister.

'I've done something really stupid,' Angela said between sobs.

'Just tell me what you've done and I'll try to help you.'

'You can't help me, no one can. If I tell you, you must swear you won't tell Mum.'

'I promise I won't say anything to Mum,' Steph replied. Surely Angela hadn't accused somebody else of raping her again? Or worse still, somebody had raped her?

Feeling terribly sorry for herself, Angela clung to her elder sister. 'I think I'm pregnant, Steph. In fact, I know I am!'

Later that afternoon, Stephanie was sitting in Old Dagenham Park repeating the conversation she had had with her sister to Tammy.

'Shit! What's she gonna do? Did she say if she'd already done a test?'

'Yeah. She said she sold some of her records to Downtown

in Romford to pay for it. She reckons her period is over three weeks late and the test came up positive,' Steph explained.

'You're gonna have to tell your old lady, Steph. I mean, Angie's gonna need to be checked out by her doctor and stuff, and if you don't tell your mum, he will. Surely, it'll be less of a shock if it comes from you?'

Stephanie flicked her cigarette butt away and put her black woolly gloves back on. The cold December air was bitter and there was a frost on the grass which made it look white rather than green. 'I can't tell me mum. She will go mental. She thinks the sun shines out of Jason O'Brien's arse because his parents go to church, and finding out he's got Angie up the spout is enough to give her a heart attack. I didn't know whether to tell Lin; she would probably know what to do for the best, but her and Angie don't really get on and I can't chance her telling me mum. I swore to Ange that I wouldn't say anything and I can't break my promise to her.'

About to remind Stephanie of all the times her younger sister had broken promises to her, Tammy opened her mouth then quickly shut it again. Slagging Angela off wasn't going to help in this particular situation, so what was the point of doing so? Deep down, Tammy was quite pleased that Angela had bitten off more than she could chew for once. If anyone deserved to be up the duff and in shit street it was that horrible little slag. 'So, has she told Jason yet?' Tammy asked.

'No, she ain't told anyone apart from me. Is that Jacko walking across the field over there? It is, ain't it?'

Tammy stood up to get a clearer view. The figure was a fair distance away, but Jacko had a distinctive swagger when he walked and there was no mistaking it was him. 'Jacko,' she yelled.

Stephanie also stood up. 'We're over here, Jacko,' she screamed, waving her arms frantically.

Tammy watched Jacko run towards them. She still thought he was gorgeous, but had convinced herself he was only interested in Steph, which helped her immensely in suppressing her feelings towards him.

Wayne was panting as he reached the girls. 'Jesus, I need to start playing football again, rather than just watching it. I'm so unfit. What yous two doing sitting 'ere? You been on the lash?'

'Nah, Steph's got a family crisis, so we've just been talking about that,' Tammy replied.

Stephanie glared at her friend to warn her not to say any more.

'What's up? Tell me and I'll try and help you,' Wayne said, sitting down on the bench in between the two girls.

'Tell him, Steph. Jacko's our mate, he won't say nothing.'

'My lips are sealed, I promise,' Wayne said, holding Stephanie's gaze.

'You'd better not tell anyone Jacko, 'cause I'll never speak to you again if you do. It's me sister; she's got herself up the duff.'

Wayne's face immediately turned a deathly shade of white. 'Fucking hell, it ain't mine, is it?'

'No. She's been going out with Jason O'Brien and the silly pair of buggers have been at it, but ain't been using nothing. What am I gonna do, Jacko? I have to help her. I'm the only one that can.'

Relieved that his nan and grandad had drummed into him the importance of always using a condom, Wayne asked Steph to give him all the information she had. When she had finished, he squeezed her hand. 'Right, first let's go to the chemist and get another pregnancy test. You can help her do it, make sure she ain't got it arse upwards, or she ain't lying.'

'She wouldn't lie about something like that, surely?' Steph said.

'Jacko's right. Look at all the lies Angie told him,' Tammy added.

'But, I've only got 50p. I spent all me pocket money on Christmas presents the other day.'

Jacko stood up. 'I've got some money. Come on, let's go to the chemist up the Heathway.'

The following morning, Angela did the test, then held Stephanie's hand as they waited for the result together. It was a Saturday, Barry would be calling soon, so to take their minds off the test result, Stephanie told her sister to read his latest letter. 'What do you think? Do you reckon he's getting off with that Sally girl?' Steph asked, when Angela handed her the letter back.

'I don't know, sis, but even if he ain't, you can't tell me Barry's gonna go all through next year and not get off with any girls. That's why I think you should have a bit of fun yourself while he's away. You ain't gotta do it with anyone, but you can still have a laugh with other boys. Eighteen months is a long while to wait for anyone. Now, let's check this test. We've waited long enough, ain't we?'

Stephanie did the honours and was horrified to find that Angela had been right and the test was positive. For once, she had hoped that her little sister had been telling one of her awful lies.

'What am I gonna do now? I don't wanna keep it. Will you help me, Steph?'

Stephanie hugged Angela close to her chest. 'Of course I will help you.'

Hundreds of miles away, Barry Franklin gingerly hauled his aching body out of bed. He'd been laid up for the past four days since hurting his back whilst lifting barrels in the cellar. His mother had barely made him a cup of tea, and if it hadn't been for his pal Sally popping in on a regular basis with food and drinks for him, he'd have probably dehydrated, then died of starvation.

'Where are your mum and Jake?' Sally asked, as she helped Barry shuffle along the hallway.

'No idea. Me muvver poked her head around the door yesterday morning and I ain't seen hide nor hair of her since.'

Sally raised her eyebrows, but said nothing. She didn't like Marlene one little bit and thought she treated poor Barry appallingly.

'Thanks for coming round and helping me get to the phone, and thanks for the sandwich and coffee,' Barry said, gratefully.

'No worries. Now, I'm gonna go and tidy up your room while you ring your Stephanie. Give me a shout when you are done and I'll help you get back into bed.'

Thanking Sally again, Barry picked up the phone. His mother had forbidden him to call Steph on her landline but, seeing as he could barely walk, it was the only way he could now speak to his girlfriend. He would tell his mum afterwards and offer to pay for any calls he'd made.

Barry grinned as he heard his beautiful girlfriend's voice. 'You all right, darling? I can talk to you for longer today as I'm ringing from home. I've done me back in and I've been in absolute agony.'

'Good, because I need to talk to you about stuff. Can you send me a picture of that Sally so I can see what she looks like for myself? Have you got a photo of her?'

Barry was furious. Stephanie hadn't even bothered asking him how he'd hurt his back. 'Don't you trust me or something? All I ever do is fucking work out here.'

'Yeah, I do trust you, but I still wanna see a picture of her. She might look like a blond supermodel with great big boobies for all I know,' Steph said, obstinately.

'So, now you're calling me a fucking liar,' Barry screamed. 'Do you know what, Steph, I don't feel well and I ain't in the mood for this today. I'm gonna hang up now before I lose my temper with you big time.'

'I'll save you the trouble,' Steph yelled, slamming the receiver back on its cradle.

Barry stared at the phone in dismay. Sally's boyfriend was coming over to Spain for a two-week holiday on Monday, and he had no designs on her – or any other bird, for that matter. He wasn't sending Steph any photographs though. If she couldn't trust or believe him, what was the point in their relationship?

Tammy and Wayne stood outside Broad Street Working Man's Club waiting for Steph to arrive.

'Well?' Tammy asked, when her pal finally turned up twenty minutes late.

'The test was positive, and I've had a row with Barry.'

Wayne put an arm around both girls' shoulders. 'I think we all need a drink, don't you? Let's go to the Elms and then we can discuss what we're gonna do next.'

Three rounds and an hour later, the discussion was still in full swing. Angela had made it perfectly clear that she had no wish to keep the baby or involve her own doctor, so when Wayne pulled the piece of paper out of his pocket that he had torn out of the Yellow Pages, it seemed like the perfect solution.

'Is it free?' Stephanie asked, dumbly.

'No, of course it ain't free. The only time she will get a free abortion is if she goes to her own doctor and gets it done on the National Health. This is a private clinic, but it's the only way that your mum won't find out. I've already rung them and they said that she can be in and out on the same day. Most of the others I phoned said they wouldn't do it unless she stayed in overnight.'

'How much is it?' Tammy asked.

'You ain't gotta worry about the cost. My dad left us plenty of dosh when he got banged up, so I'll sort it,' Wayne said, generously.

Stephanie looked at Wayne in amazement. She had no idea how much a private abortion cost, but she bet it was more than a few rounds of drinks in a pub. 'But why would you do that for Angie? Especially after what she did to you. It don't make sense.'

'I'm doing it for two reasons. Number one, I've always felt guilty about sleeping with Angie. Obviously it weren't my fault because she'd lied to me about her age, but it still don't stop me feeling bad about it. And secondly, I'm doing it for you, Steph. You're one of me best mates now, and I'd do anything for you, girl.'

As an electrifying stare was shared between Stephanie and Wayne; Tammy looked the other way. It was only a matter of time before Steph and Wayne got together now, Tammy knew that, so instead of feeling bitter, she might as well just accept the fact and deal with it.

Four days after Wayne's generous offer, Stephanie was sitting in a posh clinic in Buckhurst Hill waiting for her sister to reappear. Because Angela was quite early into her pregnancy, the staff explained that they would be using what was referred to as 'the vacuum technique'. They also said that Angela had to rest when she got home and must not do anything strenuous for the next couple of weeks. They said because of Angela's young age, her body needed time to heal itself properly.

As Steph sat in the waiting room flicking through endless magazines, she thought about how kind Wayne Jackman had been. The abortion had cost two hundred pounds, and he had also given her an extra twenty-pound note so she and Angela could travel by cab rather than use public transport. He had even offered to accompany them there, but Stephanie knew that that would cause problems with her sister. Stephanie sighed as she flicked through the pages of the magazine and came face to face with the famous actor, Matt Dillon. His cheeky smile, dark brown eyes and thick dark hair had always reminded her so much of Barry. Steph threw the magazine onto the table and fingered the jagged piece of gold heart around her neck. 'Why did you have to go away, Barry? Why?' she whispered.

Angela Crouch felt sore and woozy as she put her feet to the floor. 'I don't think I can stand up yet,' she mumbled, as she clung to the nurse for support.

'Perhaps you should rest for another hour or so. Your sister is waiting outside. Shall I bring her in?'

Feeling dreadfully sorry for herself, Angela nodded. Because they had broken up from school for their Christmas holidays, she and Stephanie weren't expected home until ten o'clock – there was plenty of time until their curfew reared its ugly head.

'Are you OK? You look ever so pale,' Stephanie remarked, as she sat beside her sister's bed and squeezed her clammy hand.

'I just feel really sore and wobbly. I feel a bit sick an' all. Say Mum notices I'm ill? What we gonna say to her?'

'I was gonna suggest you say you'd fallen over or something, especially if you're walking a bit funny, but I'm afraid Mum might drag you straight up the hospital, and then all hell will break loose. I think you're best to say you've got really bad period pains and you need to lie down. At least you can play on that for a few days. The nurse told me that you might be bleeding down below for a week or two, so we must stock up on sanitary towels.'

With tears in her eyes, Angela forced a smile. 'Thanks for everything, Steph.'

Leaning forward, Stephanie kissed Angela on the forehead. 'That's what sisters are for.'

Pam and Cathy were watching their regular Wednesday night fix of *Coronation Street* when the girls arrived home.

'There's pies and pasties in the fridge if you want to warm them up. I didn't do you a dinner 'cause you said you were having saveloy and chips,' Pam shouted out, unable to take her eyes off the screen. Mike Baldwin was her and Cathy's favourite character and they were always chatting about his latest antics.

'Look, he's gonna kiss her now,' Cathy exclaimed, excitedly.

'He's such a bastard, but a good-looking one, eh, mate?' Pam chuckled.

Stephanie helped her sister up the stairs, then ran back down and poked her head around the living-room door. 'Angie's got bad period pains, so I'm gonna heat a couple of pasties up and we'll eat 'em upstairs.'

Tearing her eyes away from Mike Baldwin, Pam eyed her eldest daughter suspiciously. It was totally unheard-of for her two daughters to go out together for the day, especially for ten bloody hours. 'Where you two been all day?'

'Christmas shopping in Romford.'

'Show us what you bought then?

'I can't. We got your presents and you can't see 'em till Christmas day,' Stephanie lied.

Pam gave her daughter an evil glare. Unlike Angela, who

had the art of lying off to a tee, Stephanie had never been very good at it. 'Go on then, warm your pasties up and get your arse upstairs. I know you're lying, by the way, and if I find out that you and Miss Period Pains have been up to any mischief, I shall ground the pair of you, for good.'

CHAPTER FIFTEEN

Christmas came and went in its usual dreary Crouch fashion. Steph found being stuck indoors with nothing to do other than eat incredibly boring, and even though her mum had let her and Angela have a small glass of Liebfraumilch with their Christmas dinner this year, the only real highlight for Steph had been watching the hour-long edition of *Top of the Pops*. Her festive spirit had also been dampened more than usual because she was still at loggerheads with Barry. They'd had another massive argument on the phone on Christmas morning which had ended with Barry cutting her off in temper.

Angela had now recovered from the trauma of having an abortion. She had been very weak for the first few days afterwards, but Stephanie had helped her pull the wool over their mother's eyes and Angela now had a spring in her step once again.

'I'm so excited. I've never been to a New Year's Eve party before,' Angela said, while carefully applying her mascara.

'Will Jason's parents be there?' Steph asked, aware that it was Jason's aunt's party that her sister was attending.

'Yeah. I ain't met 'em yet, but Jason has told me to pretend I'm a Catholic if they ask. He said they might not like me otherwise. Jase reckons the party might be shit and he says if it is, me and him can sneak off somewhere else. Where you going tonight? You seeing Tam?'

'Yeah, dunno what we're doing yet though. We'll probably just get some drink and sit over the park,' Stephanie lied. She was actually going to a disco in the Church Elm pub and was really excited about it. She didn't want to tell Angela, though, because Jacko was going with them and Steph knew that if she told her sister, it would only cause problems. They'd been getting along quite well lately and Stephanie didn't want to do or say anything that might rock the boat.

Angela stood up. 'I'm gonna shoot now. Happy New Year for later, sis.'

Stephanie grinned. 'Yep. You too.'

Wayne Jackman felt a million dollars as he stood outside the Church Elm pub with a cigarette in his hand. His nan and grandad had given him a hundred and fifty pounds for Christmas and he'd blown virtually the whole lot on clothes. Being a casual meant keeping up appearances and Wayne always took pride in himself.

'Wow, you look well cool,' Stephanie said, as she and Tammy approached Wayne arm in arm.

'Don't tell me, let me guess. Your trousers are Farahs, the jacket's Lyle and Scott and that's a Burberry scarf. Am I right?' Tammy asked, trying to remember what motif was what.

Wayne laughed. 'Nearly. The scarf is Aquascutum, but you're getting there. So, we ready to party or what? Me mate's coming as well, but he can't get here till half eight.'

'What mate? You ain't invited Potter or Cooksie, have ya?' Stephanie asked, abruptly.

'No! I hardly see them mugs any more. Danno's coming. You know, Danny MacKenzie.'

'Ain't he the one whose party you was at when you found out my sister's real age?' Steph asked.

'Yeah, but that don't matter, does it? Danno's cousin, Tanya, is the same year as your sister.'

'Yeah, I know. My sister can't fucking stand her, Jacko.'

Wayne giggled and put an arm around Stephanie's tense shoulders. 'Calm down, girl.'

By the time Danny MacKenzie arrived, Stephanie and Tammy were both well on their way to being sozzled. Danny was of medium height, had very broad shoulders, dark auburn hair, a few freckles on his nose and an extremely cheeky grin.

'What can I get you to drink, ladies?' he asked, fixing his gaze on Tammy.

'They'll have two ciders, but get 'em pints, 'cause it's rammed up that bar and you can't get served. Actually, let's get two rounds in. I'll come up there with you,' Wayne replied.

Stephanie waited until the lads were out of earshot, then turned to Tammy. 'He fancies you, that Danno.'

'No he don't! He doesn't even know me.'

'Well, he wants to know you. I could tell by the way he was staring at you,' Steph replied, giggling.

Tammy punched her friend playfully on the arm. 'You're a fine one to talk, you are. Jacko well fancies you.'

'Don't be so bloody stupid. He's Barry's best mate. He's just looking after me while Bal's away, that's all.'

Tammy shook her head. 'No, he ain't mate. He's well loved-up with you, and if you can't see that you gotta be blind.'

Two hours laters, Stephanie had to admit that her friend's prediction might be right. Wayne hadn't taken his eyes off her for the past half-hour and had just asked her to dance as the DJ slowed down the tempo.

'Come on, have a dance with me. I bet Bazza's out partying with that Sally and I put money on it he'd dance with her if she asked him,' Wayne said, knowing that Sally was a sore subject. His feelings for Stephanie were far too strong to worry about betraying his childhood pal. He even kept reminding himself that he'd once saved Barry's life to ease the odd twinge of guilt he occasionally felt.

Stephanie glanced at Tammy and Danno. They seemed to be getting along famously and Steph was pleased for her friend as she rarely had any luck with boys. She turned back to Wayne. 'Look at me, I look a right state in these jeans. I didn't realize everyone would be done up to the nines. I can't get up and dance like this.'

Wayne stared intently into Steph's eyes. 'Yes, you can. You look beautiful, and jeans or no jeans, you still knock spots off any girl in here.'

Stephanie averted her eyes from Wayne's. She felt light-headed and extremely confused. Even though she had been arguing with Barry lately, she was sure she still loved him, but she also knew she had started to develop feelings for Wayne. When the DJ played Bonnie Tyler's 'Total Eclipse of the Heart', Steph allowed Wayne to lead her onto the makeshift dance floor. When he wrapped his hands around her waist and then lowered them to her buttocks, Steph didn't push him away. Instead she responded by nestling her head into his sweet-smelling neck, which reeked of aftershave. In a strange way, being this close to Wayne kind of reminded her of what she'd had with Barry.

'When the slow dances stop, shall we go outside for a bit?' Wayne whispered in Stephanie's ear.

Whether it was the amount of alcohol she had consumed or just lust taking over, Stephanie didn't know, but she found herself agreeing. As their lips met for the very first time,

Stephanie had no idea that she was being watched by an extremely interested spectator.

Barry's sister Chantelle had never been in the Church Elm pub before and she was absolutely livid at the scene that had just unfolded in front of her. 'Fucking slag, I'm gonna glass her and that cunting Jacko,' Chantelle screamed, as she slurped the rest of her Bacardi and lemonade and made to dart towards the door with the empty glass held above her head.

Ajay, Chantelle's boyfriend, quickly grabbed hold of his heavily pregnant other half and dragged her over to the corner of the pub. 'Don't fucking start, Chantelle. I only just got out the slammer and I'm still on probation, you stupid bitch.'

'But that's Barry's girlfriend and his best mate getting off with one another. It ain't fucking right! My brother's been in bits over that no-good slag,' Chantelle yelled.

Ajay pointed a stern finger into Chantelle's face. 'You keep out of it, understand? I got all types of shit on me and if it kicks off and I get searched, you'll be bringing up our baby on your own.'

Chantelle knew when to shut up. Ajay had always been a bit handy with his fists and she didn't fancy feeling the brunt of his temper this evening. 'I'm gonna have to ring Barry in Spain tomorrow and tell him. Will you back me up in case he don't believe me?'

Ajay actually quite liked Barry and had no intention of letting him be made a fool of by some unfaithful whore. Grabbing hold of Chantelle's ever-expanding arse, Ajay squeezed it and treated her to a toothy grin. 'We'll ring Bazza first thing in the morning, and we'll tell him together, OK?'

* * *

Stephanie Crouch had never envisaged losing her virginity while standing against a wall in a dingy, dark alleyway in Dagenham Heathway, but that was exactly how it happened.

'You're fucking beautiful, Steph. I've wanted to do this for ages,' Wayne panted, as he put his hands around Stephanie's buttocks and urged her to put her legs around his waist.

Not used to drinking pints of cider, Stephanie felt drunk – very drunk, in fact. She had also had a couple of puffs on a spliff that Wayne had given her, and her body didn't feel like it belonged to her any more. She felt as though she was floating in the air, not standing up.

Wayne made lots of grunting noises, then withdrew his penis from Steph's vagina. 'That was wicked,' he said, as he took off his condom and threw it over somebody's back garden.

'Where's me knickers? I can't find 'em,' Steph said, frantically looking around on her hands and knees.

Rummaging around on the ground, Wayne found Stephanie's knickers, then helped her put her jeans back on. 'Who was better, me or Bazza?' he asked, bluntly.

Stephanie was confused. 'What you on about?'

'You know? Who was the best shag?'

'I didn't do anything with Barry. We never got that far,' Steph replied, honestly.

'Bazza told me you'd done it with him loads of times. He's such a fucking liar,' Wayne said, laughing.

'I've never done it with anyone before. That was my first time.'

Feeling like the cat that had just got the biggest plate of cream ever, Wayne put an arm around Stephanie's waist. 'You're my girl now. '

Feeling woozy and extremely light-headed, Stephanie

stared at Wayne vacantly, then promptly threw up all over his new Kicker boots.

The following morning, the realization of what she had done hit Stephanie like a ton of bricks as soon as she opened her eyes. She immediately fished around her neck for her gold heart pendant and held it tightly in her right hand.

'What's a matter? Mum said you were well drunk when you came home last night. She was proper going into one when I came in, and she reckons you ain't allowed out for a month,' Angela informed her sister.

Steph pulled the quilt over her head and burst into tears.

'Don't cry. She probably don't mean it. You know what Mum's like, she says these things and never carries out her threat,' Angela said, sitting on the edge of her sister's bed.

'I hope she does mean it, 'cause I don't ever wanna go out again,' Stephanie wept.

Angela pulled the quilt from over her sister's head. 'What you done? Has something bad happened?'

Desperate for somebody to comfort her, Stephanie threw herself into her sister's arms. 'I've done something really bad, Ange.'

Many miles away, Barry Franklin felt physically sick as he listened to what his sister had to say. 'Are you sure they were getting hold of one another? Perhaps Steph was just drunk and upset and Jacko was comforting her?' Barry said, not wanting to believe the awful truth.

'Of course I'm sure they were getting hold of one another. Steph had her tongue stuck down Jacko's throat in the pub, then I made Ajay follow them outside. He saw them at it in an alleyway, Bal. That girl's a stinking old whore and if you don't believe me, speak to Ajay yourself. He's standing here right next to me,' Chantelle explained.

Barry's eyes filled up with tears of humiliation and, unable to listen to any more of what his sister had to say, he cut her off.

'What's up with you? You soppy little fucker,' Marlene asked brutally, as she strolled into the lounge.

'Chantelle just rang up. She went out for a drink last night and saw Jacko and Steph together. They were fucking getting hold of one another,' Barry yelled.

Instead of comforting her distraught son like most mothers would, Marlene burst out laughing. 'Oh well, best I take me wedding outfit back to the shop. Told you that little slag wouldn't wait for you, didn't I? You're so gullible, Barry. You're a mug, son.'

Barry leapt out of the armchair, his eyes blazing. 'This is all your fault making me move out here and I ain't no fucking mug,' he screamed, as he grabbed his mother by the throat and pushed her against the wall.

Marlene was not only stunned, but also petrified. Jake had gone down to the bar to help clear up last night's mess, which meant she was in the house alone with her deranged son.

'Take back what you said and say sorry to me, you cunt,' Barry hissed, tightening his grip.

Seeing the look of a mad man in her son's eyes, Marlene did exactly as she was told. 'You ain't a mug. I didn't mean it. I'm sorry,' she croaked.

Barry let go of his mother's neck, then watched her splutter, hold her own throat, then fall to the floor. Her eyes were bulging with terror, and seeing the confused look on her face seemed to snap Barry out of his trance. He crouched down next to her. 'I'm so sorry, Mum. I didn't mean to hurt you. Let me help you up.'

Cowering away from the child she had given birth to, Marlene turned on the waterworks. 'Leave me alone. Get away from me you lunatic,' she sobbed.

Realizing he must have lost it completely and not knowing what to do to make amends, Barry stood up, grabbed his can of lager and bolted out of the apartment.

Back in Dagenham, Angela was intrigued to find out what Stephanie had actually done. Her sister had never exactly been the adventurous type. Steph wasn't exactly boring, but life and soul of the party she most definitely wasn't. Hearing the phone burst into life, Angela stood up. 'Let me just answer that 'cause it's probably Jase. Stay here, I'll get rid of him quick and then we can chat some more.'

Stephanie put the quilt back over her head. The memories of what had happened in the alleyway were pretty vague overall, but she was well aware that she had lost her virginity to Wayne Jackman. She had no idea how she actually felt about Wayne, but she knew how she felt about herself. A slag, that's what she was. A no-good, two-timing whore who had done it in an alleyway in Dagenham.

'Steph, it's Barry on the phone. He don't sound very happy,' Angela said, bursting into the room.

Stephanie sat bolt upright. Overcome by feelings of guilt and sordidness, she knew she wouldn't be able to speak to her boyfriend today. 'Tell him I've gone out. I can't talk to him, Ange, you're gonna have to lie to him for me.'

'I can't. I've already told him you're in. Talk to him, Steph,' Angela urged. She was desperate to listen in on the conversation.

Stephanie felt incredibly ill as she ran down the stairs. Surely Barry hadn't found out about her and Wayne? How could he? 'You all right, Bal? Happy New Year,' she said, as casually as her rapidly beating heart would allow her.

'How could you, Steph? How could you get hold of Jacko?'

Realizing that Barry knew what she had done, Stephanie

started to cry. 'I'm so sorry. I was drunk and I've been missing you so much. It just happened, but it's you I want, not Jacko. Please let's not split up over this. I'll never speak to him again. I swear on my life I won't.'

Barry laughed nastily. 'Do you honestly think I would want you now? You're a fucking slag, Steph. A no good Dagenhamite whore. As far as I'm concerned, Jacko's welcome to you. Goodbye and good riddance, you cunt.'

When the line went dead, Stephanie stared at the receiver in shock.

Angela was positioned at the top of the stairs and had overheard everything. 'Oh my God! You've got hold of Jacko, haven't you?'

'Don't be angry with me, Ange. I was really drunk and I didn't know what I was doing,' Stephanie wept.

About to tear into her sister for getting hold of her ex-boyfriend, Angela quickly decided against it. She was desperate to get to the nitty-gritty bit, and if she lost her temper she knew full well that Stephanie would clam up. 'What exactly happened? I'm not angry, honest, I'm happy with Jase now, ain't I?'

Sobbing her heart out, Stephanie ran upstairs and clung onto Angela for dear life. 'I had sex with Jacko in an alleyway, Ange. I'm so sorry. Will you forgive me?'

Absolutely seething that Stephanie had slept with her first love, Angela forced a smile. She felt like going downstairs, getting a knife out of the kitchen drawer and stabbing her slut of a sister in the gut with it, but instead she kept up the façade and hugged her. 'Of course I forgive you.'

Barry Franklin sat on the desolate beach and stared at the angry-looking waves. He found it rather therapeutic because the waves seemed to match his mood exactly. Since moving to Spain, his life had been awful, and now it had turned into absolute hell.

Picking up a pebble, Barry chucked it resentfully into the sea. The weather was bitterly cold and Barry only had a T-shirt on, but he couldn't give a toss if he caught hypothermia. Illness was the least of his problems. Unable to suppress his feelings any more, Barry put his head in his hands and, for the first time since he actually was one, sobbed like a baby. He had loved Stephanie, loved her more than anyone or anything else in the world, and how had she repaid him? By betraying him in the worst possible way, that's how.

Picturing Jacko's smiling face, Barry forced himself to stop crying. He cleared his throat and spat a mouthful of phlegm onto the damp sand. For years, Barry had considered Jacko a real hero for rescuing him when he had nearly drowned that time, but now he hated him with a passion. Wayne Jackman was a Judas, a wrong 'un, and Barry knew if he lived to be a hundred, he would never, ever forgive him for what he had done. Putting his hand on his chest, Barry fingered the gold piece of jagged heart he had once worn with pride. He hated it now, wished he had never bought it. It was meant to mean something for both him and Steph, but it was obvious his slag of a girlfriend had already forgotten about him.

Shivering, Barry stood up and walked towards the sea. He stared at its coldness and made a vow to himself. Never would he let a woman break his heart again, and never again would he shed a tear over one either. Ripping the gold necklace from around his neck, Barry threw the chain and pendant as far as he could into the ocean. He scowled as he watched it disappear under the water and chose to say a few words, as though he was speaking at a funeral. 'You might think you've seen the last of me, but you ain't Steph.

Neither has that other two-faced cunt. One day, I shall return to England, and when I do, both of yous better be watching your backs. Barry Franklin ain't no mug and I'll make sure you learn that the hard way.'

CHAPTER SIXTEEN

1994 – Ten Years Later

Pamela Crouch felt physically and mentally drained as she sat on the sofa and soaked her aching, swollen feet in a bowl of soothing warm water. Organizing her father's funeral had taken its toll on her, and attending it had brought back all the memories of her mother's death as well.

'Cooey, it's only me. How did it go?' Pam's next-door neighbour Cathy asked, as she let herself in with her own key.

'As well as can be expected. He had a good turnout and all his pals from the Rose of Denmark were ever so nice. I gave the landlord the money he asked me to in his letter, and I should imagine his wake is still in full swing as we speak.'

Seeing Pam's lip start to wobble, Cathy opened up the bottle of wine she'd brought with her. She poured her friend a glass and sat down next to her. 'You should have let me come with you, Pam. I said I didn't mind cancelling me hospital appointment. Where are the girls? Didn't they come back home with you?'

'They've gone to pick the kids up, then they're both popping back.'

'What! Don't tell me Angie's gone to pick Aidan up. That's a first, ain't it? Is she ill?'

Pam shook her head sadly. Usually, she and Cathy would have a private joke over what a terrible mother her youngest daughter was, but today Pam wasn't in the mood for cracking funnies. Her dad's death had been quite sudden. He had been taken into hospital with a suspected angina attack, and five days later had died of pneumonia. He was only seventy years old, and had been as fit as a fiddle up until two weeks ago when he had keeled over in the Rose of Denmark pub.

'Drink your drink. You look like you need one,' Cathy said, handing her pal the glass of wine she had poured her.

Pam shook her head. Apart from when he stayed with his other grandmother, Aidan was her sole responsibility, and Pam didn't like to touch a drop of alcohol until he was safely tucked up in bed at night.

Aidan's conception and arrival into the world had caused mayhem back in the day. Angela had only been fourteen years old when she had fallen pregnant by Jason O'Brien, and she had been six months into the pregnancy when Pam had finally recognized the sordid truth. For months, Angela had hidden her ever-growing stomach under baggy clothes, and it wasn't until Pam had walked into her daughter's room when she was partially naked one day that she realized the well-behaved boy Angela had been dating was actually anything but. Jason's parents were staunch Catholics, more appalled over finding out that Angela wasn't a Catholic than learning she was pregnant. Obviously, at six months, it was far too late for Pam to force Angela to have an abortion, so adoption was discussed in much detail. However, when young Aidan made his much-gossiped-about entrance into the world, both grandmothers took one look at him and made a pact to overcome their religious differences and bring up the baby between them until their own children were mature enough to cope with parenthood.

Aidan was eight years old now and, in Pam's words, was a dear little soul. He was a sturdy child who loved nothing more than playing football or riding his little bike. With his jet-black hair, he possessed a definite Irish look about him, but he had Angela's bright green eyes and petite button nose. Angela and Jason had split up three months after Aidan's birth. Both had been too young to cope with the responsibility of having a baby and their relationship had quickly become untenable. Jason was now quite a good parent, but Angela most certainly wasn't. She had little patience with her son and rarely ever saw him. Sometimes a month would pass between her infrequent visits, and even then she would never spend more than a couple of hours in Aidan's company. She proclaimed she found it too stressful.

Pam worried immensely about her youngest daughter. Angela was twenty-three now and supposedly lived in an opulent apartment in Soho with a female friend. Nobody had ever seen the apartment or the friend, and when Pam had recently asked if she could visit her, Angela had rudely refused. 'Leave it out, Mum. Look at the size of you and the way you dress. All my friends think I come from a posh house in Chigwell. I don't want 'em knowing I was brought up in a council house in bloody Dagenham, and if they see and hear you, they're bound to guess,' were Angela's exact words.

Another thing that had caused Pam many sleepless nights over the years was the career path that Angela had chosen. Her daughter insisted that she was working as a professional dancer at Stringfellows and was doing a bit of glamour modelling on the side to fund her luxury lifestyle, but since Lairy Mary had told Cathy that one of her son's friends had seen Angela cavorting partially naked around some pole in a seedy bar in Soho, Pam had often wondered if there was more to her daughter's career than met the eye.

'So, how is your Ange then? First time you've seen her in weeks, ain't it?' Cathy asked, snapping her pal out of her obvious daydream.

Pam sighed. 'Same as bleedin' usual. Turned up in a red convertible Mercedes sports car this morning, she did! You'll see it when she brings Aidan back. She said she was taking him for something to eat after school. Was rambling on about some glamour modelling shoot she's doing in Spain next week. Worries the life out of me she does, Cath. Kids, eh? Sometimes I wish I'd kept me legs bloody closed, don't you?'

Cathy nodded understandingly. She had her own worries at the moment with her youngest son, Michael. Since splitting up with his ex-girlfriend, Michael had moved back in with her and was a different person to the bubbly, fun-loving lad he had once been. Her son now spent his days alone in his bedroom, smoking dope and drinking beer in a haze of depression. 'I know how you feel, Pam. My Michael's getting worse and worse, but he still refuses to see a doctor. I'm sick of the sound of Pink Floyd, Jimi Hendrix and Led Zeppelin, but what can I do if he don't wanna help himself? I wouldn't worry too much about your Angie, mate. She's always been able to look after herself. Knowing her, I bet she's met another rich bloke and he's bought her that bleedin' car.'

Pam shrugged. Her daughter's love life was complex to say the least. Angie seemed to have a new man on the scene whenever Pam spoke to her, but Pam was yet to meet one and Angie's relationships never seemed to last long. With her long dyed-blond hair, large pert breasts, false black eyelashes, and size eight figure, Pam was only too aware of how stunning her youngest daughter was. Angela had been gifted with beauty and had the world at her feet if only she would realize it. All Pam could do was hope and pray that one day she would fall in love with a nice chap and settle down with him. Only then could she finally stop worrying.

'So, where's Lin? She still at the wake?' Cathy asked.

Pam raised her eyebrows as if to say, what do you think? Whenever alcohol was flowing freely, you could guarantee Lin wouldn't be too far away. Linda still lived with Pam, but just recently had met a man called Keith and she now spent a lot of her time around at his flat in Barking. This worried Pam dreadfully. Her sister had never had a proper relationship before and not only was Pam concerned that Lin would end up with a broken heart; she was also at her wits' end because Keith was a heavy drinker as well.

'Did Keith go to the funeral with her?' Cathy asked, reading her friend's mind.

Pam nodded. 'I dunno what to make of him, Cath. He's pleasant enough, but I just find it so weird that a geezer who's over six foot would fancy someone as tiny as Lin. I mean, is he some kind of freak?'

Cathy knew how protective Pam was over her sister, but she had met Keith a few times and believed he genuinely liked Linda. 'Lin's nearly forty now, Pam, and she ain't silly.

Pam shrugged. She rued the day that the Butterkist factory had closed down and Lin had got a job in another factory in Barking. It was there where she had met Keith, in some grotty old pub she had started drinking in after work. 'I am happy she's met someone, I just wish it weren't Keith. That Harts Lane Estate he lives on is an absolute shit hole and I know he's an alkie, he looks like one. I mean, he ain't even got a job and I don't want him dragging Lin down to his level. Next thing you know, she'll be on the dole an' all.'

'So, how's Steph? She still stressed out with all the wedding plans?' Cathy asked, cleverly changing the subject.

About to answer, Pam was stopped from doing so by Jimi Hendrix's 'Voodoo Chile' pumping through the wall.

Cathy leapt up. 'I'll get him to turn it down, mate. He's probably stoned and don't realize how loud he's got it.'

When her pal made an embarrassed dash from the room, Pam picked up her untouched glass of wine and took a large gulp. Angela and Lin she was used to worrying about, she'd had years of it, but the past week or so it was Stephanie who was causing her more sleepless nights than anybody else. Her eldest daughter wasn't herself; she seemed anxious and unhappy and Pam couldn't rest until she found out the reason why.

Stephanie and Wayne Jackman had been a couple since their schooldays. Pam had been elated at the start of their relationship as it had got her daughter over that Barry Franklin. For that reason alone, Pam had welcomed Wayne into her home with open arms, and even when Stephanie had fallen pregnant at eighteen and had had to give up her wonderful job in London with NatWest bank, Pam had accepted the situation. After Angie getting pregnant at fourteen, she could hardly tell Steph she was disappointed in her, could she?

Dannielle was six years old now and was the image of Stephanie at the same age. She had glossy, long dark hair, pale green eyes and an infectious laugh, just like her mother's. Danni, as most people liked to call her, looked nothing like Wayne, but Tyler did. He was nearly three now and with his blond hair and piercing blue eyes was the absolute spit of his father. Unlike Dannielle, who had always been a joy to look after, Pam found Tyler a bit of a handful to babysit. He had terrible temper tantrums that seemed to appear out of thin air, but Pam loved both children the same amount, like any decent grandmother would.

From a mother's point of view, Stephanie's life seemed absolutely idyllic. Wayne was a successful businessman who owned a gym in Leytonstone and a sports shop in Barkingside, while Steph had recently trained to become a fully qualified beautician. Wayne had promised to buy Stephanie her own salon as a wedding gift and Pam was sure that her daughter was more excited about that than the actual big day itself. Deep in thought, Pam didn't even hear Cathy let herself back in.

'You all right? You look like you're in a trance,' Cathy joked.

'I was just thinking about my Steph. She was ever so withdrawn again today. Something ain't right with her. I mean, you know your own kids, don't ya?'

'Fuck me, Pam, you were at your dad's funeral! Anyway, we spoke about this last week and both agreed that the wedding's probably playing on her mind. It must be ever so stressful planning a big bash like that. She's probably in turmoil over who she's gotta invite and stuff. I mean, it weren't like that in our day, was it? Fifty quid my wedding came to and I did the bleedin' catering meself. Got up at five in the morning to make me sausage rolls and poxy sandwiches, then the bastard I married had the cheek to get some old slapper up the duff.'

Pam had to smile. Cathy had a wonderful way of telling a story at times. 'I don't think it's the wedding that Steph's worried about. It's something else, I know it is, but she clammed up and changed the subject when I asked her earlier. The only thing I can think of is that she don't like where she's moved to. It can't be the house, you've seen it, it's beautiful, so I'm wondering if she ain't getting on with the neighbours or something. I know it's a posh area, but you can get arseholes living anywhere these days, can't you?'

Wayne and Stephanie had recently sold their three-bedroom house in Collier Row and were currently renting a beautiful four-bedroom property in Chigwell. It had been Wayne's idea to move, as he had wanted the kids to go to a good school in a decent area. He had suggested that they rent for six months just to make sure that they were happy with their new surroundings; then, providing they were, they would buy.

'Good job Wayne had the sense not to buy that house straight away if that's the case. How long did he sign the contract for?' Cathy asked.

'Six months with an option to buy at the end of it. The owner's living abroad apparently. Keep schtum now, Steph's just pulled up in her jeep,' Pam said as she hobbled into the hallway.

'Nanna,' Dannielle screamed as she ran up the path.

Pam hugged her granddaughter then ruffled Tyler's gorgeous blond hair. 'You all right, boy?' she asked him.

Tyler smiled and nodded. Unlike his sister who had been chatting away like there was no tomorrow at nearly three years old, Tyler's speech hadn't developed properly yet. When he did try to speak, it was extremely difficult to understand what he was saying, which seemed to make him frustrated. Pam had recently wondered if this was the main cause of his temper tantrums, but she hadn't yet broached her views to Stephanie. Her daughter had enough on her plate with the wedding.

'Now, who wants some ice cream? Nanna's got chocolate or banana. Is it OK for them to have some?' Pam asked, turning to Steph.

'Yeah, course it is. Actually Mum, I was gonna ask you a favour. A pal of mine wants me to go out with her tonight. Could you look after the kids for me and I'll pick 'em up first thing in the morning?'

'I can't, Steph. I start work at half six,' Pam replied. She had worked in the same baker's/café for years now, and she daren't be late on a weekday. The place was rammed by seven with workmen wanting their full English.

'Please, Mum. I promise you faithfully that I'll get here by six and I'll drop you off at work an' all. You don't have to worry about getting them washed or dressed. They can get in the motor in their nightclothes and I can do all that when I get them home.'

'Who's this friend then?' Pam asked, suspiciously.

Unable to control her emotions any more, Stephanie's eyes filled with tears.

'Whatever's the matter? I'm your mother and I know something's been wrong with you this past week or so, Steph. Is it Wayne? You're not having second thoughts about getting married to him, are you?'

Stephanie gave a tearful laugh and wiped her eyes on the sleeve of her black coat. 'No, me and Wayne are fine and I'm really looking forward to the wedding,' she said.

She and Wayne had come a long way since their first drunken sexual encounter in an alleyway. Steph had hated herself at the time for how she had treated Barry and had pushed Wayne away. It took six months of him pursuing her before she had agreed to give their relationship a whirl and they had been together ever since.

'Dish the kids up some ice cream, Cath, while I have a quick chat with Steph. The hundreds and thousands are in the top right-hand cupboard,' Pam shouted, as she ushered her daughter up the stairs. 'Whatever's wrong, love?' Pam asked, as Stephanie sat dejectedly on the edge of her bed.

'It's Tammy. You know I told you I ain't seen much of her since she got with this new bloke she met up town.'

Pam nodded.

'Well, she rang me last week to tell me she's jacking in

her job in the Futures market to move to Spain with him. He's a property developer, apparently, and that's where his business is based. What am I gonna do, Mum? We've been best mates for as long as I can remember and I can't imagine life without her.'

Pam sat down and held her daughter close to her chest. Stephanie and Tammy had been best friends ever since primary school, so she could understand how Steph felt. She would be distraught if Cathy ever sodded off to Spain, that was for sure.

As a child, Tammy had been slightly overweight and a bit of an ugly duckling, but as the years had passed, she had turned into a beautiful swan. Tammy's once ginger shoulder-length hair was now long and a reddy auburn. The freckles that had once smothered her face were now barely visible, and she had the most voluptuous size ten figure that Pam had ever seen.

'What am I gonna do without her, Mum?' Steph repeated. She was now twenty-five, but with her mother's comforting arms around her, she suddenly felt as if she were fifteen all over again.

'Well, with her looks and that saloon-girl figure of hers, Tammy was always gonna meet the man of her dreams one day, love. Spain ain't the end of the world. You and Wayne are hardly skint, so you can always go and visit her, and I bet she comes back to England regularly. I mean, all her family still live 'ere, don't they?'

Stephanie sighed. She knew deep down she was being selfish thinking the way she was, but she couldn't help herself. Tammy had had loads of boyfriends in the past, but had never actually moved in with any before. Steph genuinely wanted her pal to meet Mr Right and be happy like she was. She just wished Mr Right wasn't based in bloody Spain.

'So, is that where you're going tonight? Out with Tammy?' Pam enquired.

'Yeah. We're going for a meal together to have a heart to heart. I'm just a bit worried about her, Mum. That is such a good job she's got, she's on amazing money there, and I can't believe she's giving it all up for some bloke she's only known a couple of months. Tam's always been so sensible in the past, if you know what I mean?'

Pam smiled. 'Oh, I know what you mean all right, but it's obvious to me that the girl has finally found the one. I knew immediately when I met your dad – and look at you and Wayne, childhood sweethearts. You must try and be happy for Tammy, love. She'll resent you if you're not.'

'I am happy for her, Mum. I can't wait to meet him, actually. It's happened so fast, I know he must be really special.'

'Are you meeting him tonight as well?' Pam asked.

'No. He's gone back to Spain on business, but Tam's gonna introduce us when he comes back next week. All I know is that his name is Richard, he sells property and he's twenty-nine.'

'When is she moving? She'll still be here for your wedding, won't she?' Pam asked, worriedly.

Stephanie raised her eyebrows. 'I should bloody well hope so, she's my chief bridesmaid. Tam's just given three months' notice at work, so she'll be here until April, at least.'

'Good job your Wayne surprised you with a winter wedding then, eh? You might have been searching for another bridesmaid, if not.'

Remembering how Wayne had proposed to her, Stephanie couldn't help but grin. They had discussed getting married many times over the years, but what with the kids and other stuff getting in the way, they had never quite got round to it. This Christmas, however, Wayne had taken the bull by the horns, and in front of her mum, Lin and the kids, had got down on one knee.

'Steph, I'm sick of waiting for you to be my wife, so I'm asking you one last time. Will you bloody well marry me?' he'd asked, with a cheeky grin on his face.

Stephanie had thought he was drunk, so had laughed, kissed him and said 'yes'. Seconds later, she had been gobsmacked when Wayne had handed her a big envelope. He had brazenly taken the liberty of booking everything from the venue to the entertainment, bless him. The venue was a classy manor house in rural Essex, and the ceremony, meal and reception were being held there as well. Stephanie was extremely excited. Wayne's proposal had been the most romantic gesture ever and he had spared no expense. He had even paid a deposit on rooms in a local hotel so all their friends and family could stay there for the night.

'What we talking about? Oh, don't tell me, let me guess. My money say's we're talking about the wedding again,' Angela said sarcastically as she barged into the bedroom. She hadn't been with her family when Wayne had proposed, but they had spoken about little else ever since.

Pam threw her youngest daughter a disdainful look. Angela had always been jealous of Stephanie and Wayne's relationship from the very beginning, and Pam had never believed Angie's lies about her losing her virginity to Wayne at the age of thirteen. 'I swear it's true, Mum. Wayne's a pervert,' Angela had insisted on numerous occasions.

Pam hadn't wanted to upset Stephanie, but she had once confronted Wayne about the subject. He vehemently denied it all, and laughed. 'You know what your Angie's like. She's a dreamer, a chancer and a terrible fucking liar. She had a crush on me in school. She lied about her age. I met up with her a couple of times, snogged her face off, then dumped her when I found out she was thirteen. That's it,' Wayne had told her. Pam believed him, as she remembered Angela telling her the same bloody story years ago when she and Stephanie used to refer to him as Jacko.

'Where's Aidan?' Pam asked.

'Downstairs with Dannielle and that other brat,' Angela said coldly. She couldn't stand Tyler. His little tantrums did her head in.

Stephanie leapt off the bed and pointed a finger in her sister's face. 'Don't you dare call my son a brat, and what you said about Grandad earlier at the graveside was absolutely disgusting. I weren't gonna tell Mum, but I will now.'

Pam stared at her two daughters in dismay. She hated it when they argued – so much so that she was relieved that they rarely saw one another any more. 'Will yous two stop it? We've just buried your grandfather, for Christ's sake. Have some respect, the pair of you.'

Stephanie wasn't usually a grass. Angela was the master of that, but for once she couldn't help but spill her guts. 'Respect! Angela wouldn't know the meaning of that word, Mum. As Grandad's coffin was being lowered into the ground, she told me what a horrible selfish old bastard he was. She said that instead of spending his meagre bit of savings on a horse and cart and a piss-up for his mates at his own funeral, he should have left it to her.'

Unable to take any more stress for one day, Pam put her head in her hands and cried. It had been she who had forced Stephanie to ask her sister to be a bridesmaid at her wedding and she so wished now that she hadn't. They didn't get on, never had done, and Pam knew in her heart of hearts that Stephanie's big day had disaster stamped all over it. She could feel it in her aching bones.

CHAPTER SEVENTEEN

Wayne Jackman opened his overloaded wardrobe and sifted through the quality clobber he had inside. He had always been a sucker for a designer label. As a teenager he'd had a passion for Sergio Tacchini, Fila and Lacoste, but now he was a successful businessman, it was all about Gucci, Armani and Ralph Lauren. Choosing a crisp white shirt, Wayne studied his physique in the full-length mirror. He trained for hours in his own gym and his dedication had paid off big time. His stomach was taut, he had arms that were toned to perfection, and he always wore his jeans or trousers that little bit tighter to show off the rippling muscles in his legs.

Checking his watch, Wayne pulled his favourite jeans out of the wardrobe and took his expensive tan leather shoes out of their box. He was running a bit late, and didn't have time to ponce about for ages as he usually did when he was going out. Stephanie always took the piss out of him. She reckoned he was a right tart and took longer to get ready than she did. Glancing in the mirror again, Wayne added a dab more Brylcreem to his hair. Gone was the dodgy Eighties wedge style: he now wore it slicked back to give him a more sophisticated look. Finishing off his beauty regime by dousing his cheeks in aftershave, Wayne smirked as he stared at the finished article. At six foot two, he was tall, but because he was supple and fit, he didn't look lanky. His body was in perfect proportion for his height. Picking up his car keys, Wayne grabbed a jacket and sauntered out of the bedroom. Tonight he was meeting his old school pals, Mark Potter, Chris Cook and Danny MacKenzie. Danno, Wayne had kept in regular contact with since school. Cooksie and Potter he hadn't seen for years, but had made an effort to contact them because of his forthcoming wedding. Wayne grinned as he leapt into his BMW. It had been ages since he'd had a decent night out with the lads and he was looking forward to this one immensely.

Tammy looked stressed at she dashed into the restaurant. 'Sorry I'm late. Somebody chucked themselves under the train at Liverpool Street, so I had to arse about getting a cab to Mile End. Why are people so bloody inconsiderate these days? Couldn't whoever it was have just took an overdose of tablets or jumped off a cliff? Rather then ballsing up everybody else's day, mine included.'

Laughing, Stephanie stood up and hugged her best friend. Tammy's wonderful sense of humour was just one of the many things she was going to miss when her pal emigrated to Spain. 'I ordered us a bottle of Pinot, but I've already drunk half of it. Shall we have another bottle before we eat? I'm not that hungry yet and I haven't got to go home early. My mum's got the kids for the night, thank God.'

'Suits me, girl,' Tammy replied, helping herself to a glass of wine.

'So how's Tricky Dicky then? Has he been ringing you up from Spain?' Steph asked, nosily. Tricky Dicky was her nickname for Tammy's new boyfriend. His real name was Richard, but Steph rarely referred to him as that. Seeing as he'd appeared out of nowhere and was now taking her best friend away from her, Tricky Dicky somehow suited him better.

'Yep, he's been ringing me every day. Business is booming at the moment by all accounts, so it all looks promising for when I move out there. I love your hair, Steph. You've had it done different, haven't you?' Tammy remarked, changing the subject.

Stephanie ran her fingers through her bouncy dark curls. Everybody had always said she was pretty – stunning, in fact – but she had never really felt that way. Being five foot eight, she had always felt a bit gawky. She knew she had a cheeky smile, nice white teeth and cute dimples, but other than that she had always felt quite plain compared to her sister, Angela. 'I've been using heated rollers on it, but I don't put them in every day. I can't be arsed unless I'm going out somewhere. Do you think I should have it like this for the wedding? I'm not sure it will look right with that little tiara thing I've bought.'

'I'd have it like that, but you want to feel comfortable, Steph. You will look beautiful either way,' Tammy replied, honestly.

'Aah, you're so sweet, Tam. I dunno what I'm gonna do when you move. I shall be so lost without your advice. Can we try and see more of each other before you go? I've hardly set eyes on you the past six weeks.'

Tammy downed the rest of her wine and gesticulated to the waiter to bring over another bottle. 'I'll try and see you as much as I can, mate, but work's absolutely manic at the moment. They aren't happy that I'm leaving and some nights I don't get finished till eight or nine. I promise we'll go for it on your hen night, though. I've booked a couple of days off for that and we can party till we drop.'

'I won't be able to drink too much. I'll have to look after the kids the following day,' Stephanie replied.

'You said that Wayne was taking care of the kids. You've got to have a good hen night, girl.'

'I will enjoy myself, but I don't wanna go too mad. Tyler's tantrums do Wayne's head in and he can't handle him like I do. You know what men are like – they don't have much patience, do they?'

'Wayne don't hit him or anything, does he?' Tammy asked, bluntly.

'No, course not,' Stephanie lied. Wayne had clumped their son a few times just recently, but Steph had never told anyone, not even her mum. Wayne had never done any real damage to Tyler; he'd just lost his temper with the child's unpredictable behaviour. Steph could remember her mum smacking her and Angie when they were naughty as kids, so it was no big deal. 'You'll never guess who Wayne's meeting up with tonight?' Steph said.

'Who?'

'Cooksie and Potter,' Stephanie replied, laughing.

'What's he going out with them pair of plonkers for?'

'Don't ask me! You know what Wayne's like, he gets these dumb ideas in his head and won't rest until he's acted on them. Apparently, he's got in touch with Potter and Cooksie again because he wanted them to go out on his stag do with him. I reminded him what a pair of dickheads they were, but as per usual Wayne knows best. Men are strange creatures, Tam, and I'll never understand them as long as I live.'

Tammy chuckled. 'Wayne probably wants to relive his youth because he's getting hitched, Steph. I bet him, Cooksie and Potter spend the evening talking about their ICF days, their bright tracksuits and silly haircuts.'

Stephanie giggled. 'Wayne does drive me mad at times, but I do love him, Tam.'

'And the fact he's rich and you've got a nice house in

Chigwell is a bonus an' all, mate,' Tammy added, cheekily.

Stephanie leant across the table and squeezed her pal's hand. 'I know I ain't met Tricky Dicky yet, but I want you to know that I'm really pleased that you've met the one, Tam. Obviously, I wish you weren't moving to Spain, but I so want you to be happy like I am.'

Looking at the sincerity in her best friend's eyes, Tammy couldn't stop the tears from rolling down her cheeks. Her and Steph went way back, and Tammy knew when she stepped on that plane to start her new life, it would be Steph rather than her family that she would be thinking of.

Arriving in Gidea Park ten minutes late, Wayne Jackman parked his car in a side road and walked towards the Ship pub. Danny MacKenzie had done quite well for himself in life. He owned four tyre shops and had recently moved to a five-bedroom house that backed onto the local lake. It had been Danno who had tracked down Potter and Cooksie for him. It hadn't proved too difficult in the end, as Cooksie still lived locally in Elm Park. As he strolled into the pub, Wayne was shocked as he came face to face with his one-time best friends. Cooksie was skinny and as bald as a coot and Potter looked so fat he was almost unrecognizable.

'Fucking hell, Jacko, you look like an Indian waiter. You just got back off holiday or something?' Potter exclaimed, laughing.

Wayne smiled politely. Neither Potter nor Cooksie had ever had much decorum. 'No, I ain't been on holiday for ages. I've got a couple of sunbeds in me gym and I'm addicted to the bastard things.'

Cooksie gave Wayne an awkward bear hug. 'Shall we have a whip or what?' he asked him.

Seeing as Cooksie reeked of BO, Wayne used his question

as an excuse to end their hug. 'Did you sort the booze out like I asked you to?' he asked Danno.

When Danno nodded, Wayne slapped both Cooksie and Potter on the back. 'Tonight's on me, lads. I asked you to come, so this is my treat. We've got six bottles of champagne on ice here. Once we've polished them off, I'm taking us all out for a nice curry.'

Cooksie and Potter grinned at each other. Cooksie worked for London Underground, while Potter was currently unemployed, so neither were going to argue with Wayne over his generosity.

'Why the champagne? Is this some kind of special occasion, or what?' Potter asked when Wayne handed him a glass.

'Yeah! I thought the champers was a nice touch, seeing as we ain't laid eyes on one another for years, plus I'm getting married in three weeks' time. That's why I tracked you down. I couldn't have me stag night without having me two oldest muckers getting pissed with me, could I now? I thought we'd go to one of them lap-dancing clubs up town, have a bit of a giggle like. I'll be footing the bill, so you won't have to worry about dosh.'

'What's a lap-dancing club? Is it a bit like line dancing?' Cooksie asked, seriously.

Wayne, Danno and Potter all burst out laughing. 'You're such a fucking cock, mate. It's one of them clubs where you pay the birds to entertain you. They strip off and dance for you and stuff,' Potter explained.

Cooksie's face lit up. His bird, Sharon, was no oil painting and he could do with a fresh piece of meat. 'If there's gonna be tits and fanny involved, then count me in.'

'What about you?' Wayne asked Potter.

'What date is it?'

'Friday the fourth of Feb. I'm getting married the following weekend. Steph's always loved Valentine's Day, so we're getting married the weekend nearest to it. I surprised her on Christmas Day. She had no idea I'd booked it.'

Potter grinned. 'Count me in an' all. Can't miss me old china's stag night, can I? Danno was saying you've got two kids now. I'd heard you had a girl, but I didn't know you had a boy an' all.'

Wayne grinned. 'Yeah, Tyler. Looks just like me, he does – and he's got my temper. Do you remember our fisticuff days at football, lads? We were sadistic fuckers once, weren't we?'

'Do you still go over West Ham, Jacko? I live in Southend now, but I've still got a season ticket. It ain't like the old days no more, though. I hate all these middle-class pricks who have jumped on the football bandwagon. Ruining the game, they are,' Potter complained.

'I don't get time to go week in week out any more, but a pal of mine has got a box over there, so I manage to get to about half a dozen games a season,' Wayne replied.

Slurping champagne like it was going out of style, Cooksie slapped Wayne on the back. 'I can't believe you and Steph are still together after all these years. Does she still look the same? Is she still tall with dark hair?'

Danny MacKenzie spat his drink back into his glass and roared with laughter. 'No, Steph's shrunk, you dopey cunt. She's only four foot tall now.'

'You know what I mean? I meant, does she still look the same?' Cooksie replied, getting slightly agitated.

Wayne put a comforting arm around his old pal's shoulders. 'Of course I know what you meant. Yep, my Steph is still slim and even more stunning than you would remember. She's like a fine wine that's matured superbly with age, and I can't wait to marry the girl.'

'Fuck me! Never thought I'd see the day when you turned

into a nicely spoken romantic softie, Jacko,' Potter said, chuckling.

Wayne smirked. 'Don't be fooled. I ain't no mug, boys. Anyone pisses me off, they soon regret it afterwards. But when it comes to my Steph, I'm completely different. She's my life and I love her dearly.'

Over in Loughton, Stephanie had just been telling Tammy about her grandfather's funeral and what Angie had said. She hadn't stopped eating and was still picking at the numerous dishes that she and Tammy had ordered. 'Jesus, at this rate I am never going to fit into my wedding dress. What's up with you? You're normally a greedy cow with Chinese, but you've hardly eaten anything,' Steph said to her friend.

Tammy sighed. 'I was just thinking of Richard, or should I say Tricky Dicky? I wonder what he's doing now? He was going out with some business associates tonight.'

'You'll be seeing him soon enough and I'm sure he must be trustworthy. He would hardly have asked you to move to Spain with him if he were seeing other girls, would he? So, am I still gonna meet him next week? What day's he coming back?'

'I'm not sure yet, but you'll definitely meet him before the hen night.'

Stephanie grinned. 'Only three weeks now till Wayne makes an honest woman of me. I'm so excited. My mum can't wait, especially now she knows Wayne's dad's definitely not coming. She was dreading him being there because of what he did.'

Wayne's father had been locked up in 1978 for murdering Wayne's mother. He had got life, but had been let out after thirteen years and had since started a new life abroad. Wayne had had a fall-out with his dad soon after his release. They'd gone out drinking one evening, the subject of the murder had arisen and a massive argument had ensued back at the house. Wayne hadn't seen his father since. He had tried to track him down to invite him to the wedding, but Lenny Jackman had disappeared without trace. Wayne had heard through the grapevine that he had moved to Greece, but nobody knew if that was true or false.

'So, has Wayne given up searching for his old man now?' Tammy asked.

'Yeah. To be honest I don't think he would have bothered getting in touch with him again if we weren't getting married. Never mind, his nan and grandad will both be there, and seeing as they virtually brought him up, that's all that matters. I did tell Wayne to try and contact his sisters again, but he wasn't interested. He said they were adults now and if they had wanted to find him, then they would have.'

'How are the legendary Doris and Bill?' Tammy asked, laughing. She had met Wayne's dysfunctional grandparents at a couple of parties in the past, and found them highly entertaining.

'They're still exactly the same. Never sober or without a fag hanging out of their gobs. Actually, Wayne's arranged for us to go for a meal with them the weekend after next. If Tricky Dicky's about, it would be great if you and him could come along too. I'm sure Wayne wouldn't mind and you'd be doing me a massive favour.'

'If Richard's back, I'll do my best to twist his arm,' Tammy promised.

'You're definitely bringing him to the wedding with you, aren't you? Me and Wayne getting married, eh. Who would ever have thought it?'

Without any warning, Tammy started to cry.

'Whatever's wrong?' Steph asked, squeezing her best friend's hand.

Tammy took a deep breath and waved a hand in front of her face. 'Take no notice of me. I'm just pissed and thinking of how much I'm gonna miss you when I leave England.'

Stephanie stared fondly into her friend's eyes. If she didn't voice her fears now after they'd had a few drinks, then she might not get another chance. 'Please don't think I'm being selfish when I say this, Tam, but I am worried about you. You've only known this Richard for a couple of months and it is so unlike you to do anything rash. Are you sure you've thought this through? I mean, what does your mum and dad say about it all? And your sister? Being a policewoman, surely she must be worried about your welfare?'

'Richard ain't a mass murderer, Steph. He's a lovely bloke, and if I hadn't thought it through properly, then I wouldn't be going. I know I haven't known him long, but I knew he was the one the first time he kissed me. As for the sex, it's amazing. You just know these things, don't you?'

'But what about your job? You've got such a good career, Tam.'

'A career ain't everything, Steph. Look at you. You've got two beautiful kids, a handsome man, a wonderful lifestyle. That's what I want, mate. I don't wanna be sitting in an office till eight and nine o'clock every night working me tits off. I want a life!'

Finally understanding her pal's reckless decision to elope with a man she barely knew, Stephanie moved around the other side of the table, sat next to Tammy and hugged her. 'You go for it, girl. I wish you all the happiness in the world, babe, I really do.'

Danny MacKenzie looked at Wayne Jackman in amazement as he spoke of his financial difficulties. Danno had always thought that Wayne was loaded.

'I thought you'd cracked it with that gym, Jacko. You were telling me only last year how much dosh it had made you,' Danno said.

Potter and Cooksie sat quietly as Wayne explained the situation. They knew nothing about running a business, so were happy to just listen rather than butt in.

'Everything was sweet, Danno. I was raking it in up until last summer and then it all started going tits-up. That other gym opened down the road and took away tons of me custom. Then a big chain of sports shop opened up near my sports shop in Barkingside. It's got even worse this year as there's another gym just opened in fucking Wanstead. What with the wedding and everything else, I'm on me arse, mate.'

'We don't mind chipping in with the bill, Jacko,' Potter offered, as he munched yet another poppadom.

Wayne shook his head. 'Don't be daft, I ain't penniless. I've got collateral, I'm just a bit short of readies at the moment. Getting married is not cheap. But I'll pick meself up again, I always do.'

'So, does Steph know you're in schtuck, mate? Can't you postpone the wedding until next year?' Danno asked Wayne.

'I can't postpone it, Steph would be devastated. To be honest, it's all my fault we're in this position. Me and Steph had discussed getting married for years, but because of one thing and another, we never got round to it. On Valentine's Day last year, a pal of mine got hitched. Me and Steph went to the wedding and she loved it. She said getting married on Valentine's Day was the most romantic thing she had ever seen. Things were still going well for me then, so I started arranging the wedding as a surprise. By the time I told Steph on Christmas Day, my businesses were both in trouble, but I'd already organized and paid deposits for everything by then.'

'That's such a shame, mate.' Cooksie said, sincerely.

Wayne stared at his pals. They were the oldest friends he had now, so he'd chosen to spill his guts to them rather than anyone else. 'If I tell you something, promise me you won't say nothing to Steph?' he said.

When all three men vowed not to, Wayne continued. He turned to Danno. 'You know I sold me house in Collier Row to move to Chigwell?'

'Yeah,' Danno replied.

'Well, I sold it and rented because I had to. I've told Steph that we'll rent in Chigwell for six months before we buy, so we can make sure we like it before we take the plunge. But, the truth is, I was in so much debt, I didn't have much choice. When things hit rock bottom last year, I borrowed money against the gym and the shop. Even that new BMW I've bought is on the never-never.'

To say Danny was astounded was an understatement. He knew a few blokes who knew Wayne, and all of them had been under the impression that he was a millionaire at least. 'I can lend you a few bob, mate. How much do you need to tide you over?'

Wayne immediately shook his head. 'Thanks for the offer, Danno, but I'm a man not a mug. This cash-flow problem I've got is just a temporary hitch and, in hindsight, perhaps I should have come clean with Steph. She bought our little Tyler an outfit that cost two hundred sovs the other day, and the money she's spent on the bridesmaids' clobber, you don't wanna know. The price of her wedding dress was absolutely scandalous, but what can I do? I love the girl, it's the biggest day of her life and I can't spoil it for her.'

'You poor bastard,' Danno said, as he slapped Wayne on the back.

Wayne's eyes welled up. 'Look at me getting all emotional. What a prick! Seriously guys, I know we're pissed, but getting that off me chest has done me the world of good. I ain't told no other bugger and I ain't gonna. Let's just keep it between ourselves, eh?'

When Danno, Potter and Cooksie all nodded, Wayne toasted them with his glass of champagne. 'To true friends.'

Stephanie Crouch arrived home at twelve o'clock on the dot. She was merry rather than drunk and had really enjoyed her evening with Tammy. It was sad in parts but, now she understood why her mate was taking such a risk, she could finally be happy for her. As Steph put her key in the door, she could hear her home phone ringing. Guessing it was probably Wayne, she ran into the lounge to answer it. 'Hello.'

'It's me, Steph. You only just got in?' her mum asked her.

'What's up? Are the kids OK?' Steph asked, ignoring her mother's question.

'Yeah, they've been asleep for hours,' Pam replied.

'What's wrong then? Angie ain't been performing again, has she?'

'No. Is Wayne home?' Pam asked. She had something important to tell Stephanie and she didn't want to cause any trouble.

Feeling anxious and annoyed at the same time, Stephanie couldn't help but lose her patience. 'No, he ain't! For Christ's sake, just spit it out will you, Mum?'

'I would have rung you on that new mobile thing you've got, but I knew you were out with Tammy and I didn't wanna spoil your evening. It's Barry, he's come back home.'

'Barry who?' Stephanie asked, dumbly.

'Your ex-boyfriend, Barry. You know, Marlene's son. She's back an' all. They pulled up in a cab a couple of hours ago and went in their old house. They had two suitcases with 'em, so they must be planning on staying for a while.'

Feeling as if she had just been struck by a bolt of lightning, Stephanie gasped and dropped the phone in shock.

CHAPTER EIGHTEEN

The following morning, Steph was a bundle of nerves as she drove towards her mother's house. She had barely slept a wink last night and when she had finally managed to nod off, she had dreamt that Barry Franklin had turned up at her wedding with a gun in his hand and tried to shoot Wayne. Beside herself with worry, Stephanie let out a deep sigh. Wayne hadn't got in until half three this morning and had been in no fit state to have a serious conversation with. Stephanie knew she had to tell him that Barry was back home. If her ex was staying bang opposite her mother, she could hardly not bloody tell Wayne.

As Stephanie neared her mother's house her anxiety started to heighten. Whether she would ever have dumped Barry in favour of Wayne, she really didn't know, but in the end the decision had been made for her.

Swerving onto a kerb, Stephanie slammed on the brakes and repeatedly banged her head gently against the steering wheel. She had two beautiful children, would soon be marrying the man of her dreams, she was financially secure and healthy; so why did this have to happen to spoil her perfect life? Picturing Barry Franklin's face, Stephanie took the mobile phone Wayne had recently bought her out of her bag and rang her mother.

'Are you ready?' she asked, when Pam answered the phone.

'Yeah. Why? You ain't running late, are you?'

'No, I'm parked up in Ford Road. Walk the way you normally go to work and you'll see me by the crossroads,' Steph replied.

'Why can't you pick me up from home? I'll be late if I have to carry Tyler.'

'Because of Barry, Mum. If I bump into him, I'll die a death, and I really can't face the embarrassment of it all.'

Barry Franklin woke up in his old bedroom and stared at the surroundings in utter disgust. He had been rather inebriated when he'd gone to bed last night, so hadn't taken much notice of the room, but in the cold light of day it looked awful. There was dust everywhere, cobwebs hanging from the ceiling, and pieces of stale food scattered about on the carpet. Looking at the colour of the filthy, stained quilt he had slept under, Barry sat up and immediately began scratching at his skin. Compared to his current surroundings, he lived in what could only be described as a palace back in Spain, and Barry knew without a doubt that he could not spend another night at his sister's house. He would rather shell out for a hotel somewhere.

As a little mixed-race head poked out from under the quilt in the bed opposite him, Barry smiled. Chantelle had three children now, all by different men. AJ was the oldest. He was nearly ten and was the son of the Indian guy Chantelle had been with when Barry had moved to Spain. Ajay senior was now in Belmarsh. He had been caught with a big stash of heroin and was doing a fifteen stretch. The child currently staring at him with a look of bewilderment on his face was Chantelle's middle one, Jermain. His father was of Jamaican origin, but had wanted little to do with his son and had only seen him twice since his birth.

'You all right, boy? I'm your Uncle Barry.'

'Get out my room,' the child replied, glaring at him.

Barry got out of bed. The bedroom had the same odour as a public toilet, and he guessed that one if not more of the kids must wet the bed on a regular basis. Barry hadn't even met his youngest nephew yet. Daryl was only two, had an English father, and Chantelle was happy to let his dad bring him up. Apparently, she only saw Daryl every other weekend and had even cancelled the child's last visit.

'I said get out my room,' Jermain repeated, angrily.

'Chill out, boy. I'm going in a tick,' Barry replied. He walked over to the window and stared through the grimy glass at the house across the road. He knew Pam still lived there and Stephanie visited her regularly with her two children. He also knew that Stephanie and Wayne were getting married in three weeks' time. He might live thousands of miles away, but the grapevine was a funny old thing, and there wasn't much that went on that he didn't get to hear about. Barry let go of the shabby curtain. Steph had killed his faith in the female gender for a very long time, and after spending years screwing everything in sight, Barry had finally met the girl he wanted to spend the rest of his life with. Jolene, her name was. She was eighteen years old, a real stunner, and after being together for just over a year, they had recently got engaged.

'If you don't go, I'm gonna get my mum to beat you up,' Jermain growled, appearing by Barry's side.

Ruffling the child's short Afro hair, Barry chuckled and hurriedly left the room.

After disclosing her fears to her mum, and Pam reassuring her that Barry had not come back to ruin her wedding or carry out some sort of revenge attack, Stephanie drove back to Chigwell in a much better frame of mind. Wayne had still been in bed when she'd arrived home, so she had got Dannielle ready for school, dropped her at the gates and was now on the way back home again with Tyler.

'All right, babe? Cor, I was bladdered last night, girl. Did you hear me come in?' Wayne asked as Stephanie shut the front door.

'Yeah, I spoke to you, don't you remember?'

'I can't remember Jack shit,' Wayne said, hugging his wife-to-be.

'So, did you have a good night? How were Potter and Cooksie? Are they still a pair of wankers?' Stephanie enquired, genuinely interested.

'Yeah, a bit, but they're OK. Cooksie is unemployed and is living with some old bird in Elm Park who has three kids by some other geezer, and Potter works for the Underground. I dunno what he does there, he didn't say. He's got kids of his own and lives in Southend, but he ain't married. Right, I'd better get off to work now, babe. I'll probably be late tonight. I've got a business meeting with some geezer.'

'Par, Daddy, par,' Tyler said, grabbing hold of his father's leg.

'Not today, boy,' Wayne replied, ruffling his son's head. He knew Tyler's language well enough now to realize his son was asking to be taken to the park.

'I need to talk to you, Wayne,' Stephanie said, nervously.

'Can't it wait till later, or tomorrow, sweetheart? I really have got a lot on me plate today.'

'No, Wayne, it can't!'

'Wan go par,' Tyler screamed, kicking Wayne's leg, then throwing himself on the floor.

'Tough shit! You ain't going to the fucking park. Get that child away from me, Steph. I've got a banging headache, babe, and I can't be doing with his little tantrums, today of all days.'

'Just give me five minutes to calm him down, Wayne, and then we'll talk. There's something important we need to discuss.'

When Stephanie half dragged and half carried a hysterical Tyler up the stairs, Wayne sat anxiously on the sofa. Surely Steph hadn't found out about his underhandedness? Because if she had, it would ruin everything.

Unable to fancy anything to eat or drink in his sister's house, Barry offered to treat her and the boys to breakfast in a local café. Within minutes of arriving there, Barry started to regret his spontaneous suggestion. AJ and Jermain were playing up something chronic and Chantelle had a mouth on her like a sewer. Seeing Jermain pestering an old couple who were sitting on a nearby table, Barry urged his sister to control the child. 'People are trying to have a quiet bite to eat, Chantelle. Make him sit down or play outside if he's gonna be a pest in here.'

'Jermain, get over 'ere you little cunt before I rip your fucking head off,' Chantelle yelled at the top of her voice.

Barry felt himself squirm with embarrassment as he saw a tableful of workmen glance around, then snigger. Unlike himself, Chantelle had never had any style or class. She was twenty-six now, was overweight, had tattoos on her arms and an earring through her nose. Her hair was dyed a yellowy-blond colour and her clothes were far too skimpy for her size-sixteen frame. 'I'm going outside to make some phone calls,' Barry said, abruptly.

'Don't leave me sitting 'ere like a tit in a trance. Can't you make your phone calls later?'

Watching in disbelief as AJ and Jermain started throwing chips at one another, Barry glared at his scumbag of a sister. 'No, I fucking well can't.'

* * *

After three weeks of playing the grieving widow to the police and her friends in Spain, Marlene was relieved to see her best friend, Marge. When Marlene had first moved over to Spain, Marge had come out for holidays twice a year, but three years ago she had had a drunken row with Jake and he had kicked her out of his and Marlene's apartment in the middle of the night.

'Right, start from the very beginning. I know we spoke on the phone, mate, but the line was shit, you were pissed, and I couldn't make head nor tail of what you were saying,' Marge said, opening a bottle of wine.

Marlene gulped greedily at the drink that was handed to her. Jake the Snake's murder had come as a terrible shock to her. Even though she had never loved him, she would always be grateful to him for giving her the lifestyle she had always craved. Composing herself, Marlene began to explain exactly what had happened. 'Jake got himself involved in drugs about five years ago. He bumped into some old pals of his from South London. They were fugitives and he went into business with 'em.'

'Why didn't you ever tell me all this before?' Marge asked. She felt hurt that she'd been kept in the dark by her pal. They'd always told one another everything.

'Because I only found out meself recently. Barry told me. That little bastard was probably involved in it an' all. Jake was a real man's man. He was a good provider, but he never talked business with me, Marge, and I've only found out the truth since he died. I always thought the bar paid for our opulent lifestyle, but Barry said Jake just kept that to cover his arse and keep the authorities off his back. Barry reckons it only brought in peanuts.'

'What was he selling? Cocaine? That's big 'ere now, you know. It's took over from speed,' Marge informed her friend.

Marlene shook her head. 'Ecstasy tablets. They had a

factory just outside Fuengirola where they were making hundreds of thousands of the bastard things, by all accounts. They had contacts in England and were importing 'em over 'ere by boat, so Barry reckons.'

'So, why did Jake get shot then?' Marge asked, slightly confused.

'The factory got turned over and it happened to be on a day when Jake was meant to be there and he wasn't. Two of the men got away, but three others got arrested. Barry says that the other men must have thought that Jake snitched on 'em and that's why he got shot. A man on a motorbike killed him at point-blank range as we walked out of a restaurant near the harbour, Marge. Covered in claret, I was; it was awful for me. Died in me arms, Jake did. Well, sort of. I didn't actually cuddle him 'cause of all the blood. He made these terrible gurgling noises, Marge, and then he just shut his eyes and croaked it.'

'Poor Jake! And you must have been devastated. I know me and Jake fell out, mate, but I wouldn't have wished him any harm, you know.'

Unable to stop herself, Marlene burst out laughing. She'd had weeks of wearing black and crying bloody crocodile tears. 'I would! I hated the old cunt. Don't get me wrong, I'll always be indebted to him for getting me out of poxy Dagenham, but he was so ugly, Marge. Sex with him used to make me feel physically sick, and towards the end he couldn't get a hard-on by having intercourse. He could only get one if I noshed him off. Every morning he used to wake me up with a sickly smile on his face and I had to suck his little shrivelled-up cock. Used to put me off having any fucking breakfast, it did. Eating like an horse again now, I am.'

Even though Marge and Marlene went back donkey's years, Marge was bewildered by her pal's words. 'But you said his death was awful for you?'

'Well, it was, but only 'cause it happened right in front of me. Two hundred quid that silk dress I had on cost. Fucking ruined it is. I took it to the cleaner's, but they can't get the blood out. I've had to chuck it away.'

Marge roared with laughter. 'Oh, you are awful, Mar. When's the old bastard's funeral?'

'Next Monday. Will you come to it with me, mate? I'd have buried him in Spain if I'd have had my way. Waste of bloody money flying him back home, if you ask me. I dunno if you know, but Jake had two daughters. He hadn't seen 'em for years, he fell out with 'em when he split up with their mum, but because me and him weren't married, they were his next of kin and they demanded the body get buried in England. I wonder how much he's worth? He hated his ex-wife and never forgave his daughters for disowning him, so I doubt he's left them fuck all. I know he made a new will in 1991, so I reckon I've copped the lot, don't you?'

'Bleedin' hell, Mar, he must have been worth a fortune. I reckon you'll be made for life, girl.'

Slurping her drink, Marlene grinned. 'Well, after sucking his sweaty little cock for years, I reckon I've more than earned me inheritance, don't you?'

Howling with laughter, Marge agreed.

'That was a long five minutes,' Wayne said sarcastically, when Stephanie finally reappeared. Tyler's tantrums had driven him to distraction recently – so much so, he had even suggested taking the child for blood tests or a brain scan, but Stephanie had rejected the idea. She was one of these mothers who refused to believe that her son had anything wrong with him.

'Sorry, Tyler wouldn't settle. He didn't sleep well last night and I think he's been playing up today because he's tired,' Stephanie replied, apologetically.

Not wanting to listen to the usual list of excuses his fiancée always made for their son's abnormal behaviour, a hung-over Wayne came straight to the point. 'So, what's so urgent we need to talk about, that I can't go to work?'

Steph felt too stressed to put together a proper sentence, so she just blurted the crux of it out. 'Barry Franklin's back home.'

'Yeah, I know he is. In fact, I'm gonna pop over to Dagenham and see him later on today,' Wayne replied, casually.

Stephanie looked at her husband-to-be in amazement. 'How do you know that he's home? You never said nothing to me! And when did you arrange to meet up with him?'

'I knew Bazza was back in England because Martin Gowing rang me up yesterday and told me. You know that Jake the Snake geezer that Bazza's mother fucked off to Spain with?'

Stephanie nodded.

'Well, Jake got murdered by a hit man a few weeks back and Bazza and his mum have flown home 'cause of the funeral and stuff. Martin has kept in touch with Bazza ever since he moved out to Spain, so he's always kept me informed with how he's doing out there.'

'Who the hell's Martin Gowing when he's at home? And why the fuck didn't you tell me all this before?' Stephanie yelled. She had always hated secrets, especially ones like this.

'Martin is mine and Bazza's old pal from Bethnal Green. He kept in touch with Bazza when he moved out to Spain. I didn't tell you that Bazza was back as I wanted to go and see him first. Once I'd seen him, providing he was OK about me and you, I was gonna tell you everything.'

'So, when did you arrange to meet up with him?' Steph yelled.

'I haven't arranged anything. I'm just gonna turn up at

his sister's gaff and offer him a handshake. He might turn round and chin me, Steph, after what happened, but I very much doubt it. Martin told me that Bazza's recently got engaged to a stunning young bird over in Spain, so I doubt he's that arsed about me and you being together now. Don't forget, I saved Bazza's life and stopped him from drowning when we were kids, so I'm sure he'll be man enough to let bygones be bygones. Life's too short to hold grudges, eh babe?'

'I really don't think you should go round there, Wayne. Why don't you just let sleeping dogs lie, eh? Dragging up the past is never a good thing,' Stephanie said, nervously. The thought of Wayne and Barry being pals again for some reason filled her with pure and utter dread.

'I have to go and see him, Steph. When I nicked you off him I was just a boy, but I'm a man now and – whatever way you wanna look at it – I do owe Bazza an apology. This is why I never told you he was home. I knew you'd try and stop me from going to see him, but I have to smooth things over. Me and Bazza go back years and I'm sure once we have a man-to-man chat we can be pals once again. How did you know he was home, by the way? Did your mother tell ya?'

'Yeah, my mum saw him pull up in a cab last night. You just do what you gotta do then, Wayne, but if it all goes Pete Tong, don't say I didn't warn you.'

Desperate not to upset Steph before the wedding, Wayne urged her to stand up and give him a hug. 'Nothing's gonna go wrong, babe, I promise you that much.'

Stephanie was no psychic, but her innermost self told her that no good would come out of Wayne and Barry meeting up again. Clinging to her fiancé, Steph laid her worried head on his shoulder. 'I hope you're right, Wayne, for all our sakes, I really do.'

CHAPTER NINETEEN

Pam and Cathy were in their element as they discussed the comings and goings across the road. Stephanie had rung up earlier and had told her mum to keep an eye out for Wayne. 'If Barry lays one finger on him, Mum, just ring the police immediately,' she'd insisted.

'Ere's the old slapper now. Quick Pam, she's just pulled up in a cab,' Cathy screamed, as Pam walked up the stairs to use the toilet.

Pam flew down the stairs like a bat out of hell.

'She's laughing and joking with the bleedin' cab driver. She hardly looks like the grieving widow, does she?' Cathy said.

Nodding in agreement, Pam put her nose to the window as she saw Marlene go inside the house, then reappear. 'What's she got in her arms?'

Cathy squinted. 'Clothes, by the look of it. Dresses, I think, and she's got two big carrier bags.'

Pam hovered until the waiting taxi pulled away with Marlene inside it, then made a dash from the room. 'I'm busting. Keep watch for me, Cath, and I'll be back in a tick.'

* * *

Wayne Jackman's brain was working overtime as he drove towards Dagenham. His pal had just rung him to inform him that Barry Franklin was in the Church Elm pub, alone, and was awaiting his arrival. 'What did you say to him, Mart? Did he sound calm or not?'

'I just said that you were gonna shoot round and see him at his sister's, and he said to tell you to meet him in the Elms. He sounded all right; he certainly didn't have a cob on,' Martin explained.

Stopping at a red traffic light, Wayne checked out his hair in the interior mirror. He'd got showered and changed at the gym, and even though he was only venturing to some shit-hole boozer in Dagenham, he had opted to wear his best clobber. Barry had always had style himself and Wayne certainly wasn't going to mug himself off by turning up like a tramp. As the lights turned to green, Wayne continued his journey. He didn't think he was nervous about meeting up with Barry again, so he put his palpitations down to excitement, although couldn't help feeling that Barry's choice of venue had been chosen just to make him feel awkward. Why else would Barry want to meet him in the Church Elm pub if it wasn't to bring home to him his wrongdoings of the past?

Barry Franklin was sitting in the Church Elm pub at a table near the window. He had quite enjoyed sipping a couple of bottles of beer, while watching the traffic and shoppers go by. The Heathway had changed in the ten years since he had left Dagenham. There was a much bigger ethnic community and the shops now all looked tatty and extremely old fashioned. As Wayne Jackman bowled across the road, Barry spotted him immediately. With his suntan and designer clothes, he stood out like a sore thumb in Dagenham Heathway. Since moving to Spain, Barry had kept tracks on Wayne's life. Wayne thought that Martin Gowing was his pal, but he wasn't really. Gowing hated Wayne with a passion for stealing Steph off him, and he had only pretended to be friendly with Wayne as a favour to Barry. 'I wanna know everything that cunt Jacko does, 'cause one day, when the time's right, I'm gonna get me own back,' Barry had explained to Gowing many moons ago.

Barry smirked as Wayne approached him with an outstretched right hand. He could sense that Wayne was dubious over the welcome he would receive. Ever the gentleman, Barry stood up to greet his old friend.

'It's been a fucking long time, ain't it, Bazza?' Wayne said, with more than a hint of anxiety in his voice.

Staring at Wayne's slighty quivering right hand, Barry smirked, then shook it. 'It's been far too long.'

Stephanie was a bag of nerves when she set off to pick Dannielle up from an after-school birthday party. Waiting for the phone to ring when something important was at stake was the worst feeling in the world, and she had spent half the day staring at the plastic object.

'Swee, Ma, swee,' Tyler said, poking his mother in the arm.

Steph was more than used to her son's unconventional language and managed to understand his every want or need quite clearly. 'We'll stop for some sweeties in a bit, darling. But first we must pick Dannielle up from her party, else we'll be late, OK?'

Tyler grinned in approval. Even at his tender age, he knew that if his mum made a promise, she would deliver. His father was a different kettle of fish entirely.

'Pass Mummy her phone,' Stephanie asked, pointing to the object that was ringing on top of her handbag in the footwell. Tyler always sat in the front of the car with her, because he would kick off if she forced him to sit in the back.

As her son bent down and handed her a hairbrush, Stephanie wanted to scream with frustration, but chose not to. 'No, the phone Tyler, the phone,' she said, as calmly as she possibly could.

When Tyler looked at her blankly, Stephanie bumped the car onto the kerb and picked up the phone herself. She punched in her mother's number. 'Did you just ring me, Mum?'

'Yes. I rang to tell you that me and Cath have been glued to the window for the past three hours and there's been no sign of Wayne. The old slapper came home, then went out again, but that's about all I've got to report.'

'What about Barry? Have you seen him go in or out at all?' Stephanie asked.

'Nope. Not seen hide nor hair of him. Chantelle's there though. She's just ordered a pizza and paid the man at the door.'

Thanking her mother for keeping look-out, Stephanie ended the call and punched in Wayne's number. She had rung him six times in the past couple of hours but he hadn't answered any of her calls. 'Bollocks,' she mumbled, as the phone rang and rang once again. She felt desperately inadequate. Say Barry had done something awful to Wayne? If he had it would be all her fault. She was the one who had forced both men to become part of a sordid love triangle in the first place.

'La you, Mummy,' Tyler uttered softly, as the tears rolled down Stephanie's cheeks.

Stephanie held her son close to her chest. 'I love you too, boy. Let's just both pray that Daddy will be OK, eh?'

Tyler had no idea what his mother meant by the word pray, but seeing that she seemed so upset, he decided nodding was the best thing to do.

Stephanie ruffled his hair. Tyler was such a handsome

boy. With his blond hair and piercing blue eyes, he would have made a fabulous child model had he been better behaved.

'Da be OK,' Tyler said, trying to repeat his mother's words.

Stephanie smiled. Her son might not know what he was saying, but he was right. Of course his father would be OK. Wayne was no man's fool and Steph was sure that any mud Barry Franklin chose to throw at him, her big, strapping fiancé was more than capable of slinging back twice as hard.

Wayne Jackman stared at the paralytic man and woman who were getting louder and louder on the next table. There was so much he wanted to say to Barry and it was only the surroundings that were stopping him from doing so. 'Are you in a rush to get back to your sister's, Bazza? You gotta be anywhere later on?'

'Nope. I ain't gotta be nowhere.'

'Look, tell me to fuck off if you want, but I know a cushti little Indian restaurant over in Chadwell Heath. The geezer who owns it used to train down my gym and I get treated like a king whenever I eat there. Why don't we go there? We can order a nice curry and a few bottles of bubbly. It's got to be better than sitting in this dosshouse, eh?'

'Yeah, fuck it, why not?' Barry replied. Anything was better than going back to the refuge tip his sister called home. Barry downed the rest of his lager in one, urged Wayne to do the same, and then led him to where his car was parked.

'Nice set of wheels, Jacko,' Barry said, as they approached Wayne's flash new BMW.

Wayne nodded. He couldn't believe how nice Barry was being towards him. He hadn't really known what to expect, but Barry was acting as though the Steph love triangle had never happened, and Wayne couldn't help thinking that his old pal's acceptance of the way he had once betrayed him was slightly too good to be true. Wayne started the engine and drove over Heathway Hill in silence. Barry hadn't mentioned Stephanie yet, neither had he, but he knew the subject would have to be discussed sooner or later and decided to broach it in the restaurant, rather than in the car. 'So, tell me about Jake the Snake. I know you told me bits in the pub, but I couldn't concentrate on what you were saying because of that lairy pair of pissheads next to us.'

'To put it in a nutshell, Jake upset some extremely heavy people. He was involved in a bit of this and that and, apparently, had his hands in the till. I've no idea who actually bumped him off, but I keep hearing the rumours why. I think one or two of the lads he was involved with thought he was a snitch an' all, hence the bullet through his head, I suppose.'

'What was he dealing in? Drugs? Were you involved an' all?' Wayne pried.

'Yeah, I think so, and no I weren't! Not my scene, that shit,' Barry replied, honestly. As a lad, Barry had envisaged ending up in that type of world, but in the end he hadn't needed to. He'd saved his earnings from the bar and had an eye for a run-down property. Since buying and selling his first for a tidy profit, he had never looked back, and even though some of his dealings were shady, especially when it came to the taxman, Barry always described himself as a self-made property entrepreneur.

'So, is your mum proper upset over his death? What about you? Were you close to him?'

'You know what my muvver's like, Jacko. I think she was more upset about her dress being ruined by bloodstains, than poor old Jake getting shot. I shall miss him though. I wouldn't say we were exceptionally close, but he was OK. My old girl's dated worst geezers in her time, put it that way.'

'How's your old man, Bal? He must be due out again soon?' Wayne asked, changing the subject.

Barry's father, Smasher, had been in and out of prisons all his life. His most recent stretch was for GBH and he was due for release in April. 'Got about ten weeks left to serve, he has. I'm going to visit him next week and I can't wait. It'll be the first time I've seen him in over two years. What about your old man? He's out now, ain't he?' Barry asked Wayne.

'Yeah. He got out last year, but we had a big barny and he fucked off abroad somewhere. I tried to find him 'cause I wanted him at the wedding, but . . .' Realizing that he had just mentioned his forthcoming nuptials, Wayne stopped in mid-sentence.

'It's OK. I know you and Steph are getting married,' Barry said, trying to defuse the awkward moment.

Wayne knew that now he had brought the topic up, it was only right that he apologized. 'I'm really sorry about what happened, all them years back, Bazza. I didn't mean to fall for Steph, but when you left and we carried on spending time together, it just happened if you know what I mean? You must have thought I was such a cunt at the time and I can't say I blame you.'

Barry stared out of the window at the passing traffic. He could never forgive Wayne for what he had done to him, what real man would? But he would never give his old pal the satisfaction of knowing how he felt.

'This is the restaurant. Are you OK, Bazza?' Wayne asked, nervously.

Managing to compose himself, Barry turned to Wayne and grinned. 'Of course I am, mate. Listen, what happened with me, you and Steph was donkey's years ago and I'd nigh on forgotten all about it until you just mentioned it.'

Wayne breathed a huge sigh of relief. When Barry had gone quiet on him, Wayne had glanced his way and was positive he had seen a vicious expression on his old friend's face. 'Thanks for not hating me, Bazza. It means a lot.'

Barry stared deep into his pal's eyes. 'How could I hate the geezer who saved my life, eh?'

Over in Chigwell, Stephanie was completely beside herself. She wasn't that much of a drinker since she'd become a mother, but was now so worried about Wayne's whereabouts that she had managed to sink a whole bottle of wine by herself. Dannielle and Tyler were both fast asleep, and after trying Wayne's phone for what seemed like the hundredth time, Stephanie rang her mum again. 'What am I gonna do? His phone is still switched off. Do you think I should call the police?'

'You know what Wayne's like, love. I know he don't go out that much, but when he does, he's a sod for coming home at a decent hour. Me and Cath have still been keeping tabs across the road and there's been no sign of Barry either. You can bet your bottom dollar that they're pissed and having a whale of a time somewhere, so if I was you I'd stop worrying.'

'But say Barry's done something bad to him? For all I know, Wayne could be lying dead in a ditch somewhere with a bullet through his brain.'

'Oh, don't be so silly, Steph. You sound like bloody Angela! Of course Barry hasn't done anything bad to Wayne. Why don't you get yourself to bed, love? I can tell you've had a good drink because you're slurring.'

Stephanie said goodbye to her mum, then rang Tammy. There was no answer and Steph guessed, with it being Friday, that Tammy had gone out with the city crowd after work as she usually did. Deciding to take her mother's advice, Stephanie went upstairs and got into bed. She shut her eyes and, not for the first time since she had heard Barry Franklin was back home, pictured his face. She had no idea what he looked like now, but she could remember his cheeky smile, his kiss, and his touch – as though it were only yesterday that she had last seen him. Stephanie leapt out of bed and rummaged about in the bottom of her wardrobe. She had never thrown it away. Taking the half of the jagged gold heart out of its black velvet box, Stephanie held it in her right hand and stared at it. She knew how much she loved Wayne, but Barry returning to England had stirred up all sorts of weird emotions for her and she wished he would just sod off back to Spain, pronto. Putting the heart back in its box, Stephanie snapped the lid shut and put it back in its hidey-hole. She had never really believed in God. How could she when he had taken her father away from her in such a cruel manner? But, for once, Stephanie decided to see if the Lord above did actually exist. Clasping her hands together, she shut her eyes and tilted her head towards the ceiling. 'Please God make Barry go away because, putting it bluntly, I would rather die than ever have to see his face again.'

Unaware that Stephanie was currently kneeling on the floor praying, Wayne was busy discussing her in the restaurant. Barry seemed cool with the conversation and also genuinely interested.

'Well, I'm glad it's worked out for the pair of you. You seem ever so loved-up and happy, and I know how that feels now I've met Jolene. Do you wanna see a photo of her?' Barry asked.

Wayne nodded, then stared at the snap of the pretty blond-haired girl who was standing next to a boat wearing a skimpy red bikini. 'Fucking hell, no wonder you're happy, she's a right sort! The boat's a beauty an' all. Who's that belong to?'

'It's mine,' Barry replied, casually.

'Is it? Jesus, you must be doing all right for yourself, Bazza. What is it – a houseboat?'

'Yeah, a fifty footer. I'm doing OK. And Martin tells me you've cracked it an' all. To be honest, me and you were always destined to be cakeo. Even as kids we knew how to earn a few bob, didn't we?'

'We sure did, but things ain't been good for me lately. Between me and you, I'm in shit street at the moment.'

Barry was shocked as Wayne began to go into details over his financial difficulties. Martin Gowing had always kept him up to date on Wayne's business activities, and even though Barry was sure that Wayne was nowhere near as rich as himself, it was still a surprise to learn he was in dire straits.

'Even the car's on credit and I don't know what I'm gonna say to Steph when I have to explain that we ain't got no money to buy another house. I will have to sit her down and tell her everything, but not until after the wedding. I would never forgive myself if I spoilt her big day for her, so please keep what I told you to yourself,' Wayne said, solemnly.

'See no evil, hear no evil, me. Surely you must have some dosh left if you've sold a massive chunk of the gym, though? How much did you get for it?'

Wayne suddenly clammed up. 'Not as much as you'd think. The geezer I sold it to knew I was desperate for readies and took full advantage of the fact. Let's talk about something else, eh? If not, I'll only get on a downer.'

Barry nodded. 'How's your nan and grandad? They are still alive, I take it?'

'Yep. Still drink like fishes, smoke like chimneys and bet like dockers. They don't change and are still as fit as fiddles.'

Remembering Doris and Bill from when he was a small boy, Barry chuckled. 'Do you remember when we used to do your nan's weekly shopping and she would give us fifty pence each?'

'Yeah, we used to nick all the dear stuff and put it in her shopping trolley. Then we'd tell her we lost the receipt and pocket the money for what we'd chored. We had a right little earner out of that, didn't we? And we never got caught.'

'Do you remember when we used to nick all the empty Corona bottles and sell 'em back cheap to the geezer on the float? And what about when we used to pick the lock of that market trader's van who sold the toiletries. We used to stagger down the road with dustbin liners full of kitchen rolls, bleach and hairspray. The bags were that fucking heavy, our knees used to buckle under us,' Barry recalled, chuckling.

Wayne sniggered. He and Barry had been right little sods as kids. From the age of seven, they had always had their fingers in one pie or another. 'Why don't you come round for a meal tomorrow night, Bal? I'd love you to see the kids. Dannielle's definitely her mother's daughter, but Tyler's a ringer for me.'

'Oh, I dunno, Jacko. Don't get me wrong, I'd love to come round, but you better check it's OK with Steph first. I don't wanna cause any unnecessary problems.'

'Steph would love to see you again, mate, I know she would. She's a good cook an' all, so I'll get her to rustle us up something nice. If you do, I know that we've truly laid the past to rest and we can be good mates again.'

Not wanting to give Wayne any reason to believe that he hadn't forgiven him, Barry grinned. 'OK then. Dinner it is.'

Wayne was absolutely elated. This was all working out

much more perfectly than he ever could have imagined. 'I'm just going for a slash. Order another bottle of bubbly, and don't worry about the bill – I'll sort it. I eat and drink in 'ere for peanuts.'

Watching his once best friend swagger towards the toilets like he owned the gaff, Barry allowed himself a wry smirk. If Wayne Jackman honestly thought he had forgiven him for his awful act of betrayal, then the mug had another think coming.

CHAPTER TWENTY

Wayne Jackman woke up the following morning on the sofa. He had an awful headache and vague memories of ending up in a nightclub somewhere, then having an argument with Steph on his arrival home.

'Daddy,' Dannielle yelled, leaping on top of him.

'Get off me, babe. Daddy don't feel too good. Where's your mum?'

'Getting Tyler dressed. Why did you sleep on the sofa, Daddy? If you sleep on there again, can I sleep downstairs with you?'

Remembering that he had invited Barry around for dinner this evening, Wayne put his head in his hands. He had no idea if he'd told Steph when he had come home last night, but if he hadn't, then best he did so quick.

'Daddy, I said, can I sleep down here with you?' Dannielle repeated.

'Don't ask me now, babe,' Wayne said, as he gingerly stood up. Feeling his stomach rumbling with hunger, he headed up the stairs. Steph wasn't going to be happy, he knew that, and he was desperate not to start World War Three.

'You all right, babe? Sorry I didn't get in till late. Me

and Bazza had plenty of catching up to do, and you know what it's like.'

Wrapping a bath towel around Tyler, Stephanie turned to Wayne and glared at him. 'No, I don't know what it's like! Worried sick I was, and I rang you about a hundred bloody times. Why don't you ever answer your fucking phone, eh? There's no point in you having a mobile, is there?'

'I'm sorry. I left the phone in the car, then when I went to ring you later in the evening, the battery had died a death. Don't be angry with me, sweetheart. We're getting married in a few weeks' time, so just give us a hug, eh?'

'It's only because I love you, Wayne, that I worry so much,' Steph said, trying to hold back the tears.

Wayne held Stephanie tightly. He obviously hadn't yet told her about Barry's planned visit, as he knew she would have mentioned it immediately.

'So, how did you get on? I take it Barry doesn't hold any grudges? Did you tell him that we're getting married?'

'Bazza was sweet. He definitely ain't got no grudges and was asking all about you and the kids. He's engaged himself now, to a girl called Jolene. She's beautiful, he showed me a photo of her. Done right well for himself, he has an' all. You wanna see the boat he owns. I hope you don't mind, but he was so nice about everything that I invited him round for dinner this evening?'

Stephanie felt her whole body seize up with fear. This had to be one of Wayne's little jokes, surely? 'You're not serious, are you?' she mumbled.

'Course I'm serious! Why? What's the problem?'

'I don't want to see Barry, Wayne, and I certainly don't want him coming round our house. This is exactly why I didn't want you to contact him in the first place. I knew it would stir up a hornet's nest and I would somehow end up getting involved. You better uninvite him, sharpish.'

'I'm not uninviting him. I've been pals with the bloke since I was four years old, so why should I? I dunno why you're so bothered about him coming round. You only went out with him for a matter of weeks and it ain't like nothing sexual happened between you, is it? Or have you been lying to me all these years?' Wayne asked, accusingly.

'You know I never had sex with Barry. How dare you ask me that when you know full well that the only man I've ever slept with in my life is you.'

'Well, what you so worried about him coming round for then? Have you still got feelings for him? Is that it?'

'Of course I haven't still got feelings for him. You know I love you,' Stephanie replied, bursting into tears.

Wayne held Stephanie in his arms again. 'And I love you too. Look, let's not argue over this, it's ridiculous. Bazza's an old pal and he's popping round to see us, it's no big deal. I tell you what, why don't you invite Tammy round as well? Her bloke will probably be back by now and it'll give you a chance to meet him before the wedding.'

'Pa, Daddy, pa,' Tyler said, holding his arms out to Wayne and dropping his towel.

Wayne let go of Stephanie and picked up his naked son. 'If you wanna go to the park, Tyler, then Daddy shall take you there. You never know, the fresh air might even clear his hangover.'

Drying her eyes with a piece of toilet paper, Stephanie managed a smile. 'I'd best ring Tammy then.'

Wayne grinned. He was far too cute for Stephanie and always knew the right things to say to ensure that he got his own way. 'You just worry about sorting some grub out. It ain't gotta be nothing fancy, lasagne and salad will do. I'll ring Tammy. If I beg her and say I fucked up by inviting Bazza round when I was pissed, there's far more chance of her coming. I'll take the kids to the park for a couple of hours, get 'em out your way while you're preparing the food.'

Feeling a bundle of nerves, but desperate not to show it, Stephanie smiled. 'Thanks, Wayne, that'll be great.'

Over in Soho, Angela Crouch was sitting in a café with her new best pal, Roxy. The girls had met through working in a local lap-dancing club and had since moved in together. It wasn't exactly the luxury apartment that Angela had told her mother it was, but their two-bedroom flat was extremely trendy with lots of home comforts.

'We don't want no butter,' Angela snapped at the waitress, as she put the one slice of toast and two mugs of coffee on the table.

Roxy tutted when the waitress took the disgusting-looking butter tray away. In her and Angela's job, it was unusual for them to eat carbohydrates, let alone plaster them with something as evil as butter. Roxy cut the toast in the middle and handed half of it to Angela. 'So, how did you do last night? I earned a hundred and fifty and you seemed far busier than me.'

'I earned about twenty-five more than you, but it was bloody hard work. Fucking perverts most of my clients were, especially that fat, bald-headed old bastard that kept mauling me all night. He offered me five grand to sleep with him and I told him exactly where to poke it.'

Roxy laughed. Neither she nor Angela were slags. Some of the girls who worked at the club were, and would sleep with anything that had a pulse for five hundred quid plus, but Roxy and Angela were both very choosy. Their men had to be rich and good looking to even be considered for any extras. 'I met a nice chap last night. His name was Mark, he owns a club in Islington and he was very handsome. I gave him my number and he said he'd call me this afternoon,' Roxy said.

Angela smiled at her friend. With her long dark curly hair and perfect features, Roxy was an absolute stunner. Her mum originated from Mauritius and Roxy's dark skin only added to her beauty. But, unlike Angela, Roxy was very un-streetwise and had a habit of believing every yarn any man told her. 'Don't get too involved this time until we've checked him out, eh?'

'No, I won't, but I'm sure he weren't no Billy Bullshitter, Ange. He was dripping with money from his watch to his shoes. You can just tell the wealthy ones, can't you?'

'Yeah, you can, but don't forget the last one you fell for, Rox. He told you he was single and had a chain of betting shops, then he turned out to be a married bus driver,' Angela reminded her pal.

Roxy giggled. 'I suppose I was a bit naive then, but it didn't take long for the penny to drop, did it? So, what you up to today? You're seeing Aidan, aren't you?'

Angela sighed. She had promised to take her son to the pictures today, but the very thought of the boredom she would have to endure filled her with dread. 'I'm gonna ring me mum up, tell her I've got a sore throat. I can't be arsed schlepping all the way over to Essex, and the thought of spending two or three hours watching some crappy kids' film don't even bear thinking of after the amount we had to drink last night. Why don't we go shopping instead? Let's go up the King's Road and check out that new boutique Pippa told us about.'

Roxy grimaced. She adored Angela as a friend, but thought she was an absolutely diabolical mother. When she was in her early twenties, Roxy had given birth to a still-born baby and it had all but torn her heart to shreds. How Angie could treat Aidan with so little regard, Roxy would never know. 'You can't just blow your son out, Ange. He's probably really looking forward to seeing you. Why don't

I come with you and we can both take him out? We haven't got to go to the pictures, if you don't want to. Why don't we go to that Lakeside Shopping Centre. That's in Essex, isn't it?'

Angela felt herself blush. She had told Roxy that her mother was well-to-do and lived in a posh house in Chigwell, so how was she meant to explain the crappy council house in Dagenham?

'Look, I know your mum don't live in no posh gaff, and I know you were bought up in Dagenham as well, if that's what you're worried about. You've slipped up a couple of times when we've been drunk, but I knew before that anyway.'

Angela immediately relaxed. 'How did you know?'

'By the way you talk and by the way you act, Ange. You told me you went to a private school and I know people who went to private schools and they don't talk like you, mate. I don't know why you feel the need to lie. You're such a nice person and it's not as though me or any of the other girls are posh.'

'I'm sorry, but you won't tell the other girls, will you? My mum's fat and common and Dagenham is such a dive. I'm just embarrassed by my upbringing, that's all.'

Roxy squeezed Angela's hand. 'I won't tell a soul, I promise, but you shouldn't be embarrassed of your mumma no matter what she is or looks like. You should also try and see more of Aidan, Ange, 'cause if you don't, some day you might just regret it.'

Feeling sorry for herself because the truth had been blatantly pointed out to her, Angela felt her lip begin to tremble.

'Don't get upset, mate. I'm only telling you all this for your own good. Now, dry your eyes and let's go and pick that lovely little boy of yours up, shall we?'

Wiping her eyes with the cuff of her fake-fur jacket, Angela nodded.

Stephanie could feel her hands shaking as she tried to hold the wine bottle to pour herself a sneaky glass. She had cooked two big dishes of lasagne, but her mind had been so all over the place, she wasn't even sure if she had added all the usual ingredients.

'You all right, babe? Is everything prepared?' Wayne asked, poking his head around the kitchen door.

'Yes. I've chopped all the salad up and all that's left to do is the garlic bread, which I'll cook fresh,' Steph replied, trying to hide her glass of wine by putting a screwed-up carrier bag in front of it.

Wayne had eyes like a hawk and spotted the half-hidden glass immediately. 'Why you necking the wine? It's a bit early, ain't it?'

Not wanting to admit that she was desperate for something to relax her and instil a bit of Dutch courage into her terrified body, Stephanie scowled at her fiancé instead. 'Give me a bloody break, Wayne, will you? I've been slaving away in this kitchen for the past couple of hours because you decided that we were having a dinner party this evening, so please don't begrude me one glass of poxy wine.'

'Sorry, babe. I weren't getting on your case, honest I weren't. It's just unusual for you to drink this early in the day, that's all. Pour me one as well. The kids are ready and looking the part. I dressed 'em in the outfits you told me to.'

'Thanks. Now ring Tam and see where she is for me,' Stephanie replied, glancing at the clock. She had rung her pal a couple of hours ago after Wayne had already spoken to her, and Tammy had promised her faithfully that she would arrive before Barry did. 'I'll die if Barry turns up and there's just me,

Wayne, and the kids here. I need your support to get through it, Tam,' Stephanie had whispered down the phone.

'She's five minutes away in a cab,' Wayne said, reappearing.

'Is Tricky Dicky with her?'

'Yep.'

'Ooh, I can't wait to meet him. Apart from his name and what he does for a living, Tam's told me very little about him. She wouldn't even tell me what he looked like. She said he's that handsome, she wanted to surprise me.'

Tyler's screams stopped Wayne from answering. 'Let me sort him out. I ain't having him playing up when people arrive.'

'Don't hit him, Wayne. Just be gentle with him,' Stephanie urged her fiancé.

'Don't hit him! I'll fucking brain him if he shows me up in front of Barry, let me tell you. He needs a bloody good hiding, that's what he needs. He don't need pampering, Steph.'

Stephanie downed her drink in one and quickly poured a refill before Wayne returned. She had showered earlier, but was purposely waiting for Tammy's arrival to get herself glammed up. She wanted to drag her mate up the stairs and chat to her alone. Tammy was the only person who would understand the way she felt.

'The cab's just pulled up outside. Take this kid upstairs and do not fucking bring him back down until he has learnt how to behave himself,' Wayne demanded, handing Stephanie their hysterical son.

'Send Tam upstairs while I'm getting changed. I don't want Richard to see me looking like a bag lady,' Stephanie said, while trying to calm Tyler down by stroking his head. Her son was a little sod when he kicked and thrashed his arms about, and had given Steph many a bruise over the past year or so.

Wayne opened the front door and smirked as Tammy walked up the path with a tall, strapping six-foot hunk. He held out his right hand. 'So, finally we get to meet Richard.'

Tammy glared at Wayne. Coming over to the house and meeting up with Barry again was the last way she had wanted to spend her evening. She would much rather have introduced Stephanie to Richard in a restaurant or a wine bar somewhere, without Wayne or Barry being involved.

'Steph's upstairs. Go up and chat to her, so me and Richard can do a bit of male bonding,' Wayne said, grinning at Tammy's obvious annoyance.

Tammy's lips curled up with contempt. Stephanie was dreading seeing Barry again, so was she, and Wayne should have known better than to invite him over for dinner. 'Pour me a drink, make it a large one, then I will.'

Barry Franklin picked up the huge bouquet and bottle of champagne off the back seat. 'Cheers, mate,' he said, as he slammed the door of the taxi. He stood on the pavement and took in his surroundings. He wasn't overly familiar with Chigwell, but he could see that it was a sought-after area and stank of money. Barry felt no nerves as he sauntered up the driveway. He was actually looking forward to seeing his slut of an ex again.

Wayne answered the door with a big grin on his face. 'Bazza, let me get you a drink, pal. What you having?'

Barry handed Wayne the bottle of champagne. 'Either open that, or I'll have a scotch.'

Wayne checked out the label on the bottle. 'I'll open this when the girls come down. They're upstairs powdering their noses at the moment. This is Richard, Tammy's boyfriend,' he said as he led Barry into the lounge.

Barry was a bit taken aback as Richard stood up. The chap was extremely well built and, even from a man's point of view, incredibly handsome. He was suited and booted nicely as well, and remembering Tammy with her ginger ponytails and freckles, Barry could hardly believe that they were a couple.

Walking over to the drinks cabinet, Wayne poured out three scotches. 'Cheers, lads,' he said, handing one to Richard and one to Barry.

'So, how long have you and Tammy been together?' Barry asked, sitting down opposite Richard.

'We only met just over a couple of months ago. I'm a property developer and I was over in London on business when I met Tammy in a bar up town.'

Wayne sat on the arm of the sofa. 'You won't recognize Tam now, Bal. She ain't 'arf changed since we were at school, mate. Richard and Tammy are moving to Spain soon. Richard's just been telling me about his business out there. This is the first time we've met tonight as well.'

'Whereabouts in Spain you moving to?' Barry asked Richard.

'Alicante. It's where most of my business is based.'

'I know a lot of massive property developers over in Fuengirola and Marbella. You heard of Johnny Duncan?'

'For fuck's sake, Bazza. We're meant to be reminiscing, not talking business. Let's have a toast, eh?' Wayne suggested, holding his glass aloft.

Barry stared at his old friend and couldn't help but grin. Here he was, sitting in a posh house in Chigwell that didn't belong to him, clad from head to foot in designer clothes, when he didn't have two pennies to rub together, yet he still had the brass neck to be giving it the large.

'To old and new friends,' Wayne said in earnest.

About to reply, Barry was stopped from doing so as a little girl in a red dress ran into the room.

'Who are these men, Daddy?' Dannielle asked, sitting on her father's knee.

Barry stared at the child who was lowering her eyes shyly. She was incredibly beautiful and looked like a younger version of how he remembered Stephanie.

'Hello, my name's Barry and I'm an old friend of your mum and dad's. You gonna tell me your name?'

Giggling, Dannielle climbed off her father's knee. She walked over to the armchair that Barry was sitting on. 'My name's Dannielle and I'm six,' she said, her eyes twinkling. She liked Barry already.

Barry smiled at her. Dannielle's nose, eyes, ears, even the colour of her hair, were all replicas of the Stephanie he had once known and loved.

'Looks like Steph, don't she, Bazza?' Wayne said, chirpily.

'Yep, she's definitely her mother's daughter.'

'Speak of the devil and it appears,' Wayne said, when Stephanie walked into the room behind Tammy.

Barry was temporarily lost for words as he focused on both girls for the first time in years. Tammy looked stunning, totally different from how he remembered her, and Stephanie's beauty would have shone out at him like a lighthouse on a cold, dark sea, had he not hated her so much. Knowing that Wayne's eyes were firmly on him, waiting for a reaction, Barry took a deep breath and stood up.

'Steph, Tam, the pair of you look beautiful, and I can't tell you how brilliant it feels to see you both again.'

'What about me? Am I beautiful?' Dannielle asked, tugging at the leg of Barry's trousers.

Barry was pleased to have the distraction. He crouched down, picked Dannielle up, and swung her around in his arms. 'You, my little sweetheart, are the most beautiful girl in the whole wide world.'

CHAPTER TWENTY-ONE

Upset that she was seeing less and less of Linda as every week passed, Pam had taken Cathy's advice and invited her younger sister to bring her boyfriend around for dinner. 'Now who wants what for dessert? Strawberry trifle or black forest gateau?' Pam asked, cleaning away the dinner plates.

'I'll have the gateau, mate. What do you want Michael?' Cathy asked, nudging her son. She had only managed to entice him out of his bedroom by telling him how much he had in common with Keith.

'I'm full up, thanks,' Michael replied.

'I haven't got a sweet tooth, but I'd love another bottle of Pils,' Keith said, cheekily grinning at Pam.

'I'll just have a beer an' all,' Lin chipped in.

'So, what bands you into?' Michael asked, turning to Keith.

Thrilled that her usually depressed son seemed so chirpy, Cathy followed Pam out into the kitchen.

Pam shut the door behind them. 'I can't take to that Keith, Cath, I really can't. He's so skinny, he looks like a bleedin' beanpole, and he don't smell very wholesome either. Have you seen the state of his fingers? Bright yellow, they are, where he chain-smokes, and his teeth are gammy and look too big for his mouth.'

Cathy shrugged. 'He's no oil painting, mate, but he seems to be making your Lin happy. Surely that's all that matters?'

'My Lin's been drinking too much again. I can tell by her eyes and her complexion. Keith's no good for her, Cath. He's only been here an hour and he's already drunk six bottles of lager. I knew they'd been to the pub before they arrived an' all, I could smell it on the pair of 'em's breath.'

'Where's the beers then?' Lin asked, opening the kitchen door.

When Pam handed her sister three bottles of Pils, Linda smiled. 'I've got something really exciting to tell you.'

'What?' Pam and Cathy asked in unison.

'Keith's asked me to move in with him permanently and I said yes.'

Pam's heart lurched. 'That's not a very nice area where Keith lives, love, and what about getting up for work and stuff? Surely you're better to stay round Keith's of a weekend and here in the week. You know you're not very organized of a morning without me helping you.'

Linda's expression turned from happy to sheepish. She had got sacked from her factory job two weeks ago for taking too much time off sick. 'I don't work there any more,' she mumbled, awkwardly.

'What do you mean you don't work there any more?' Pam asked, angrily.

'They had to lay people off and because I was one of the new girls, I got the bullet. It weren't just me, four others got made redundant as well,' Linda lied.

'Just take the beers in the other room, Lin.'

'She's fucking lying! Made redundant, my arse! Got the sack for lying in bed all day with that pisshead more like,' Pam said to Cath, when Linda took the beers in the other room.

'She's a grown woman, Pam. You can't rule her life for her, she has to learn by her own mistakes, mate.'

The doorbell rang before Pam could reply. 'That must be Angie bringing Aidan back. Turned up out the blue this morning to take him out for the day,' Pam said, marching up the hallway.

'Look what I got, Nanna,' Aidan said, thrusting an enormous shiny toy car her way.

'That's lovely. Did you have a nice time, boy?'

'Yeah! I got loads of toys and I ate a whole pizza by myself.'

'All his other toys are in that bag, Mum. I'd better go, because Roxy's waiting in the motor.'

Pam had met Angela's friend, Roxy, when she turned up to collect Aidan earlier, and had been rather surprised at how nice the girl seemed. Angela had only ever had one real friend in her life before, and that had been Chloe, who Pam had disliked immensely. 'Why don't you bring Roxy in for a glass of wine? Lin and her boyfriend are here and so is Cathy and Michael.'

Angela sneered and shook her head. Whenever she bumped into Michael he had a habit of leering at her breasts. He gave her the creeps. She kissed her mum on the cheek, then bent down to hug her son. 'Get Aidan ready earlier next Saturday, Mum. Me and Roxy are going to take him to the zoo.'

Pam couldn't help but smile as she shut the front door. For years she had wished that Angela would become a better mother to her son, and finally it seemed as though her wish might have been granted.

Clocking Stephanie frantically gesticulating at her, Tammy followed her friend out into the kitchen. 'Tricky Dicky's gorgeous, Tam. No wonder you're all loved-up, mate. He seems a really nice guy as well. Good for you, you deserve to be happy.'

'Thanks, babe. Sod me though, let's talk about you. How does it feel seeing Barry again after all these years? He looks well, don't he? '

'I felt a bit awkward at first, but I'm OK now I've had a few drinks. Yeah, he does still look good, but he looks more like John Travolta now than Matt Dillon. Don't get me wrong, I still think he's good looking, but he ain't a patch on my Wayne, is he?'

'I think Barry and Wayne are both really nice-looking blokes, mate, but neither are as handsome as my Richard, of course.'

Stephanie punched her friend playfully. 'Dannielle's took a right shine to Barry, hasn't she? Tyler hates him though. He went ballistic when Barry tried to pick him up, didn't he? I wanted to laugh when he started kicking him, but I daren't in case Wayne got the hump.'

'Yep, Danni is certainly besotted by Barry. And are you sure you don't still just fancy him an eenie-weenie bit?'

'I swear, Tam, on my kiddies' lives, I don't fancy Barry at all.'

Barry Franklin smirked as Wayne Jackman cracked open yet another bottle of vintage champagne. Like himself, Wayne seemed to have an exquisite taste in bubbly. If he treated all his guests as well as he had him, no wonder the poor man was skint.

'Not for me, thank you,' Richard said as Wayne tried to top up his empty glass.

'You've only had two drinks since you arrived. Go on, have another one,' Wayne urged.

'No honestly, I'm fine. I'm not much of a drinker now, although I was in my younger days. Tammy, are you coming to meet my friends with me? Or would you rather stay here?'

'You're not going yet, are you?' Stephanie asked, hopefully. It was only 9.30 and she didn't want to spend the rest of the evening with only Wayne and Barry for company.

Tammy stood up. 'We've got to go, Steph. I told Wayne when he rang me earlier that we couldn't stay all night. We'd already made arrangements to meet some of Richard's friends up town.'

'Do you want me to call you a cab?' Wayne asked Richard.

'No, it's OK. We passed a train station on the way here. Grange Hill, I think it was called. The Central Line takes us exactly where we need to go, so we might as well jump on that.'

'No probs. Well thanks for coming, Tam, and it was really nice to meet you, Richard,' Wayne said, shaking his hand.

'Likewise,' Barry said, standing up and doing the same.

'Can we sing Incy Wincy Spider again?' Dannielle pleaded, looking up at Barry adoringly. She wasn't used to playing games with men, her dad was always too busy, and she loved the way Barry pretended that his hand was the spider and tickled her until she screamed with laughter.

'Don't drive Barry mad, Danni,' Steph said, sternly.

'She's fine. I love kids and am hoping to start a family of my own soon,' Barry replied, looking Stephanie in the eyes.

Stephanie ignored Barry's comment and walked to the front door with Tammy and Richard. 'I wish you didn't have to bloody go so soon. I'm gonna feel a right plum now,' Steph whispered in her pal's ear.

Tammy's earlier jovial expression suddenly turned serious. 'Barry still fancies you, I can tell by the way he keeps looking at you. Be very, very careful. I don't trust him one little bit,' she whispered back.

Stephanie nodded fearfully, then watched Tammy and Richard hold hands as they walked up the driveway. 'Enjoy your evening. I'll bell you tomorrow, Tam,' Steph shouted as she shut the front door. Tammy had been fine with Barry's presence earlier. She had been laughing and joking with him all evening, so what on earth had changed her mind?

Wayne and Barry were deep in discussions about the old days when Stephanie walked back into the room. Tyler was asleep on the floor and Dannielle's eyes were shutting as she sat next to Barry with her head leaning on his arm. 'I'm going to put the kids to bed, Wayne. They're knackered, bless 'em.'

Wayne stood up. 'I'll take 'em up. You have a chat with Barry.'

'No, I'll take them up,' Stephanie insisted, glaring at her fiancé.

Wayne had been necking the champagne as though it was going out of style and took no notice of Stephanie's look of hatred. 'Don't be rude, babe. Bazza's our guest and you've barely spoken to him yet. You've been so busy with the dinner and stuff,' Wayne said, lifting Tyler off the carpet. 'Come on Danni, bed,' he said, prodding his daughter's arm.

Dannielle stood up and rubbed her tired eyes. 'Will you come to visit us again?' she asked Barry.

Barry smiled at her. 'Hopefully, but I'm not sure when. I live in another country, you see.'

'You'll see Barry again, don't worry,' Wayne said, as he ushered his daughter out of the room.

Stephanie felt incredibly uncomfortable as she sat in the armchair opposite her ex-boyfriend. Should she apologize about betraying him in the past? Or should she just let sleeping dogs lie? 'I'm sorry to hear about Jake the Snake. How is your mum?' she asked, saying the only other thing she could think of.

Barry stared at Stephanie intensely. 'You know my mum,

Steph. I think she's more worried about what Jake's left her in his will rather than his actual death.'

'Wayne said that you've done well for yourself in Spain. What exactly do you do?'

'I rent out properties. I bought my first one at eighteen and I now own a dozen or so. What about you? Did you ever get that good job up town that you always used to bang on about? You talk posher now, so I guess you did.'

'I worked in a bank for a couple of years. But very soon I will be setting up my own beauty salon, and I can't wait. I've done all the training, passed all my exams and Wayne is buying me the salon as a wedding present. I've chosen that instead of a honeymoon,' Stephanie replied, proudly.

Barry raised his eyebrows. How the hell was Wayne going to afford a beauty salon if he was as boracic as he proclaimed to be? Not wanting to piss on Stephanie's parade just yet, Barry grinned at her. 'I wish you all the luck in the world with that, girl. You always had a good brain on you, so I'm sure it will be a roaring success.'

'Wayne said that you're engaged now. Do you and your girlfriend live together?' Stephanie asked, genuinely interested.

'No, we don't live together yet, but she stays round mine most weekends. Jolene, her name is, and she still lives with her parents in the week. Do you wanna see a photo of her?'

Stephanie nodded, then sat next to Barry on the sofa so she could look at it. 'Wow, she's really gorgeous.'

'Cheers. She's a good girl actually.'

'So, when you getting married?'

'I don't know yet. We've not long got engaged. Jolene's only eighteen, so we'll probably wait a year or two,' Barry explained.

'Well, I'm glad you've met the girl of your dreams. She is seriously pretty.'

'She ain't as pretty as you though, is she?' Barry said, winking at Steph just to make her feel awkward.

Feeling unnerved by Barry's cheeky comment, Stephanie stood up. 'Let me get you another drink, your glass is empty.'

Barry grinned as Stephanie topped him up with champagne. He was determined to make her feel as uncomfortable in her own home as he possibly could. It appealed to his warped sense of humour. 'Ere, do you remember when we used to hop over all them back gardens to get to my muvver's house? I know we weren't together long, but we did have a laugh, didn't we, Steph?'

Stephanie didn't know how to reply. Reminiscing about her past relationship with Barry somehow seemed entirely inappropriate, although she had no idea why. Nothing sexual had happened between them, so what was her problem? 'Yeah, we did have some giggles, but we were only kids, Barry. Times change and people move on, don't they?' she replied, coldly.

Barry smirked. Steph's reluctance to elaborate over their relationship only proved one thing to him. She was too frightened to reminisce, in case she awoke feelings inside herself. 'So, how's your mum and her sister? I know they're still living over the road to Chantelle, but I ain't clapped eyes on 'em since I've been home.'

'My mum's fine and she still works in that baker's. Lin's hardly there now; she's got herself a serious boyfriend, believe it or not.'

'And what about the lovely Angela?' Barry asked, chuckling.

'Angie don't change. Did you know she had a son with that Jason O'Brien?'

Barry had been kept up to date with everything that had happened in Stephanie's family over the years, but he wasn't going to admit it. 'No, I didn't,' he lied.

'Aidan's eight now and he's a lovely little boy. Angie rarely sees him. She's an awful mother.'

'Now, why doesn't that surprise me? Does she graft?' Barry asked, knowing full well that Angela was a stripper.

'Yeah, she works in Stringfellows as a lap dancer. How's your dad? Wayne said that he got locked up again.'

'My old man loves a bit of porridge,' Barry replied, laughing. 'He's due out again soon – though how long for is anyone's guess. Do you remember when we used to sneak up that Bishop Bonner to have a drink with him instead of going to school?'

'Yeah, course I do.'

'We would have made a sound couple, me and you, you know. If things had turned out differently, little Dannielle could have been mine and yours,' Barry said, trying to keep a straight face.

Feeling herself blush, Stephanie was relieved when Wayne reappeared. 'Tyler never woke up and Danni fell asleep after three lines of her bedtime story,' he said, laughing.

'They're beautiful kids, both of 'em. Yous two must be really proud of yourselves,' Barry said, looking at Stephanie rather than Wayne.

'Oh, we are, ain't we, babe?' Wayne replied, sitting down next to Steph and squeezing her hand lovingly.

Stephanie was feeling more ill at ease by the second. Was Barry taking the piss? Or was he just being too nice and sickly?

'Do you know what? I've really fucking enjoyed tonight. How long you in England for, Bal? I'd be over the moon if you could come to my stag night,' Wayne said, slurping his champagne.

'What date is it?' Barry asked.

'Fourth of Feb.'

'I reckon I'll still be about, you know. I've got a few loose ends in England that I need to tie up while I'm here,' Barry said, catching Steph's eye once again. He had thoroughly enjoyed winding her up.

'Well, if you're gonna be about for the stag do, surely you can prolong your trip for one more week and come to the wedding?' Wayne asked.

Stephanie wanted to strangle her husband-to-be, but instead smiled at him falsely. 'Don't drive Barry mad, love. I'm sure he's got far more important things to do than be hanging about in England for our wedding.'

'To be honest, Steph, I haven't. I've left a pal of mine in charge of my properties, so I ain't got to worry about that, and I was gonna doss for a bit in England anyway, so I can spend a bit of time with me old man when he gets out. I'd love to come to the wedding, Jacko, thanks for inviting me, mate. Is it OK if I invite Jolene as well?'

Wayne leapt up from the sofa. 'Yeah, course it is, and thanks so much for agreeing to come. It means a lot to us, don't it, Steph?'

Clocking Stephanie's horrified expression, Barry smirked and grasped Wayne's hand. 'How could I say no to the bloke who saved my life, eh?' Picking up his glass of champagne, Barry raised it in the air. 'We might not have seen one another for years, but we can never forget the good times, eh? To old pals.'

'To old pals,' Wayne repeated, holding his glass in the air.

As Wayne nudged her arm, Stephanie also lifted her glass into the air. She tried to say the words, but none would come out of her mouth. For the first time in her life, Steph was left totally speechless.

CHAPTER TWENTY-TWO

'How do I look?' Marlene asked, as she walked into Marge's lounge and did a little twirl.

Marge stared at the over-the-top outfit and laughed. Marlene was clad from head to foot in black, and even though the skimpy minidress, fishnet stockings, thigh-length boots, fake-fur coat, oversized hat and dark sunglasses were probably, in most people's opinion, way too over the top for a funeral, the film-star look suited Marlene to a tee. 'You really do look the bollocks, mate. Does this look OK, what I've got on?'

Even though Marge was classed as obese, she had a bubbly personality and a pretty face, therefore could get away with being fat to some extent. 'I love the trouser suit, and that scarf really sets it off,' Marlene replied, honestly. She was thrilled that Marge had agreed to attend Jake's funeral with her, as she was dreading facing his family alone.

'What time's Barry picking us up? Is he still at your Chantelle's?' Marge asked.

Apart from the first night they had arrived back in England, neither Marlene nor Barry had stayed at Chantelle's house. Marlene had once kept a frowsy home herself, but since living in Spain and having a cleaner do all the hard graft, she had got used to cleanliness. Chantelle lived in squalor, which is why she had chosen to stay with Marge instead of her daughter. 'Barry's staying in a hotel in Brentwood. He's hired a car as he said he's gonna stay in England for a few weeks. You'll never guess where he went the other night. Do you remember that bird he was knocking off over the road in Dagenham? Used to live bang opposite me – Stephanie her name was. Her mother was the fat, stuck-up bitch that I used to call Porky the Pig.'

'I don't think I ever saw the girl, but I remember you mentioning her and I remember Porky. Didn't the girl run off with one of his mates or something?'

'Yeah, that's the one. She got with that Wayne Jackman, he was Barry's old pal from Bethnal Green. Horrible family they were, the Jackmans. The mother was an old bag and the father knifed her to death after catching her at it.'

Unable to stop herself, Marge burst out laughing. Over the years, her and Marlene had had more pricks between them than a second-hand dartboard, yet Marlene still had the front to call other women old bags.

'What you laughing at?' Marlene asked, in a cross voice.

'You! It's the way you tell a story, mate, you do make me laugh,' Marge said. She daren't say what she was really thinking as, unlike Marge, who was fully aware of what she was, Marlene liked to class herself as a lady.

'Well, that's where Barry went the other night, round that Wayne and Stephanie's house. I couldn't believe it when he told me, Marge. That girl broke his fucking heart and he was in bits over her for a long time in Spain. The dirty little whore wants shooting if you ask me.'

'Knowing your Barry, that's probably what he's planning to do,' Marge joked. Marlene had once proclaimed that Barry had tried to murder her by strangulation, but knowing what a drama queen her friend was, Marge had never actually believed her.

Marlene raised her eyebrows. 'If I tell you something, swear you won't say a word to anyone.'

'Go on, you know you can trust me, mate.'

'Well, I have no proof of this, but I've got a gut feeling that it might have been Barry that killed Jake. They had an argument and never spoke for a few days before his death. The day before Jake got shot, I went out for a drink with Barry and told him how unhappy I was with the old cunt. I said that I'd be really elated if he keeled over one day. I also said that I was positive he'd left everything in his will to me.'

'Christ, that's heavy stuff, Mar. Do you think Barry actually shot Jake himself, then?'

'No. He had a good alibi the night Jake was shot. He was in some posh restaurant with his girlfriend, Jolene, and her parents. Convenient, don't you think?' Marlene replied.

'Why don't you just ask him outright, mate?'

'No! Barry tells me nothing. He thinks I'm fucking silly, Marge, but I ain't. My Barry's absolutely cakeo and I'm sure he's involved in drugs out in Spain. He's a little fucker, always has been.'

Hearing a car engine, Marge looked out of the window. 'Barry's just pulled up, mate. We'll continue this conversation later.'

Seething that Wayne had asked Barry to their wedding without first asking her permission, Stephanie had barely spoken to her husband for the past thirty-six hours.

'We can't carry on like this, babe. Let's call a truce, eh? How about I skip work today and take you out for a slap-up lunch to say I'm sorry for being such a dickhead?' Wayne asked Stephanie.

Steph glared at her fiancé. A slap-up lunch wasn't the answer to this particular problem. Uninviting Barry to the wedding was the only way to solve it. 'You're gonna have to ring Barry up and tell him he can't come, Wayne. You'll have to say that we rang the venue and they said that we can't have any more guests.'

'I can't do that, babe. I'll make meself look a right mug.'

'Please, Wayne, I'm sure he was taking the piss out of us the other evening. You were too drunk to notice, but I clocked it. I don't trust him one little bit.'

Wayne put his arms around Stephanie's waist. 'Bazza's all right and I would have noticed if he was taking the piss. You're just being paranoid because of what's happened in the past, that's all.'

Stephanie nuzzled her face into Wayne's neck and took in his sweet-smelling aftershave. She loved him so much, he always seemed to get his own way with her. 'Where you gonna take me for this posh lunch, then?'

Wayne grinned. 'I take it that means Barry can come to the wedding then?'

'I suppose so.'

Marlene had thought it an insult that she wasn't invited to travel to Jake's funeral in one of the cars behind the coffin. Jake's family had organized everything, and she only knew the date and time of the service because one of Jake's friends had informed her. Because of the snub, Marlene decided it best that she go straight to the crematorium in Streatham and, as she got out of the car, she felt that all eyes were on her.

'Shit, I can see Donkey Dave staring at us. Trust my luck to spot that pervert immediately,' Marge hissed.

Remembering her pal's night of debauched passion with Donkey Dave, Marlene wanted to laugh, but couldn't. She had to play the grieving, loving partner. It was what today was all about. She held Barry's arm one side, Marge's the other, and promptly turned on the waterworks.

'You OK, Mum?' Barry asked.

'Of course I'm bloody OK. I'm acting, you idiot. Where's the family? Can you see 'em anywhere?' Marlene spat.

Barry shrugged. 'None of us know what they look like, do we? I doubt his ex-old woman is here anyway, Jake always said she fucking despised him. Most people are going inside the chapel now, so we'll have to clock the front row to work out who's who.'

'I should be sitting in the bloody front row. I'm the poor bastard that had to suck his sweaty little cock for years,' Marlene whispered in Marge's ear.

When Marge burst out laughing, Barry looked at her and his mother in horror. 'For fuck's sake, yous two, show some respect. You're at a man's funeral, not his birthday party.'

Marlene let out a huge racking sob and pretended to almost faint as she walked into the packed chapel.

'Stand up straight, Mother, everybody's looking at us,' Barry hissed.

Aware that she had definitely now got everybody's attention, Marlene continued to sob loudly throughout the whole service.

'That's gotta be the daughters, ain't it? Front pew on the right,' Marge said.

Marlene nodded. She had spotted the two women scowling at her a few minutes ago. Both were skinny, plain and had great big noses just like Jake's. They were definitely their father's daughters, all right. 'Do you reckon that's his ex-wife next to 'em?' Marlene whispered, dabbing her eyes with a hankerchief.

'Dunno, but she looks a right old dragon, whoever she is,' Marge replied.

As the service ended and the curtains closed, Frank

Sinatra's 'Fly Me to the Moon' came blaring out of the speakers. Sinatra had been Jake's favourite singer and he used to regularly croon his songs on stage in their bar over in Spain. The senile old sod had even thought he sounded like his idol.

Marlene walked out of the chapel, acting as though she was being physically supported by Barry and Marge. Once she started a bit of role play she had always found it very difficult to switch back off. 'I need to see if my beautiful wreath is here,' she said loudly, in an overly dramatic voice.

'Tone it down, Mother, you're making yourself look a right cunt,' Barry whispered in her ear.

'Marlene! How wonderful to see you again, though what a shame it has to be under such awful circumstances. How are you bearing up? What happened must have been the most awful shock for you?'

Marlene squeezed the tall, thin man's hand. Slippery Joe had been one of Jake's lifelong friends. He had visited her and Jake out in Spain a couple of times every year, and Marlene had always found him quite charming. Unlike Jake, Joe was quite handsome and extremely charismatic and Marlene had never forgotten Jake telling her how he had earned his nickname. 'Back in the old days, when banks were easy to get into and rob, Joe was the master of it. He was so skinny and agile he used to slip through the hole in the vaults that people would dig, then he would pass the money through and slither back out like an eel,' Jake had explained.

'I miss my Jakey boy so much, Joe. He was my life: I don't know how I'm going to cope without him,' Marlene said, her voice full of sorrow.

Unable to listen to any more of his mother's crap, Barry lit up a cigarette and walked over to where the flowers lay.

'Marlene's been in a terrible state, Joe. She's been staying with me, bless her,' Marge said, joining in with the deceit.

'And do you know what hurts the most, Joe? Ten wonderful years I spent with my Jake, yet I never had any say in his funeral and I only found out when and where it was because Eddie Spurling rang me up to tell me. For years I told Jake we should get married because I knew one day something like this would bloody well happen,' Marlene wept.

Slippery Joe put a comforting arm around Marlene. Jake had never had any intention of marrying Marlene, he knew that for a fact, but it was neither the time nor place to say so. 'Jake loved you very much, Marlene. You made him very happy,' he assured her. The last time Joe had spoken to Jake, he had been anything but happy with Marlene, and had even spoken briefly about leaving her.

'I take it that's Jake's daughters over there? Who's that woman and man with them?' Marlene asked, spotting the people who had been sitting in the front pew on the left.

'That's Jake's ex-wife, Anne, and her brother, Thomas.'

'What's she doing here? I thought she hated his guts,' Marlene spat.

'Anne probably came to support Miranda and Isabelle.'

'But Jake always said that his daughters hated him an' all. Two-faced bastards,' Marlene mumbled.

'Some people have got no morals, mate – but to turn up here, lapping up all the attention when they haven't spoken to the poor man for years, is beyond belief if you ask me,' Marge said, supporting her friend.

'I must go and say hello to a few old faces now. I take it you are both coming to the wake, girls?'

'Wake! What wake? Eddie Spurling said that all Jake's pals were just doing their own thing back at one another's houses or in their local pubs.'

Realizing that he had just put his foot in it, Slippery Joe

had no choice but to tell Marlene where the wake was. 'It was a last-minute change of plan, Marlene. We were just going to have a drink at a pal's house, but the numbers got out of hand. The wake is now being held in a pub not far from here called the Bedford Park. You must come; in fact I insist you come.'

'Yes, we will bloody come, won't we?' Marge said, nudging her friend. She guessed that the drinks would be free, and missing out on a good piss-up was not in Marge's nature.

'I'll see you there,' Joe said, keen to make his escape.

Marlene linked arms with Marge and dragged her over to where Barry was standing.

'Are we gonna go?' Marge asked her pal.

Marlene smirked. 'I wouldn't miss it for the fucking world.'

Stephanie and Wayne had just enjoyed a first-class lunch in Smith's fish restaurant in Ongar. It had been ages since they had been out as a couple and Steph had thoroughly enjoyed herself. 'We must do this more often once we've got the wedding out of the way, Wayne. I can't remember the last time you and I went out without the kids, can you?'

Wayne squeezed Stephanie's hand. 'It's my fault, I'm always working lately, but I promise you faithfully, once we're wed, we'll do shit like this at least a couple of times a month.'

Stephanie looked lovingly into her man's eyes. Because of Wayne being a workaholic and the children's presence, it had been ages since they had made love. Apart from the odd late-night fumble, their sex life had suffered from the stresses of everyday monotony over the past year or so. 'I've got a fab idea,' Stephanie suggested.

'What, babe?'

'Why don't I get Dannielle's friend's mum to pick her up from school, so we can go home and have a bit of me and you time? I told my mum that I wouldn't pick Tyler up until sixish, so what do you think?'

'Why didn't your mum go to work today? Is she ill?' Wayne asked.

'No. Both her and Cath booked a day off work so they could watch the comings and goings across the road for Jake's funeral. Gutted, my mum was when I dropped Tyler off. She reckons Marlene must be stopping elsewhere,' Steph said, laughing.

'Serves her right for being so bleedin' nosy. Shall we go mad and order another bottle of champagne?' Wayne asked.

'Don't you fancy a bit of us time?' Stephanie asked, slightly dismayed that Wayne hadn't done somersaults over her romantic suggestion.

'Yeah, course I do. I just thought, if we ain't in no rush, we could have a bottle of champagne first.'

Stephanie smiled. 'OK, whatever.'

Within five minutes of arriving at the wake, Marlene and Marge clocked Donkey Dave heading towards them.

'Nice to see you again, Marlene. I'm so sorry for your loss. How have you been coping?' Dave asked, completely ignoring Marge's presence.

'Fucking brilliantly! Her partner gets his brains blown out right in front of her, so how do you think she's coping?' Marge asked, sarcastically. Dave had nearly ripped her insides in half, so how dare he bloody blank her as though she were invisible?

'You look well, Marge. Have you lost some weight?' Dave asked, mockingly. She looked even more obese than when he had shagged her.

'No I ain't, you cheeky bastard. Look, we don't wanna talk to you, so why don't you go and nuisance somebody else?' Marge replied, glaring at him.

'I don't particularly want to talk to you either, but I was asked to come over here by the family to politely ask the pair of yous to leave.'

'I beg your fucking pardon?' Marlene asked. She was absolutely astounded.

'Jake's family arranged this wake as a private function for their close friends and family, and yous two are neither,' Dave said bluntly.

'You cheeky fucking wanker,' Marge screamed.

Dave held his hands up, palms facing outwards. 'Listen, this has nothing to do with me, I'm just the mug that's been asked to give out the orders. If it were up to me, you could both stay, but it ain't.'

'Go and find my Barry, Marge,' Marlene ordered. Barry hadn't wanted to attend the wake, but Marlene had begged him to. Now he had disappeared, which was just like her son. He was never there when you needed him. When Marge stomped off, Marlene turned back to Donkey Dave. 'You can go back over there and tell Jake's family of grim reapers that I ain't going fucking nowhere.'

Marge returned a couple of minutes later with Barry in tow and two large glasses of wine in her hand. Marlene snatched at the wine, downed it in one and grabbed another off a nearby table. 'I have never been so insulted in all of my life. I'm fucking going over there in a minute to give them cunts a piece of my mind. Who do they think they are, eh?' she said to Barry.

'Why don't we just go, eh Mum? I said it was a bad idea us coming here, so why don't I take you and Marge for a nice meal somewhere? We can have a toast for Jake there, can't we?'

'If I'm gonna leave then I'm leaving in style,' Marlene announced, pushing her son out of the way.

'Go with her, Marge,' Barry ordered. He knew what an acid tongue his mother possessed and there was no way he was embarrassing himself by standing in on one of her little slanging matches. A man of his ilk did not get involved in crap like that.

Miranda and Isabelle, Jake's daughters, and his ex-wife, Anne, looked at Marlene in horror as vulgar words and insults spewed out of her mouth. They had never seen or met Marlene before, but every vile description they had ever been given of the woman was actually worse in the flesh.

'I want you to leave now. You're upsetting my daughters and making a complete show of yourself and us at the same time,' Anne said coldly.

'Making a show of myself! You've got some brass neck, you have, and so have them two ugly fuckers,' Marlene said, pointing at Jake's daughters. 'None of you would give my Jakey the time of day when he were alive, you all hated him, so what you making yourself busy at his fucking funeral for, eh?'

'How dare you call my daughters ugly, you tasteless old tart, and for your information, my daughters spoke to their father regularly, way before his death. Whenever he was over in England, Jake would visit them and me. For my girls' sakes, I decided to put any grievances I had with Jake to one side. He was their dad, after all.'

'You lying fucking whore. My Jakey would have told me if he had visited you or them. I ain't stupid, you know. I know exactly why you've reared your ugly, venomous heads now. It's because you're hoping to cop some money in his will, that's why.'

'I want you to leave this very minute,' Anne's brother demanded, grabbing Marlene by the arm.

'Get off her,' Marge screamed, throwing a right hander Thomas's way and catching him full on the chin.

When Thomas went sprawling, all hell broke loose, and Barry had no option but to run over to the fracas to try and rescue his mother.

'I loved my Jakey with all of my heart and I've been treated worse than a leper today by everybody. I hope you're all ashamed of yourselves,' Marlene screamed, as her son dragged her out of the building.

'Marlene will have the last laugh, you bunch of no-good cunts,' Marge shouted, before Barry bundled her out through the door as well.

'What is the matter with yous two? I have never felt so embarrassed in all my life,' Barry said.

'Shut it, you soppy bastard. You might think you're upper class now, boy, 'cause you have a few bob in your pocket and a posh tart on the go, but you ain't. I'm your mother and I know exactly what you are.'

'And what's that meant to mean? On second thoughts, don't even bother telling me. Just get in the car, will you?' Barry said. He hated his mother in drink; she was an arrogant cow and he couldn't be bothered arguing with her, today of all days.

Marge got into the back of the car with Marlene. 'Well, you said if you had to leave you were going in style, and you sure did that, mate,' she said, laughing.

Marlene wasn't in a very jovial mood. All she could think of was what Anne had told her and she didn't like it one little bit. 'Did you know anything about Jake being back in contact with his daughters, Barry? I know he used to talk to you.'

'He never said anything to me about it. His ex-old woman was probably just trying to wind you up.'

'That woman was a fucking liar, mate. Don't be listening to anything she said,' Marge assured her friend.

'Well, she had better be lying, because if I find out that shrivel-cocked, good-for-nothing old bastard has left his family one penny in his will, as God's my judge, I will go ballistic.'

Back in Chigwell, Stephanie and Wayne had just finished making love. 'I don't arf love you,' Stephanie said, as Wayne rolled off her.

'And I love you too,' Wayne replied, getting out of bed and putting his jeans on.

'Don't get up yet. Let's have a cuddle for a bit,' Stephanie said, grabbing Wayne's hand.

'I need to shoot down the gym, babe. I just wanna check that everything's OK.'

'But you said you were taking the day off,' Steph replied miserably.

Wayne smiled, leant across the bed and kissed his wife-to-be. 'I have taken the day off, you dopey cow. It's nearly five o'clock and you need to pick our kids up. I'll be back by the time you get back.'

Stephanie grinned. She'd had such a fabulous day alone with Wayne, she didn't want it to end. 'Go on then, sod off and leave me,' she joked.

Wayne laughed. 'You should be so lucky. You're stuck with me for the rest of your life, sweetheart.'

CHAPTER TWENTY-THREE

Stephanie felt anything but excited as she got ready for her hen night the following Friday. She hated fuss, detested being the centre of attention, and if it wasn't for Tammy forcing her to go out, she wouldn't have had a hen do at all.

'Wow, you look amazing, babe,' Wayne said, poking his head around the bedroom door.

Stephanie smiled. She hadn't bothered buying anything new for what was meant to be her big night. Instead, she had chosen to wear her long sleeveless red dress, silver sandals and diamante jewellery that she had bought last year. 'I really don't feel like going out, Wayne. I might just have the meal, then come straight home. Tam's talking about going clubbing afterwards, but I know I won't enjoy meself.'

'Don't be such a misery guts. Your hen night's like your last night of freedom, so you've gotta have a good one. Anyway, I've invited the lads round for a beer tonight, so you don't wanna be coming back too early.'

'What lads? And what about the kids?' Stephanie asked, annoyed. She hated leaving Tyler with Wayne at the best of times, even more so if he had been drinking.

'Bazza and Danno are coming round. Don't worry, the kids'll be fine and we ain't planning on getting shitfaced.

We're just gonna have a few cans, a takeaway, and plan next week's stag do.'

'But I thought you'd already planned your stag do. You said you was going to a club up town,' Steph asked, in a distrustful tone.

'We are going to a club up town, but the lads wanna do it properly and book a hotel and stuff. The thing is, I doubt we'd get back until six the next morning, so what is the point of me coming in pissed up and waking you and the kids? We might as well book a couple of rooms somewhere. You know me, Steph, I don't like the kids seeing me too drunk and I'm bound to get completely rat-arsed on me stag night, ain't I?'

'Please don't stay out all night, Wayne. You might trust Barry Franklin, but I don't, and I shall really worry if you're out with him all night.'

Wayne laughed. 'Chill out, for fuck's sake, Steph. Bazza's cool and he ain't gonna murder me, babe. I'm sure if he were going to blow my brains out for stealing you off him, he would have done it years ago.'

Feeling a bit silly, Stephanie put her arms around Wayne's neck. 'Just think, in two weeks' time from now, I'll be twenty-four hours away from becoming Mrs Jackman.'

Wayne grinned and kissed Steph on the forehead. 'All the more reason why you should celebrate until you drop tonight, girl. I mean, can you imagine how many other women would kill to be in your position?'

Stephanie playfully punched Wayne on the arm. Wayne had rated himself highly even as a schoolboy and had never lost any of his confidence over the years. 'Do you remember that time I first asked you out when I was sitting opposite the station on Heathway Hill?'

'Yeah, sort of.'

'Well, after mugging me off in front of Tammy like you

did, you're the one who should be thinking yourself lucky, big man.'

Wayne chuckled. 'Yeah right, darling.'

Angela Crouch was not in the best of moods. Not only had she been forced to take the night off work to attend Stephanie's poxy hen night, her mother was now giving her grief over Aidan.

'What do you mean, Mum? I ain't unreliable, I just got the dates mixed up. I've turned up tonight, ain't I?'

'That little boy has been so looking forward to going to the zoo tomorrow. What am I meant to tell him now, eh?' Pam shouted.

'Why don't you tell him that you made his mother go on his Auntie Stephanie's fucking hen night and she had to lose a night's wages, therefore has to work tomorrow. I'm sorry, Mum, but I can't afford to take two days off work. Just tell Aidan I'll take him to the zoo some other time,' Angela replied coldly.

'You don't even work in the daytime. You are such a selfish bitch, Angie. You really don't deserve kids,' Linda piped up.

Relieved when the cab pulled up outside the restaurant, Pam turned around in the front seat. 'We're here now, so please let's not argue no more. This is Steph's big night so let's all go in there with smiles on our faces, shall we? I'll take Aidan out somewhere tomorrow, OK? He'll be fine, I'll make sure of it.'

Angela's false smile turned to a look of dismay the moment she walked into the restaurant. When her mother first suggested that she be Stephanie's bridesmaid, she had only gushed with delight, saying 'she would love to be one' because she had known how much it would wind her sister up. Now, because of her own stupidity, here she was, stuck in some shitty Greek restaurant in Waltham Abbey with her horrendous family and a four-foot inflatable penis.

Giggling like a naughty schoolgirl, Linda ran over to the penis and picked it up. At four foot, the penis was the same height as Linda. 'I wish my Keith had one this size,' she yelled.

When everybody burst out laughing, Angela couldn't even manage to crack a smile. This had the night from hell stamped all over it and she couldn't wait for it to be over.

Wayne Jackman ended the phone call, turned to Barry and Danno and grinned. 'All sorted, boys. I've booked us three rooms and they've got an all-night bar there as well.'

'When shall we square up with you? Now, or next week?' Danno asked.

'The hotel's my treat. Potter and Cooksie ain't got no dosh, so I can't expect them to pay, and young Lee who works for me is always boracic because of his addiction to prostitutes. He'll have a field day in Soho, he will,' Wayne said, chuckling.

'Well, I'll pay me own way,' Barry insisted.

'Me too,' Danno added.

'No, you won't. I know I'm having a few financial problems at the moment, but one night out ain't gonna make no difference to the mess I've got meself in. I'm only gonna get married once, so I'm determined to enjoy me stag. I'll worry about all the other shit after the wedding.'

'Are things still that bad?' Danno asked, concerned.

'Nah, mate, they're even worse! My sports shop is closing down tomorrow. I owed a load of money to a geezer and he's been on me case for it. I can't mess him about no more, so I've had to sell the shop to pay him back. I ain't told Steph yet, so for fuck's sake don't put your foot in it at the wedding. I'm gonna tell her afterwards, if I can manage to pluck up the courage.'

Remembering what Steph had told him about her wedding present, Barry couldn't help but pipe up. 'So, have you already bought Steph's wedding present, Jacko? She said you were buying her a beauty salon instead of going on honeymoon.'

Wayne sighed. He'd had no idea that Stephanie had told Barry that piece of information, but knew he must answer the question. 'There is no salon yet, but that is another reason I've sold the sports shop. I can't let Steph down and I reckon I can sort something out for her within the month. I bet she's expecting the salon keys on her wedding day, bless her heart, but you can't get blood out of a stone, can you?'

'Can I have a drink, Daddy? I'm thirsty,' Dannielle asked, opening the lounge door in her nightdress.

'Hello Princess,' Barry said, smiling at her.

'Uncle Barry,' Dannielle screamed, running towards him excitedly.

Barry hugged her.

'Come on then. Drink, then back to bed,' Wayne said, grabbing his daughter's hand.

Barry winked at her. 'Sweet dreams, angel.'

Over in Waltham Abbey, Stephanie had got over her earlier reservations and was now thoroughly enjoying herself. She had wanted to keep her hen night low-key so apart from her family, Cath and Tammy, she had only invited two of her friends from Collier Row. Tina was her old next-door neighbour and Jenny was the mother of Dannielle's best friend, Poppy.

'So, how's life in Chigwell, mate? I really miss you being next door to me. It's so quiet now because there's no kids living there. I used to love watching your Dannielle and Tyler playing in the garden,' Tina told Steph.

'Chigwell's OK. We haven't really got to know any of the neighbours there yet and I don't think we will somehow. It doesn't seem as friendly an area as Collier Row. I think people tend to keep themselves to themselves more in Chigwell.'

'You ain't talking about kids and bloody houses again, are you? Tonight's your hen night, Steph, we're meant to be having a laugh, so let's all talk about sex,' Lin shouted out.

'Stop it, Lin. Behave yourself,' Pam said, embarrassed.

Linda chuckled. Behaving herself wasn't in her nature and she had no intention of changing a habit of a lifetime. 'Me and Keith sometimes do it six times a day,' she said, proudly.

Cathy burst out laughing. 'Lucky you. My old man could barely manage it once a week and even then he did it with the local barmaid.'

As the unrefined conversation continued, Angela turned to Stephanie. 'What about you and my ex-boyfriend, sis? How many times do you shag per week?' she asked, sarcastically.

'Who's your ex-boyfriend?' Tina asked Angela.

'Wayne, of course! Oh sorry, has Steph forgotten to tell you that the man she's getting married to next week took my virginity from me when I was thirteen years old. Didn't you know he was a paedophile?'

Stephanie had never told any of her neighbours or friends about Angela's fling with Wayne. Not only was it old news, but it was also extremely embarrassing. Apart from Tammy, she had never really discussed it with anybody. Wishing that the floor would miraculously open and swallow her up, Stephanie burst into tears.

'You are one evil fucking bitch, Angie,' Linda screamed at her niece.

'And you're one foul-mouthed, drunken little dwarf,' Angela screamed back.

Furious with Angela, Pam stood up. Her face was red with rage as she pointed her finger at her youngest daughter. 'How dare you spoil Stephanie's hen night and insult your Auntie Lin. You are one nasty piece of work, even though I've spent years trying to convince myself otherwise. You'll never change your ways. You're a horrible sister to poor Steph and an even worse fucking mother to your own son. Now get out of my sight, and don't even think of turning up at the wedding because you're uninvited as a bridesmaid and a guest.'

Stunned by her mother's cutting speech, Angela ran from the restaurant in tears.

Barry Franklin had never been so bored in his entire life. For the past two hours all Wayne had been rambling on about was his lack of funds and it was becoming extremely tedious. Did Wayne actually think that he was going to offer to bail him out after stealing his girlfriend from him? Because if he did, he had a hell of a long wait. Barry was no man's fool, and he had only agreed to attend the wedding because he knew how awkward it would make Stephanie feel. He still wanted her to pay for what she had done to him, but it would be Wayne that copped the bulk of his revenge, because in Barry's eyes it was he who deserved it the most. Faking a yawn, Barry stood up. 'I'm gonna shoot off and leave you to it now, lads. I was up early this morning and I'm cream crackered.'

'Don't go yet. I've just opened another bottle of bubbly. I wanna hear all about Jake's funeral and stuff. How did it go?'

Barry sat back down and allowed Wayne to top his glass up again. 'It kicked off at the wake, as it always does when my mother's involved, but other than that it was OK. I've got to attend the reading of the will next week. Same day as the stag, it is, but it's in the morning.'

'What was Jake worth, Bal? Do you reckon he's left you anything?' Danno asked, bluntly.

'I dunno what he was worth, but he certainly weren't short of a few bob. I got on pretty well with him, but not well enough for him to leave me his worldy goods. Having said that, he owns an old Jaguar classic car out in Spain. I always loved it, and he always told me that when he popped his clogs, it was mine. The rest of his estate, including the bar, is bound to be left to his beloved partner, who just happens to be my wonderful gold-digging fucking mother,' Barry chuckled.

'Perhaps a bit of inheritance dosh might just help her with her grief,' Wayne said, laughing. He stood up. 'I'm gonna have a piss and check on the kids, boys. Who's hungry? We ain't ordered sod all to eat yet.'

'I could murder an Indian, could you?' Danno asked Barry.

'I ain't that hungry, to be honest, and I'm gonna shoot off in a bit anyway.'

'Is that yours?' Danno asked, as the mobile phone that was perched on the edge of the sofa sprang into life.

'No, it must be Jacko's,' Barry replied.

'Was that my phone ringing? Who was it?' Wayne asked, bursting back into the room.

'Dunno, mate. I didn't like to answer it,' Barry said, handing the phone to his so-called friend.

Wayne stared at the phone then put it to his ear. 'What's up?'

When Wayne walked out of the lounge, Barry stood up and stretched. 'Right, I'm off.'

Danno stood up and shook Barry's hand. 'You take care, mate.'

Wayne walked back into the room and slung his phone onto the sofa. 'That was fucking Angela. It all went off in the restaurant, apparently. Steph's in tears and all sorts. She's on her way home, I think.'

'That's women for you,' Danno joked.

When Wayne started to spout off about what a bitch Angela was, Barry couldn't help but smirk. He had been seconds away from sodding off home, but now it had all kicked off and Steph was on her way home, he'd decided to stay instead.

'I feel like one of them poor Ethopians that Bob Geldolf's always banging on about, Jacko. Can we order something to eat now or what?' Danno asked, bluntly.

'Yeah, of course we can. Order a selection of stuff for the three of us,' Wayne said, chucking Danno three menus out of a drawer.

'I fancy an Indian and Barry's shooting off,' Danno replied.

Barry grinned at Wayne. 'Do you know what? All of a sudden I feel ravenous, so think I'll stay and eat with yous after all.'

CHAPTER TWENTY-FOUR

On the morning of his stag do, Wayne was awake at the crack of dawn. He turned onto his side and stared at Stephanie, who was still asleep. She had calmed down over the past few days over the hen-night fiasco, but had vowed never to speak to Angela ever again. 'For as long as I can remember, all I have ever done is given love and support to Angela, but received nothing in return. In my heart, I will always love her and I shall miss her not being part of my life, but by cutting her out completely, at least she can't hurt me any more,' Steph had tearfully decided.

'You're up early,' Steph whispered, as she heard Wayne get out of bed. She always slept lightly in case the children were ill or needed her.

'I've got shitloads to do today, babe, so I thought I'd make an early start.'

'Come back to bed and give me a cuddle first. I've barely seen you this week. You've been running around like a blue-arsed fly, and seeing as you've got your stag do tonight, I probably won't see you again until tomorrow evening.'

Wayne got back into bed and put his arms around Stephanie. Feeling himself becoming aroused, he immediately pulled away from her and lay on his back.

'Somebody's very excited this morning,' Stephanie said, tenderly stroking Wayne's penis.

Wayne sighed as Stephanie kissed his chest, then moved her mouth further down his body. As her lips locked around the tip of his manhood, he let out a huge groan of pleasure. 'Kneel on all fours,' he ordered, huskily.

Stephanie did as Wayne asked, then gasped as he entered her doggy style. Their sex life had been crap just recently, but as Wayne shafted her harder and faster than he had for many years, Stephanie allowed herself a wry smile. Finally, Wayne's libido had returned. And it was back with a vengeance.

Jake's solicitor was a Jewish chap called Hymee Michaels, and it was he whom Jake had appointed to be executor of his will. Marlene knew very little about the formalities of such a procedure, but she was quietly confident that she was travelling to Bermondsey as a poor woman, to be told that she would soon be very rich.

'So, did you ring this Mr Michaels yesterday to ask him if we were going to be the only ones here today, like I told you to?' Marlene asked her son.

'I did ring him, Mum, but Michaels was out of the office all day yesterday. His secretary sounded like a proper dimwit, but the one thing that I did find out off her is that this is actually a formal will reading, which apparently Jake insisted on. It's written in his own words, so she reckons.'

'I thought everybody who had money had a formal will reading. I've seen 'em on telly loads of times,' Marlene said.

Barry shook his head. 'I dunno about America and places like that, but they're pretty unusual over here. I've seen 'em on TV and in films, but that is usually just to dramatize the effect. Will readings spoken in the words of the deceased are fictional. They ain't reality, Mum.'

'So, why is Jake having one then?' Marlene enquired, becoming more confused by the second.

'Your guess is as good as mine, but you can bet your bottom dollar that me and you ain't the only ones there. There is no way he would have demanded a proper reading where his actual words are spoken by his brief if it was just us two involved.'

'Well, who else is gonna be there then? We were the only real family the old fucker had. You don't reckon he's left any dosh to any of his mates, do you?'

'I don't know, muvver, but do me a favour. If any of his other family are there, please don't kick off and make a complete show of us, will you?'

Suddenly feeling anxious, Marlene fished around in her handbag for the small bottle of brandy she kept in there for emergencies. The thought of anybody else coining in on her hard-earned inheritance had left a bitter taste in her mouth, and the quicker Marlene gargled it away, the better she would feel.

The pawnbroker looked at Wayne in amazement as he emptied the contents of his bag onto the counter.

'Christ, you certainly have some nice pieces of jewellery here, but I won't be able to take that amount off you unless you've got some receipts or identification,' he said, fingering an extremely heavy gold chain with glee.

Over the years, Wayne had sort of collected gold. He had taken it as payment if anybody had owed him money and, back in the Eighties, when gold was the height of fashion, he had often treated himself to a chunky ring or necklace whenever the mood had taken his fancy. 'There's my ID,' Wayne said, showing the pawnbroker his driving licence, 'and there's two utility bills with me name and address on 'em as well. I'll be honest with you, mate, I own a gym in

Leytonstone which is struggling at the moment and I'm also getting married next week. Being the decent chap that I am, I have promised to buy my wife her own beauty salon as a wedding present, and seeing as I haven't worn gold since the late Eighties, I thought I might as well shove it in here to get some readies to pay for my Steph's little dream. I can come and collect it as soon as things have picked up for me again.'

The pawnbroker smiled. 'Do you want to go and grab a coffee while I work out a price?'

Wayne shook his head. 'I ain't got time to arse about, mate. I've got a business meeting up town at one o'clock, then tonight I've got my stag do. You and I both know that what you've got there is worth at least five grand. Just give me half of that for the lot to save time, eh?'

'I'll have to check the hallmarks out first, and if I'm paying that sort of money, I'll have to charge you a higher rate of interest. Is that OK?'

Wayne grinned and held out his right hand. 'You've got yourself a deal, pal.'

Marlene glared at Jake's ex-wife and his two daughters as she sat herself down. As usual, Marlene had chosen her outfit carefully for the occasion. Today, she had on her black leather miniskirt, black basque, fishnet stockings, suede ankle boots, and to finish the look had worn her beige fur jacket and put a red bow in her hair to match her lipstick. Marlene might have celebrated her fortieth birthday just a month before Jake's death, but in her eyes, she was still a stunner. 'I feel like Cinderalla sitting here with them two,' Marlene whispered to Barry, pointing at Miranda and Isabelle. 'They're definitely the two ugly fucking sisters.'

'Just shut it, will you?' Barry hissed.

'Are we all comfortable? If so, I shall begin,' Mr Michaels said.

'Excuse me, Mr Michaels. Can I ask you a question first?' Marlene piped up.

'Yes, of course, and please call me Hymee.'

'Why are we having one of these formal will readings, Hymee? My son said that they only have 'em on the telly and in America,' Marlene enquired, feeling rather pleased with herself for asking such an intelligent question.

'I didn't say they had 'em in America; I said I didn't know if they did,' Barry said, embarrassed. His mother could never just sit there and listen. She always had to put her two penn'orth in and make a complete show of herself and him at the same time.

Hymee Michaels smiled at Marlene. He knew all about her. Jake had given him lots of information about the woman he lived with, and Marlene was exactly how Hymee had imagined her to be. 'Readings like this are fairly unusual, but I have performed two in the past. Jake was a man of few words when he was alive, and I think there were certain things he wanted to say to people which he felt unable to. I'm sure that's why he was insistent on a reading of this kind. He would never want to pass over to the other side with so much left unsaid.'

Marlene nudged Barry. 'Pass over to the other side. What fucking other side?' she said, laughing.

'Put a sock in it, will you, muvver?' Barry snapped, embarrassed.

Anne, Miranda and Isabelle glanced at one another, but said nothing. They had far too much class and respect to get involved in another argument with a foul-mouthed old tart such as Marlene.

Hymee picked up the papers in front of him and smiled wryly. When he had helped Jake write this over an extremely boozy lunch, they had had a right old laugh over it. Hymee had liked Jake. He was a funny character, one of his nicer clients, and Hymee was determined to do his old friend proud today. Clearing his throat, Hymee adjusted his reading glasses.

'To Barry Franklin, who I always classed as the son I never had, I leave my beloved classic Jaguar car and my bar in Spain. I know and trust Barry will take good care of both for me.'

'How comes he got the fucking bar? It's called Marlene's, so surely that should have been mine?' Marlene yelled, callously.

Barry was shocked. The bar didn't make fortunes, but it was certainly worth a few bob if he ever decided to cash in and sell it.

'What have I got?' Marlene asked Hymee.

'I was told by Jake to read this in a specific order, Mrs Franklin, so I'm afraid you will have to wait your turn,' Hymee replied. 'To my daughters, Miranda and Isabelle, I leave my property in England and fifty thousand pounds each. Both of my—'

'What? You're having a fucking laugh, ain't ya?' Marlene shrieked, stopping Hymee mid-sentence.

As his mother went to stand up, Barry grabbed her by the arm. 'Sit down, shut up, and stop being so bloody rude. Let the man finish what he's saying, else I'm walking out and leaving you 'ere.'

When Marlene sat back down, Hymee nodded, then continued. 'Both of my daughters are very dear to my heart and I truly regret all the wasted years that we spent apart. I am so glad that we managed to put our differences to one side and become friends again, as I would never have been able to rest in true peace if we hadn't been able to achieve that.'

Marlene took her bottle of brandy out of her bag and took a large gulp to calm herself down. Anne had obviously been telling the truth at the funeral when she had said that Jake had been in contact with her and his daughters for the past few years. Marlene was absolutely livid. 'The lying fucking old bastard. Good job someone else shot him 'cause I could quite easily have done it meself now,' she said loudly.

When Isabelle burst into tears and was comforted by Miranda, Barry asked Hymee to continue. The quicker this was over with and he got out of here, the better.

'Would you like a couple of minutes' break, Isabelle?' the solicitor asked.

'No, I'm fine,' Isabelle replied, blowing her nose with a tissue.

'Of course she's fine. Who wouldn't be fine if they'd just been left fifty grand and half a house?' Marlene grumbled.

'To my ex-wife, Anne, I leave the sum of twenty-five thousand pounds. I know we rarely saw eye to eye, but I hope you will accept the money as an apology for the diabolical way that I sometimes treated you in the past. I am truly sorry for my actions.'

'I've got the apartment in Spain and the rest of the estate,' Marlene whispered in Barry's ear.

'And last, but not least, out of the people who are present, we come to you, Marlene,' Hymee continued, smirking at what in his opinion was an absolutely horrific excuse for a human being. 'To my loving girlfriend, Marlene Franklin, I leave the sum of one thousand pound and my ashes. I would be grateful if Marlene—'

Marlene had no choice but to interrupt Hymee. 'You've obviously read that wrong, love. Do you mean a hundred thousand pounds and you ain't mentioned the apartment yet?'

Hymee wanted to laugh, but knew that he musn't. 'No,

I've read everything correctly, Mrs Franklin. It clearly states here one thousand pounds. Now, would you like me to continue? I haven't quite finished yet.'

For once Marlene was lost for words, so sat open-mouthed instead.

'Now, where were we?' Hymee said, staring at the piece of paper. 'I think I'd better read your part from the beginning again, as I've now lost track of where I was up to.'

Marlene nodded dumbly.

'To my loving girlfriend, Marlene Franklin, I leave the sum of one thousand pounds and my ashes. I would be grateful if Marlene would spend her money wisely and also cherish my remains. Perhaps she would like to invest her inheritance in some clothes that aren't two sizes too small for her, or a wooden shed which she can live in. Or, if she wishes, she can spend it on her two fancy men – Louie, our one-time gardener, or Fernando, the young waiter who works in our bar, or perhaps doesn't by the time this will is read. Enjoy the rest of your life, Marlene; it was truly a pleasure knowing you, darling.'

'You didn't, did ya? Not with Fernando?' Barry spat, looking at his mother in absolute disgust. The boy in question was years younger than he was and was barely out of nappies.

Marlene burst into uncontrollable tears. 'Where am I gonna live? The old cunt can't take my home away from me, I live there. Do something Barry, do something,' she screamed.

Barry didn't know whether to laugh or cry. One part of him thought the whole thing was hilarious, but the sensible side of him was concerned about where his mother was going to live, because there was no way she was moving in with him.

Miranda and Isabelle were totally stunned. Anne wanted

to burst out laughing, but was too frightened of having another nasty altercation with Marlene to actually do so. She would dine out on this story for many years to come with her friends, and her deceased ex-husband had suddenly gone up immensely in her estimation.

'There must be something in there about the apartment in Spain? Me mum and Jake lived there together,' Barry said to Hymee.

'That's in the final part of the will. Would you like me to read it to you now?'

Barry nodded. 'Stop crying, Mum, and listen to the man.'

'The rest of my estate, including my property in Spain, I wish to split equally between my two grandchildren, Molly and Abigail, and any other future grandchildren that may be born after my death. I insist it be held in trust for the kids until they are twenty-one years old and are old enough to spend it wisely. My last wish is that twenty thousand pounds be taken out of the estate fund and be given to Battersea Dogs Home. My beloved dog, Fido, came from there, and it would give me great delight to give something back to such a worthy cause.'

'Dad was such a kind man,' Miranda said, tearfully.

Miranda's statement was like showing a red rag to a bull to Marlene's ears. 'Kind! Fucking kind! Your cunt of a father has just left me penniless, you ugly, hooked-nosed prat.'

'Don't you dare speak to my daughter like that, you repulsive, gold-digging whore,' Anne replied, forgetting about her earlier wariness.

Marlene leapt out of her seat like a kangaroo. 'I'll talk to your moose of a daughter however I fucking wanna talk to her. As for you, did all right for yourself making up with Jake, didn't ya? Twenty-five grand you got, yet it was me who had to suck his sweaty little cock for the past ten years and I got fuck all. Even Fido's fucking pals in the dogs' home got more than me and I ain't bastard well having it. I want what's mine.'

'Come on, Mum, we're going,' Barry said, grabbing his mother roughly by the arm.

'I ain't going nowhere until I get what's rightfully owed to me. As for you, you conning little cunt, you did all right an' all, didn't ya?' Marlene yelled, punching her son on the chin.

When Marlene lunged at Anne and knocked over a plant pot in the process, Hymee grabbed his phone. 'Please get her out of here as I don't want to have to call the police,' he said, worriedly. Hymee had sort of expected fireworks just by the description he had been given of Marlene, but he hadn't expected the deranged woman to start smashing up his office.

Miranda and Isabelle cowered in the corner as Marlene tried to lunge at their mother once again. Marlene's eyes looked totally insane, and she reminded them both of a wild animal who had just been let out of its cage after years of being held in captivity.

'I'm afraid I really must ask you to leave now,' Hymee insisted, as Marlene broke free from Barry and ran towards him.

'Give me them fucking ashes,' Marlene screamed.

Petrified, Hymee bent down and picked up the black urn.

'Let's go, muvver. You can pick the ashes up another time,' Barry said, grabbing Marlene's arm once again.

'I want them now,' Marlene screamed, in a hysterical-sounding voice.

Barry turned to Hymee. 'Give us the ashes, mate, then we'll go.'

Hymee handed Barry the urn and then watched in horror as Marlene snatched it off her son and took the lid off. 'There you go, you fucking vultures. You've had all me cash, so you might as well have that old cunt an' all,' Marlene screamed, as she directed the ashes in the direction of Anne, Miranda and Isabelle.

Hymee grimaced as most of the black dust landed all over poor Isabelle. Jake wasn't a silly man, and had known Marlene would do something awful with his ashes. 'Hymee, my daughters might have sort of forgiven me, but they ain't gonna bloody want my remains. Anne still hates me, I can see it in her eyes. I insist you give the ashes to Marlene for a laugh. If there is anything in all that life-after-death bollocks, I shall piss myself from up above as I watch her pour my ashes down the nearest drain,' Jake had ordered.

'Get Daddy off of me. Please get Daddy off of me,' Isabelle screamed, hysterically. She was waving her arms like a lunatic as she desperately tried to remove the remains of her father from her hair and clothes.

Anne and Miranda couldn't speak, such was their shock over what Marlene had done.

Hymee wasn't the most manly of men, but he stood up and confronted Marlene nethertheless. 'Get out of my office now, you awful woman. You have thirty seconds to leave before I call the police and have you both arrested.'

'Say hello to Daddy for me, you cunt,' Marlene cackled, as Isabelle continued to scream blue murder.

'Call the police, Hymee. I demand that you call the police and have that woman arrested for what she has done,' Anne insisted.

Barry grabbed his mother from behind and managed to bundle her out of the room. Before shutting the door, he poked his head back around the frame and pointed his finger at Hymee. 'If them three involve the Old Bill, you deny everything that my mother's done. If you don't and she or I get nicked, you'll have me to deal with, understand?'

Shaking like a leaf, Hymee fearfully nodded his head.

The look of evil on Barry's face had told him all that he needed to know. Ending up with a bullet through his head, like his old friend Jake had, was not the kind of death that he had planned for himself. Natural causes suited Hymee just fine.

CHAPTER TWENTY-FIVE

'Par, Dadda, par,' Tyler yelled excitedly, toddling over to Wayne with chocolate cake all over his hands and face.

'Oh, no you don't. You'll ruin Daddy's suit, you messy little pup,' Stephanie exclaimed, grabbing her son just in time. 'Can you wash Tyler's hands and face for me, darling?' she asked Dannielle.

'I wan go par,' Tyler screamed, when Dannielle tried to lead him out of the room.

'I suppose I'd best get going in a minute. I can't be late for me own stag do, can I?' Wayne said.

'Where you meeting the lads?' Stephanie asked.

'Liverpool Street Station. I hate bastard trains, but everyone lives so far away from each other, it sort of made sense to meet there.'

'How many of yous going now?'

'There's only six of us. I wanted to keep it small, 'cause I'm footing the bill,' Wayne replied.

'It's not like you to worry about money. You usually spend it like water,' Steph said, laughing.

Wayne felt very sheepish and could barely look Stephanie in the eye. 'We all have to pull our horns in sometimes, babe. I'll see you tomorrow. Say goodbye to Danielle for me.'

'You can say goodbye to her yourself,' Steph replied, as she heard their daughter plodding down the stairs.

Bending down, Wayne kissed both his children on the forehead.

'Where you going, Daddy, and why you taking a big bag with you?' Dannielle asked, inquisitively.

'Daddy's going out with his friends and while he's staying in some posh hotel, me, you and Tyler will all be stuck here, bored,' Stephanie said, chuckling.

'Will Uncle Barry be there, Daddy?' Dannielle asked.

'Yep. He'll be there,' Wayne replied, stroking his daughter's long, dark hair.

'Can I come too?' Dannielle pleaded.

'Not tonight, love, it's adults only, but I'm sure Uncle Barry will pop round and see you again very soon.'

'What you got in this? It weighs a ton,' Stephanie asked, picking up Wayne's sports bag.

Snatching if off Steph, Wayne grinned. 'You know me, girl, I never travel light. I've got me jeans, leather jacket, and all me toiletries in there. I ain't travelling home stinking tomorrow in dirty clothes, that's for sure.'

Throwing her arms around her fastidious fiancés neck, Stephanie hugged him. 'You're such a bloody poser, but I do love you, you tart. Have a fab time and please be careful, won't you? You might trust Uncle You-Know-Who, but I bloody well don't, and I wouldn't put it past him to leave you stark-bollock-naked in Scotland somewhere as an act of revenge.'

Wayne loosened Stephanie's grip from around his neck. 'Bye, babe. I'll be careful, I promise.'

Marlene Franklin was usually far too concerned about her appearance to ever allow herself to get paralytic. However, after the day she'd had, she decided to make an exception for once. 'Pour me another brandy, Marge,' Marlene ordered. She had purchased a litre of Napoleon on the journey home from Bermondsey and had drunk half of it on the District Line train after Barry had ordered her to get out of his car.

Marge felt dreadfully sorry for her pal. Marlene always kept herself immaculate, but with her mascara all round her face, and her usually perfect blond hair looking like she had been dragged through a hedge backwards, Marge thought her friend suddenly looked sixty rather than forty. 'So why did your Barry chuck you out the car? You haven't told me that bit yet,' Marge asked, handing Marlene her drink.

'Because I accused him of murdering Jake. Seems funny how that little cunt was left with the bar and I got sod all, don't it? I bet Jake had told Barry that when he popped his clogs the club was his, and that's why the devious little bastard organized a hit on him. He's a nasty little schemer, Marge – always has been, always will be.'

'So, what did Barry say to you when you accused him? Did he look guilty?'

'He went ballistic and gave me some load of old bollocks about how much he had thought of Jake. He then stopped the car, told me what an awful mother I was, and slung me out. I mean what boy leaves their distressed mother in the middle of nowhere, eh? I didn't have a clue where I was, and I even had to take me high heels off to walk to the nearest station,' Marlene said, feeling dreadfully sorry for herself.

'I ain't sticking up for Barry, Mar, but I honestly can't believe that he would want Jake dead. I know Barry's no angel, but he ain't no cold-blooded murderer either, mate.'

'You don't fucking know him like I do, Marge. What about when he tried to throttle me, eh? Seconds from death that night I was. Evil little bastard, he is, and I'm sure he's only staying in England for a while so he can get his revenge on that Wayne and Stephanie. My Barry won't rest until he's got his own back, trust me, and it wouldn't surprise me if that Wayne ends up with a bullet through his bonce an' all. Capable of anything, that boy is, and how something that awful ever came out of my fanny, I shall never know.'

Over in a bar in Liverpool Street, Wayne and rest of the lads were in hysterics as Barry told them the story of what had happened at the solicitor's office earlier.

'So, did your mum actually try to throw the ashes over the people?' Cooksie asked. He wasn't quite as bright as the other lads and hadn't got the gist of story.

'She didn't just try. She opened the fucking urn and chucked Jake's remains all over his ex-wife and two daughters. One of the daughters copped it full in the face. "Get Daddy off of me," she was screaming.'

'That has to be one of the funniest stories I've heard in years,' Wayne said, holding his sides. He had been laughing so much that it had given him a stitch.

'The classic bit for me was when the old Jew-boy of a solicitor read out about me muvver shagging the gardener and the barman. You know when you just want the ground to open up and swallow ya? She must have had more fucking men than I've had hot dinners.'

'So, where is she now?' Wayne asked.

'I dunno. After we left Bermondsey, she got in the motor and started accusing me of murder. She said I organized the hit on Jake because I had a silly row with him just before he died. She reckons I knew that he'd left me the club and I did it in case he changed his will. Pissed, she was. She'd been necking the brandy in the solicitor's office, so I slung her out the fucking car. I got on well with Jake and I certainly didn't know anything about him planning to leave me the club.'

'When you going back to Spain, Bal?' Wayne asked.

'I dunno to be honest. I've struck a couple of good business deals while I've been over here and, even though I love it in Spain, it's still nice to be back home. I've even been thinking about buying a place over here, so I can flit backwards and forwards.'

'Where's all the strippers and whores then? I can't see any in here?' Lee asked.

Wayne chuckled. Lee was only nineteen and had worked for him doing odd jobs around the gym for the past year or so. 'I have never known anyone with a cock that wanders as much as yours, Lee. Didn't that dose you caught put you off, boy?'

Lee grinned. 'Nah, that's all cleared up now. The clinic gave me antibiotics for it.'

Wayne picked his glass up. 'Shall we down our drinks and then head off to Soho then, lads? We'll stop off at the hotel, drop our bags off, then we'll party properly, eh?'

'Me and Potter never brought any bags with us,' Cooksie said.

'Neither did I,' Lee added.

'Oh well, yous three soapy bastards can have a drink in the hotel bar while me and Bazza put our bags in our room. Danno's meeting us at the hotel, so once he's arrived, we can paint the town red.'

'Whey-hey. Tits, beers and fanny,' Cooksie shouted at the top of his voice.

Wayne stood up. 'Come on, then. Let's get this stag night on the road.'

Back in Dagenham, Marlene was having severe mood swings. One minute she would be snarling with anger and planning her revenge on all those who had wronged her, then the next she would be crying her eyes out while insisting that her life was now over and it would be better for everyone if she just killed herself.

Marge walked over to Marlene, sat down on the sofa next to her and held her in her arms. 'Now, you listen to me. I don't wanna hear any more of this silly talk about you topping yourself. You're like me, Marge, you're a tough old bird and you'll get through this. Look at all the knocks we've had in the past. We've been to hell and back over the years, me and you, yet we've always picked ourselves up again, ain't we?'

'I ain't never been through anything this bad before. Years, I searched for a rich man who would look after me and give me the life I deserved, and now he's been cruelly snatched away from me.'

'But you didn't even like Jake, let alone love him, mate,' Marge reminded her friend.

'I liked his fucking money though, didn't I? I still can't believe that he left twenty grand to that fucking dogs' home for Fido's mates, and I ain't even got a roof over me head.'

'I've got a spare room here. Why don't you move in with me? We'll have a scream, mate, and I get ever so lonely here since me mum died, so you'll be doing me a favour an' all,' Marge offered.

'What about all me lovely clothes and stuff? Most of me good clobber is all still out in Spain.'

'I'm sure Barry will organize something and send them over here somehow.'

'I ain't asking that murdering little fucker for any help. It's all his fault that I'm in this position in the first place,' Marlene snarled.

'You don't know that for sure, Marlene. You can't go around accusing people of murder until you have some proof, love. Why don't you ring Barry tomorrow and ask him if he can organize your clothes being sent home, eh?

You'll feel much better once you've got all your bits and bobs around ya. In the meantime, me and you can even decorate your bedroom, if you like?'

'I don't fucking like, but what cunting choice have I got, eh?' Marlene screamed.

Marge stood up and poured herself another drink. Marlene could be such an ungrateful cow at times, she really could.

Having finally got to Soho, Barry and Wayne were standing at the bar sharing a bottle of champagne, watching Potter, Cooksie and Lee parade around the club like complete imbeciles.

'So, did Danno say what was wrong with his kid?' Barry asked Wayne. Danno had been meant to meet them at the hotel, but had rung Wayne to say that he couldn't make it.

'His youngest son fell down the stairs, apparently. Danno reckons he's broken his arm and has got concussion. Danno's already been sat up the hospital for hours, the poor bastard. He said he was gonna try and meet us later, but I told him not to worry. His kid's health is more important than my bloody stag night, eh?'

Watching Potter and Cooksie literally drooling at the mouth over the strippers, Barry nudged Wayne. 'How the fuck did you ever hang about with them pair of mugs? Look at 'em. Anyone would think they'd never seen a naked bird in their lives before. I can understand Lee's excitement, he's only a kid, but them pair are embarrassing.'

'I don't like it in 'ere. It's shit and their champagne tastes like fizzy vinegar. Let's fuck off now to that lap-dancing club I told you about, shall we?' Wayne suggested.

'Sod you! I've just paid fifty sovs for that bottle of vinegar and I'm gonna sink it first. Why don't you like it? It just tastes like the normal crap bubbly that they serve in these clubs to me.'

'It's rotten. You drink it, mate. I'm gonna get meself an orange juice,' Wayne said.

Barry shook his head and sniggered. 'You've turned into a right boring bastard, Jacko. This is meant to be your stag night and you've hardly even had a drink yet. You've been dead quiet as well. What's a matter? You ain't having wedding jitters, are you?'

'Nah, course I ain't. I can't drink as much as usual because of these,' Wayne said, pulling a strip of tablets out of his trouser pocket.

'What are they?'

'Antidepressants. I've been on 'em over a month now and you ain't meant to drink with 'em.'

'Well, you certainly didn't shy away from the booze last weekend, mate,' Barry said, remembering how much they'd had to drink on the evening of Steph's hen night.

'I know and I felt like shit for two days afterwards. That's why I don't wanna get blottoed again. These tablets and booze just don't seem to mix.'

'What you taking 'em for?'

'What do you think? I'm in shit street up to me eyeballs, mate.'

Not wanting to get into another conversation about Wayne's financial difficulties, Barry pretended he needed to use the toilet.

Barry smirked as he reached the Gents. Given that he was disclosing all his secrets to Barry, Wayne obviously must think that the past had been forgotten and they were now best buddies again. If only he knew the truth.

Angela Crouch smiled politely at the two overweight old leches as they helped themselves to drinks off the silver tray she was holding. The skimpy bikini she was wearing barely covered her vital assets, but Angela didn't care. She had a good body and carved a good living out of perverted old men looking at it.

'You'll do for me, baby, you'll do for me,' one of the men said, as he tried to put his dumpy hands on her breasts.

'Get off me,' Angela said forcefully, as she pushed his hands away with her elbow.

The club in Soho where Angela worked was run by an Irish ex-boxer called Daniel O'Flannigan. Mr O'Flannigan, as he insisted on being called, was the best boss that Angela had ever worked for. He had a no-nonsense attitude, therefore the club had strict rules. The entrance fee was a hundred pounds, with free wine or beer included in the price. Any other drinks had to be bought and paid for at the bar. The dancers were expected to mingle with the clients between the hours of nine and eleven o'clock. After that, they were allowed to dance in private booths for money. Mr O'Flannigan didn't charge his dancers any fee for working there, but he did expect them to walk about in bikinis serving drinks as payment for his kindness.

As the man tried to touch Angela's breasts once again and this time succeeded, Angela gesticulated to security. There was a strict look-but-don't-touch rule in the main part of the club, and anybody who broke that rule was firstly warned, and if their behaviour continued, thrown out.

'What's up?' asked Leroy.

'This gentleman here has twice tried to grab my breasts.' Angela explained.

'You wouldn't be dressed like that if you didn't want to be touched, darling,' the man said to Angela.

'Apologize to the lady, else you're leaving,' Leroy ordered, glaring at the man in question.

'I'm not apologizing to that tart. Anyway, you can't chuck

me out without giving me my money back. I've just paid a hundred quid to get in this dump and I've only had one drink.'

'Tough shit! Out you go,' Leroy said, grabbing the man by the shoulder and literally dragging him towards the door.

'You OK?' Roxy asked, walking over to where Angela was standing.

'Yeah, just some old perv trying to grab me tits, that's all.'

'Come on. It's gone half ten. Let's take the trays back and go and freshen up, eh?'

Angela followed Roxy back towards the bar area. 'Oh, my God!' she exclaimed, grabbing her pal's arm.

'What's a matter now?' Roxy asked her.

'I've just seen Wayne Jackman,' Angela replied, excitedly.

'Is that the bloke your sister's with?' Roxy asked.

'Yep, and the one I lost my virginity to.'

'Blimey! Do you reckon he knows you work here, Ange? What you gonna do if he wants you to dance for him?'

Angela laughed. 'Show him what he's been missing all these years.'

Barry Franklin hadn't seen Angela Crouch for years. Even though he had heard she was working as a lap dancer in a seedy club in London, he was shocked when Potter pointed her out to him. Wayne had apparently spotted her when Barry had gone to the toilet, and Wayne was now having a nice, cosy chat with her by the looks of things. Barry craned his neck and smirked. Wayne had been insistent on coming to this particular club, so surely he must have known that Angela worked here?

'Wait 'ere, I'll be back in a tick,' Barry ordered Cooksie and Potter. Young Lee was in a drunken trance and had just half collapsed on a nearby seat.

'Where you going?' Cooksie asked. Wayne had paid for everybody to get into the club, and he only had a score on him. There was no way he could afford to drool over the dancers unless Barry or Wayne paid for the pleasure.

'I'm just gonna check that Wayne's OK. He might not have known that Angie worked here, so don't you pair come over in case he feels a bit awkward.'

'He didn't know she worked here. He was well shocked when he saw her. We all were,' Potter informed him.

'What a coincidence!' Barry said, as if to agree, before walking over to where Wayne and Angela were standing. Potter and Cooksie might both be as thick as two short planks, but he most certainly wasn't. It was far too much of a coincidence that – out of every club in the whole of London – Wayne had chosen this particular one where Angie worked. Now, all he had to do was find out what was going on.

'Look who I bumped into,' Wayne said awkwardly when he spotted Barry.

Angela stared at Barry. He was extremely handsome, looked familiar, but she couldn't quite place him. 'Do I know you?' she asked, flashing her most seductive smile.

'You bloody well should do! You used to live opposite me. Barry Franklin's the name and it's a pleasure to see you again, Angela. My, my, haven't you grown.'

Angela grinned. Her sister's first love and fiancé were both in her club. This night was just getting better and better. 'Where you sitting? I'll come over later and give yous a dance. I've got some gentlemen over there that require my unique talent first, though, so give me about half an hour or so.'

'So, didn't you know she worked here?' Barry asked when Angela walked away.

'You don't think I'd have fucking come 'ere if I did, do

ya? No, I didn't have a clue she worked 'ere. That's all I need. Steph will go apeshit if she finds out and Angie's bound to tell her. As if I ain't got enough on me plate as it is.'

Barry studied Wayne. If he wasn't telling the truth, then he was certainly a wonderful liar. 'What do you wanna do, then? We don't have to stay 'ere if you don't want to.'

'Bit late for that now. Not only has it cost me five hundred sovs to get us in 'ere, Angie's already seen us. I'll worry about what I'm gonna say to Steph in the morning, so let's just get pissed, shall we?'

Barry chuckled. 'I thought you weren't drinking much.'

'I weren't, but I've changed me mind now I've seen fucking Angie. Honestly, Bal, my life couldn't get any worse at the moment.'

'Grab a waitress then, and I'll treat you to a bottle of bubbly,' Barry said, smirking. Wayne's last comment had tickled him somewhat. If Wayne honestly thought that his life couldn't get any worse, then he had no idea of his quest for revenge.

The rest of the evening turned into a usual stag-night fiasco. Potter and Cooksie had an argument over football, which nearly escalated into a fight. Lee had been sick all over one of the dancers and had been thrown out of the club by security. Wayne had gone off to look for Lee, but had never returned, and Barry had spent a fortune paying one girl to dance for him purely because he was bored shitless. Glancing around the club, Barry spotted the mixed-race girl who Angela had pointed out as her flatmate earlier. He walked over to her. 'Where's Angie, love? I'm looking for Wayne and I wondered if they were chatting somewhere.'

'She left about an hour ago. She felt ill,' the girl replied.

Smirking, Barry made his way back over towards Potter

and Cooksie. It had been about an hour ago when Wayne had disappeared as well, which was another strange coincidence. 'I'm going back to the hotel now,' Barry told the lads.

'Don't go yet. Wait till it shuts,' Cooksie replied. He and Potter were both skint, and without Barry they couldn't afford any more dances.

'Nah, I gotta go. Yous two stay here and have fun.'

'Why you gotta go, then?' Potter asked, nosily.

'Because I need to see a man about a dog.'

'What's that mean?' Cooksie asked, perplexed.

Laughing, Barry turned on his heel and sauntered out of the club.

CHAPTER TWENTY-SIX

Barry woke up early the next morning with a muzzy head. He stood up, stretched, looked at Wayne's empty bed and smirked. Feeling absolutely ravenous, Barry had a quick shower, threw on the change of outfit he had brought with him and headed downstairs for some breakfast.

'Bazza,' he heard a voice shout.

Barry looked around and saw Cooksie and Potter both tucking into a full English. 'That's not lager you're drinking, is it?'

Potter laughed. 'We ain't been to bed yet. Jacko said to order whatever we wanted at the bar and put it on his tab, so we did. We haven't took the piss, mind. We've only had four pints each.'

'Where is Jacko? Still in bed, is he?' Cooksie asked.

'I dunno where he is. He never made it back to the hotel. His bed ain't been slept in and his sports bag is still in his room.'

'The lucky bastard! I wonder who he copped off with,' Cooksie said, wistfully. He had tried to pull at least a dozen birds last night and each and every one of them had all but told him to fuck off.

'I think I know who he copped off with, but if I tell you,

don't say nothing, will ya?' Barry said, knowing full well they were both gossips.

'We won't say nothing, honest we won't,' Potter replied, with an innocent look on his face.

'I think he spent the night with Steph's sister, Angie. She disappeared early, faked an illness apparently, and he went off the radar at exactly the same time. It's too much of a coincidence, if you ask me – and remember, they've already got history.'

Stephanie Crouch hadn't had the best of mornings, Tyler had had one of his little tantrums and had broken her favourite plant pot. Dannielle had been sick three times. Then, to top it all, the alterations lady had brought her wedding dress back and Stephanie still wasn't happy with the way it fitted. Trying Wayne's number again, Stephanie began to feel the first stirrings of unrest. Wayne had known how worried she was about him going out with Barry, and her husband-to-be had promised to ring her the moment he opened his eyes this morning. It was noon now, and his phone was still bloody well switched off. Guessing that he had probably got plasterered and was currently sleeping it off, Steph rang Tammy. 'Where you been? And why ain't you been answering my bloody calls, you inconsiderate bitch?' she asked, laughing.

'Sorry, mate. Richard paid me a surprise visit and we went to a party last night. I didn't take my phone with me, so never got any of your missed calls until this morning. Was you pissed? You must have rung me about six times,' Tammy replied.

'No, I was just bored and wanted a chat. It was Wayne's stag do last night, weren't it?'

'Shit! I'd forgotten about that. How did it go? Is Wayne home yet?' Tammy asked.

'No, I can't get hold of the bastard. Probably still pissed out of his head somewhere,' Steph said, chuckling.

'Why don't you ring one of his pals? Make sure he's OK. I don't trust that Barry Franklin. He's a wrong 'un, I'm telling you, Steph. I bet he's tied Wayne up and left him somewhere, or even worse.'

Stephanie sighed. Ever since the night Tammy had come over with Richard, her friend had kept harping on about how she didn't trust Barry and how she thought he was out for his revenge. 'I haven't got any of his mate's numbers. Wayne'll be fine. I bet his phone battery has run out. The drippy bastard forgot to pack his charger and is probably on his way home as we speak. Why don't you and Richard come round tonight? Wayne will definitely be back by then and I'm sure a nice takeaway will cure his hangover. There's a lovely Indian I've just found near here and they deliver.'

'I'd have loved to, Steph, but Richard's flying back to Spain this evening. I've promised to take him to the airport. He only came over for a flying visit. He had an important business meeting up town somewhere.'

About to tell Tammy about the fiasco with her wedding dress, Stephanie heard Dannielle calling her name. 'I'm gonna have to go, mate. Danni's got a bug and I think she feels sick again. Let me go and see to her and I'll call you straight back.'

'Don't worry about ringing back, Steph. Richard's taking me out for lunch, so I'll call you tonight after I've dropped him off at the airport.'

After tending to her sick daughter and making her son a sandwich, Stephanie picked up the phone and rang Wayne again. The phone was still switched off and, remembering Tammy's words of warning, Steph immediately rang her mum.

Pam was in no mood to listen to her daughter ramble

on about Wayne's whereabouts. She'd had the morning from hell herself, what with Angie not turning up to collect Aidan. 'I'm gonna kill that selfish little mare when I get my hands on her, Steph. I know I told her I wanted nothing more to do with her, but how can she treat that little boy like that, eh? He's been sitting 'ere crying his eyes out, bless him. Look, I'll have to go. I'll call you back a bit later. Don't worry too much about Wayne. I bet he's on his way home as we speak.'

'OK. As soon as I hear from him, I'll let you know, Mum,' Stephanie said, ending the call. Dialling Wayne's number again, Stephanie swore at the receiver in temper as the recorded message informed her that his phone was still switched off. If Tammy was right and her ex had played some stupid, evil prank on Wayne, she would kill Barry bloody Franklin with her own bare hands.

Back at the hotel in Soho, Barry was at a loose end at what to do next. The rooms had to be vacated by twelve noon, so he had collected his and Wayne's bags and had sat at the bar awaiting his return. Potter and Cooksie were both well hammered and about as much use as a chocolate teapot so, running out of ideas, Barry decided to search Wayne's bag. 'Bingo, lads,' he said, as he pulled out Wayne's mobile phone.

'No wonder you couldn't get through to him,' Potter slurred.

Barry switched on the phone and was relieved that it still had battery life left.

'Who you gonna ring?' Cooksie asked, struggling to sit upright.

'Steph. Jacko might have felt guilty spending the night with Angela and fucked off straight home,' Barry replied, smirking. He punched in the contact that read home, then gleefully waited for an answer. 'Is that you, Steph?'

'Yeah, who's that?'

'It's Barry.'

'What do you want? Where's Wayne?' Stephanie asked, frantically.

'To be honest I was about to ask you the same question. I take it he hasn't rung you or been home yet? It's Wayne's phone I'm calling you on.'

Stephanie felt her stomach lurch. 'No, what have you done to him, Barry? If you've played some dumb prank on him, you're gonna have me to deal with.'

'I ain't done nothing, mate. We ended up in a club last night in Soho and Wayne left early. Actually, let me ring that young fella Lee who works for him. Lee got slung out the club for puking up and Wayne went off to look for him. Perhaps he took him home in a cab and stayed round his or something. I'll ring him now and call you straight back, OK?'

'No, I'm not OK, and why have you got Wayne's phone?' Stephanie asked, in an extremely distressed voice.

'Because he left his bag in the hotel room and the phone was in it. I remember him ringing Danno when we dropped our bags off before we went out last night, and he must have switched his phone off and left it in the room. I've only just found the poxy thing, otherwise I'd have rung you earlier, Steph.'

'Ring Lee then, and ring me straight back,' Stephanie ordered.

Barry turned to Potter and Cooksie. 'Jacko ain't at home, so I'm gonna ring Lee to see if he's with him.'

'Why don't you ring Angie? She's probably got his cock in her mouth as we speak,' Potter said, laughing.

Barry grinned, then scrolled through the phone once again. He found Lee's number and rang it. 'Is Jacko with you?' he asked.

'No, why?'

'When you got slung out the club last night, he came looking for you. No one's seen him since, so we wondered if he took you home or something?'

'I can't even remember leaving the club, let alone seeing Wayne. I remember trying to get a black cab, but none would take me, then I think some foreign geezer pulled up, said he was a minicab and he took me back to Woodford for twenty quid.'

Barry ended the call and, as promised, rang Stephanie straight back. 'I've just spoken to Lee and he hasn't seen Wayne either. I dunno what to do, Steph. Me, Potter and Cooksie can't sit 'ere all day waiting for him. We got chucked out of our rooms ages ago.'

'So, where the hell is he? What have you done to him?' Stephanie asked, panic-stricken.

'Calm down. We ain't done nothing to him. Wayne left the club long before me and the others did. Ask the others if you don't believe me. Cooksie and Potter are both sitting here beside me.'

'No, I don't want to talk to them. Do you think I should call the police?' Stephanie asked, near to tears.

'You can't ring the Old Bill, not yet anyway. If you tell them that Wayne was out on his stag night, they will laugh you off the phone. I'm gonna grab a cab in a minute. Do you want me to come round?'

Debating whether to say yes, Stephanie remembered Tammy's distrustful opinion of Barry. 'No. I'm fine,' she snapped.

'Do me a favour, then. Can you write down my phone number and ring me as soon as you hear anything from him?'

'Yep. Fire away.'

Barry gave her his number, then ended the call abruptly. He'd only treated himself to a mobile phone a couple of days ago and was now bloody glad he had. They were a handy invention and more and more people were starting to use them. In fact, Barry had watched a programe the other evening where they predicted in the next ten years, half of the households in the UK would own one.

'What's happening, then? Shall we get another drink?' Cooksie asked, grinning greedily.

'No, we're going,' Barry informed him, picking up his and Wayne's overnight bags.

'Who's gonna pay the bill? We ain't got no money,' Potter said, with a look of dismay on his face.

Barry sighed. 'I'll suppose I'll have to sort it. Listen, yous two shoot off and I'll get Wayne to bell you as soon as I hear from him.'

'How you getting home?' Potter asked.

'I'll jump in a cab.'

'Can't we jump in with you? We're well pissed and it'll take ages to get home on a train. Potter lives in Southend and I've gotta get to Elm Park,' Cooksie asked, brazenly.

Barry stared at the two drunken fools. If it wasn't bad enough that he now had to pay for a room they hadn't even used, and for their bar bill, did they honestly expect him to pay for their cabs home as well? 'I ain't going your way home, lads. I've got some business to attend to south of the water, so you're gonna have to jump on a train, I'm afraid,' he lied.

'Can't you lend us some money to get a cab? Jacko will give it back to you,' Potter asked bluntly.

'No, I fucking well can't! Now get out my face before I change me mind about paying your hotel and bar bill, you cheeky pair of cunts.'

Potter grabbed his pal by the arm, and without a backward glance or even a thank you, he and Cooksie staggered out of the building.

* * *

As every minute ticked by, Stephanie's worries only heightened. She tried to call Tammy, but got no reply, so rang her mother instead.

'Try to stop crying, darling. I can't understand what you're saying properly,' Pam said, worried.

'Can you come over, Mum? I ain't got a clue what to do and I can't go looking for him 'cause I've got the kids here. Ring a cab and I'll pay for it. I've got plenty of wine and you and Aidan can stay here tonight. Hopefully, by the morning, Wayne will be back and then I'll drop you back home.'

'OK, I'm on my way.'

Barry Franklin was deep in thought as he sat in the back of the black cab. The driver was an old boy, a talkative type, and kept rambling on about Arsenal having a crap season.

'You got a pen and a bit of paper, mate?' Barry asked, interrupting him.

When the driver handed him both, Barry started to write down any number that might be useful to him from Wayne's phone. He then gave the driver his pen back and shoved the piece of paper into his pocket. 'Change of plan, mate. Sorry to mess you about, but can we go to Chigwell first? I might be getting out there, but I won't know until I've knocked at someone's door. Between me and you, a pal of mine's gone missing. I wanna drop his bag off and make sure his bird and kids are all right.'

'No probs, pal. Christ, I hope your mate's OK,' the cab driver said, his voice full of concern.

Barry smirked. He didn't, but he had to play the game. 'Me and you both, mate.'

Pam gave Stephanie a motherly hug as soon as she walked through the front door. Her daughter looked dreadful and her eyes were red raw through crying. 'Where are the kids?' she asked.

'In the lounge. Go and play with Dannielle and Tyler, mate,' Stephanie replied, ruffling Aidan's hair.

When Aidan scampered off to join his cousins, Stephanie turned to her mum. 'I haven't said anything to the kids about Wayne yet. Tyler's too young to understand and I don't want to worry Dannielle. '

'So, where do you reckon Wayne is? It's so unlike him not to contact you, isn't it?'

Stephanie led her mother into the kitchen and poured them both a much-needed glass of wine. 'I'm so glad you're here 'cause it takes my mind off it a bit. I haven't got a clue where he is, but let's talk about something else, eh? It's only half two and we can start worrying again later if he still hasn't turned up,' Stephanie said, forcing a smile.

'What's the betting the bastard walks in in the next hour or so, as bold as bloody brass?' Pam joked.

'So, how's Lin? Have you seen her lately?' Stephanie knew how worried her mother was about her Auntie Linda moving in with Keith.

'She's rung up a few times, but I ain't seen her since she came round for Sunday dinner with him. She seems happy enough, mind. But I just can't help but worry about her, Steph. I can't help but picture them sitting drunk in that shithole of a flat every night, especially now she hasn't got a job.'

Stephanie squeezed her mum's hand. 'If it makes you feel any better, I think Lin is the happiest she's ever been in her life. She rang me the other night, full of beans, honest she did. Keith even chatted to me on the phone and I'm positive he adores Lin, you know.'

Pam smiled. 'Well, I know you wouldn't lie to me, so I suppose I'm just gonna have to accept that Lin's a grown woman and is living the life of her choice, aren't I? I've always felt so protective of her though, Steph, I think that's why I've found it all so hard to deal with. I always worry about people taking the piss out of her and I imagine in my mind that in that crappy area where's she living, that's what people are doing.'

'They aren't, Mum. Lin's got a new best friend, the next-door neighbour, and she's incredibly happy, I just know she is,' Steph said.

'Mum, can me, Tyler and Aidan have some Coke and crisps, please?' Dannielle said, skipping into the kitchen.

Stephanie took the crisps out of the cupboard and then dropped the bag on the floor as the doorbell rang. Perhaps Wayne had got so drunk that he had lost his keys? She ran into the hallway. 'What do you want?' she asked, as she came face to face with Barry Franklin.

'I thought I'd better bring Wayne's stuff back. I take it you ain't heard nothing yet?' Barry asked, handing her the phone and sports bag.

Stephanie shook her head dejectedly.

'Look, all his numbers are on his phone. Why don't you let me come in and we'll do some searching together, eh?'

'Uncle Barry,' Dannielle screamed, running into the hallway with her arms outstretched, hoping for a cuddle. She had recognized her idol's voice.

When Barry picked up her daughter and swung her around, Stephanie started to soften. Her mum was here, and any help finding Wayne was better than none, even if it was from Barry. 'Go in the kitchen. My mum's in there and you can tell us everything that happened last night.'

'OK, just let me pay the cab first.' Strolling down the path, it was a struggle for Barry to keep the big grin off his face. Wayne going missing wasn't just good news as far as he was concerned. It was the fucking *crème da la crème*.

CHAPTER TWENTY-SEVEN

Barry politely kissed Pam on the cheek, then sat down opposite her at the kitchen table.

'Go in the lounge now, Dannielle. The adults need to talk and I need you to look after your little brother for me,' Stephanie said.

'Can't I stay out here with Uncle Barry? I want him to sing "Incy Wincy Spider" with me,' Dannielle pleaded, her lips pouting with disappointment.

Barry grinned at Dannielle. 'You do as your mum says and look after your little brother and I promise we'll sing "Incy Wincy Spider" later on.'

'OK then,' Dannielle said, smiling shyly.

When her daughter skipped out of the kitchen, Stephanie got straight down to business. 'I want to know everything that happened last night from start to finish,' she demanded coldly.

'Offer the boy a beer or a coffee first then, Steph,' Pam ordered her daughter.

Barry stared at Stephanie as she poured a can of lager into a glass for him. They had been so close once upon a time, but he felt as if he barely knew her at all now. She had definitely changed over the years; seemed much more cynical and harder than the soft, fresh-faced girl he had once known and loved.

'Fire away then,' Steph said, sitting down next to her mother.

Apart from admitting that they were at a lap-dancing club in Soho, or mentioning Angela, Barry spoke truthfully about everything that had happened the previous evening.

'So, how drunk was Wayne when he followed Lee out the club?' Stephanie asked.

'He weren't that drunk at all. He wasn't really drinking until the latter part of the evening.'

'Why not? That don't sound like Wayne,' Steph asked, supiciously. If Barry was lying to her, he was wasting his time, because Steph knew Wayne better than anybody did.

'I dunno if you know, but Wayne's been on tablets, antidepressants, and that's why he wasn't drinking much. He told me that the tablets and booze don't mix very well.'

Stephanie scowled at Barry. Wayne taking antidepressants was the most ridiculous yarn she had ever heard in the whole of her life. 'Antidepressants and Wayne, don't make me laugh. You're lying, Barry, I know you are, and if you don't tell me where my fiancé really is, I'm going to call the police and have you arrested.'

Barry shook his head. 'I'm telling the truth, Steph. I wouldn't lie over something serious like this. Wayne had a small strip of tablets in his trouser pocket. He showed them to me and told me what they were. Have a look in his sports bag or upstairs in his bedside drawer. He must have more of 'em hidden somewhere.'

Stephanie unzipped Wayne's sports bag and angrily tipped its contents all over the kitchen floor.

'Now, don't lose your temper, love,' Pam said, softly.

'I bet you planted them there,' Stephanie shouted, picking

up a packet of tablets that were in a small white pharmacy bag.

Barry stood up. 'I'm going. I came round to help you, not to be abused. Apart from fishing around in that bag for Jacko's phone, I haven't even looked through his stuff. I just guessed he might have the tablets in there, because the strip he had in his pocket looked almost empty.'

Pam snatched the tablets out of her daughter's hand. 'Is Wayne registered with a Doctor Patel in Collier Row?' she asked.

Stephanie nodded her head. 'Me and the kids have registered with a new doctor in Chigwell, but Wayne hasn't changed his yet.'

'Well, in that case I think you should apologize to Barry, because they are definitely Wayne's tablets. They have his name on the box and your old address is printed on the pharmacy bag,' Pam said sternly.

'I'm sorry, and please don't go. We need your help,' Stephanie mumbled.

Barry sat back down again and, as he did so, his mobile rang.

'Is it Wayne?' Stephanie asked, hopefully.

Barry shook his head. 'No, it's my girlfriend. I'll call her back in a bit.'

Steph put her head in her hands. 'It's gone three now. What time should I leave it to until I call the police?'

'Give it till tomorrow morning, and if he still ain't home, ring 'em first thing. I'm sure the Old Bill have some policy where people have to be missing for twenty-four hours before they do anything, and they certainly ain't gonna bust a gut to find some geezer who's just been out on his stag night,' Barry said bluntly.

'When is Daddy coming home, because Tyler wants to go to the park?' Dannielle asked, walking into the kitchen again.

'Daddy is at work I think, love. How about if I take you, Aidan and Tyler to the park? I could do with some fresh air,' Stephanie offered. Why her son had such a fixation with parks she would never know, but ever since he had learned to say the word, there wasn't a day went by when he didn't demand a trip to one.

'Can Uncle Barry come with us?' Dannielle asked.

'No, Uncle Barry's going to stay here and keep your nan company. Now go and get your and Tyler's coats and we'll go,' Stephanie said, in a none-too-happy voice. It really pissed her off that her daughter had taken such a shine to Barry and kept referring to him as her uncle. If she didn't have bigger things to worry about, she would have put a stop to it, there and then.

The moment Stephanie and the children walked out the front door, Barry's phone burst into life once again. Pam said a silent prayer that it would be Wayne, but when she heard Barry utter the words, 'Marge' and 'Mum', she knew that it wasn't.

'I'm gonna have to shoot off, Pam. Me mum's in a bit of a state by all accounts, and the mate she's staying with don't know what to do with her. You remember my mother, I take it?'

About to refer to her as the old slapper, Pam stopped herself just in time. 'Course I remember Marlene.'

'Well, if you remember her you'll know she's a nightmare. Bane of my life, that woman is, but she's always gonna be me mother, so I'm lumbered with her, unfortunately.'

Pam smiled. She liked Barry. He seemed a decent, honest kind of chap. 'Before you go, is there anything else you can tell me about last night? If Wayne went off with a bird, please say so. I won't tell Steph unless I have to.'

Barry took a deep breath and sighed, as though breaking the news was extremely hard for him. It wasn't, not one little bit, but he had to play the game. He had very nearly blurted it out to Steph when she had accused him of lying over Wayne's tablets, but being clever, he had managed to bite his tongue. 'I dunno how to tell you this, Pam, and there was no way I could have told Steph the truth.'

Pam's heart lurched. 'What is it?'

'We went to a lap-dancing club in Soho. I didn't really want to go there, neither did the other lads, but Wayne was insistent that we did. When we got there, it turns out that your Angie was one of the dancers. I went off to the toilet, and when I came back Wayne and Angie were in some deep conversation. Next thing I knew, both had disappeared. Angie's flatmate works there also – Roxy, I think her name was. Anyway, when I realized Wayne had gone missing, I asked her where Angie was, and she said that she had suddenly felt ill and had gone home. I dunno about you, Pam, but I would say that that was one hell of a coincidence, eh?'

Pam was stunned. She knew Angela wasn't a very nice person, but how could she do something so vile to her own sister?

'Are you OK, Pam? Would you like me to get you a drink or something?' Barry asked, politely.

Pam shook her head. Even if Wayne did turn up in the next hour or so, how could she let Stephanie marry him next week when she now knew what he had been up to? She took a deep breath to try to steady her emotions. 'Go on, love. You get off and see to your mum. I can deal with this.'

'What you gonna do?' Barry asked, solemnly.

'I'm gonna confront Angela; then if your suspicions turn out to be true, I shall have to tell Stephanie. It's gonna break her heart, I know it is, but I can't let her marry him, Barry. I would never forgive myself if I did.'

Barry squeezed Pam's hand. 'Well, if it's any consolation, I think you're doing the right thing telling Steph. I know if it were me about to get married, then I'd want to know. Having said that, this is all just speculation at the moment. For all we know, Wayne could have ended up elsewhere and might walk in as right as rain any minute. Perhaps Angela was genuinely ill, who knows?'

'I very much doubt it, but I'll get to the bottom of it if it kills me. Go on, love, you shoot off. Thanks for coming round and thanks for being honest with me.'

Pam found Stephanie's address book. She was relieved when the cab firm only quoted her ten minutes, as she couldn't wait to ring Angela and give her a piece of her mind.

Barry chatted away politely as he finished the rest of his beer. He had given Pam his phone number and she had promised to contact him personally the moment she had some news, whether it be good or bad. 'Do you know what, Pam? You're a lovely lady and I'd give my right arm to have a mother like you. I hope your Stephanie realizes how lucky she is.'

Pam forced a smile. Considering that Barry had been reared by the horrendous Marlene, he had certainly turned into a lovely lad. He was handsome, polite, honest and charming, and for the first time ever, Pam wished he hadn't moved to Spain all them years ago, and it was he that Stephanie was planning to marry rather than Wayne.

Within seconds of returning from the park with the kids, Stephanie knew that something had happened. She knew her mother like the back of her hand and could tell that Pam was hiding something. Not wanting to create a scene in front of the children, Steph put the McDonald's they had begged for onto three plastic plates and ordered them to eat it in the lounge.

'Right, what's going on?' she said to her mother as she shut the kitchen door.

Pam didn't know if she was coming or going. She had tried to ring Angela, but her mobile phone was switched off and she had no home number for her. Cathy, who she would usually ask for advice, was at Bingo, so that was a no-go. Then, in pure desperation, Pam had rung Linda, and there had been no answer from her either. Not wanting to make a mountain out of a molehill in case Wayne walked in at any second, Pam decided to lie. 'Nothing's wrong apart from the obvious. You got any more wine, love? I could kill another glass.'

Stephanie went into the conservatory, grabbed a bottle of Chardonnay and poured the majority of it into two large glasses. 'Why did Barry go before I got back? Did he say something that upset you?' Steph probed, her voice full of suspicion.

'No, of course not! Barry left because his mother is creating havoc, I think. How an old slapper like that ever gave birth to a decent lad like Barry, I shall never know.'

Looking at the clock on the kitchen wall, Stephanie shook her head in despair. It was nearly five p.m. now and would soon be dark outside. Waiting until the morning to ring the police was ridiculous. The sooner she rang them and reported Wayne missing, the better. 'I'm gonna ring the Old Bill now, Mum, I have to. No matter how drunk Wayne was last night, he would have definitely rung me by now if he was OK. Something's happened to him, I just know it has, and at least if I report him missing, the police can check the hospitals and stuff.'

'No, don't ring them yet,' Pam said, alarmed. She hadn't worked out how to break Barry's news to Stephanie yet and she didn't want to send her daughter over the edge. 'Barry's right. The police will laugh at you if you ring them now and say Wayne hasn't come home from his stag night yet.'

Stephanie had tried to be strong all day, but couldn't hold the tears back any longer. 'What am I gonna do if we can't find him, Mum? How long am I meant to leave it until I cancel the wedding and ring all the guests?'

Pam held her sobbing daughter in her arms. If Wayne didn't arrive home to sort out this mess very soon, she would personally fucking strangle him.

Barry Franklin had no intention of going to visit his mother. Marge had rung him, but only to inform him that his mother was 'sorry for what she had said' and had asked 'could he please send her clothes home from Spain?'

Strolling into the boozer in a side road just off Brentwood High Street, Barry queued up at the bar. Today had gone to perfection for somebody as desperate for revenge as he was: it was the stuff that dreams were made of. Not only was Wayne on the missing-persons list and thought to be with Angela, he also had Pam eating out of his hand, which was a proper added bonus.

The young dark-haired barmaid smiled at Barry. He had been in a few evenings recently and, unlike most of her other punters, was always generous in offering her a drink. 'A bottle of Bud, is it?' she asked.

Barry grinned. 'Nah, I fancy something different tonight. Give us a bottle of champagne, sweetheart.' Barry laughed. 'I'm in the mood for celebrating.'

By nine p.m., Stephanie had become rather hysterical and Pam knew she couldn't hold her secret piece of knowledge back much longer. 'Come and sit down, darling,' she said sadly, as Steph trawled through the Yellow Pages to try to find out phone numbers of local hospitals.

'I can't fucking sit down. I've got to do something.'

'Sssh. The kids probably aren't asleep yet. You don't want to worry them, do you?' Pam said, sensibly. It was less than half an hour since she had tucked the poor little mites up in bed and Pam was positive that Dannielle had sensed that something was amiss when she had asked if she was 'still going to be a bridesmaid next week?'

Deflated, Stephanie sat down on the armchair opposite her mother. She had been trying to call Tammy all evening to ask her advice. Her best friend's sister was a policewoman and Stephanie was sure that she could be of some help, if only Tammy would switch her bloody phone on.

'Who's that you're trying to phone – Tammy again?' Pam asked.

Stephanie nodded. 'She's taken Richard back to the airport, Mum. She rarely has her mobile on when she isn't at work, but she did say she would call me once she'd dropped him off. Look, I'm sick of waiting for people to switch their fucking phones on. I don't care if the Old Bill laugh at me. I'm gonna ring 'em now, Mum.'

As Stephanie began dialling 999, Pam snatched the phone out of her daughter's hand.

'What you doing?' Steph yelled.

Knowing that awful time had come when she had to break Stephanie's heart, Pam urged her to sit down again.

'What's a matter?' Steph asked, fearfully.

Pam sat next to her daughter on the sofa, and with tears in her eyes said the sentence she had been dreading disclosing. 'I'm so sorry, Steph, but I think Wayne might have run off with our Angela.'

Letting out one almighty scream, Stephanie grabbed the framed photo of her and Wayne off the wall and threw it across the room. Aware of the sound of breaking glass, she then sank to her knees and sobbed like a baby.

CHAPTER TWENTY-EIGHT

Stephanie felt like a zombie when Tammy arrived the following morning. She had been unable to sleep a wink and had spent all night tossing, turning, and crying. The more she thought about it, Wayne being with Angela just didn't ring true. Her partner had always hated her sister, ever since their teenage fling, so why would he suddenly run away with her?

'I'm so sorry you couldn't get hold of me last night, mate. I was going to ring you after I'd dropped Richard off, but my battery went dead. What's been happening? Have you rung the police yet?' Tammy asked, sitting next to Stephanie on the sofa.

'Come on kids, let's go and play in the garden,' Pam suggested to her grandchildren. They knew something was wrong. Dannielle had been crying earlier, and Pam wanted to shield them from the awful truth for as long as she could.

'Me wan weeties,' Tyler screamed, pummelling his little fists against the carpet in temper as Pam tried to lift him up.

'Walk 'em down the shops and get them some sweets, Mum. Take the money out of my purse.'

When the front door slammed, Steph breathed a sigh of relief.

'So, have you rung the police?' Tammy asked again.

'I rang them about an hour ago and they said that they would send someone round, but they haven't yet. They asked where Wayne had been and when I said he had been out on his stag night, I'm sure they were laughing at me.'

'What about Angie? Have you got an address for her yet?' Tammy asked. Steph had told her on the phone what Barry had said to Pam.

'No. My mum's been trying to ring her all morning, but Angie's phone is still switched off. We don't have an address for her or a home number, but Mum reckons the police will be able to trace her because she must have registered her mobile phone at her new address. What about your sister, Tam? Can't you ring her and see if she can help us? I'm at my wits' end, I really am.'

Tammy's sister and brother-in-law were both in the police force, but had recently moved to Colchester. 'Worse comes to the worst, I'll give my sister a bell, but I doubt that she will be able to do much, mate, as she is working at a station out in Essex now. See what the Old Bill say when they come round, but I don't believe for a minute that your Wayne would run off with Angela. I reckon Barry's got something to do with his disappearance, you mark my words.'

Steph put her distraught head in her hands. 'But why would Barry have agreed to come to the wedding if he hated Wayne's guts? And why would he turn up round here yesterday and be so helpful and nice?'

'Because he is bloody clever, Steph. I never liked Barry Franklin that much, even when we were at school, and I wouldn't trust the bastard as far as I could throw him now.'

'You never said you didn't like him at school,' Stephanie replied. Her mind was all over the place and she really didn't know what to think any more. Her mum seemed to think that the sun shone out of Barry's arse, and she was rarely ever wrong about anyone.

After buying the children a bag of goodies, Pam stopped at the nearest phone box. 'Hold Tyler's hand and go and play on that bit of green with him,' she ordered Dannielle and Aidan. Pam rang Cathy first, explained what had happened, and was relieved when her friend said that she was on her way over. Pam then rang Linda and explained Wayne's disappearance to her.

'I'm gonna kill that fucking Angela. Don't you dare have no more to do with her after this, sis. I think me and Keith should come over. Steph will need her family around her.'

'OK,' Pam said. She ended the call, then tried Angela again. She was surprised when her daughter actually answered. 'Where the hell is Wayne?' Pam screamed psychotically.

'How the hell should I know where Wayne is? I take it you've heard that he came to my club, then?'

'This ain't funny, Angela, so don't you dare lie to me. If Wayne is there with you, you have to tell me now because Stephanie has just called the police.'

'Called the police! What the fuck you on about, Mum? Wayne ain't with me. I saw him at the club, briefly, and that was it.'

Pam sighed. Her youngest daughter had always been an extremely convincing liar, and Pam could never tell if she was pulling a fast one or not. 'If you are telling the truth, Angie – and with your track record, I very much doubt it – then you'd best get yourself round to your sister's house and tell her and the police exactly what happened.'

'What do you mean, what happened? All I did was go to work, felt ill, and came back home. Yes, Wayne was there on his stag do, but I barely spoke to the bloke for more than five minutes.'

With the pips going, Pam quickly stuffed some more coins into the slot. 'Barry said you chatted to Wayne for ages, and he said that you and Wayne disappeared at the same time. Wayne's missing, Angela. He hasn't been seen since he was at your club – so for once, just tell me the bastard truth.'

'I am telling the bastard truth! I tell you what, Mother. You get Barry shit-stirring Franklin round Steph's, and me and Roxy will drive straight over. I've been sick as a pig for the past twenty-four hours and I've only just dragged meself out of bed. You call the Old Bill back and tell 'em I'm on my way round now, and don't forget to ring Barry an' all. I refuse to be accused of something I ain't done, Mum. It's bang out of order.'

Pam was stunned when Angela slammed the phone down on her. For once, it seemed like her youngest daughter might actually be telling the truth.

Stephanie was furious when firstly Cathy, then Linda and Keith turned up. She knew people were only there to support her, but with her life and wedding seemingly in tatters, she really wasn't in the mood to be talking to anyone. Steph followed her mother into the kitchen. 'Can't you get rid of everyone, Mum? I only want you and Tammy here.'

Pam tried to hold Steph in her arms, but was pushed away.

'Just get off me, Mum. All I want is Wayne back, not to be treated like a fucking child.'

Pam sighed. She hadn't yet told her that both Barry and Angela were also on their way round, but she knew she had to soon. 'Look, people are only here because they love you so much. I rang Cath and Lin when I was out, and I rang

Barry, Angela, and the police again. They'll all be here soon, and the quicker the better if you ask me. Wayne needs to be found, love, and after speaking to Angela, I truly believe she's in the dark about his disappearance as well.'

'What did the bitch say? You know she's always been the liar of all liars,' Stephanie screamed.

'Your sister swears blind that she spotted Wayne at the club, spoke to him briefly, then felt ill and went home, alone. She's bringing her flatmate, Roxy, round here with her. You haven't met Roxy yet, but I have and, surprisingly, she is a really decent girl. Angie was fuming when I told her what Barry had said, so that's why I rang him. The police are coming round at five to take statements off the whole lot of 'em. I know it's stressful for you, darling, but the quicker we find out what's really happened to Wayne, the better, eh?'

Wondering if she was having a bad dream, Stephanie picked up a saucepan and began banging herself over the head with it to see if she would wake up.

'Stop it! What you doing?' Pam shrieked, grabbing the handle out of her daughter's hand.

Bursting into tears, Stephanie sank to her knees. 'I think I'm going off my head, Mum. I honestly don't know what I'm doing.'

Barry Franklin was in a rather buoyant mood as he drove towards Stephanie's house. He was amazed that Wayne hadn't been found yet, but thrilled that he could now shove the final nail in his old pal's coffin. As the current number one song, D:Ream's 'Things Can Only Get Better', came on the radio, Barry cranked the volume up and laughed as he joined in with the lyrics. Things most certainly weren't going to get better for Wayne Jackman, because Barry was about to make sure they became decidedly worse.

* * *

Linda was livid as Angela strolled into the lounge with the attitude from hell. 'Don't be giving it the large, Ange. Don't you realize that your sister's in bits? You selfish bloody cow,' she shouted.

'Calm down, Lin. Let me get you a beer, eh?' Keith said, squeezing his partner's hand.

'I don't want a fucking beer. I want to tell this no-good, conniving little bitch her fortune,' Linda yelled, as all four foot of her lunged at her neice.

'Stop it. Just bloody well stop it,' Pam shouted, as Dannielle and Tyler both started to scream.

'Can I have a cuddle, Mum?' Aidan said, holding his arms out to Angela.

About to say no, Angela remembered she had Roxy standing by her side, so instead gave her son a false motherly hug.

Feeling a bit awkward, Cathy stood up. 'I'll put the kettle on. Who wants tea and who wants coffee?'

Before anybody had a chance to reply, the doorbell rang and Pam dashed off to answer it. 'Do come in, officers. My daughter is in the living room,' she said nervously.

Stephanie felt incredibly edgy as she stared at the uniformed man and woman. Their presence made Wayne's disappearance seem all the more real somehow. 'Take the kids upstairs with Cath, Mum. You and Keith go with them as well, Lin,' Steph ordered.

'I don't want to go, Mummy. I want to stay here with you. Where's Daddy? Has he died?' Dannielle asked, clinging to her mother's leg.

Stephanie held her daughter's head in her hands and kissed her on the nose. 'Daddy's not dead. He's just got lost somewhere and the police have come to see us to help us find him. Now you be a good girl and go upstairs with Nanny while Mummy talks to them, OK?'

Pam ushered the three children out of the room. 'Just shout if you need me.'

As Linda walked out behind Keith and Cathy, she prodded the male officer in the arm. 'And don't be believing anything that lying little mare tells you,' she said, pointing at Angela.

Roxy squeezed her friend's hand. 'Just take no notice.'

Angela sensibly smiled at the two police officers. She was far too clever to retaliate.

'Do you want to start questioning us now? Or shall we wait for Barry Franklin to arrive? Barry was with Wayne the night he went missing,' Stephanie explained.

'I'd wait for Barry. Bet he knows more than anybody else does,' Tammy stated abruptly.

Stephanie glared at her friend as if to urge her to shut up. Tammy shouldn't start insinuating that Barry had done something to Wayne in front of the police until they had some kind of proof at least. 'That's probably Barry now. Go and answer it, Tam,' Stephanie said when the doorbell rang.

Dressed in a trendy tan leather jacket, matching tan shoes and faded jeans, Barry Franklin strolled into the lounge and shook both police officers' hands.

'What they doing here?' Stephanie asked horrified, as she spotted Cooksie and Potter bowl into the room behind Barry.

'Well, seeing as they were both with us the other evening, I thought the police might want to speak to them as well. I also rang Lee, but I couldn't get hold of him,' Barry replied.

'Right, let's get started. Firstly, we need a description of what Mr Jackman was wearing on the evening in question, and also the names of any places you might have visited,' the female officer said to Barry.

While Barry, Potter and Cooksie filled the police in with details, Stephanie furtively glanced at her sister. Her mum was positive that for once Angela was telling the truth, but

Stephanie wasn't quite so sure. Angela was sly and manipulative, and Steph had always been under the impression that her sister had held a grudge over her relationship with Wayne.

Angela smirked as she heard the policewoman ask Barry if Wayne had been chatting any girls up. 'Do you mind if I say something, please?' Angie asked, putting her hand up as though she was still at primary school.

The policewoman turned to her. 'Not at all. Any help to find Mr Jackman would be much appreciated.'

'I spoke to Jacko – sorry, I mean Wayne. Jacko's his nickname, and I had a rather in-depth chat with him, actually. He was telling me how skint he was and how he regretted asking my sister to marry him, as he now couldn't afford to give her the wedding that she had dreamed of.'

Unable to control her fury, Stephanie leapt up and pointed her finger in her sister's face. 'You are one twisted, nasty piece of work, Angela Crouch. You've always been jealous of me and Wayne having such a comfortable lifestyle, and no one will believe your vicious lies, so why bother telling them?'

When Roxy and Tammy both jumped up, Barry quickly moved to calm things down.

'Bundle,' Cooksie shouted, nudging Potter. Potter laughed, but then quickly reverted to serious again when he clocked the policeman glare at him and Cooksie.

'Just calm down, Stephanie. Angela isn't lying. Me, Cooksie and Potter can vouch for that,' Barry said softly.

'Wayne isn't skint. We've got a wonderful lifetstyle,' Stephanie insisted.

Glaring at Barry, Tammy pushed him out of the way and held Stephanie in her arms. 'They're not lying, Steph. Wayne did have money problems, babe.'

Stephanie was not only furious, but also mortified. How

come everybody else knew about Wayne's financial difficulties, yet she didn't? It was her who was meant to be getting married to him, so why had he spoken to every other bastard about it, but not her? Feeling like a complete and utter fool, Stephanie flopped onto the armchair in despair.

'Would somebody like to tell us about Mr Jackman's financial affairs?' the policeman asked. He had his pen and his notebook in his hand and was raring to go.

'Jacko was telling us that he'd sort of lost everything, weren't he, Potter? He took us out for a curry a few weeks back and spilt his guts. He reckoned he was up to his neck in it and was scraping the bottom of the barrel. He was proper upset, though, because he adored Steph and was worried about letting her down,' Cooksie said, honestly.

When everybody else started chipping in about the state of Wayne's finances, Stephanie felt that her head was about to explode. 'Why didn't you tell me? You of all people, I thought I could trust, Tam,' she screamed at her lifelong best friend.

'I didn't tell you because Wayne begged me not to. He loves you so much, Steph, and he was so worried about not being able to buy you the salon that he had promised you. I thought it was just a temporary blip for him; I didn't realize he had told anybody else, mate. He was going to tell you after the wedding, and if he hadn't, I swear I would have. Nobody wanted to spoil your big day for you, Steph, including me,' Tammy explained, breaking down in tears herself.

As Angela watched both her sister and Tammy cry, she felt nothing but happiness within. Deciding to put the boot in even further, Angela knew she had to first put on an act because Roxy was with her.

'Are you OK, Ange?' Roxy asked, as the tears began to drip down Angela's cheeks.

'No, not really. I feel I should tell the police about my relationship with Wayne all them years ago. Say he don't get found, then they start pointing the finger at me,' Angela whispered in her friend's ear.

Roxy shrugged. She didn't really see the need to tell the police about that yet, but she didn't want her flatmate to worry over it. 'Well, if you think you should, then you tell them,' she said supportively.

'I think there is something I should tell you, officers. It's probably not important, but I feel if Wayne isn't found soon and you dig deeper with your enquiries, you may start to look at me in a suspicious manner for not saying anything.'

Stephanie clocked the falseness in Angela's overly dramatic voice and immediately knew what she was about to say. 'Just shut it, Ange, that has nothing to do with Wayne's disappearance,' she spat.

The female officer glanced at her colleague, and then glared at Stephanie. 'We will be the ones to decide that. Now, would you like to tell us your concerns?' she asked, turning her attention back to Angela.

Dabbing her eyes with a tissue from her handbag, Angela nodded. 'Wayne Jackman was my boyfriend before he got with my sister, Stephanie. In fact, he took my virginity from me when I was only thirteen years old.'

About to start shouting and screaming about how her sister had lied about her age to Wayne, Stephanie decided not to bother. She had already been humiliated beyond belief in front of the police, so what was the point in her making matters worse for herself?

When the police began to question Angela over the details of her and Wayne's relationship, Barry glanced at Stephanie and wanted to laugh. In his eyes, she deserved everything that had happened to her in the past day or two. She had broken his heart and this was payback time.

CHAPTER TWENTY-NINE

Purgatory would be the best way to describe the days that followed for Stephanie. Initially, the police had thought that Wayne would reappear with a stag-night hangover and an apology, but as Stephanie's wedding day approached with still no word from the groom, the constabulary became increasingly concerned about Wayne's wellbeing.

Apart from popping home to pick up some more clothes and toiletries, Pam had barely left her daughter's side. Pam's boss at the baker's had told her to take as much time off as she needed, and Pam was extremely grateful to him, as Stephanie's frail state of mind certainly wasn't up to coping with two young children on her own.

On the morning of what was meant to be her daughter's wedding day, Pam got up at the crack of dawn and had a nice, relaxing soak in the bath. She was dreading the day ahead. Over the past couple of days she'd had the awful task of ringing around all the guests to tell them that the wedding had been cancelled. Cathy and Linda had both been brilliant and were coming around again later to support Stephanie on such a traumatic day.

Barry Franklin had also been a tower of strength and had popped in regularly to try and keep Steph's spirits up. The more Pam saw of Barry, the more she liked the lad. He was charming, funny, very thoughtful, and had even taken the kids over to the park yesterday so she could rest her tired legs. Immersing her body into the hot, soapy water, Pam thought about Wayne and sighed. She had always got along with her daughter's partner, but in her heart of hearts, she had never really liked him that much. In Pam's eyes, Wayne's qualities as a father left a lot to be desired, and she also found the man to be rather cold. Wondering what on earth had happened to him, Pam leant her head against the edge of the bath and shut her eyes. She was pleased that the police were coming around again this morning to update her and Stephanie on their enquiries, and she imagined they were bound to ask more questions. Wayne's disappearance was the most baffling thing that Pam had ever encountered; but one thing she did know: if Wayne was ever found safe and well, there was a good chance she would end up murdering him herself.

Stephanie opened her wardrobe door and took out the wedding dress. The alterations lady had bought it back on Thursday and Steph hadn't even looked at it yet. She knew she was torturing herself by trying it on, but she couldn't stop herself from doing so. She had paid the woman another fifty pounds, so had every right to check that the sleeves now fitted as they should.

'Is Daddy coming home, Mummy? Can I wear my bridesmaid dress now?' Dannielle asked excitedly.

Through lack of sleep, Stephanie felt as though she were in a trance as she stared at her daughter. Tyler was too young to even miss Wayne. He didn't have a clue what was going on. Dannielle, on the other hand, had been tearful, off her food, and acting very clingy.

Not wanting her daughter to be affected any more than

she already had been, Stephanie decided to end the saga once and for all. Steph had made a pact to herself that if Wayne wasn't home for their wedding day, she would snap out of her trauma for the sake of her children, and that's exactly what she intended to do. She snarled as she ripped off her wedding dress and then grabbed the pair of scissors she kept in her bedside drawer.

'No Mummy. No,' Dannielle screamed, as Stephanie hacked at the beautiful dress with the scissors, like a woman possessed.

'Daddy isn't coming home, Dannielle. It's just me, you and Tyler from now on, OK?' Steph screamed.

'What are you doing, love?' Pam asked, horrified, as she opened Steph's bedroom door.

'Well, I'm hardly going to be needing it now, am I?' Stephanie yelled, before bursting into tears.

Dannielle was petrified. 'I want my daddy,' she cried, clinging to Pam's midriff.

Pam had tears in her own eyes as she urged Stephanie to move away from the dress.

Steph couldn't. Instead, she lay face down on top of it. 'I miss Wayne so much, Mum. Where is he?' she sobbed.

Pam sat on the bed and held Stephanie tightly to her chest. Her daughter was so vulnerable at the moment, it reminded Pam of when she was a little girl all over again. 'The police will find out what's happened to him, love. They are so clever these days, so dry them eyes and get yourself ready for their visit. They might even have some news for you.'

'If I ask you something, Mum, will you tell me the truth?'

'Of course I will,' Pam said, moving a strand of her daughter's hair away from her wet eyes.

'Do you think Wayne's dead?'

It was an impossible question to answer, so Pam had no

choice other than to sit on the fence. 'I don't know, sweetheart, I really don't know.'

Barry Franklin was seated at a table in the Bishop Bonner pub in Bethnal Green. His father, Smasher, had only recently come out of prison, and Barry was enjoying listening to him and his old cronies reminiscing about the good old days.

'It's proper changed in this boozer. Do you remember when we used to get all the old boxers in 'ere? I bet Henry Cooper wouldn't set foot in the shithole now,' Smasher said, gloomily. The pub had really altered since he had gone inside and he didn't like the atmosphere of it now one little bit.

'It ain't been the same since Freddie and Rita had it, if you ask me. Those were the good old days – when we used to have Chas and Dave down here on a Thursday night and everybody got up and sang. Do you remember the old boy who had the fish stall down the Roman? He used to bring the house down, and you certainly don't get characters like him in here any more,' Smasher's pal, Charlie, told Barry.

Barry raised his eyebrows. He hadn't had a beer with his father for Christ knows how long and had been expecting a jovial piss-up, not a melancholy look back in time. 'Yeah, I do remember Chas and Dave singing in 'ere when I was a kid, but now they're famous I doubt they'd wanna be slumming it round 'ere again. Times have changed, lads, and we have to move with 'em, unfortunately.'

'Gonna have a little chat with me, boy. We need a bit of a one-to-one,' Smasher said to Barry.

Barry followed his father outside. 'What's up?'

'Nothing, lad, unless you wanna include your whore of a mother spreading rumours. She's been going around telling people that you killed Jake the Snake.'

'Oh, for fuck's sake. She sprang that one on me in the motor on the way home from the brief's office. I thought she was just talking drunken bollocks, I didn't actually think she would start telling people. Who did she tell? Do you know?'

'It's Fat Carol who's been mouthing it off round 'ere. I went and knocked on her door yesterday and, apparently, Lairy Mary, who now lives in Dagenham, had told her. I've warned Fat Carol that she better keep her gob shut else she'll have me to deal with. You didn't have anything at all to do with the old boy's death, did you, Bal?'

'What do you take me for, Dad? I've told you many a time that I quite liked the geezer, so course I never. Anyway, I've got bigger fish to fry than poor old Jake, ain't I?'

Smasher smirked. He was well aware of Barry's quest for revenge against the two people who had betrayed him in the worst way possible. 'Has Jacko been found yet?'

'No sign of him,' Barry replied, grinning.

'And how's it going with the bird?' Smasher asked, referring to Steph.

'Sweet! I've got her and the mother eating out the palm of me hand and it won't be long before I strike. What goes around comes around, eh, Dad?'

Smasher laughed. 'That's my boy.'

Stephanie felt her heart pounding nineteen to the dozen as the two coppers sat down on the sofa opposite her. They seemed much more important than the two who had visited her the other day. These were plain clothed and had an air of power about them. One of them introduced himself as DI Jobson and told Steph that his colleague was DC Moore, then Jobson spoke directly to her.

'I'm afraid we have had little success in tracing Mr Jackman's movements after he left the club that he was drinking in. One of the doormen gave us a statement saying that he saw Mr Jackman leave and cross the road, but from there the trail goes cold. We do have some other news for you, though. We have conducted a thorough search of Mr Jackman's business activities and we now know that he had recently sold most of his assets. Were you aware that the money your fiancé received from the sale of your house in Collier Row had been taken out of his account and was supposedly used to pay off debts?'

'No, I wasn't aware of that – and what do you mean by "supposedly"?' Stephanie asked, anxiously. She had ordered her mum to take the children to the park and now wished she hadn't.

'I say "supposedly" as we cannot find any proof of Mr Jackman actually paying off these debts. It's all very much hearsay at the moment. We have taken statements from quite a few of Mr Jackman's friends and work colleagues, and apparently he had spoken quite openly of the financial difficulties he had found himself in. Did you know that he had recently sold a part of his gym, and had also taken out a massive loan against it?'

'No, I didn't, and I just can't believe all this is true. Wayne never showed any sign of being in debt to me, although he did say a couple of strange things to me just before his stag night.'

'What did he say?' DI Jobson asked.

'I can't remember to be exact, but he did drop a hint that he had a cashflow problem. Actually, I do remember it now. As Wayne was about to leave for his stag do, he made a comment about how he'd only invited a few people to it because he was footing the bill.'

DI Jobson pulled out a notebook and jotted something down. 'Anything else you can remember about that conversation?'

'I think I said to Wayne that it was unusual for him to worry about money; then he said something about everybody having to pull their horns in sometimes. I didn't take much notice of what he said, to be honest. I just thought that Wayne was referring to the cost of the wedding.'

'How would you describe your relationship with Mr Jackman? Did he seem different recently? Distant perhaps?' Moore asked.

Stephanie glared at both officers. What were they trying to insinuate, for Christ's sake? Were they hinting that Wayne had fallen out of love with her and had disappeared of his own accord? 'I'm not sure exactly what you're getting at, but I can assure you that there was nothing wrong with Wayne or our relationship,' she replied, angrily.

DI Jobson sighed. It was part of his and Moore's job to ask these types of questions, so why did people always seem to take them as a personal insult? 'Look, Stephanie, all we are trying to do is find out what has happened to Wayne. His disappearance is rather baffling, to say the least, and I'm afraid that we have to explore every avenue possible. Some questions we ask you, you might not want to answer, but it would help us enormously if you did.'

Stephanie immediately saw the error of her ways. Jobson was right. He and his colleague were only trying to find Wayne, so she quickly decided to speak from the heart. 'Wayne and I have been together since school. We've had a few ups and downs over the years, but who hasn't? I would say that our relationship was really good overall, but to be perfectly honest, over the past six months or so, I did feel that we had become like ships that pass in the night. Wayne was always at work so, apart from first thing in the morning and sometimes last thing at night, I rarely saw him some days. We did still socialize at weekends, though. We didn't really go out any more because of the kids, but just recently we had friends over quite a few times.'

'Where did Wayne work in the evenings?' Moore asked Stephanie.

'At his gym. It didn't shut until ten at night, therefore by the time Wayne had locked up and that, he didn't get home until after midnight. Between me and you, I think he and a couple of the lads used to have a few drinks after work. I smelt alcohol on his breath a few times when he got home late, and he admitted to me that he liked to de-stress after a long, hard day.'

Jobson glanced at Moore. They had already spoken to Wayne's employees from the gym and, apart from on the odd occasion, the employees reckoned that Wayne had rarely been there of an evening. Something didn't ring true. Determined to get to the bottom of it, Jobson carried on with the questioning.

Stephanie answered as best as she could, but she found the experience extremely unsettling, and breathed a sigh of relief when she heard her mum and the kids return from their trip to the park.

'Are you policemen? Have you found my daddy yet?' Dannielle asked, as she bounded into the room and stared at Jobson and Moore.

'Yes, they are policemen, and no, they haven't found Daddy yet. Now, take your brother upstairs for a minute, Danni. Me and Nanny need to have a little chat.'

'Why aren't you wearing policemen's clothes?' Dannielle asked. She had always been an inquisitive child, and could not understand why Jobson and Moore were not in uniform.

'Take Tyler upstairs now, darling,' Stephanie urged, raising her voice. Dannielle was far too clued-up for her age to be listening in on what the police had to say. That is why she had wanted her mum to take the kids over to the park in the first place.

When Dannielle did as she was told, Pam turned to

Jobson. 'So, what's happened? Is there any more news?' She could tell by Stephanie's face that whatever news her daughter had received wasn't particularly good.

'Your daughter will explain what we've already spoken about to you later, Mrs Crouch. There are a few more questions myself and my colleague need to ask Stephanie, though, and then we'll be out of your way.'

Pam sat on the armchair next to Stephanie and supportively squeezed her daughter's hand. When her own husband had been killed in an accident, Pam had felt as if her whole world had fallen apart, but at least she had known what had happened to him. What Steph was going through was a hundred times worse, unless it had a happy ending, of course.

Jobson cleared his throat. 'In the sports bag that Wayne had with him on the night of his disappearance, we found some receipts amongst other things. One was from a pawnbroker's and it stated that Wayne had pawned a lot of jewellery earlier that day. I take it he never mentioned anything about this to you?'

'No, nothing,' Stephanie replied, grasping at her mother's hand for support. How many more secrets had Wayne kept from her?'

'And how was Wayne acting on the day of his disappearance? Did he behave in an unusual manner at all? Or perhaps say or do something that he wouldn't normally do? Were you actually here when he left to go to his stag party?' Moore asked.

Remembering her and Wayne's frantic sex session that morning, Stephanie felt herself blush, but said nothing. The way Wayne had made love to her that day had been rather unusual, but there was no way she was going to discuss something as intimate as that with the police. 'Wayne was completely normal on the day of his stag do, and yes, I was here when he left to go out. There was nothing odd about his behaviour at all as far as I can remember.'

Jobson nodded. 'Please do not worry when I ask you my next question, as I have already told you that we have to cover every bit of ground. Enemies. Were you aware of any that Wayne might have had?'

Wondering if she should mention to the police that Tammy thought that her fiancé's disappearance had something to do with Barry Franklin, Stephanie decided against it. Deep in her heart, Steph could not believe that her ex had anything to do with Wayne going missing. Barry had been absolutely wonderful throughout all of this trauma, and Steph was sure that Tammy was barking up the wrong tree. 'My Wayne didn't have any enemies as far as I know. Wayne's always been a good partner, a good father and a good man, and I can't imagine anybody disliking him, can you, Mum?'

Pam didn't agree with the good father bit, but decided to sing Wayne's praises anyway. 'You speak as you find, officers, and Wayne has certainly always made my daughter happy. And, Steph's right. I can't imagine anybody having it in for him, either.'

Hearing one of Tyler's familiar screams coming from upstairs, Stephanie leapt up. 'I'm gonna have to see to my kids now. My mum will talk to you for a minute.'

'We're actually done, for now. Thank you, Stephanie, you've been most helpful. We'll pop round again in the next couple of days to speak to you again. Obviously, if we have any news in the meantime, we'll inform you immediately,' Jobson said.

When Steph dashed out of the room, Pam stood up and shut the lounge door. 'I couldn't say anything in front of my daughter because I don't want to upset her any more than she already is. Why were you asking all those questions about Wayne acting differently?'

'We just need to build a picture of Wayne's mood and his movements to help us further our enquiries,' Jobson replied.

'Well, what do you think has happened to him then? Because if it is something bad, I would much rather you told me so I can prepare my daughter for the worst,' Pam said.

Jobson glanced at his colleague before answering her question. 'We really can't speculate at the moment, but as soon as we have any concrete news regarding Wayne or his whereabouts, I can assure you that you and your daughter will be the first to know.'

Pam led the two officers to the front door, then leant against it as she closed it. She was sure that the police knew more than they were letting on, but what that was, she didn't know.

CHAPTER THIRTY

As the weeks turned into a month and there was still no news of Wayne's whereabouts, Stephanie began to lose all hope of finding her fiancé alive. The police had sent one of their trained counsellors around to speak to her and prepare her for the worst, but Steph had found the experience extremely upsetting and had refused to have any more to do with the counsellor afterwards. In Stephanie's eyes, the constabulary had not pushed the boat out as much as they could have to find Wayne. They had appealed for information via a local newspaper, put posters up around Soho, and had interviewed Wayne's employees, friends and family numerous times, but other than that they had done very little else. Stephanie wasn't stupid and she knew what the police thought had happened. Wayne had told numerous friends and his grandparents of the debt he had got himself into, and the police had already insinuated that they believed the pressure of losing his business and the cost of the wedding might have tipped Wayne over the edge – so much so that he had taken his own life. Wayne's GP had also verified that Wayne had been to visit him twice in the month before his disappearance and he had been extremely anxious and depressed. His GP had also said that Wayne had spoken about having suicidal thoughts, which in the eyes of the police made their theory more probable than ever.

Stephanie had learned the art of holding her emotions within herself. Smashing and ripping things up was not going to make Wayne walk back through the door and she had needed to get her act together for the sake of the kids. Her doctor had prescribed her some sleeping pills, and since Steph had been taking them she had behaved much more rationally. This had obviously rubbed off on Dannielle, as her daughter now seemed brighter and far less clingy. As for Tyler, he was in a little world of his own, and since Steph had been taking him to the park on a regular basis, he hadn't mentioned his father at all.

Tammy still insisted that Wayne's disappearance had something to do with Barry Franklin, but Stephanie didn't believe so. Since her mum had gone back to live at her own house just over a fortnight ago, Barry had become Stephanie's rock. Every day he popped round to help her with the kids and give her some moral support, and Steph didn't believe his kindnesses were the actions of a guilty man. Tammy, on the other hand, had been of little help. She was so busy working and planning her new life in Spain with Richard, that Stephanie had barely seen her best friend. Tonight, however, they were going out for a farewell meal together. Tammy was moving abroad next week, so it would be the last get-together they would have for God knows how long. In a way, Steph was pleased that she and Tammy had drifted apart over the past six months or so. Tammy's high-flying career, then meeting Richard, had spelt an end to their regular routine of spending lots of time together, and in a way it kind of made Tammy's departure easier for Stephanie to deal with.

Hearing the phone ringing, Stephanie dashed into the

lounge to answer it. When Wayne had first gone missing, her heart had leapt every time the bloody thing had rung, but as the weeks had passed, Steph refused to build her hopes up any more.

'All right, darling? How are you today? I bet you're looking forward to your night out with Tammy, aren't you?' Pam asked her daughter.

'Not really, Mum. It's another person I'm losing and I know it's gonna be sad.'

'Now don't think of it like that, love. I'm sure Tammy will want you to visit her regularly in Spain, and a couple of holidays a year in the sunshine will do you the world of bloody good.'

'What am I meant to travel out there with, Mum? Shirt buttons? Apart from the few grand that I have in my bank account, I'm penniless, and I've only got three months left in this place until I'm turfed out. I can't work because of Tyler, so it looks like I'll be going cap in hand to the council and the social soon, unless a miracle happens,' Stephanie reminded her mother. Wayne had paid the first six months' rent up front for their house in Chigwell, but after that she was in shit street.

Pam sighed. Being a loving mother, it was her duty to help her children in any crisis which might befall them in life, but for once she was stumped on how to help Steph. The mystery of Wayne's disappearance had ripped the heart out of her beautiful daughter's life, and for once there was sod all that Pam could do to rectify the situation. 'What time you dropping the kids over to me, love? And don't be worrying about picking 'em up early tomorrow – I'll cook a nice roast dinner for 'em. I can do you a little dinner if you want as well?'

'Don't worry about cooking for me, Mum, but it'd be great if you can keep the kids until late afternoon tomorrow.

Barry's gonna take me out for lunch. He said it will cheer me up after saying goodbye to Tammy tonight.'

'Aw, that's kind of him.'

'I'll bring the kids over as soon as the police have been and gone. They're popping round in a minute to drop the bits off they took from the house,' Steph told Pam. The police had taken several pieces of paperwork and Wayne's mobile phone to see if they could find any clues as to what might have happened to him.

'Will you be OK speaking to the police on your own? Or is Barry gonna be there with you?' Pam asked, worriedly.

'Barry's going over to Dagenham to see Wayne's grandparents again. He said they're a crafty pair of old sods and might know more than they're letting on. He reckons they must know where Wayne's dad is in Greece, but there's no way that Wayne can have gone there as he never had his passport with him. Anyway, he would never just leave me and the kids in the lurch. Even the police said that Wayne had told everybody they had spoken to how much he loved his family.'

Pam didn't know what to think. Barry had spoken to her on the quiet and he believed that there was no way in the world that Wayne would take his own life. 'Between me and you, I reckon he's done a runner,' Barry had said.

'I'd better go now, love. Aidan'll be here soon and I want to get me housework done first. I'll see you later on.'

Barry walked up to the bar to buy Wayne's grandparents another drink. He had known Doris and Bill since he was a kid, and rather liked them, therefore had delivered his 'concerned friend' act with absolute precision. Barry hadn't asked all the questions he had told Stephanie he was going to but, over lunch with her tomorrow, he would pretend that he had. Barry put the two pints of Guinness down on the table, then shook Bill's hand and kissed Doris politely on the cheek.

'Ain't you having another one, son?' Bill asked.

'Nah, I can't. My lunatic of a mother, who has barely spoken to me for weeks, has demanded that I take her and her pal out for dinner. Bloody dreading it, I am.'

Doris chuckled. Her and Bill had lived in Bethnal Green for years before they had moved to Dagenham and knew Marlene well.

Bill stood up and shook Barry's hand. 'Well, thanks for coming to see us again, lad. Me and Doll were saying what a good bloody mate you've been to our Wayne, searching for him and taking care of his family like you have. We'd have liked to have got more involved, but me and Doll have never got on brilliantly with that Stephanie. Between us and the kitchen sink, we've never really forgiven her for ruining yours and Wayne's friendship.'

Thanking Bill for the compliment, Barry strolled out of the social club. The moment he got into his car, he laughed loudly. God sure did move in mysterious ways.

Pam opened the front door and was rather taken aback to see Angela standing there rather than Stephanie. 'What do you want?' she asked coldly. Pam hadn't yet forgiven her youngest daughter for the fiasco she had caused at Stephanie's hen night, nor what she had said to the police to embarrass her sister.

'I've just come to say goodbye,' Angela replied haughtily.

Pam looked her daughter up and down. In her black, cropped leather jacket, tight faded jeans and black leather boots that came over her knee, Pam thought how tarty she looked, but decided not to comment. 'What do you mean you've come to say goodbye?'

'Mummy,' Aidan screamed with delight as he ran towards

the front door. Twice his mum had taken him out in the past six weeks, and both times she had bought him loads of new toys. Wondering if Angela was taking him out again today, Aidan held his arms out for a cuddle.

'Your hands are filthy, Aidan, and this is Mummy's new jacket. Go and sit in the lounge while I speak to your nan for a minute,' Angela said unfeelingly.

Seeing her grandson's face crumple, Pam glared at her daughter. 'Say what you've come to say and then go, Ange. That poor little mite is crying now, you wicked mare.'

'I'm going to live in Greece for a while.'

Pam looked at Angela in bewilderment. Was this another one of her little games? 'Greece is hundreds of miles away, ain't it?'

'Yes, and that's exactly why I'm going there. I can't get over the hurt and the pain of being accused of running away with Jacko. So, as far as I'm concerned, I haven't got a family any more. I'm off to pastures new.'

'Get in the kitchen, now!' Pam growled at her daughter. She knew Angela's tricks of turning things around and Pam couldn't believe she was trying to blame the family for her selfish decision to depart to a foreign country.

'You ain't gonna make me change my mind. Roxy's moving over there with me and we've got a good job to go to.'

Pam wasn't very good with geography. The Isle of Wight was the furthest she had ever been in her life, but she knew Greece was nowhere near England. 'You can't go! What about Aidan? I know you don't put yourself out to see him very much, but you're still his bloody mother.'

'Well, you can look after him for me, can't you? Or, if you don't want him, Jason will have him.'

'We're not talking about a fucking dog, Angela. This is your son, you heartless cow. He's registered to you by the authorities, remember?'

'Look, I ain't arguing with you, Mum. I've made my mind up and I'm going. I dare say I might come back for the winter, and I'm not gonna inform the authorities I've gone, so you can still cash the child allowance. I'll even send some money home every couple of months, if you want me to?'

As Pam looked at the coldness in her daughter's eyes, and for the first time in her life, she could honestly say that she hated her. 'I don't want anything from you, Angela. Now get out of my house and don't you ever, ever darken my doorstep again, understand?'

Angela shrugged. 'Suits me, but I wanna say goodbye to Aidan before I leave.'

'You leave that boy alone,' Pam warned her.

Ignoring her mother's orders, Angela marched into the living room. 'Have you washed them chocolatey hands yet?'

'Yeah, I wiped them with Nanny's tissues,' Aidan mumbled apologetically.

Pam couldn't bear to be in the same room as Angela asked Aidan to sit on the sofa next to her and said, in a fake loving voice, 'You know Mummy took you shopping recently, Aidan, and bought you all them lovely presents?'

'Yeah! Do you wanna play with my car with me, Mummy?' Aidan asked excitedly. The remote-controlled Porsche his mother had bought him was the best present he had ever had.

'No, darling. Mummy has to leave soon and she won't be able to see you for a while. I've got a new job, you see, and it's a long way away.'

'Can I come with you?'

'No. I'd love to take you with me, but little boys aren't allowed there,' Angela lied.

Earwigging outside the door, Pam shook her head in repugnance. How she could have given birth to two such different daughters she would never know, and not for the first time in her life, Pam briefly wondered if the nurse had given her the wrong baby when she had taken Angela home.

'When will you take me out again then, Mummy?'

'I don't know yet, but I promise you when I do I'll buy you lots and lots of lovely presents. That's why I'm going away to work. It's not for me, I'm doing it for you. The money is much better where I'm going and it means I can buy you much better presents than ever before.'

Aidan threw his arms around his mother's neck and held her tightly. All his friends at school had mums that picked them up every day and came to their nativity plays and sports days, and he really wished that his could be there too sometimes. 'I love you, Mummy,' he said.

Realizing that her son was crying, Angela stood up quickly. She felt a bit tearful herself and, in that split second, knew she must love him. Roxy had been shocked when she had taken the job abroad, and Angela had broken down as she had explained her reasons to her friend. 'I ain't a bad person, Rox, but I'm a crap parent, and Aidan is far better off being bought up by my mum, his dad, and his other grandparents,' she had told her friend bluntly.

'Please don't go yet, Mummy,' Aidan sobbed, as Angela put her hand on the handle of the door.

Bending down, Angela kissed her son on his forehead. 'I have to go now, Aidan, but don't you ever forget that Mummy loves you.'

Stephanie was dismayed when she walked into the restaurant in Buckhurst Hill and saw Richard sitting at the table alongside Tammy. She had said to her friend the other evening that she felt as though she barely knew Richard, but she hadn't expected Tammy to bring him along with her. She had thought and wanted it to be just the two of them. A proper girlie farewell.

Tammy grinned as Steph walked towards her. 'Don't look so glum. Richard's only staying with us for a little while as he's off up town with his mates. He wanted to treat us to a nice bottle of champagne to start our evening off, didn't you, babe?' Tammy said.

Richard stood up and kissed Stephanie on the cheek. 'Here, let me take your coat for you.'

Steph sat down and watched Richard stroll over to the coat stand. He had a dark grey suit on, a crisp white shirt that he wore unbuttoned to reveal his toned chest, and expensive-looking tan leather shoes. With his floppy dark hair, perfect teeth and killer smile, he really was a looker. 'Well, I have to say, Tam, he is even more handsome than I thought he was when he came round mine. I was so worried about seeing Barry again for the first time in years, I didn't take enough notice of Tricky Dicky. Wow, no wonder you're giving up everything for him, mate.'

'I am so sorry to hear about Wayne going missing, Stephanie. Tammy's been telling me all about it, and I do hope he is found safe and well,' Richard said, sitting back down at the table.

The mention of Wayne being found safe and well, along with Tammy lovingly squeezing Richard's hand, was enough to make Stephanie's eyes well up. She had been with Wayne since she was fifteen years old, and not being part of a couple any more was one of the hardest things she had ever had to deal with. Wayne had never been at home that much, but it was the intimacy of sharing a cuddle or a conversation about her day and the children that Steph missed the most. The thought of living the rest of her life as a lonely single parent worried Steph even more than the financial difficulties that were heading her way.

'Are you OK?' Tammy asked.

'Yeah. I'm just thinking about how much I'm gonna miss

you,' Steph replied. She didn't want to get into another long conversation about Wayne.

'Let's make a toast to the safe return of Wayne, shall we?' Richard said, holding his glass aloft.

Stephanie joined Tammy in holding hers aloft and then made a toast of her own. 'To Richard and my best friend Tammy. Wishing you all the best for your new life in Spain.'

Tammy and Richard both looked at one another and laughed. 'To us,' they said in unison.

Barry walked into the Indian restaurant in Chadwell Heath and immediately knew why his mother and her friend had changed their original plan of him picking them up from Marge's house. He only had to glance at the pair of them to know they had been out drinking for most of the day.

Spotting Barry walking towards her, Marlene glared at the four ugly men that were sitting at the next table. They had been trying to chat her and Marge up for the past half an hour, but when Marlene had suggested they treat her and her friend to a bottle of wine, the miserly gits had refused. 'This is my handsome toy boy, the one I told you about. Now, yous tight bastards can fuck right off,' Marlene said, throwing her arms around her son's neck.

'Get off me. Everyone's looking at us,' Barry hissed.

'Me and Marge'll have a nice bottle of wine, boy,' Marlene said, flopping back down on her chair.

'Let's have red, like my arse. Look Barry, I burnt it on one of them bleedin' sunbeds,' Marge said, standing up, turning around, and pulling the waistband of her black leggings down to reveal all.

Hearing the four blokes on the next table laugh, Barry's face turned as red as Marge's backside. He leant across the table. 'If yous two show me up once more, they'll be no wine, no meal – there'll be fuck all. Understand?'

'Gertcha, you miserable little sod. Becoming more like that father of yours as every day passes, you are,' Marlene said, chuckling.

'Come on, let's behave ourselves. I'm bloody well gasping and starving,' Marge said, nudging Marlene to urge her to tone it down a bit. She didn't want to miss out on her free meal and drinks.

'Shall I order a selection of grub for all of us?' Barry asked, studying the menu. The quicker they ate and he got out of the restaurant, the better. His mother when sober was bad enough, but pissed she was an absolute nightmare.

'Oi, Gunga Din, we want two bottles of wine, one red and one white and whatever my toy boy's having,' Marge shouted to the young waiter.

Barry jumped up and walked over to where the open-mouthed waiter was standing. 'I'm really sorry. That woman's my mother. She has recently suffered a family bereavement, therefore has got herself a little bit drunk today. Just bring the two bottles of wine over, a bottled lager for me, then I'll order the food. We'll be out of your way in no time, I promise.'

As the young waiter scuttled off like a frightened mouse, Barry sat back down. 'So, why the phone call, Mum? Last time I saw you, you accused me of murdering poor old Jakey. Then, next thing I know, you're ringing me up telling me how much you love me and what a fantastic son I am. What you after, dosh?'

'Would madams like to taste the wine?' the waiter asked, quickly reappearing.

Barry shook his head. 'Nope. They'd drink petrol if it came in a bottle, mate. Can you just bring us up a selection of rice and bread? I'll have Tandoori chicken. What do yous two want as your main?' Barry asked. He waited for the order to be taken, then stared at his mother. 'Well, what you after then?'

Marlene grinned. 'I could really do with some readies, boy, and I also need you to get all me beautiful clothes sent over 'ere from Spain for me.'

Previously guessing that his mother was going to be on his earhole for cash, Barry had come well prepared. Pulling a thick wad of money out of his back pocket, he began counting off fifty-pound notes. 'Will a grand be OK?'

'I suppose it will have to be,' Marlene replied, ungratefully. 'What about me clothes though? Walking about in the same half a dozen outfits, I am. How quick can you get 'em back to England for me?'

Barry handed Marlene the wedge, then sighed. 'I don't think I'm gonna be able to get your clothes back for you. Your old gaff in Spain has already been sold, Mum.'

Marlene felt the hairs stand up on the back of her neck. 'Sold! Sold! Whaddya mean it's been fucking sold?'

'Someone bought it within days of it going up for sale. Jolene rang me to tell me a week or so back.'

To say Marlene was in a state of unadulterated shock was putting it mildly. 'I want my clothes, I want my ornaments and I want my fucking furniture back,' she screamed.

'Well I'm sorry, Mum, but apart from buying you some new clothes, I can't really help you,' Barry replied, bravely.

Leaning forwards, Marlene pointed her forefinger in her son's face. 'If I was you I'd take that statement back, because I'm telling you now, if you don't get your arse back to Spain and sort out my belongings, I shall be making a phone call to the Spanish Old Bill and I'll be telling 'em that it was you who ordered the hit on Jake. And that ain't all I'll do. I know that it's you responsible for Wayne Jackman's disappearance, you scheming little bastard. You've done him in, I know you have. Want me to go and have a chat with that little slapper Stephanie who you can't keep away from, do you? 'Cause if I don't get my stuff back, I will, you know.'

Barry shook his head in disgust. 'Now you listen to me and you listen very carefully, muvver. I had sod all to do with Jake getting killed or Jacko's disappearance, and if you don't stop spreading vicious fucking lies and spouting that vulgar mouth of yours off to every Tom, Dick and Harry, me and you are gonna come to blows. Understand?'

Marlene stood up and began waving her arms about like a lunatic to attract people's attention. She turned to the four men on the next table who she had insulted earlier. 'Did you hear what my son just said to me, lads? He has just threatened to kill his own mother and I want yous to be my witnesses. He has already tried to end my life in the past.'

'You said he was your toy boy,' one of the men replied. The other three blokes immediately started to chuckle. They had all thought that Marlene was quite attractive in a tarty sort of way earlier, but they could now tell she was a liability.

'Sit down, mate. You can't be shouting out things like that. Barry didn't mean it that way,' Marge said, grabbing Marlene's arm.

When she went into full actress mode and started to cry, Barry looked at his mother in horror. 'Sit down, for fuck's sake,' he spat.

The restaurant wasn't packed to the rafters, but Marlene was well aware that she now had everybody's attention. 'My son has already murdered my partner and his ex-girlfriend's fiancé. Now he is threatening to kill me also,' she shouted, in a posh, overly dramatic, tearful voice.

Marge put her head in her hands. She loved Marlene, but when she got a bee in her bonnet, especially when this drunk, there was truly no stopping her. Marge liked Barry. He was a good lad and, in her opinion, Marlene didn't realize how lucky she was to have such a charming, generous son.

As Marlene carried on with her amateur dramatics, Barry calmly polished off his lager. His mother going around spreading rumours that he had been responsible for Jake's murder was one thing, but her spouting off about him being responsible for Wayne's disappearance was another. Barry stood up and turned to his mother's rather stunned-looking audience. He could see the young waiter standing there with their tray of food, far too frightened to bring it over to the table. 'I am so, so sorry, everybody, for my mother's outrageous behaviour. As you have probably already realized, she is an old lush with a severe alcohol dependency, which makes her talk utter rubbish and behave in this appalling manner.'

When his mother's posh voice turned into her usual coarse one, Barry couldn't help but smirk as he clocked the shocked look on the other diners' faces.

'You muggy little cunt,' Marlene screamed at the top of her voice.

'This is my mother's true self. This is what I've had to put up with since I was a child,' Barry said loudly.

Livid that her son had not only made her look a joke, but had also caused her façade to slip, Marlene picked up Barry's empty lager bottle and threw it as hard as she could at his cocky little face.

Unfortunately for Marlene, the bottle completely missed Barry, but hit a grey-haired woman on the table behind. When the woman fell onto the floor clutching her head, all hell seemed to break loose. Two waiters grabbed hold of Marlene, Marge lashed out at them, and all Barry could do was the sensible thing. He legged it.

CHAPTER THIRTY-ONE

Ever since they were young, Stephanie and Tammy had always enjoyed spending time alone together. As kids they would sit in one another's bedrooms and learn the words to their favourite pop songs from the magazine, *Smash Hits*. Then at Sunday teatime, they would sing along and dance while listening to the top-forty countdown. When they reached their teenage years, standing on a street corner, or dossing about over the park with a bottle of cider and a packet of cigarettes was their preferred way of whiling away their time together. When they were old enough to get served in pubs, that's what they did, but just recently, they loved nothing more than going out for a nice meal. Whatever they did together, Stephanie and Tammy had always had fun, but tonight was an exception. When Stephanie had first been told that Tammy was leaving England for sunnier climes, obviously she had been heartbroken at the thought of losing her best friend. However, with Wayne vanishing off the face of the earth, having to cancel her wedding, money worries, and the disappointment of not being able to open her own beauty salon, Tammy's departure was now the least of Stephanie's problems. In fact, she rather liked Richard and genuinely wished Tammy well in her new life, which is why Steph couldn't understand her friend's bolshy attitude since her boyfriend had left the restaurant earlier.

As Tammy yet again interrupted her reminiscing about old times to start banging on about how positive she was that Barry Franklin had murdered Wayne, Stephanie started to get rather annoyed. This was her first night out since Wayne had disappeared, her last night out with Tammy for the foreseeable future, and with no kids to worry about until tomorrow afternoon at least, all Stephanie had wanted to do was let her hair down and forget about her troubles, even if it was only for one evening. She turned to Tammy. 'Can you stop going on about Barry murdering Wayne, please? I've come out to enjoy myself tonight for a change, Tam. The Old Bill came round earlier asking loads more questions and I'm sick to death of talking about it. What is it with you and Barry Franklin? You used to like him when we were at school, so why do you hate him so much now?'

Tammy took another big slurp of wine. She had been drinking like a fish ever since Richard had left earlier. 'I'm sorry, Steph, but Wayne hasn't just miraculously vanished into thin air, has he? Don't you think it's strange that your ex-boyfriend returns from Spain and a couple of weeks later the bloke you left him for goes missing?'

'Well yeah, if I was an outsider looking in, I suppose it might sound suspect, but the police have spoken to Barry numerous times and they don't think he had anything to do with Wayne's disappearance. Neither do I, neither does my mum. Since Wayne went missing, I've barely seen you, Tam. I know you've been busy wrapping up your job and stuff, but that ain't the point. Apart from my family, Barry has been the only person who has supported me through all this. There isn't a day goes by when he doesn't ring or pop round. He's helped me with the kids; in fact he's helped me with everything, and that certainly ain't no behaviour of a guilty man, if you ask me.'

With a snarl on her face, Tammy shrugged her shoulders. 'If you wanna bury your head in the sand then that's your prerogative. Wayne's your fiancé, not mine, and if you think being pals with his murderer is the right thing to do, then carry on doing what you're doing, Steph.'

Stephanie was furious. How dare Tammy accuse her of betraying the man she loved and was about to marry. On the point of tearing into her best friend, Stephanie took a deep breath and somehow managed to restrain herself. 'Look Tam, I don't wanna fall out with you, so can we just please talk about something else? I haven't told you about Angie yet, have I?'

Tammy sighed. 'I'm sorry, mate. It's just that I'm going away, and I hate to think of Barry sniffing around you when I'm not there to protect you any more. You do know I only warn you of these things because I care so much about you, don't ya?'

Stephanie nodded. Part of her wanted to remind Tammy that she hadn't been there protecting her recently while she still lived in England, but she decided to say nothing. 'I know you care. I love you and you love me. Now, let's change the subject.'

Tammy grinned. 'Tell me about Angie, then.'

When Stephanie began telling the story of Angela moving to Greece, Tammy gesticulated to the waiter to bring over another bottle of wine. 'What a terrible fucking mother that sister of yours is. People like her should have their fannies sewn up,' she said, giggling.

Relieved that Tammy had now stopped going on about Barry, Steph began to knock the wine back as quickly as her friend was. 'So are you and Tricky Dicky gonna have kids? Have you spoken about it yet?' she asked.

'Yeah, I'd like one straight away, but Richard wants us to wait a bit. I think he want us to settle in Spain properly first and be together for a bit longer before we take the plunge of including children in our lives.'

'You never know, he might even propose soon,' Steph replied. Even though her own wedding had been so cruelly snatched away from her, she would still be happy for her friend if she was to get engaged to Richard.

'So, whereabouts in Greece is Angie going to work?' Tammy asked, changing the subject.

'My mum don't know, Ange never told her. I know we're laughing about it, Tam, but it ain't funny really. Say something bad was to happen to Aidan while she was away. I mean, he could fall ill or have a bad accident, and we wouldn't even be able to contact Angie and tell her. I know Ange is a crappy person and an awful mother, but my mum did hear her tell Aidan she loves him. He adores her, that little boy, he's such a little sweetie, so I really hope for his sake that she rings up and writes to him from time to time.'

'Don't you think it's a bit strange that she's all of a sudden darting off to a foreign country without giving an address?' Tammy asked.

'Not really. Angie has always been a selfish bitch, hasn't she?'

'Look, please don't have a go at me for saying this, but you don't think she's running away to be with Wayne or something, do you? I mean, the police did say that she left the club that night the same time as him, didn't they?'

Stephanie nearly choked on her drink, and for the second time that evening was absolutely livid at her friend's stupid comments. Did Tammy think that Wayne didn't love her or something? Did she honestly think that he would opt out of their forthcoming marriage and abandon his own two children to run off with her airhead of a sister? 'I can't believe you just said that. What sort of fucking mate are you, eh Tam?'

'What do you mean? I'm sorry if I've upset you, but Wayne and Ange did have a thing going years ago, didn't they? She lost her virginity to him, didn't she? Or have I got the wrong bloke?' Tammy asked sarcastically.

Stephanie looked at her pal in total disbelief. She knew Tammy was drunk, but even so, that was no excuse for what she had just said. Steph stood up, rooted through her handbag and threw thirty quid on the table.

'What's that for? What you doing?' Tammy asked.

'That's to pay for my meal and drinks. I'm going home.'

Tammy grabbed Steph by the arm. 'Please don't go. At least let's finish our drinks first.'

Aware that people were staring at them, Stephanie moved her face closer to Tammy's. 'Let go of me,' she hissed.

Tammy let go, and as Stephanie stormed out of the restaurant she was vaguely aware of two things. One was Tammy sobbing, and the other was her yelling out, 'I'm sorry.' Ignoring both, Steph carried on walking.

Barry pulled up in the car park at the Harrow pub in Hornchurch. He had got sick of living in a hotel and driving a hired car, so had recently taken out a three-month lease on a flat in Emerson Park, and bought himself a cheap motor. He couldn't wait to get back to Spain now, and as soon as his mission was complete, he would be off like a shot. Picturing his stunning girlfriend, Barry dialled her number. 'Hello sweetheart. How are you today?'

Stephanie let herself indoors, collapsed on the sofa and sobbed. Could her life get any worse at the moment? Somehow, she didn't think so. Desperately needing someone to talk to, Steph debated whether to ring her mother, but quickly decided against it. Her mum had enough on her plate looking after Aidan and it wasn't fair to keep worrying her. Realizing that she now only had one true friend in the world who would understand the way she felt, Steph picked up the phone and rang him.

'Can you come round, Barry?' she wept.

'What's up? Is it Jacko? Have they found him?'

'No. I've fallen out with Tammy and I really feel like getting drunk and having a good old chinwag. You ain't gotta go home. You can stop here the night in the spare room. Please say you will, Bal.'

Barry smirked. 'I'm on me way.'

Over at Dagenham East Police Station, Marlene and Marge were in opposite cells to one another. When the police had been called to the restaurant, both women had tried to do a runner. Marge was so fat, though, she'd barely been able to waddle, let alone run, and Marlene hadn't wanted her pal to take all the blame for something that was her fault.

'You all right, Patsy?' Marge shouted out. She and Marlene still hadn't given the police their real names. Because they were inebriated, they had thought it quite hilarious to give the police the names of the characters out of their favourite TV programme, *Absolutely Fabulous*. Marlene had told the Old Bill that she was Patsy, while Marge had called herself Eddy. The police hadn't got the joke and had thought Marlene and Marge were actually giving their real identities. In the end, short-staffed and unable to trace any address for the two women, officers slung Marge and Marlene into the cells to sober up.

'Yep, I'm fine, Eddy. Don't fancy spending all night in here though, do you?' Marlene replied.

'Why don't you ask if you can ring your Barry, mate? They offered us a phone call, didn't they? He can send a solicitor down 'ere for us, so we can go home. I'm dying for a crap and I can't shit in 'ere, can I?' Marge shouted out.

At the mention of her son, Marlene's face twisted with anger. She was disgusted that he'd run off tonight and allowed her and Marge to be arrested. 'I ain't asking that little bastard for any help tonight, but I tell you what I am gonna do for us, mate.'

'What?'

'I'm gonna blackmail him so we can go on a nice holiday. I'm gonna tell him if he don't give me five grand, I'm gonna tell the Spanish authorities what he did to Jake the Snake.'

'You can't do that, mate. Your Barry ain't a bad lad. I'm sure you've got it all wrong,' Marge replied, horrified.

'I can do what I fucking well like. But he ain't bad, you got that bit right – my Barry's pure evil. The boy's a mass murderer.'

'Don't be so bleedin' stupid,' Marge said.

'And who's this mass murderer we're talking about?' a young PC asked cockily as he approached Marlene's cell.

Marlene snarled at the fresh-faced PC. 'Mind your own fucking business, you spotty-faced little cunt.'

Over in Chigwell, Stephanie had just greeted Barry with open arms.

'It's OK, babe. You let it all out. How you've been so brave recently I'll never know,' Barry said, hugging Stephanie and stroking her hair. Even though Steph had relied on him over the past month or so, she had never been touchy-feely with him up until now, and he guessed he was finally winning her over, just like he'd hoped he would. 'You said you wanted to get drunk, so look what I bought us,' Barry said, gesturing to the two big carrier bags he'd put down by the door.

Stephanie peered inside the two bags. One contained a big bottle of Strongbow Cider. The other, four cans of Holsten Pils and twenty Benson and Hedges. 'Talk about memories of our youth. I haven't drunk cider for years, nor do I really smoke any more,' Steph said.

'I don't drink Holsten any more and I only ever smoke socially now, but what the heck? I bought a couple of Eighties tapes with me as well. I thought a night reliving our youth and doing the stuff we used to might cheer you up a bit.'

Stephanie couldn't help but grin. 'You are so thoughtful, Barry.'

'Yep, I know I am. Now, tell me about Tam while I pour us both a drink. Do you wanna slurp the cider out the bottle like you used to? Or, you gonna use a glass like the lady you are now?'

Stephanie opted for a glass, then sat down next to Barry on the sofa.

Barry listened intently as Stephanie explained what had happened with Tammy earlier. His ears pricked up when Steph told him that Tammy had been insistent for the past few weeks that it was he who was responsible for Wayne's disappearance, but he said nothing until Steph had finished telling her story in full. 'I'm really shocked Tammy seems to have it in for me so much. I always got on all right with her while I was going out with you. It was Jacko, Potter and Cooksie who took the piss out of her being ginger and stuff, not me. She's bang out of order blaming me for Jacko going missing. I didn't even leave the club with him, you know that, so do the Old Bill.'

'I know you didn't, but Tam has this stupid theory that you somehow bumped into him on the way back to the hotel, topped him, then buried him in a nearby forest. I know it's mental, but Tammy's always had a vivid imagination. I wouldn't worry about it too much, Bal, as when I told her that Angie was going to live in Greece, she said that she was running off to live with Wayne as well. Tam's changed so bloody much since she met that Richard, I'm glad she's emigrating now. Good riddance is what I say.'

Putting a casual arm around Stephanie's shoulders, Barry kissed his ex-girlfriend on the top of the head. 'Fuck Tammy and her ponce of a boyfriend. Chin up, you've still got me, babe. I'll be your new best friend.'

Stephanie stared into Barry's soft brown doleful eyes and, for the first time since she had got with Wayne, she saw what she had seen all those years ago. A handsome, kind, honest person, who would one day make a wonderful husband and father to some lucky girl.

Aware of the nostalgic way that Stephanie was looking at him, Barry debated whether to go in for the kill, but quickly decided against it. He knew Steph was warming to him, but she hadn't completely fallen hook, line and sinker for him yet and he didn't want to jeopardize the outcome of his plan. He stood up. 'Right, I'll put on the Eighties music while you pour us some more drinks. Tonight, Miss Crouch, you will forget all your troubles, because me and you are gonna party, girl.'

And party Stephanie and Barry most certainly did. Over the next few hours, they sang along to all the songs that reminded them of their teenage years, drank two bottles of Wayne's expensive champagne after they had polished off the cider and lager, reminisced about old times and even got up and danced to a Duran Duran record for a giggle.

Stephanie knew that she was very drunk, but for the first time in weeks the smile on her face was genuine. Tomorrow, she would probably wake up and have the weight of the world on her shoulders once again, but tonight she was having a blast and that was all down to Barry Franklin. In her heart of hearts, Steph was sure that Wayne wasn't ever coming back home again. What had happened to him would play on her mind forever, but one day she would have to move on with her life, whether she learned the truth or not. When Barry began singing along to 'The Love Cats' by The Cure, Stephanie laid her head on his shoulder. It had been years since she and Wayne had spent a night laughing, drinking, singing and chatting intimately like she and Barry just had, and it made Steph wonder if her relationship with Wayne had been as good as she thought it had.

Barry tilted Stephanie's chin towards him. 'What's up? What you thinking about?'

Not wanting to slag off her relationship with her missing fiancé, Steph shrugged her shoulders. 'I'm just thinking about how much I've enjoyed myself tonight. Do you have nights like this with your girlfriend, Barry? What's Jolene like? Tell me more about her.'

'Jolene's only a baby and she wouldn't be interested in the music we listen to or the subjects we talk about. She's a lovely girl, but I wouldn't say I have as much in common with her as I do with you.'

'So, why are you with her then? Why don't you go out with someone older who you have more in common with, like me?'

Treating Stephanie to his killer, intense stare, Barry smiled. 'Do you want the truth?'

Steph could feel her heart beating at double its usual speed. 'Yeah I do.'

'The reason I don't go out with someone older who I have more in common with, like you, is because there is only one you, Steph.'

About to ask Barry exactly what he meant, Stephanie stopped herself from doing so. Barry's penetrating gaze told her all she needed to know. Over the course of the evening,

Stephanie had drunk an enormous amount of alcohol so whether it was that, or the thought of spending the rest of her life alone that was affecting her judgement, she really didn't know. What she did know was that, as she locked lips with Barry for the first time in years, it not only felt good, it also felt so bloody right.

CHAPTER THIRTY-TWO

Stephanie felt mortified when she woke up the following morning. Her last memory of the previous night was of her asking Barry to go to bed with her, and then bursting into tears when he said no. Gingerly sitting up, Stephanie put her aching head in her hands. She was fully clothed, thank God, but she could recall the heavy petting session with Barry getting rather heated at one point. Stephanie stared at the photo of her and Wayne on the bedside cabinet. It had been taken on her twenty-first birthday at the party Wayne had organized for her as a surprise. Feeling incredibly guilty and absolutely disgusted with herself, Steph felt the watery bile reach the back of her throat. She dashed to the toilet, and moments later was violently sick.

Barry Franklin was inside Dagenham East Police Station. He had received a phone call from his mother at seven a.m. this morning to inform him that she and Marge were getting charged with being drunk and disorderly and affray. With it being a Sunday, Barry had told his mother to use the duty solicitor, and then he had driven straight to the nick. Steph had still been in bed when all this had happened, so Barry had left her a note telling her he would call her later this afternoon. Last night was a bit of a blur for Barry as well. They had sat up boozing until four a.m., and even though Barry had been tempted to go to bed with Stephanie and shag her brains out, he knew he'd done the right thing by saying no. Taking advantage of Stephanie while she was drunk wasn't part of his plan. He needed to reel her in more first, and it was a tad too early for him to make his move just yet. As his mother and Marge walked towards him looking rather bedraggled, Barry stood up. 'Was the solicitor OK? What did he say?'

'He just advised us to say no comment. He reckons we'll get a hefty fine, but that's all. No thanks to you running off and leaving us in the lurch, may I add,' Marlene said, obnoxiously.

Barry led them around the corner to where he had parked the car. 'Look, don't be worrying about your fines, 'cause I'll pay 'em for both of you. As for me leaving the restaurant, I can't afford to be getting meself nicked over 'ere. Say it had turned really nasty and I'd got nicked for GBH or something? I can't be having my passport taken away from me. I need to get back home to Spain soon.'

'I can't understand why you're still hanging around in England? I thought you'd have gone back to Spain like a shot to get your grubby little maulers on my bloody bar. It's that slag, Stephanie, that's keeping you 'ere, ain't it? You poking her, or what?' Marlene asked crudely.

'No, Mother. I'm not "poking her", as you so daintily put it. I'm still over here because I have a few loose ends to tie up. Once that's done, I'll be heading back to Spain immediately.'

'What loose ends you got to tie up, then?'

'Nothing for you to worry your pretty little head about. Now, do you want me to drop you back at Marge's gaff or somewhere else? You didn't lose that dosh I gave you last night, did ya?'

'The money's still in my bag, I checked, and yeah, take us to Marge's. I was saying to Marge while we were stuck in those pissy-smelling cells last night, that me and her could really do with a nice holiday abroad somewhere. Really cheer us up, that would.'

'Don't you dare blackmail him,' Marge hissed in her friend's ear. She had been appalled last night when Marlene had said she was going to. In Marge's eyes, blackmailing your own flesh and blood was as below the belt as anything.

Barry sighed. He knew his mother was on his earhole for more money, and because he still felt guilty about nearly strangling her years ago, decided to be generous once again. 'I'll tell you what I'll do for you. Meet me in Romford outside the Royal Bank of Scotland at midday tomorrow, and I'll take you to a travel agent and book you an all-inclusive somewhere nice. I'll pay for you and Marge and I'll give you a bit of spending money. But, only on one condition.'

'What?' Marlene asked, sulkily.

'If I treat you to this holiday, then I want you to stop banging on about me murdering Jake and Jacko. It's bollocks, Mum, you know it is, and it's embarrassing when people keep coming up to me saying you've said these things.'

'Say yes,' Marge urged, nudging Marlene's arm. She hadn't had a decent holiday for years and couldn't wait to get stuck into all the free drink and food on an all-inclusive. Some people might not get their money's worth on those types of trips, but she bloody well would.

'OK, I won't say it no more.'

'Ain't you got anything else to add to that?' Barry asked, taking a sharp right turn.

'Like what?' Marlene asked, stroppily.

'Like I'm sorry for saying it in the first place, and thank you son for paying for me and my friend to go on holiday,' Barry replied. His mother was such an ungrateful cow at times. Always had been, always bloody would be.

Marlene felt her lip curl into a snarl. She had just spent the whole night stuck in a cell because her son had run off and allowed her to be arrested, yet she was now meant to grovel and thank him. 'If it weren't for me you'd never have been born, boy, so if I were you I'd just shut your trap and fucking drive.'

Barry smirked. That was exactly the kind of reply he had been expecting.

Pamela Crouch knew her daughter like the back of her hand. After trying to call Stephanie for the past few hours, as soon as she finally got through to her, she knew by the tone of Steph's voice that something was dreadfully wrong. 'Whatever's the matter, love? Have you heard some news about Wayne?'

The mention of her missing fiancé immediately sent Stephanie into a blubbing mess. The guilt she felt was immense. Poor Wayne could be lying dead in a ditch somewhere, for all she knew. Too embarrassed to admit to her mother what had happened with Barry, Steph blamed the argument with Tammy for her upset.

'Why don't you come over 'ere and stay with me tonight, love? Aidan's gone to Ireland with his dad and grandparents, so you can stop in your old bedroom. Lin's coming for dinner and I know she'd love to see you. I ain't at work tomorrow, either, so we can go out for lunch or something before you go home, if you want?'

Stephanie had read Barry's note twice, then screwed it up and threw it in the bin. If Barry was going to ring this afternoon, she knew full well that if he didn't get any answer he would turn up at her door, and she couldn't bring herself to speak to him, let alone face him. She made her decision there and then. 'I'll have a quick shower, then I'll be over, Mum.'

An hour later, Stephanie was driving over Dagenham Heathway hill when her phone started to ring. She pulled over. Seeing the caller was Barry, she waited for it to stop ringing, then turned the bloody thing off. She closed her eyes. 'Dear God. I can't be alone, I'm not strong enough. Please find my Wayne and send him home to me. Amen.'

Stephanie waited for her tears to subside, then continued her journey.

'Mummy,' Dannielle yelled, running out of the house to greet her.

'You all right, darling? Where's your brother? Has he been behaving himself?'

'No, Mum. Tyler's been naughty,' Dannielle replied, honestly.

Pam gave her daughter a big hug as she walked into the hallway. 'You OK, love? Don't be worrying about Tammy. I'm sure she'll be in touch before she goes to Spain.'

'I'm not bothered if she rings me or not, to be honest. Has Tyler been OK?'

'He had one little tantrum earlier, but he's been fine other than that,' Pam replied. She had marks on her already swollen ankles where the little sod had kicked her, but she wasn't about to tell Steph that. Her daughter had enough on her plate as it was. 'Do you want a cup of tea, love?'

'No, but I could kill a glass of wine,' Steph said, handing her mum a carrier bag. She had stopped at the off-licence on the way over and bought a couple of bottles.

'Try and find out what's a matter with Lin for me. She's been ever so quiet since she got 'ere and she asked for a cuppa rather than a beer. Keith's gone up the Vernon for a pint with Michael and I don't think they'd had a row as they seemed friendly enough towards one another. She'll talk to you,' Pam whispered in her daughter's ear.

Pam made sure everybody had a drink then sat down on the sofa. She was in hysterics as Cathy told Linda and Stephanie the story of Barry's sister Chantelle, who'd had a fight in the street earlier with her ex-boyfriend. Pam and Cath had found it compelling viewing. It was pure comedy gold.

'Talk about like mother like daughter. How that poor Barry ever got lumbered with Chantelle as a sister and Marlene as a mother, I will never know. He's such a lovely boy compared to those two,' Pam said.

Stephanie didn't answer and was relieved when Dannielle asked, 'What time will dinner be ready?'

When her mum and Cathy dashed out to the kitchen to start dishing up, Steph moved over to where Linda was sitting. 'What's up with you? Why aren't you drinking?'

Linda took a deep breath. 'If I tell you, don't say nothing to your mum until Keith gets back, will ya?'

'What's a matter? You're not ill, are you?' Stephanie asked anxiously.

Linda grinned. 'No. I'm up the duff.'

Barry was sitting in a restaurant in Hornchurch, tucking into a bit of steak. He had been trying to ring Stephanie for the past three hours and knew she must be purposely avoiding his calls. Pushing his plate to one side, Barry took a sip of his lager. As a lad he had fantasized over what it would be like to make love to Stephanie many a time, and for a long time after he had split with her, Barry had still had some weird obsession about her. He had hated Steph with a passion, yet he'd always slept with girls who reminded him of her in some way. He had slept with loads of other birds, too, ones who hadn't reminded him of Steph, but it was the ones who had, whom he'd enjoyed the sex with more. Picking up his mobile, Barry tried both of Stephanie's numbers once again. He knew she must feel embarrassed over what had happened the previous evening, so he motioned to the waiter to bring him the bill. Barry downed the rest of his drink and ran his fingers through his hair. Last night's shenanigans had disturbed him slightly, and he knew that the quicker he did what he had to do and sodded off back to Spain, the better. Leaving thirty quid on the table, Barry stood up. It was time to pay Stephanie a little visit.

Back in Dagenham, Pam was in a state of incredulous shock. 'Pregnant! Whaddya mean, you're pregnant?'

Keith squeezed Linda's hand. 'Lin means that me and her are going to have a baby, Pam. What do you think she means?' he asked.

Pam started to laugh. 'You're winding me up, you pair of sods, ain't ya?'

It was now Stephanie's turn to squeeze her mother's hand. 'Lin isn't joking, Mum. She really is pregnant.'

'But you can't have a baby. You're forty next month and how you gonna cope with your size, Lin?' Pam stuttered.

Linda shook her head in annoyance. Seconds later she gave her elder sister what for. 'You're just like Mum deep down, ain't ya, Pam? You pretend you ain't, but I know that you are. I will always be grateful to you for letting me live with you when Mum died, but whenever I'm around you, I know you see me as different. And why? Because I'm a dwarf, that's why. What you seem to forget, sis, is that I'm still a woman. A woman that unbeknown to you has craved to have the love of a good man and a child of my own for many years. I never told you that, why would I? I always knew you'd behave like this if I ever mentioned the fact that I wanted a baby. Well, let me tell you something. After years of being treated like a freak and a fucking outcast, my dreams have finally come true. So don't you dare try and spoil this happy moment for me, Pam. Don't you dare!'

Pam's eyes welled up. 'I'm not trying to spoil anything for you, Lin. I just worry about you, that's all. Both you and Keith are heavy drinkers and surely there's a fifty-fifty chance that your child might be born a dwarf. Have you even thought about that?'

Absolutely livid, Linda walked over to where Pam was sitting and pointed a stubby finger in her face. 'Have I had a drink today? No, I fucking haven't! As for the chances of my baby being born with dwarfism, so what if it is? I'm gonna love my baby whatever size, shape or deformity it might have. Even if it was born with no fingers or toes, or had Down's Syndrome or something, I would still love that child more than any mother could. And do you know why? Because I know what it's like to be different.'

'I'm sorry, Lin. Let's not fall out over this,' Pam said, wiping her eyes with a tissue.

'Stick your sorrys up your arse, 'cause I ain't in the mood for 'em today,' Lin said bluntly. She walked over to her boyfriend and grabbed him by the hand. 'Come on, Keith, we're going home.'

Barry pulled up on Stephanie's driveway. Wayne's hire-purchase car had gone back last week, but Steph's car wasn't there either, and Barry wondered if she had hidden it around the corner because she was trying to avoid him. He knocked on the front door. The house was in darkness, so he put his ear to the letterbox to see if he could hear the kids at all. He couldn't hear a dickie bird, and after numerous knocks and rings on the bell, he was sure that no one was home.

Kicking at the gravel in frustration, Barry got back in his car. The only other place he could think of where Steph could be was her mother's house. Debating whether to drive straight round there, Barry decided not to. He would go to a nearby pub, and if Stephanie wasn't home in the next couple of hours, he would then take a little trip over to Dagenham.

When Cathy and Michael left, Steph put the kids to bed, then she and her mum shared a much-needed bottle of wine between them.

'I'm so worried about Lin, Steph, and it ain't just her height. She's nearly forty, for Christ's sake. I never knew my mum's sister, but I remember my mum telling me that she had a kid in her forties and died in childbirth. Say that happens to Lin. I mean, say her little frame can't cope with pushing a baby out?'

Stephanie said nothing. She could understand why her mum was concerned about Lin, but she had so much going on in her own life at the moment, her aunt falling pregnant was the least of her worries.

Sensing that Steph had other things on her mind, Pam squeezed her daughter's hand. 'Do you want to tell me why you and Tammy fell out?' she asked.

Stephanie explained in detail what had happened at the restaurant. She was still furious with Tammy for ruining what should have been a great farewell evening for both of them.

'Well, I dunno what to say, love, but the only reason I can think of why Tam has got it in for poor Barry so much is that she's worried he's after you. I mean, it would take a blind person not to see that he's in love with you, Steph. I've seen the way he looks at you and it's more than just friendly glances. I've watched him, and sometimes he can't take his eyes off you. I think he's actually besotted with you.'

Stephanie felt her heart pounding in her chest. 'Barry doesn't think like that. He's too much of a gentleman, Mum. Anyway, he knows how much I love Wayne. How could I even think of moving on while I have no idea where my fiancé is or whether he is dead or alive?'

Pam sighed. She was under no illusion that Wayne was ever coming back. The police had all but said so themselves the last time she had spoken to them. 'Do you want my honest opinion, love?'

Stephanie nodded.

'I don't think Wayne's gonna be coming home, darling, so if I was you I wouldn't look a gift horse in the mouth by turning Barry down. You ain't got to rush into anything. Just take things one day at a time. Barry's ever so good with the kids; Dannielle adores him. So why don't you just take things slowly and see how it goes? Men like Barry don't come along every day of the week, and he'll always provide for you, I know he will. Surely that's better than being a one-parent bloody family in council accommodation, relying on handouts from the social?'

Stephanie looked at her mum in astonishment. Was she saying what she thought she was saying? 'Didn't you like Wayne or something, Mum? And what makes you think he ain't ever coming back home? Do you know something I don't?'

'Of course I liked Wayne, but if you want the truth, I never thought that you and him were particularly well suited. I thought his fathering skills left a lot to be desired, an' all, if you want total honesty. He was never there for them kids, if you ask me. As for him not coming back, the police said that to me. I don't think they know whether he's taken his own life, had a breakdown and sodded off or what, but I know they don't think he's ever coming home again.'

With her brain feeling as though it were about to explode, Stephanie held her head in her hands. She had loved Wayne with all her heart and had thought that their relationship had been idyllic, but the time she had recently spent with Barry had put a different light on matters. Had her and Wayne's relationship really been that good? Or, had she thought they were the perfect couple because she had settled down so young and didn't know any bloody different? The one thing she did know was that Barry was far more attentive towards her and the kids than Wayne had ever been.

'Are you OK, love? Shall I pour us another drink?' Pam suggested, putting a comforting arm around her daughter's shoulder.

Stephanie lifted her head up and smiled sadly. 'You pour us some drinks, Mum, but can you give me five minutes? I need to make a phone call.'

Pam immediately stood up. 'Who you ringing? Tammy?'

Stephanie shook her head. 'No, Mum. I need to speak to Barry.'

Grinning, Pam left the room.

CHAPTER THIRTY-THREE

With her mum's wise words firmly in her mind, over the next couple of weeks Stephanie spent more and more time in Barry's company. She had completely accepted now that Wayne wasn't coming back, although she could never truly rest until she had found out what had happened to him. The police had turned up unexpectedly the other day with a few pieces of useless information. They had informed Stephanie that they had questioned hundreds of cab drivers in and around the Soho area, but there were no sightings of Wayne. They had also said that some of Wayne's business dealings didn't quite add up and they were looking into the matter further.

'Where we going today, Mummy?' Dannielle asked, jumping up and down on the bed in the new pretty red dress that Barry had bought her last week.

Stephanie smiled. Dannielle was far more beautiful than she had ever been. Today, Barry was taking them all out once again, and since he had been spending every day with her and the children, even Tyler's behaviour had improved dramatically. Her son was even speaking better now as Barry had spent so much time reading children's books to him to help him pronounce his words properly.

Whenever Steph felt as though she was betraying Wayne by spending too much time with Barry, she consoled herself by remembering she was doing it mainly for the children's sake. They needed the stability of having a man in their lives, just as much as she did, and if she did decide to take her relationship with Barry to the next level, at least her kids would never have to suffer the trauma of living on some rough council estate. Barry had even said that he would help her set up a salon and finance it, so one day if it took off like she hoped it would, she could send her children to private school. He told her that it was what Wayne would have expected and wanted him to do.

'Barry'll be here in a minute. Now stop jumping up and down, else you'll ruin your nice outfits,' Stephanie ordered her children.

'Why aren't you and Uncle Barry staying at Nanny's with me and Tyler?' Dannielle asked, nosily.

At the mention of Barry and the evening ahead, Stephanie felt jittery. Apart from the odd friendly kiss, nothing had happened between herself and Barry since that night they'd got drunk together. Their inebriated fumble had rarely been mentioned since, but Stephanie knew that as every day passed, her feelings and longing for Barry had grown stronger and stronger. She was sure he also felt the same way about her: women could just sense these things. Tonight they were having dinner alone indoors together, and Stephanie knew that if the inevitable didn't happen this evening, then it probably never would.

'You not answered me, Mummy,' Dannielle said, poking Steph in the arm.

'Sorry, darling. Me and Barry can't stay at Nannys with you because Aidan will be there and there isn't enough room. Now, let's go downstairs and wait for Uncle Barry, shall we? He'll be here in a minute.'

As both of her children ran down the stairs screaming excitedly, one thing crossed Stephanie's mind. Neither child had mentioned or asked about their father for weeks.

Busy polishing Aidan's school shoes in the garden, Pam didn't hear the phone ring.

'Nanny, Auntie Lin wants you on the phone,' Aidan yelled, opening the back door.

Pam felt her heart lurch as she dropped her brush and ran into the house. She had apologized to Lin two or three times since the night her sister had first told her she was pregnant, but Lin had been quite wooden towards her and this was the first time she had rung Pam since the falling out. Praying that nothing was wrong, Pam's hands shook as she held the phone to her ear. 'You all right, Lin? What's up?'

'Nothing. It's just that Keith's gone on a beano to Margate with our mates from the pub and I didn't wanna go because I couldn't drink. Keith offered to stop at home with me, but I told him to go and bleedin' enjoy himself. Is it all right if I come round yours for a bit? I don't know the first thing about pregnancy or babies and I thought you might be able to give me some useful tips.'

'Of course I'll give you some tips. You gonna stay for a bit of dinner? I've made a nice minced beef and onion pie.'

'Yes please. I'm starving! I'll be leaving to get the bus in about ten minutes.'

Replacing the handset, Pam grinned like a Cheshire cat. After two weeks of barely speaking, she finally had her sister back.

Dannielle and Tyler were in their element as they studied all the different animals. Wayne had always banned the kids from having a pet, so Dannielle and Tyler had rarely had any contact with cats and dogs, let alone sheep, cows, pigs and chickens.

'Moo, moo,' Tyler yelled, running towards the fence where the cows were.

'No, Tyler. You're not allowed to go too close,' Stephanie said, grabbing her son's hand. It had been Barry's idea to come to the farmyard. They had an open weekend and, because it was such a glorious, sunny day, the place was packed with families making the most of the freak April weather.

'Can I have an ice cream, Uncle Barry?' Dannielle asked, putting her little hand in his.

Barry felt sad as he glanced down at Dannielle. He had grown to love the child almost as much as if she was his own and he was going to miss her dreadfully when he headed back to Spain. He forced a smile and turned to Stephanie. 'Tyler's arms look a bit sunburnt. Shall we head off to a nearby pub? We can have a couple of drinks and the kids can have an ice cream in there.'

Stephanie nodded. She had thoroughly enjoyed all the family days out she'd had recently with Barry and the kids. Wayne had never been very family orientated. He had always been too obsessed with work to spend any quality time with her and the children. Steph was now positive that she should make a go of it with Barry, but she needed to ask him some important questions first. Jolene was still Barry's fiancée, and Steph was desperate to know whether he planned on ending his relationship with her before she gave him her all. Getting her heart broken again was the last thing that she needed.

Over in Dagenham, Pam and Lin were having a lovely afternoon. Cathy had gone round to her eldest son and daughter-in-law's house with Michael. Aidan was out with his father, and Pam was pleased that for once her house wasn't like Casey's Court and she could spend some quality time alone with her sister.

'So, have you thought of any names yet?' Pam asked Lin. She was still inwardly worried about how her sister would cope with childbirth and looking after a baby, but Lin was so full of it, Pam couldn't help but feel pleased for her.

'Keith said if it's a boy we should name it after him. I told him bollocks. I ain't having no son of mine called bleedin' Keith. Anyway, I got me own way as per usual, and if it's a boy we're now gonna call him David, after your David.'

Pam felt full of emotion as she squeezed her little sister's hand. Her husband, David, had meant the world to her, and they had been so happy before he had been killed in a freak work accident. 'That's one of the nicest things anyone has ever done for me, Lin. I'm a bit lost for words, to be honest.'

Aware that Pam was near to tears, Lin put her little arms around her neck. 'No more arguing between us, eh? I hate falling out with you. I'd rather lose me right leg than lose you as a sister.'

Pam immediately starting blubbing. 'Sod you, Lin! I invited you round for a bleedin' laugh.'

Lin chuckled. 'You heard anything from Angie yet?'

Pam shook her head. 'Poor little Aidan keeps asking when he's gonna see her next. He know's she working away, but I could kick meself for not getting a contact number or address off her. I know she's a bastard, Lin, but I still worry about her. Say she bleedin' disappears like Wayne did or something? A young girl doing all that raunchy dancing in a strange country with a load of foreign men leering at her has to be in danger, surely?'

Lin chuckled. 'Knowing Angie she'll punch any bloke

who even looks at her in the wrong way. Seriously, Pam, I wouldn't worry too much about her. If anyone can take care of themselves, your Angie can. The one thing I will say, though, is she should be bloody ashamed of herself for how she's treated that little boy. She's a terrible mother, an absolute disgrace of a parent. I will be the exact opposite of her with my child. You just watch me.'

Pam put an arm around Linda's shoulder and kissed her on the top of her head. 'You'll be a brilliant mum, little sis. I just know you will.'

After dropping the kids off at her mum's house, Stephanie felt incredibly nervous as she headed back home. Barry had insisted that she didn't cook. He had said he wanted to do it. Steph was really looking forward to having Barry all to herself for the evening, but she was extremely anxious about the questions she needed to ask him. She was also scared about the possibility she might have sex with him. Steph had never made love to anyone other than Wayne, and she had a feeling that she wasn't the most exciting lover in the world. Feeling her stomach churn as she swung into her driveway, Steph got out of the car and let herself into the house.

'Wow,' she exclaimed as she walked into the lounge.

Barry had pulled the dining table into the centre of the room. He had laid a red tablecloth and had lit a big candle in the centre. The lights in the room were all turned off and Steph thought it looked ever so romantic. Wayne had never put himself out for her like this; and apart from organizing her a surprise twenty-first birthday party at a hall in Collier Row, she could barely remember him doing anything spontaneous.

Barry popped a champagne cork. 'You sit yourself down.'

'Where did you get the candles from at this time of night?

And that tablecloth?' Stephanie asked. She couldn't believe Barry had gone to all this trouble. He had done the same sort of thing for her when they were young, just before he had left for Spain, and the fact he had taken the trouble to do it again just proved to Steph how much he must really like her.

'They were in the boot of my car. I wanted to make tonight special, Steph,' Barry explained, staring at her with an intense look on his face.

Stephanie averted her eyes and gesticulated towards the kitchen. 'Dinner smells lovely. What have you cooked?'

'You'll soon find out. I'm gonna dish it up right now.'

When Barry left the room, Stephanie downed her champagne and quickly poured herself another. She walked over to the photo of Wayne she had recently had blown up, kissed her fingertips and placed them on the frame. 'Please don't hate me. I will always love you, but I have to move on for the sake of our children.'

Another person completely bowled over by Barry's wonderful gestures was Marge. She and Marlene were currently sitting in a bar at Heathrow Airport and were waiting to board their plane for their two-week, all-inclusive holiday in Barbados.

'I still can't believe we're going. I've always dreamed of a holiday in the Caribbean, but unless I'd had a win on the bloody football pools or at the Bingo, I could never see meself going there,' Marge said.

Marlene took a sip of her wine. She was done up to the nines in a tight floral dress and big mauve hat, and from an outsider's point of view, she must have looked as if she was on her way to Ascot, rather than Barbados. 'You'll be in your element out there, Marge. You know you like a bit of black cock and most black men love big women. It wouldn't even surprise me if you found yourself a husband.'

Marge roared with laughter. She had always been rather partial to black men. Not only did she find them incredibly sexy, the ones she'd actually got hold of had all been hung like donkeys. 'You can fucking talk! I can count quite a few black men you've been out with as well. What's the betting you find yourself a bit of black cock with a husband attached to the end of it an' all.'

Guffawing like a crow being strangled, Marlene held her aching sides. She had a very good feeling about this holiday. A very good feeling indeed.

Stephanie put her fork down on the table. Barry had cooked a beautiful paella and had served it up with Spanish bread. In normal circumstances, Steph would have wolfed the lot and possibly asked for seconds, but she had so much on her mind, she just couldn't think straight, let alone eat.

'What's up? Don't you like it?' Barry asked her.

'It's lovely, Barry, but we really do need to talk about stuff.'

'Go on,' Barry said, laying his own fork on the table and topping up their drinks.

As Stephanie tried to search for the right words, she felt a hot flush come over her. She could also feel her hands start to shake. 'It's me and you, Barry. Where are we heading? Only, I've started to have feelings for you, the kids have become extremely attached to you, and I need to know what's going on inside your head. What do you want from me, Barry?'

Licking his lips with anticipation, Barry leant across the table and held Stephanie's trembling hands in his own. He stared deeply into her eyes. 'I think you know exactly what I want, Steph. I want something that I've waited for and craved for a long, long time.'

'But what about Jolene? I'll feel awful if me and you get it together while you're still engaged to her.'

Clocking the look of longing in Stephanie's eyes, Barry knew it was the right time to strike. He stood up, grabbed Steph by the hand, thrust her up against the wall and urged her to put her legs around his waist. 'Let's not worry about Jolene right now. I want tonight to just be about the two of us.'

Stephanie groaned as Barry kissed her and pushed his rock-hard penis against her groin. She was so desperate to be held and wanted again. Dropping her legs to the floor, Stephanie took Barry by the hand. Feeling overcome by lust, she then led him up the stairs.

Unaware that her daughter and Barry were currently in the first throes of passion, Pam was busy discussing their relationship with her sister. 'I wish Steph would just stop faffing about and make a go of it with him. She's gonna regret it if she don't and Barry sods off back to Spain. Between me, you and the kitchen sink, I think he is far better suited to Steph than Wayne ever was. Don't get me wrong, Wayne weren't a bad lad, but there was something about him that I could never truly take to, if I'm honest. He was always polite enough, but I always got the impression that he weren't into the family side of things and sort of wanted Steph all to himself.'

Lin nodded. 'Wayne was always OK towards me, but we never saw a lot of him really, did we? I remember him being round 'ere quite a lot when they first got together, but after him and Steph moved to Collier Row, he never seemed to come round again, did he? I always thought he'd got a bit above himself when he started raking it in, to be honest. I often wonder what's happened to him though, Pam. God, if my Keith ever went missing, it would kill me. I know your David's death was a terrible shock for you, but can you imagine how you'd have felt if he'd just disappeared off the face of the earth? Not knowing what has happened to someone you love must be the worst feeling in the world, and perhaps that's why Steph's not ready to move on just yet.'

'I often wonder if Wayne's done a runner, you know. Perhaps he got cold feet because of the wedding, or something. The police asked Steph a few weeks ago if they knew where his dad was in Greece. I mean, why would they be trying to trace his father if they thought Wayne had committed suicide in England? I reckon the Old Bill must be suspicious,' Pam said, bluntly.

'I shouldn't think he's run off to Greece, Pam. If Wayne didn't wanna be with Steph, surely he would have just ended their relationship? I mean, he'd still want to have contact with his kids, surely?'

'Yeah, I suppose he would. I didn't really think much of it at the time, but when Angie went off to Greece as well, it did make me wonder if she and Wayne had run off together and were being harboured by his father.'

'Surely even Angie wouldn't stoop that low?' Lin replied, shocked at her sister's suggestion.

'To be truthful, I don't think my Angie could be bothered to give Wayne the time of day now, but I'll tell you something, Lin, if I ever find out that her and Wayne had run off together, I would find 'em and – may God be my judge – I'd kill the pair of 'em with me own bare hands.'

'Barry, I'm ever so thirsty. Let me go downstairs and pour us both a drink, eh?' Stephanie suggested. She and Wayne had been quite rampant when they had first got together, but their lovemaking sessions had never gone on for hours on end, as this one with Barry seemed destined to.

'Go and grab that bottle of champagne. I bought three and there's one still in the fridge. Don't you be too long though. I've waited a long time for this moment and I ain't finished with you yet.'

When Stephanie skipped happily from the bedroom, Barry put his hands behind his head, lay back on the pillow and grinned. He was an expert when it came to making love to women and Stephanie's cries of delight only added to his glee. Another few hours, he would be out of here, and he couldn't wait to see the look on Steph's face when he said his piece and left. It would be truly and utterly priceless.

Marlene and Marge had been so excited about their holiday that they had got to the airport three hours before their check-in time. Bored with sitting with the two blokes who had latched onto them, but were too tight to buy them any drinks, Marlene put her hat back on and went to look at the information board. Thrilled when she spotted the words, BOARDING NOW, Marlene tottered back to Marge as fast as she could. Her five-inch stilettos definitely weren't designed for running. 'Come on, let's go.'

'But these men are just gonna get us a drink,' Marge said. She quite fancied the dark-haired one with the moustache.

'Sod the drink. We've been sitting with 'em for the past half-hour and the tight bastards never offered to buy us one then, did they?' Marlene hissed in her friend's ear.

Marge stood up.

'Perhaps we can all meet up when you get back off holiday?' the man with the moustache suggested to Marge.

Sensing that her pal was about to give her phone number out, Marlene had another little word in her ear. 'What do you want, some big, strapping handsome black geezer whose cock is eight inches when soft? Or, that skinny, tashy-faced twat who has probably only got four inches on the hard?'

Marge immediately turned her back on the men. She and Marlene had been drinking all day and had earlier made up their own lyrics to the old Seventies classic by Typically Tropical.

'You didn't say where you was going?' the man with the moustache shouted out.

Turning around, both Marge and Marlene broke into song. 'Woh, we going to Barbados. Woh, to find big black man. Woh, we like big penis. Woh, near the sunny Caribbean sea.'

Roaring with laughter at the shocked look on the men's faces, Marlene and Marge linked arms and strutted off.

Barry smirked as he ejaculated inside Stephanie for what he'd planned to be the very last time. She was on the pill, had even showed him the packet, so he'd decided to ride her bareback to give himself maximum pleasure.

If Steph had any doubts beforehand about whether what she was doing was wrong, she certainly didn't have them now. The sex between her and Barry had been fantastic – mind-blowing, in fact – and even though Steph felt incredibly guilty having sex with another man while her fiancé was still on the missing list, she knew she would never have allowed herself to fall for Barry in the first place if she hadn't been so intent on giving her children the life they deserved. That's what mothers were meant to do, weren't they? Put their children's needs before their own. Falling for Barry and enjoying the sex was just an added bonus. 'I've got something to show you,' Steph said, leaping out of bed.

Barry laughed as Steph produced the half of the jagged gold heart Barry had given her all those years ago. He could not believe that the silly bitch had done what she had done to him, yet still had the brass neck to keep it. Knowing now was the perfect time to leave, Barry stood up.

'Why are you getting dressed? Don't tell me you've kept the other half of it and you've got it in the car?' Steph asked, happily.

Barry ignored the question. 'Do you feel guilty about Wayne at all?' he asked, as he zipped up his jeans.

'Yeah, I wouldn't be human if I didn't. But, as my mum said, Wayne isn't coming back, so I need to get on with my life. Why do you ask? Do you feel guilty?'

'No. I just wanted to know how you felt.'

Throwing her arms around Barry's neck, Stephanie grinned. 'I think you know the answer to how I feel, and to prove how serious I am about you, why don't you move in with me? I know it's early days, but I hate being here on my own of a night. I get really nervous. I'm sure the kids would love it if you moved in permanently as well. They adore you, so do I, and I don't care what other people think, do you?'

'Yeah, I do actually. Unlike you, I have standards, Steph. Anyway, I'm going back to Spain to marry my beautiful girlfriend,' Barry said, icily.

Positive that Barry was joking, Stephanie playfully punched him on the chest. 'Give me a big kiss,' she said, throwing her arms around his neck.

Grabbing her wrists, Barry squeezed them tightly and stared coldly into her eyes. 'Know how it feels now, you slag, do ya?'

Stephanie froze as she noted his chilly expression. 'Whatever's wrong, Barry? Have I said or done something to upset you?'

Barry laughed nastily. 'Yes, darling. Many years ago you did something that upset me immensely. Remember?' he said, letting go of her wrists.

Feeling faint, Stephanie sat on the edge of the bed and made a grab at Barry's hand as he tried to put his T-shirt on. 'Why are you being like this? I thought we had something special? I thought you loved me.'

Seeing the distress in her eyes only added to Barry's pleasure. 'Oh, we did have something special once, Steph. I loved you so much all them years back, but you didn't honestly think I was going to give up my wonderful life in Spain and my stunning girlfriend for an untrustworthy slut like you, did ya?'

Bursting into tears, Steph grabbed a pillow to cover up her nakedness. 'Please tell me this is a joke, Barry. What about the children?'

Barry secured the clasp on his watch, bent down, and tilted Stephanie's chin towards him. 'I feel sorry for them kids of yours – they'd be better off without you. Their dad ain't been missing five minutes and you're already out there whoring yourself out, ain't ya? You've always thought you were better than your sister, Steph, but I tell you now, you are not. Angie don't pretend to be anything she ain't, but you, you're the dirtiest slag of all.'

When Barry picked up his keys to leave, a distraught Stephanie forgot about her nakedness and fell at his feet. Sobbing uncontrollably, she grabbed both his legs. 'Please don't go, Barry. I love you, the kids love you; please don't do this to me. I am so sorry about what happened all them years ago. I was only a kid and I didn't know any different. I have always loved you deep down, I know I have. Please don't go, I beg you.'

Looking at the naked wreck grovelling at his feet, Barry smirked. He picked the gold piece of heart up and secured it around Stephanie's neck. 'You weren't a bad fuck, babe, I'll give you that much. Enjoy the rest of your life, sweetheart.'

'No Barry. Please don't leave me,' Stephanie screamed, as he moved her hands away from his ankles and bolted down the stairs.

When she heard his car pull away, Stephanie knew there was only one thing left for her to do. She hated herself and knew there was no way she could live with betraying Wayne in such an awful way. She had made a complete and utter fool of herself and Barry was right, the kids would be better off without her.

Steph put her dressing gown on and sobbed hysterically as she shuffled into the bathroom. She opened the cabinet and stared at the masses of tablets. Suicide might be deemed as a coward's way out, but unfortunately, she'd left herself with no choice.

CHAPTER THIRTY-FOUR

Ten Years Later – 2004

Double-checking that she had set the alarm, Stephanie Crouch locked the salon door and pulled the shutters down. She had set up her beauty business exactly five years ago next week and, apart from her children, it really was her pride and joy in life. A government grant had given Steph the opportunity to achieve her dream. She had called the shop 'Danni's' after her stunning daughter, and it had been so successful that she was seriously considering opening up another salon because she could no longer cope with the amount of bookings she was getting.

Considering suicide had been a massive wake-up call for Steph, and if it hadn't been for Tyler having an accident at her mum's house that fateful evening, she wouldn't be here now. She had already swallowed a dozen or so tablets when the phone had rung. Tyler had fallen down the stairs and knocked himself unconscious, and it was only because she had heard her mum's frantic voice leave an answerphone message that she had snapped out of committing such a selfish act. After putting her fingers down her throat, Stephanie had dashed off to the hospital. Tyler had woken up by the time she arrived and was being monitored for concussion. Steph had never told a soul about what she'd attempted, but she knew in her heart that it was her son who had saved her life.

Stephanie got into her car. She had recently treated herself to a BMW M3 convertible and loved driving about in luxury. The car was alpine white with a black leather interior and had proved to be a real man-magnet. Trouble was, Steph wasn't interested in men. In fact, she hated them with a passion. Barry had destroyed her trust in the male gender forever more, and Steph knew she could never fall in love again for as long as she lived. Sometimes, Steph would have nightmares, and the one that kept reoccurring the most was a vision of Wayne being throttled by Barry. Wayne had never been seen or heard of since his disappearance on his stag night over ten years ago and, after learning of Barry's thirst for revenge, Steph was now positive that it was he who had murdered Wayne. The police had stopped looking for Wayne ages ago. They thought he had taken his own life and Stephanie had never told anybody about her own suspicions. Barry was evil and she was scared to open her mouth in case it opened up a can of worms. What had happened between Barry and herself, Steph had never disclosed to anyone. It had made her feel guilty, naive and cheap, and keeping it a secret was the only way Stephanie could cope with it. At the time, her mum had been devastated when she had told her that she wouldn't be seeing Barry any more. 'But why? He's a lovely young man and yous two are so well suited,' she'd said.

Steph had wanted to tell her mum that Barry was anything but bloody lovely, but instead had kept her mouth shut and came up with the only viable excuse she could think of. 'I asked him to choose between me and his girlfriend in Spain. He said he wasn't ready to make that decision, so I sent him packing.'

Aware that her phone was ringing, Steph fished through her handbag to find it. Unable to do so, she tipped the bag upside down on the passenger seat in annoyance. 'You OK, love?' she asked her daughter, Dannielle.

'Hurry up home, Mum. A woman called Mrs Woodcock has just knocked here. She reckons Tyler has threatened her son, James, with a knife of some kind and she's fuming. I told her you'd be home soon and she's waiting outside in her car.'

Stephanie sighed. Unlike her sixteen-year-old daughter who had never caused Steph any worry or trouble in her life, Tyler was, to put it bluntly, a little bastard. Her son had just turned thirteen, and had been diagnosed with a medical condition called ADHD at the tender age of five. The doctors had said that Tyler had an inbalance of chemicals in the management of his brain, which was the reason for his tantrums and learning difficulties.

Frustrated that the driver in front hadn't realized that the traffic lights had turned from red to green, Steph put her hand on her hooter. She had no idea who this Mrs Woodcock was, and all she could do was hope that the woman didn't involve the police. Tyler was a good boy at heart. He was very protective of her and Dannielle, and having never really had a father figure in his life, had taken it upon himself to play the man of the house. With a bit of luck, once Mrs Woodcock realized that Tyler suffered from ADHD and Steph apologized profusely, that would be the end of the matter. In Stephanie's eyes, her son wasn't a violent boy. He might be a little bastard at times, but other than that, he was just extremely misunderstood.

Pam roared with laughter as she caught up with today's episode of *Loose Women*. It was Pam's favourite TV show ever, and she loved listening to the antics of the female presenters. Carol McGiffin was Pam's favourite of the panellists. She was always talking about getting drunk and falling over, and she so reminded Pam of her sister, Lin. Lin would be fifty next month and her son David, who had thankfully been born without dwarfism, was now nine. Lin had promised when she had fallen pregnant that she was going to be a fantastic mum, and up until recently she had been. However, six months ago, Lin's partner Keith had died of liver failure, which had sent Lin spiralling back to the clutches of alcohol herself. Keith was the only proper relationship that Lin had ever had and Pam's heart went out to her little sister. She knew what it felt like to lose the only man you had ever loved, but Lin needed to learn that the answers to her grief didn't lie at the bottom of a bottle. Dealing with the loss itself was the only true way to move on in life.

Pausing *Loose Women*, Pam went into the kitchen to make herself a cuppa. Due to her obesity, she had given up her job in the baker's a few months ago. Her GP had warned her that if she carried on the way she was, she wouldn't make old bones. Food had always been the one thing in life that Pam could not say no to, therefore working in a baker's was no good for her at all. That's why she couldn't say too much to her Lin about her drinking at the moment. Everybody had their vices in life, didn't they?

About to reach for the biscuit tin out of habit, Pam heard the phone ring and darted into the lounge. 'You all right, Steph? Were you run off your feet at the salon again today?'

When Stephanie explained that Tyler had threatened to stab someone, Pam said what any decent mother would say. 'Calm down. I'll be over within the hour.'

Over in Hornchurch, Angela was sitting in a restaurant called Jailhouse Rock. There was a fat bloke on stage who imagined he looked and sounded like Elvis Presley, but watching him prance around like a penis, *so* wasn't Angie's cup of tea.

'Do you like it in here, Mum?' Aidan asked, hoping that she did.

Angela smiled, then nodded. She might have been an awful mother years ago, but she idolized her son now, and if he was happy, then so was she. Angela had moved to Greece ten years back with her pal Roxy. She had loved getting away from England and her family at the time, and the first contact she had made with her son again was when she had turned up at her mother's door three years later. Pam had been furious by her unexpected visit. She had called Angela every name under the sun, accused her of being the worst mother ever to walk the earth, and had implied that she had run off with Wayne. It had taken Angela more than a week to convince her mother that she had nothing to do with Wayne's disappearance. Then, when she had returned to Greece, she had kept in regular contact with her son. Angie wasn't one for writing letters, but she had rung Aidan every week and sent expensive birthday and Christmas presents his way.

Angie had been back in the UK permanently for just over a year now. Roxy had married a Geordie fella she had met, who had been working as a holiday rep in Greece, and she now lived in Tyneside. Angela had discovered true love for the first time herself while working in Greece. She had fallen head over heels for the extremely wealthy son of a Greek shipping tycoon. Theodore was five years younger than Angela. His name meant 'Gift of God' in Greek mythology, and to Angela that is exactly what he was. Theo, as she liked to call him, was six foot two, had jet-black greased-back hair, an air of power about him, and a body to send shivers down any woman's spine. As a lover, he was a genius, and Angela would have married him at the drop of a hat – if only he didn't already have a Greek wife and two small children.

Their affair was intense and extremely passionate, and even though Angela had ended it twice, neither she nor Theodore could keep away from one another. It had been Theo's idea that he buy Angela a flat and she move back to England. He said that if his parents were ever to find out about their relationship, his mother would disown him and would force his father to sack him from the family empire.

Angela was reasonably happy with the way things had turned out. Theo flew over to England at least twice a month and would spend at least three or four days with her at a time. He also paid her rent, bills, and gave her two thousand pounds a month living allowance. Obviously, being so in love with Theo, Angela would rather be with him every day of every week, but she could not live without him and beggars couldn't be choosers. At thirty-three years old, Angie was far too old to be doing erotic dancing any more, and she now quite enjoyed being a lady of leisure. Whenever Theo was in London, he would take her to Harrods or Harvey Nic's and buy her whatever she wanted. He had also bought her a brand-new Mazda sports car for her to cruise around in.

'Shall we order some food now? And I don't want no arguing about the bill, tonight is on me,' Aidan said in a manly tone.

Angela smiled. She might have her mum to thank for bringing her son up, but that didn't mean she couldn't still be proud of him. Aidan was eighteen now, and with his jet-black hair and bright green eyes, was an extremely handsome boy. He had a very Irish look about him, but unlike Jason, who was a shortarse, Aidan was just under six feet tall. He was also a gym freak, and for a young boy had a wonderful physique. Whenever Angie went out with her son, she was well aware of the admiring glances from groups of young girls, and that made her as proud as punch. Aidan had left school at sixteen and had taken a job as a trainee mechanic. The company he worked for had sent him to college two days a week and he had recently passed his exams with flying colours. He was no longer an apprentice now. Aidan had been offered a permanent position just last week, which was why he'd insisted on taking his mum out for a meal tonight.

'I'll let you pay for everything, but only if you let me treat us to a bottle of champagne first. It's my way of saying how proud I am to have you as a son,' Angela said, jovially.

Aidan beamed from ear to ear. He knew both his nans were rather vexed over how close he now was to Angela, but he didn't care. For years he had craved his mother's love and attention; now finally he had it.

Pam got off the Central Line train at Loughton and walked towards Stephanie's house. Her daughter's beauty business had been such a roaring success that Steph had managed to buy herself a posh four-bedroom house just a few minutes' walk from the station. Pam was extremely proud of her eldest daughter's achievements, but she would never stop wishing that Steph would find a nice man to share her life with also.

Tyler was a real bloody handful and, in Pam's eyes, the guidance of a level-headed man was exactly what her grandson needed at this point in his life. Pam let herself into Steph's house with her own key. 'Sorry I'm a bit later than I said I'd be. I waited ages for both bleedin' trains. Where's Tyler now? What happened with the woman?'

Stephanie and Dannielle were seated side by side on the red leather sofa. 'Let me get you a drink, Nan? Do you want a cup of tea?' Dannielle offered.

'No, we'll have wine,' Stephanie replied, her face etched with worry.

When Dannielle returned with a bottle of Chardonnay, Stephanie urged her daughter to go upstairs and get herself ready. Danni had finished her final exams this week and had now officially left school. She had chosen to follow in her mother's footsteps and go on to beauty college, which Stephanie was extremely pleased about. Her daughter already worked in her salon as a Saturday girl and had a natural talent and interest in the job. Dannielle was tall, slim, sexy, and stunning, and when she finished her college course, Steph planned to buy her daughter her own little salon. She might even surprise Dannielle with the keys on her eighteenth birthday if all went to plan.

'Are you sure you don't mind me going out, Mum? I'm happy to stay in, if you need me here?'

Stephanie smiled at her daughter's thoughtfulness. Danni's best friend, Mimi, had extremely wealthy parents who had organized a big bash for the girls' leaving party this evening. It wasn't a school prom – Danni had that to look forward to in a couple of weeks' time – but this was a lovely gesture and an important night in her daughter's life. 'Go and get yourself glammed up and off you go. Nanny's going to stay here tonight, so she'll be with me when your naughty brother decides to show his face.'

'So, what happened then?' Pam asked, when Danni left the room.

'Oh Mum, it was awful. That Mrs Woodcock was such a nice woman. She said that she'd heard that Tyler had behavioural issues due to an illness and that was the reason she'd come here rather than involve the police. Tyler had the knife with him at school, apparently. Mrs Woodcock's son, James, is in the year above Tyler and she said they accidentally bumped into one another in the corridor yesterday. James admitted that when Tyler was abusive towards him, he swore back at him, but he said that although there was a slight bit of pushing and shoving, no real violence actually occurred. Mrs Woodcock said that James thought that was the end of the matter, until Tyler waited outside the school for him today with a knife in his hand. He followed James, then told him that if he didn't apologize, he would stab him until he did.'

Pam put her hand over her mouth. 'Gordon Bennett! That's awful! Is this woman gonna tell the school?'

'No, but she has told me if Tyler threatens her son in any way in the future, she will involve the school and the police. She has another son who was in Dannielle's year called Jack. Danni said that her and Jack are quite good friends, so perhaps that's another reason why Mrs Woodcock didn't involve the authorities. I know if one of my kids was threatened by someone with a knife, I'd be straight on the phone to the Old Bill, wouldn't you?'

Pam nodded. 'So where do you think Tyler is now? Has he not been home at all since this afternoon?'

'No. The little bastard probably knows he's in trouble, that's why he's avoided coming home.'

'Do you think we should go out and look for him?' Pam asked, concerned.

'Not yet. I rang around his friends' mums. Tyler was round his mate Brad's house earlier, but they've gone out again. He'll be home around ten. The little sod always strolls in about that time when he's done something wrong,' Stephanie replied confidently.

Pam's heart went out to her daughter. She knew what it was like to have one good and one bad child. 'Don't worry about things too much, Steph. When Tyler gets home, me and you will give him a proper good talking-to. He'll grow out of this violent stage he's going through. It's probably just his hormones playing up. He is a teenager now, ain't he?'

Stephanie sighed. The learning difficulties Tyler had experienced as a young child had improved immensely over the years. He was by no means as bright as most of the boys in his class, but his teachers had told Steph that he had a real talent for drama and art. Unfortunately for Steph, the domineering side of her son's nature seemed to be getting worse. This was the fourth time in the past year that she had suffered the humiliation of another child's parent knocking on her door to complain about his behaviour. Tyler bullying other children was something Steph had got used to hearing about but, to her knowledge, he had never threatened anybody with a knife before.

Pam put her arm around her daughter's shoulders. 'Chin up, babe. Ty ain't all bad, you know that.'

Stephanie shook her head in total despair. 'I hope you're right, Mum. For all our sakes, I do.'

Marlene checked her appearance in the full-length mirror and, not happy with the red miniskirt, decided to change her outfit once again. She was fifty now, and if there was anything she despised in life, it was getting bloody old. Marlene had been living back at her old house opposite Pam for over two years now. Chantelle had got back with her Indian boyfriend, Ajay, and they now lived in Wolverhampton where Ajay had family. Rumour had it, Ajay had upset a few big-time drug dealers around the Ilford area, and he and Chantelle had scarpered for their own safety. Marlene rarely saw her daughter these days, but once a week they would chat on the phone. Chantelle's eldest two children, AJ and Jermain, were both now banged up. They had been part of a robbery that had gone dreadfully wrong and a man had died in the tussle that followed. Both lads had been sentenced to three years in a young offender's institution and were only three months into their stretch. Chantelle's other son, Daryl, was twelve now, and was by all accounts an extremely talented footballer.

Deciding to go with the red miniskirt after all, Marlene quickly got changed again. Hearing her phone ringing, she ran to pick it up.

'Hi baby. So sorry, but I'm running about half an hour late. Is that OK with you?' Dennis asked politely.

'Yep, that's fine. I've not even started dinner yet, so you just get here when you can.' Marlene had only been seeing Dennis for the past fortnight and this would be his first visit to her house. That is why she had offered to cook, and had cleaned the place from top to bottom this morning. Years ago, Marlene had been quite happy to live in squalor, but not any more. Having a cleaner whilst living with Jake the Snake in Spain had given her a taste for cleanliness, and since her son Barry had bought this house off the council for her to live in, Marlene was determined to make it look as nice as she possibly could. She hated those nosy pair of cows, Pam and Cathy, who lived opposite her, and making her house look better than theirs was something that now pleased Marlene greatly.

Turning her attentions back to her evening with Dennis, Marlene grinned with expectation as she pictured his handsome face. Dennis was ten years younger than herself, six feet two; as black as coal and as fit as a butcher's dog. They had been introduced by Marge's other half, Frederick, and had hit it off almost immediately. Many years ago, when she and Marge had flown off to Barbados on holiday, they had joked that they would both find themselves husbands. Marge had. She had met Frederick, but he hadn't lived in the Caribbean. He was over there on holiday visiting family. He lived in bloody Tooting. Marlene poured herself a drink and sat down to touch up the varnish on her false nails. It had been nearly a year since she had last had sex with a man, and Marlene had a very strong feeling that tonight was the night she would finally end her long celibacy.

While waiting for her dysfunctional son to show his innocent-looking face, Stephanie and Pam chatted about most things bar the weather. Linda was at the forefront of their conversation, and when Pam blurted out the concerns she had over her sister and nephew's welfare, Stephanie came up with a suggestion. 'Why don't you ask Lin and David to move in with you? Obviously, Lin's probably only drinking again because she's grieving for Keith. She must be lonely. I hate that estate in Barking where she lives. It's such a shithole, and it can't be much fun for her and David being cooped up in a flat on their own there.'

Pam paused before answering. Aidan had moved in with his father on a permanent basis just under a year ago. Jason now had his own council flat up at the Fiddlers in Dagenham and, because it was only a ten-minute walk from where Aidan worked, that had been her grandson's excuse for moving out. Pam had been gutted at the time to lose the boy she had all but brought up single-handedly, but Aidan was all grown-up now and Pam could understand why living with his gran wasn't such a cool option for him any more. 'I don't know, Steph. You know what Lin's like, she'll probably bite me head off if I as much as suggest her moving in. Not only that, I'm too old and set in me ways now to be having young kids in the house again. I've already done my fair share of bringing up nippers, don't you think?'

'Lin hasn't got to give her flat up, Mum. The social pay all her rent for her, so she can just stay with you until she gets her head together again. David's a good boy. I'd swap him for Tyler tomorrow if I could,' Stephanie said, half jokingly, half serious.

Pam mulled over her daughter's suggestion. When Keith had first passed away, Linda and David had stayed with her for over a fortnight and Pam had thoroughly enjoyed looking after them both. She had been born to be a mother hen. But, even though she now enjoyed having the house to herself at times, unless Cathy popped in of an evening, Pam did find it a bit boring. 'OK, I'll bell Lin tomorrow and put the idea to her. At least it'll save me worrying about her if she stops with me for a bit. I shall watch her like a bleedin' hawk . . . 'Ere, you know what I forgot to tell ya.'

'What?'

'The old slapper has just had new windows put in over the road. Lairy Mary told Cathy that the house belongs to Barry now. Mary reckons Barry bought it for Marlene to live in.'

The mention of Barry's name made Steph feel rather queasy. The thought of him always sent shivers of terror down her spine. 'Didn't Dannielle look beautiful when she went out, Mum?' Steph said, changing the subject completely.

'She looked like a model, bless her little heart. Ain't she got herself a boyfriend yet? With her looks, she must have 'em queuing up.'

Stephanie chuckled. Dannielle had plenty of boy mates, who Steph could tell were besotted by her daughter. Thankfully, Dannielle didn't seem that interested in them. 'I want to be a successful businesswoman like you, Mum. One day I would love to settle down and have kids, but not until I'm at least thirty. Anyway, the boys at my school are so childish, I would much prefer to meet an older man, someone who's already successful and has their own business. I don't see why I should have to scrimp and save if I don't have to in life,' was Dannielle's take on matters.

Stephanie was thrilled by her daughter's maturity. At least she wouldn't have to worry about Danni getting pregnant young, like she bloody well had, and if her daughter ended up with a rich man five or ten years older than her, who was Steph to judge after the mistakes she had made? 'No, Mum. Danni is far more clued-up than me and Angie ever were,' Steph replied, honestly.

'Did the kids mention Wayne's birthday yesterday, love?' Pam asked.

'I took 'em both for a meal, like I do every year on Wayne's birthday. We only went for a pizza, and to be honest they barely mentioned him. Tyler doesn't remember him at all and I think Danni's memories of Wayne have faded as well. I made them say a little prayer for him as I always do on these special occasions, but that was about it really. To be honest, I rarely think of Wayne myself now. He's been missing so long, I don't see the point of keep going over old ground. The only thing I do wish is that the police would find his body so that we could give him a proper funeral. It would be nice for the kids to have a grave where they could visit him and lay flowers and stuff, especially now they're older.'

'But, you don't even know if he's actually dead,' Pam reminded her daughter.

Thinking of Barry's evil face, Steph gave a solemn half-smile. 'Oh, Wayne's dead all right, Mum. I just know he is.'

Tyler Jackman said goodbye to his pal, Brad, and dawdled towards home. He could picture the scenario now. Either his mum and sister would be sitting on the sofa waiting for him, faces like thunder. Or, even more likely, his mum and his nan. Tyler didn't deem himself to be a bad person. He had a vicious temper, he knew that, but if he saw an old lady struggling with her shopping bags, he would offer to help her. His mum had always drummed it into him how important it was to respect his elders, therefore he did. What Tyler couldn't bring himself to respect was anybody who tried mugging off him, his friends, or his family. Since moving to secondary school, Tyler had got himself a reputation as being the hardest boy in his year. It was a reputation that had certainly made him popular with both sexes. Boys were desperate to be his pal and girls were desperate to become his bird. Tyler enjoyed his new-found popularity. As a youngster, his learning difficulties hadn't enabled him to make friends or socialize in the way that the other kids had. Therefore, he'd been picked on and had few friends.

Spotting an empty beer can, Tyler kicked it along the street as though he were playing with a football. James Woodcock had spoken to him like he was a piece of shit in front of all his friends the other day, and Tyler had no regrets over the way he had dealt with the matter. Woody had grovelled, screamed and cried like a baby when Tyler had pointed his knife at him. Walking into his mother's driveway, Tyler hid his flick knife in the bush where he always hid anything he didn't want his mother to find. Whether it be items he'd nicked from local shops to sell on, porn magazines, or even the odd can of lager, he would stash it in his secret hidey-hole. Creeping up to the front door, Tyler got his key out. As he put it in the lock, he heard the exact words he had been fully expecting to hear.

'Tyler! Get your arse in here now, you little bastard.'

CHAPTER THIRTY-FIVE

Tyler Jackman got out of bed and stretched his lithe young body. Tyler had light blond hair which he wore short and spiky. His eyes were the colour of a deep blue sea and his mum had told him recently that, facially, he was the spitting image of how his dad had looked when he was at school. Hearing a knock on his bedroom door, Tyler made a grab for his Nike tracksuit bottoms. 'Hang on a sec, I ain't dressed yet,' he shouted out. Last night's telling-off had gone pretty much as expected for Tyler. His mum and nan had given him a real stern talking-to, which had ended up with him being grounded for the foreseeable future.

Thinking it was his mother at the door about to give him another earful, Tyler opened it cautiously. 'Oh, it's you,' he said to his sister.

Dannielle was extremely close to Tyler. For brother and sister they got on very well. 'So, what happened, Ty?' Dannielle asked, plonking herself on the edge of his bed.

Tyler explained truthfully about his original altercation with James Woodcock. 'Honestly, sis, he was laughing at me and all sorts. He really mugged me off in front of me mates and I had to show him who was boss. I had no intention of using the knife on him, honest I didn't, but the look on his face was priceless when he saw it. Crying like a baby, the prick was. He won't be larging it with me again, I'm telling ya.'

Some of Tyler's expressions and foul use of language shocked Dannielle at times. Most of the lads in Loughton were reasonably well-to-do and spoke quite nicely, but Tyler didn't. He sounded like a little gangster. Her mum blamed herself for that, as they had lived on a council estate for a large chunk of Tyler's life, before they'd had enough money to move into the nice house they now lived in. It wasn't her mum's fault, Dannielle knew that. After her dad had disappeared into thin air, their money had run out; being rehomed by the council had been the only road her mum could go down. Putting an arm around Tyler's shoulders, Dannielle smiled at him. 'What we gonna do with you, eh Ty?'

'I tell you what you can do for me, sis. Have a word with Mum for me, will ya? I tried to explain that James ain't the nice, shy boy she seems to think he is, but Nan was chirping in and neither of 'em would listen to me properly. Just tell Mum what I've told you, Danni, otherwise she'll make me stay in forever more. I hate being stuck indoors, you know I do.'

'I'll smooth things out with Mum for you, on one condition.'

'What?'

'That you promise me you will never carry a knife about with you again. It's so dangerous and you don't want to end up in some borstal somewhere, do you? I don't know if you know this story, but our grandad, our dad's dad, stabbed our nan and ended up doing life in prison.'

Tyler's eyes opened like organ stops. This was the first time he had ever heard of this story. 'What, did our grandad kill our nan, then?'

'Yes, and Mum said he then spent most of his life in prison. Now, will you promise me that you won't carry a knife around again with you?'

Tyler immediately nodded. 'I told Mum I'd already thrown the knife away, but I haven't really. I will though, I promise. I don't want to get into bad trouble. I'm too young to go to prison, Danni.'

Ruffling her brother's hair, Dannielle stood up. The story she had told Tyler was all true. She had wanted to shock him into seeing sense, and seemingly she had. As his big sister, Dannielle felt that it was her duty to keep Tyler on the straight and narrow and, hopefully, for the time being, she might have succeeded.

Pam had been expecting nothing less than a barrage of abuse when she rang up Lin and suggested that she and David might move in with her for a while. Instead, all she got was a sweet, seven-word answer. 'Are you sure you don't mind, sis?'

When Pam had given up work, Stephanie had insisted she had Sky TV installed. Pam had flatly refused, saying it was a waste of bloody money, but when Steph had surprised her with it on her birthday, saying she was footing the monthly bills, Pam had got hooked on it almost immediately. She loved *The Jerry Springer Show* and often watched back-to-back episodes for hours on end, but Pam knew that losing herself in other people's problems was no substitute for dealing with her own. About to change the quilt cover in the room that Lin would be sleeping in, Pam darted into her own bedroom to answer the phone.

'Look out the window,' Cathy said, excitedly.

Thankful that Stephanie had recently bought her one of them cordless phones in case of emergencies, Pam did exactly what Cathy had asked. 'Oh, my giddy aunt,' she exclaimed, as she watched Marlene and the big black man virtually having sex in the middle of the street.

Cathy laughed. 'What time your Lin and David arriving?'

'Late afternoon,' Pam replied, her face pressed to the window. Marlene was waving frantically in her direction and, not wanting to make herself look a fool, Pam opened the bedroom window. 'Do you want me for something?'

'I was gonna ask you the same thing,' Marlene yelled.

'Whatever do you mean?'

'I mean why are you and that nosy old bat next door both staring at me out the fucking window? Ain't you got lives of your own?'

'Who you calling an old bat? You fucking old slapper,' Cathy shouted, opening her window as well.

Absolutely incensed by the brass neck of Marlene, Pam didn't even notice Angela get out of her car.

'For your information, my mother has a wonderful life of her own. She has daughters who think the world of her, and three grandchildren who absolutely idolize her. I wonder if the same can be said for you, Marlene. Hardly mother and grandmother of the year, are you now?' Angela said sarcastically.

When Marlene began screaming abuse at her daughter, Pam ran down the stairs to get Angela inside the house. Pam didn't know what had shocked her the most, Angela sticking up for her, or her daughter having the front to slag off Marlene's parenting skills when she had been the mother from hell herself. 'Get in here now, Ange. She ain't worth it,' Pam hollered, as her daughter started to march across the road to have a face-to-face altercation with Marlene.

Angela immediately came to her senses and changed direction. She had a pretty face and didn't fancy having it damaged in a Dagenham street brawl. 'You're right, Mum. She isn't worth it,' she shouted.

'Fucking old slapper,' Cathy added, before shutting her window.

'So, what you doing here?' Pam asked coldly as she shut the front door. Aidan saw more of Angela now than he did of her and, even though Pam was pleased for her grandson, after bringing the boy up almost single-handedly, she found his closeness to Angela a bitter pill to swallow.

'Well, that's a nice greeting, isn't it?'

Pam stood with her hands defensively on her hips. Angela rarely visited her, so she must want something. 'Come on then, spit it out. What you after?'

Angela sat down on the sofa. 'I've actually come to see you to try and build some bridges, Mum. Spending time with Aidan has kind of made me realize just how important family is, and I wondered if you could have a word with Steph for me. I know I was a bitch in my younger days, and I can't blame Steph for hating me, but I've changed now. I can see the error of my past ways and I feel as though I am not only missing out on a relationship with my sister, but also my niece and nephew. I would like to wipe the slate clean and start all over again. I thought perhaps we could all go out for a family meal or something. I'll pay for it, of course.'

Pam was so shocked by her daughter's heartfelt speech that, rather than sit on the armchair, she sort of fell on top of it. Was Angela playing another one of her devious little games? 'So, what's brought all this on, then?' she asked suspiciously.

'As I said, spending time with Aidan has just got me thinking about things. You've only got one family, Mum, I realize that now, and Steph and I haven't spoken for bloody years. My fault, I know, but I wanna make things right if I can. Will you help me do that?'

Pam stared at Angela's pretty face. Her daughter certainly

seemed to have changed for the better since returning from Greece, and for once Pam believed that she was being genuine. 'Your sister's got enough on her plate at the moment, but I will have a word with her in the next week or so and try to sort out a truce between yous. I dunno how Steph will feel about it, but I'll do me best.'

Angela smiled. 'Thanks, Mum. I had a lovely time with Aidan last night, by the way. He insisted on taking me out for a meal out of his first wage packet. He's bought you a present and is bringing it round on Sunday. You should have seen all the girls in the restaurant looking at him, Mum. Aidan could have had his pick of 'em, honest he could.'

Pam couldn't help but chuckle. She was pleased that Aidan had bought her a present and was coming to visit her. At least he hadn't forgotten about her completely. 'What restaurant did you go to?'

'Jailhouse Rock in Hornchurch. 'Ere, you know who I bumped into in there? I didn't recognize her, but she recognized me. Tammy's sister, the copper. Apparently, she came out of the actual police force and now just answers the emergency calls. She said that her and her husband had split up, so she had moved back to stay with her parents. She asked how Steph was and then told me that Tammy had just found out she was pregnant. She said since moving to Spain with Richard, Tammy had distanced herself from her family and was a bit up herself.'

'Ooh, I'll have to tell Steph that. Do you fancy a bit of lunch?'

Angela stood up. 'No, I can't, Mum. Roxy and her husband are coming to stay with me for a couple of days and I need to get home and make a start on the dinner. I learnt how to cook whilst living in Greece and I really enjoy tampering with new dishes and stuff now. Tonight, I am attempting Lobster Colorado for the very first time. Christ knows what Roxy's bloke will make of it. Dean is a typical chips-and-gravy northerner.'

Pam chuckled. She had no idea what Lobster Colorado was herself, so could imagine the look on this poor Dean's face when he was presented with it on a plate. She stood up and was stunned when Angela gave her a daughterly hug. 'Christ! You ain't ill, are ya?' she asked, jokingly.

'No, Mum. I'm not ill. I'm just grateful for the way you brought my son up for me, and I can't thank you enough for being there for him when I wasn't. You truly are a wonderful woman.'

Absolutely gobsmacked by the change in Angela's attitude, Pam was too choked up to reply.

Stephanie listened in earnest as Dannielle explained Tyler's version of events over his altercation with James Woodcock. 'Honest, Mum, I know Ty's not lying, but I still gave him a real big talking-to. He seriously didn't have any intention of using that knife, I know he didn't. He is just a typical lad who doesn't like to lose face in front of his pals. You know how cocky young boys can be?'

Remembering how Wayne was at school, Stephanie nodded sadly. 'Tyler's very much like your dad, in more ways than one. When I first met your father, he was a football hooligan, you know. He used to go over West Ham and get into gang fights and all sorts. I don't ever recall him carrying a knife about with him, though. That's what has scared the life out of me, Danni. Boys will be boys and all that, but carrying knives is not only stupid, but bloody dangerous as well.'

'Tyler knows that now. Between me and you, I told him about our grandad ending up in prison for stabbing our nan to death. It frightened the life out of him, I know it did. Ty won't be carrying no more knives, trust me. Don't ground him though, Mum. You're at work till late most days, I'm always round my friends houses or out gallivanting, and it's not fair for him to be stuck indoors all alone. I can guarantee you, after my little speech, Ty will be the best-behaved boy in Loughton for a good few months.'

Stephanie couldn't help but smile. Dannielle was not only an angel sent from heaven as a daughter, she was also a godsend as a sister for Tyler. 'OK. Tell him he's allowed out, but he's got to be in by eight. If he proves that he can behave himself, then after a month or so, I'll let him stay out until his old curfew, nine.'

'Thanks, Mum. Oh, and while I think of it, I want to ask a favour off you for myself.'

'What now?' Stephanie replied, pretending to be cross.

'You know I told you my friend Mimi's sister owns a pub in Chigwell?'

'Yeah,' Stephanie replied, half guessing what was coming next.

'Well, Mimi's sister said me and the girls can go in there now that we've left school. She said that we're not allowed to be served alcohol, but as long as we behave ourselves we can have soft drinks in there. Can I go, Mum, please? The other girls have already asked their mums and they all said yes. You know you can trust me, don't you?'

Part of Stephanie wanted to say no. Danni was still a little girl in her eyes, but remembering that she and Tammy had been visiting pubs and drinking alcohol long before they were sixteen, Steph nodded. 'Just be careful, though, and never leave your drinks unattended. There was some woman in the salon the other day telling me that her niece had got her drink spiked, and had then been sexually assaulted by some boy.'

'Mum, I'm not stupid. I'll only have a couple of Cokes and they won't leave my side, I promise. I'm going to have a shower in a bit and start getting ready. I haven't a clue what I'm going to wear.'

'Are you going to this pub tonight, then?' Steph shouted out as Danni galloped excitedly up the stairs.

'Yes.'

'Well, give me the name and address of it before you go. I don't mind you enjoying yourself, darling, but I need to know where you're gonna be.'

'I will, Mum,' Danni yelled, as she shut the bathroom door.

Stephanie let out a deep sigh. Children were the most wonderful gift in the world, but with that gift came worry.

Pam had expected Lin to be in a reasonably melancholy mood, but within a couple of hours of arriving, she seemed quite chirpy considering the circumstances. David was upstairs messing around on his PlayStation, which Steph had bought him to cheer him up a couple of days after his dad had died.

'I'm a bit peckish, are you? I think I'll make us all some sandwiches,' Pam said to Cathy.

'How's your diet going?' Lin asked her sister.

Pam grinned. She had recently joined Weight Watchers and had now lost nearly two stone. 'Yeah, good. I lost another three pound this week. Getting there slowly but surely. I've saved some of me points so I can have a couple of glasses of wine tonight. Anyone wanna join me in a tipple?'

'Does the Pope pray?' Cathy said, laughing.

'Wine makes me depressed lately, so I'll just stick with a beer, sis,' Lin added, sensibly.

'I'll rustle us up some grub, then I'll sort the drinks out afterwards,' Pam said, heading off to the kitchen. Just about to butter the bread, Pam heard an excited yell.

'Pam, quick. Come and look who's just pulled up in a cab.'

Thinking she had an unexpected visitor, Pam dropped her bread knife and ran into the lounge. 'Oh my gawd! Looks like he's here to stay for a while by the size of that suitcase an' all.'

'He's more handsome than ever, ain't he? I wish I was thirty years younger,' Cathy said, chuckling.

'He reminds me of an older version of Robbie Williams,' Lin said, joining in with the fun.

Grabbing her phone, Pam darted back into the kitchen and rang her eldest daughter.

'You all right, Mum? How's Lin?' Steph asked.

'Lin's absolutely fine. 'Ere, you'll never guess who's just pulled up outside in a cab.'

Steph had been dozing on the sofa and hadn't really come to her senses yet. 'Who?' she asked, yawning.

'Barry Franklin.'

Stephanie leapt off the sofa as though she had just received an electric shock. 'What the hell is he doing back?' she hissed.

'I don't know, love, but by the size of his suitcase, he's staying for a while.'

Stephanie felt a griping fear inside her stomach. Barry Franklin had toyed with her feelings, used and abused her, and left her emotionally scarred for life.

'Are you OK, love?' Pam asked.

Stephanie was anything but OK. Dropping the phone, she ran to the toilet and was violently sick.

CHAPTER THIRTY-SIX

After a sleepless night, Stephanie tried her hardest to act as normal as possible the following morning.

'Are you OK, Mum? You don't seem yourself,' Dannielle asked, concerned. She had been chatting away about her great night out for the past half an hour now, and she could tell that her mum had barely listened to a word she had said.

Hearing that Barry was back in England had knocked Stephanie for six. Every bit of pain and humiliation Barry had ever caused her had come flooding back into her mind, as if it had happened only yesterday. He had killed her fiancé, Steph was sure of that now, and had she not fallen for Barry's deceit and slept with him, Stephanie would have told the police the truth. However, having her name dragged through the court, and the jury looking at her as though she were some stupid tart, was not something that Steph could have handled. Her children were her top priority, and if they had ever found out the awful truth of her sleeping with Barry just months after their father had gone missing, Steph would probably have tried to top herself again with the shame of it all. 'I'm fine, darling. I just feel a bit peaky this morning, that's all. There's been a bug going around the salon and I think I might have caught it,' Steph lied.

Dannielle swallowed the fib and carried on chatting about her night out. She had found going to the pub with her friends for the first time ever extremely exciting. It had made her feel like an adult for once. She had told her mum the truth about them only being allowed to buy soft drinks in the pub. What she hadn't told her mum was that she and her friends had drunk four alcopops each before they had even gone inside the boozer.

'So, did any boys in the pub try to chat you or your friends up?' Steph asked, warily.

'No. Well, a few tried to talk to us, but none of us were interested.'

Breathing a massive sigh of relief, Stephanie put the bacon on the grill. 'Call your brother, darling. Tell him his breakfast will be ready in five minutes.'

'Did you let Ty go out last night, Mum?' Dannielle asked, remembering their conversation.

Even though her daughter had had a word with her about not grounding Tyler, Steph had still been keen to keep him in for a week or so, to make sure her son was fully aware of the error of his ways. 'No. I made him stay in and he sulked all evening in his bedroom. However, he can go out today as long as he comes and eats this bloody breakfast I'm cooking. The little sod refused his dinner last night and he must be starving.'

Dannielle grinned. 'I'll go and tell him – and is it OK if I go to the pub again tonight? They are having a karaoke night.'

Under usual circumstances, Stephanie would not have allowed Tyler to go out gallivanting or her daughter to spend two consecutive evenings in the pub. However, after hearing that Barry was back in England and was less than ten miles down the road, what her children got up to was the least of her problems. Stephanie turned to Dannielle and forced a smile. 'Of course you can go to your karaoke evening.'

Barry Franklin felt surprisingly at ease when he woke up at his mother's house the following morning. He and Marlene had never particularly seen eye to eye, but when he had turned up yesterday evening, they'd knocked back a bottle of Scotch between them, had a good in-depth chat, and had got along better than they had in years. Barry had come back to England for two reasons. Number one was that Jolene had done his head in and he'd recently got rid of her, and number two was his father had been diagnosed with throat cancer. Barry wanted to spend as much time with his old man as possible before the inevitable happened.

'Morning, boy. Now, 'cause I never knew you were coming, I haven't got any proper breakfast stuff in. Because I'm knocking on a bit now, I have to really watch my figure, so I don't usually eat shit like fry-ups any more. But we did sink a few last night, and I dunno about you, but I think we need to soak it up with something. Shall we shoot up that café in the Heathway and stuff our faces in there?'

Absolutely starving, Barry readily agreed. When he had spent some time in England just over ten years ago, he had purchased a couple of properties in Essex to rent out. One was in Chigwell, not too far from where Steph had lived at the time, and seeing as the current tenants were moving out next week, that was where Barry was planning on living for the time being. Residing in Spain wasn't an option any longer, not after everything that had happened; and in all truthfulness, Barry was pleased to get back to England. He had thoroughly enjoyed his twenty-odd years in sunny Spain, but it had never really felt like home to him. Pie and mash in Kelly's at Roman Road was far more his scene than paella on the veranda.

Barry followed his mother out of the front door and gave a furtive glance at the house opposite. Barry still despised Steph for what she had done to him and probably always would. But, making love to her that time was something that would stick in his mind forever. It had been perfect, just like he had always known it would be, and he was sure it was because of his night of passion with Steph that he had never been able to make a proper go of it with Jolene afterwards. There was an old saying that there was a thin line between love and hate, and Barry now believed in that. Steph had ruined his life, and even though he had got his revenge, he still couldn't completely move on from her. He probably never would.

'So, what exactly happened with you and Jolene then? Why didn't you ever get married or have kids?' Marlene asked, inquisitively. She could sense that Barry had been slightly reluctant to talk about this relationship with Jolene last night, so she had spoken about her own life instead.

'We were really happy for a while, Mum, but it was never right, if you know what I mean. Jolene was very immature in her ways. Twice we organized the wedding, then had a massive barney and called it off. I fell out of love with her quite a while back and, to be honest, I thought she felt the same way about me. Just recently, though, she kept banging on about getting married again and having kids and stuff, so I knew I had to end it for good,' Barry explained.

'And was she OK when you called it a day?' Marlene asked.

'No, not at all. I dunno if I went the wrong way about it, but I took her out on the boat for the day, cooked us a nice lunch and told her after we'd eaten it. She went absolutely ballistic and tried to strangle me and all sorts. I steered us back to shore and then had her father on me case. Jolene's now fucked off somewhere apparently, and I'm sure her old man thinks that I've done her in or something. I told him I've heard from her. She's rung me twice, but her mum and dad have been telling people otherwise. All the expats over in Spain started looking at me as though I was some kind of a fucking murderer. Then, some bastard set fire to me boat. Poured petrol over it, they did, and burnt it to cinders. Gutted I was. Don't get me wrong, that ain't the reason I've come back to England. You know me, Mum, I ain't frightened of no bastard, including Jolene's scouse prick of a father. I've come back because I wanna spend some time with me father before he croaks it. Not only that, I'm sick of living in a foreign country. Home is where the heart is and all that, eh Mum?'

Marlene smiled politely, but said nothing. Jake the Snake's killer had never been found; neither had the mystery of Wayne Jackman's disappearance ever been solved. Now, all of a sudden, Jolene had gone missing after a day out on Barry's boat with him, and then the boat had mysteriously been destroyed. Marlene was no prude. Barry's father had been a wide boy when she had first met him and she'd always mixed in a villainous kind of circle, even before ending up with Jake the Snake. However, wondering if she had given birth to a mass murderer was something different. As Barry led her into the café, then turned to her and asked her what she wanted to eat, Marlene suddenly felt rather nauseous. Not wanting Barry to be aware of her suspicions, she grinned at him falsely. 'I'll just have a coffee, boy.'

Barry looked at her in bewilderment. It had been his mother's idea to go out for breakfast. 'But I thought you were hungry, Mum. Don't you still want a fry-up?'

Marlene shook her head. 'You order what you want, Bal,

but honestly I couldn't eat a thing now. It must be all that Scotch we drank. Made me feel proper sick it has.'

Pam had just popped round to her local newsagent to get the Sunday papers when she bumped into Barry Franklin on the short walk home. 'Hello, love. How are you?' she asked, fondly.

The warmth in Pam's voice told Barry that Stephanie had never disclosed to her mother what had happened between them, so Barry politely leant forward and kissed Pam on both cheeks. 'I'm fine, thank you, Pam. How about yourself? You're looking well.'

'I'm fine thanks, love. My Steph ain't half done well for herself, you know. Got her own beauty salon in Essex and has bought herself a nice big house for her and the kids to live in. What about you? Are you married with children now, Barry?'

'Nope. I'm officially single again now, Pam. I've recently split up with my girlfriend, which is one of the reasons I've moved back to England. My dad unfortunately has cancer, so that's another reason I've come back home.'

'Sorry to hear about your dad, love. Terrible disease that cancer. So, are you home for good?' Pam asked, hopefully. She wasn't silly, and had guessed that there had been some kind of fall-out between Stephanie and Barry all those years ago. However, people have silly tiffs all the time, and Pam was still sure that Barry and Steph would make the perfect couple. Pam would love to see her daughter settled, and Barry would sort Tyler out, she was sure of that.

'Yep, I'm home for good now. I've sold most of my properties in Spain and I'm gonna start buying land over here and building flats. That's where the money is these days, Pam. How are Stephanie's children? They must be all grown-up now.'

'Dannielle's beautiful, Barry. Sixteen now, she is, and looks just like Steph. She's ever so bright and is gonna work in the beauty business like her mum. Tyler's a good lad deep down. He's the spit of Wayne, but between me and you, Steph has had a few problems with him over the years. I think Tyler needs a man in his life to knock him into shape, but my Steph has been single for years now. Not looked at another man since Wayne disappeared, bless her.'

'I take it Wayne's never been found then?' Barry asked, knowing full well that he hadn't. Barry had kept in touch with a few old pals back in England while he was living in Spain, and one of them gave him regular updates on everything.

'Nope. Wayne's never been seen or heard of since his stag night, Barry. I doubt we'll ever find out the truth of his disappearance now. Too many years have passed and the police gave up looking for him yonks ago. I'm sure my Steph would love to see you again, Barry. Why don't I give you the address of her salon and you can pop in and surprise her one day, eh?'

Well aware that Pam was trying to fix him and Stephanie up, Barry nodded politely. He already knew where Stephanie's salon was, as his pal lived down the road from it.

Pam scribbled the address down on the back of an old receipt and handed it to Barry. 'Do me a favour, love. If or when you do pop in and see my Steph, don't tell her I sent you, will ya? She's very business-minded now and quite set in her ways. I would hate Steph to think I was trying to fix her up or something. She'd bleedin' well kill me,' Pam said, chuckling.

Not wanting to inform Pam that there was more chance of hell freezing over than he and Stephanie becoming a couple, Barry tucked the address away in his pocket. 'Don't you worry, Pam. If I do pop in the salon to see Steph, your secret's safe with me, darling.'

Worried about her mum being so lethargic and quiet, Dannielle wondered whether she should ring her nan or not. Steph hadn't eaten any breakfast or dinner, but Dannielle had caught her drinking a glass of wine earlier, which had made her think that her mother was lying about having some kind of bug. Something or someone had upset her and, determined to find out what or who, Danni decided against ringing her nan and planned to confront her mother herself. 'What do you think I should say to her, Ty?' Dannielle asked her younger brother.

Tyler had just spent the past ten minutes listening to his sister rambling on about his mum's strange mood. Not only was he bored shitless, he was also desperate to go out with his mates. 'I don't know what you can say to her, Dan. You're better with words than I am. If it was me, I'd just ask her if she was on the blob.'

'You really are a disgusting little boy at times, do you know that, Ty?' Dannielle said, punching him playfully on the arm.

Giggling like the naughty schoolboy that he was, Tyler stood up. 'I'm going out now. Good luck with Mrs Blobby.'

Dannielle chased Tyler down the stairs and out the front door. She then went in the lounge to confront her mum. 'Ty's just gone out, Mum. Shall I put your dinner in the microwave for you now?'

Stephanie, who had been lying horizontal on the sofa, immediately sat up. 'No, I'll have it a bit later, babe. Wow, you look fab! Is that the new dress you got the other day?'

'No. It's the one you bought me in Bluewater ages ago. Do you think it's a bit short for me to wear to the pub? I don't look tarty, do I?'

The dress was a floral chiffon and, even though it was way above Dannielle's knees, because of its puffy style it looked pretty rather than tarty. 'No, you look fine. Are you going out now, love?'

'Well, we're meant to be meeting around Mimi's at six, but I'm only gonna go if you tell me what's up with you, Mum. I know something's wrong. I'm not a child any more, you know.'

Annoyed with herself for worrying her daughter, Stephanie knew it was time to pull herself together. So what if Barry Franklin was back in England? He was hardly going to knock on her door after the way he had treated her, was he now? Also, Barry must know that she knew that it was he who had been responsible for murdering Wayne, and Steph doubted he would want to open that particular can of worms, in case she decided to involve the police again. Perhaps Barry had just popped back to England for family reasons, or even a flying visit? Stephanie smiled at her daughter. 'Honest, I'm fine now, darling. I did feel a bit down earlier, I don't know why, but everybody has their off days. I'm due on, so it's probably PMT. What you giggling at?' Steph asked Dannielle.

'Just something Tyler said earlier. He seems to know more about women's time of the months than I do, Mum.'

Stephanie stood up and gave Dannielle a motherly hug. 'I'm actually quite hungry now, so I'm gonna warm that dinner up after all. You get off and have a good time, darling.'

When Dannielle picked up her clutch bag and skipped happily out of the front door, Stephanie couldn't help but smile. She remembered what it was like to be a teenager as clearly as if it were yesterday. She and Tammy had started swigging alcohol as young as thirteen, and she would put money on it that Danni and her friends were doing the same before they got to the bloody pub. Steph put her dinner in the microwave and sighed. 'Oh, to be young again and know what I know now,' she mumbled.

Barry Franklin hadn't seen his old mate Martin Gowing since Martin had visited him in Spain last year.

'So, where we going then, mate? I dunno about you, but I fancy a beer, then a curry,' Martin said, as he got into the cab and gave Barry a friendly smack on the back.

'Yep, that sounds good to me. Let's shoot down Chigwell Row, eh? I wanna check out the new local for when I move in me gaff next week,' Barry suggested.

'It's your call, mate.'

Barry told the foreign cab driver the name of the pub and, seeing as the guy had barely spoken any English, or a word to him as he had travelled to pick up Martin, Barry was surprised when he finally entered into a conversation.

'Busy, busy night, dat pub. You do singing?' the cabbie asked.

'No, I ain't their singer, mate. I'm just going in there for a pint,' Barry replied politely.

Unable to stop himself, Martin burst out laughing. 'I think he's trying to tell you it's karaoke night, Bazza.'

Dannielle and her three best pals were having the time of their lives at their first-ever karaoke night in a pub together. They had just got up and sang Beyoncé's 'Crazy in Love' and had got a massive round of applause for their efforts.

'We were great, weren't we? What shall we sing next?' Dannielle asked Mimi.

'You choose the song this time, Gem, then you Danni, and then Carly,' Mimi ordered.

Being a karaoke night, the pub was full of youngsters. There were a few older people in there, but not very many, and as the door opened and Barry Franklin walked in, Dannielle spotted him immediately. Unlike any of the other men or lads in the pub, Barry had class and he really stood out in his dark jeans and crisp white shirt.

'Wow, he's dishy,' Dannielle commented, nudging Mimi.

Mimi looked at her pal in horror. 'He's well old, Dan. He looks as ancient as my dad.'

Dannielle laughed and then studied Barry again. There was something about his handsome face and the way he had swaggered in that looked vaguely familiar to her.

'Put your tongue away, you perv, and stop looking at him,' Mimi said, laughing.

'I'm not perving over him. I'm just looking at him because I'm sure I know him from somewhere and it will bug me all night if I can't remember where.'

Carly and Gemma immediately joined in the banter. 'Don't lie, Danni, we all know you like 'em old,' Carly joked.

'Yeah. We all need to lock up our grandads when Danni's about,' Gemma added, chuckling.

Dannielle giggled and held her hands up in surrender. 'OK, I admit it, I do like older men, but not as old as him. As Mimi said, he's ancient.'

Barry Franklin wasn't overly impressed with his new local. It was noisy, rough-looking and full of youngsters. 'Well, I can't see meself drinking in 'ere much, Mart. I feel like I'm back in the fucking school playground.'

Martin chuckled. 'I should have warned you, mate. I knew it was young in 'ere. The Camelot's only down the road and it's much quieter. Shall we shoot down there for a couple? I can't hear meself think in 'ere, let alone talk.'

About to agree, Barry clocked the stunning dark-haired girl staring at him. The resemblance to Stephanie as a teenager was incredible – so much so, Barry felt the hairs on the back of his neck stand up. He turned to Martin. 'Do you know what Stephanie's daughter looks like?'

'Yeah, sort of. I've seen her with her mother a couple of times. And I'd definitely recognize the boy 'cause he's a ringer for Jacko. Why, mate?'

'Don't look now, but there's a bird sitting at the second table on the right from the door facing us. She's got long dark hair and a flowery type of dress or top on. She's with three other young birds. I'm gonna shout us up a drink and, while I do so, have a sly butcher's and see if you recognize her.'

Barry could feel his heart beating nineteen to the dozen as he stood at the bar. The girl in question was absolutely breathtaking and, even though she looked like Stephanie had when Barry had first met her, this girl was far more beautiful. 'Well?' Barry asked, as Martin joined him a minute or so later.

'I couldn't say one hundred per cent, but I'm ninety-nine per cent sure that it is Steph's daughter,' Martin reported back.

Barry took his change from the barmaid and glanced around furtively. Whoever the girl was, she couldn't take her eyes off him, so he decided to test the water by grinning at her. She smiled back, then seconds later, stood up and walked towards him. 'Go for a piss or something,' Barry hissed at Martin. He could see the girl approaching, and up close with her lithe young body, she looked even more stunning than she had from a distance. Pretending to be watching the three fools who were prancing about on the stage trying to sing a Madness song, Barry feigned surprise as Dannielle tapped him on the shoulder.

'Excuse me, but I have to ask you this. Do I know you from somewhere?' she asked.

Barry was unsure which way to play it. If he told Dannielle

who he was, then she might run a mile. 'I don't know, babe. But, seeing as you're the prettiest girl in this pub, you must let me buy you a drink,' he said, deciding to be cautious.

Dannielle felt her heart flutter as she looked into Barry's soulful brown eyes. His stare was penetrating and was making her feel all funny inside.

Aware of the effect he was having on the girl, Barry touched her arm gently. 'What's your name, sweetheart?'

'Danni. What's yours?' Dannielle replied, feeling suddenly shy.

'I'll do a deal with you. You let me take you out for a meal tomorrow night and I'll tell you my name and everything else about me. What do you say?'

Apart from kissing a couple of boys from school, Dannielle was a complete novice when it came to the male sex. 'I don't know if I should. Where will you take me?' she replied, nervously.

When Martin reappeared by his side, Barry leant forward, squeezed Dannielle's hand and whispered in her ear. 'I'll take you anywhere you wanna go. Meet me outside this pub tomorrow night at seven, OK?'

Without waiting for a reply, Barry winked at her, then sauntered out of the pub with his pal.

Open-mouthed, Dannielle stood fixated to the spot.

CHAPTER THIRTY-SEVEN

Stephanie was woken early the following morning by the phone ringing next to her bed. She knew without even looking at it that the caller would be her mother.

'There you are! You OK? Worried the life out of me when I couldn't get hold of you all day yesterday,' Pam said, in a relieved tone.

'You wasn't trying to call me all day yesterday, Mum. You didn't even start ringing me until after teatime.'

'Well, if you knew I was ringing, why didn't you answer the bloody phone?' Pam asked, getting annoyed.

'Because I wasn't well, Mum. I had terrible period pains and was lying in bed with a hot-water bottle and a packet of anti-inflammatories. I'm sorry I didn't pick up the phone, but I felt too rough to talk,' Stephanie lied. She hadn't gone to bed early at all last night. She just hadn't really felt like talking.

'So, are you well enough to go into work today?' Pam asked.

'Yeah. Maria's opening up for me and I'll go in about twelve.'

'That's good, 'cause me and Lin are popping down to see you later. David's staying over his friend's house tonight, so we thought we'd spend the evening with you. Lin was a bit down yesterday, she kept crying, so I cheered her up by telling her you'd give her one of them facials and a makeover. It did the trick; she's ever so excited. If we get to you about four, we can have a couple of hours in the salon with you and then go out for a bite to eat. Me and Lin wanna treat you and the kids for once.'

As much as Stephanie loved her mum and her aunt, she really wasn't in the mood to socialize, but what could she say? Her mum sounded so buoyant over her and Lin's spontaneous plan, she could hardly say no. 'OK, Mum. I'll see you both about four-ish then.'

Dannielle Jackman had had the most restless night's sleep she could ever remember having in her life. She couldn't stop thinking about the good-looking older man she had met in the pub and had spent most of the night debating whether she should go out for a meal with him or not. The sensible side of Dannielle told her how stupid and dangerous it might be to go with a man she didn't know. Yet her adventurous side told her how romantic and exciting the evening could be.

'You awake, Danni?' Stephanie asked, gently tapping on her daughter's bedroom door. Dannielle quickly pulled the quilt over her head and pretended to be asleep. Her mum would kill her if she knew that she was considering going out for a meal with some strange man, and Danni didn't want to face her in case the guilt of what she was debating showed in her eyes.

As she heard the sound of her mother's footsteps traipsing down the stairs, Dannielle sat up and put her head in her hands. She was an extremely indecisive person – she always had been. Danni hadn't told any of her friends the previous evening that she was considering going out for a meal with the man she had met. They would have ribbed her something chronic, so she had decided to keep schtum. Knowing that she needed to get advice from someone, Dannielle considered speaking to her brother, then quickly dismissed the idea. Tyler was so protective over her when it came to her love life, he'd probably have found fault if she told him she had a date with Robbie Williams. Grabbing her mobile phone from her bedside cabinet, Danni got back under her quilt and dialled Mimi's number. 'Are you awake?' she asked stupidly, as the phone was answered.

'Well, I wasn't, but I obviously am now, you div, if I've just answered me own mobile. What's a matter? Is something wrong?' Mimi asked.

'Yes and no. Look, I really need to talk to you in private, but you must promise me you won't tell the other girls. Can I come round yours about lunchtime?'

'Yeah, course you can, but please don't tell me this is something to do with the old wrinkly you met in the pub last night, Dan?'

'I can't talk now, but I'll explain everything when I get there.'

'Oh my God! It is, isn't it?' Mimi exclaimed.

Dannielle couldn't help but giggle. 'You'll just have to wait and see.'

Barry was shocked and upset to see how ill and thin his father now looked. Barry hadn't expected throat cancer to give his old man a glowing complexion, but seeing as the last time Barry had met up with his dad he had been built like a brick shithouse, his now skeletal appearance and gaunt expression nigh on brought tears to Barry's eyes. 'So, what do you wanna do today, Dad? I treated meself to a Range Rover this morning, so shall we go for a spin then and have a bit of lunch in a nice boozer somewhere quiet afterwards?'

'Can't really eat normal food no more, boy. I've been living on soups and milkshakes. Your Auntie Jean has been good, mind. She keeps bringing dinners round that she's mixed up in one of them food processors. I can't eat much of 'em though. Reminds me of fucking baby food.' Clocking the worried expression on his only son's face, Smasher gave him a playful punch on the arm. 'I can still bloody drink, smoke and have a bet though, so it ain't all bad. I'll tell you what, why don't we go for a spin in this flash new motor of yours, then we'll stop at the bookie's and go to the Working Man's Club and watch the horse racing in there? Got one of them big screens, they have, and I could murder a few whiskies.'

Barry chuckled. His old man might resemble a walking corpse, but at least he still had his fighting bulldog spirit.

Mimi ushered Dannielle inside her house and told her to go into the lounge. 'My mum and dad are going out in a minute, so we can sit in there, have a chat, and listen to *Kiss FM* on me dad's new stereo system,' she whispered.

Dannielle kissed Mimi's parents, then said hello and goodbye all in one sentence. As soon as the front door slammed, Mimi turned to her friend. 'Come on then, tell me the gossip.'

Dannielle had told her friends very little about her conversation with the man in the pub the previous evening, but as she explained to her pal exactly what he had said to her, Mimi sat open-mouthed. 'I'm sorry, Dan, but I am not letting you go out alone with some old bloke when he wouldn't even tell you his name. He might be a paedophile or a rapist. He sounds well dodgy, if you ask me.'

'Mimi, I'm sixteen not twelve, so you can't call him a paedophile. Anyway, I wasn't going to go for a meal with him alone. I want you to come with me.'

Mimi was aghast. 'You don't honestly think that I'm spending the evening sitting in a restaurant with you and some old pervert, do you?'

'Don't be like that! I'd do it if the boot was on the other foot, you know I would. Honestly, Mimi, he was such a nice guy and I just know we'll have a fab night with him. I've definitely met him before somewhere, and if I don't go tonight, it's gonna bug me forever where I know him from. He was rich, I could tell that by his clothes, so I know me and you won't have to pay for a thing. And, because he's older, we can get served lots of alcohol. Please Mimi, say you'll come? I will never ask you another favour in my life if you do this for me. Pretty please?'

Mimi sighed. She could tell how important this evening was to Danni and the thought of sitting in a nice restaurant, eating free food and drinking lots of alcohol, was enough to make Mimi change her mind. 'OK, I'll do it. But, remember Dannielle Jackman, you owe me one.'

Lin felt like a cross between Victoria Beckham and the Queen as she was pampered and fussed over by her niece and her staff. Stephanie's salon mainly did beauty treatments, but she had recently employed a girl who solely did makeovers, and when Lin looked in the mirror, she squealed with glee. 'Christ, I can't even recognize meself,' she said, grinning at her older sister.

Pam put an arm around Lin's shoulders. 'You look absolutely stunning, don't she, Steph?'

'Aw my gawd! What was that?' Lin asked, as she heard a loud bang behind her.

'It's champagne for the lady,' Stephanie said in a posh voice as she handed Lin a glass. 'We only give this to our most important clients.'

'Christ, I could get used to this, love. When can you book me in again?' Lin asked, laughing.

Pam winked at Steph as a sort of a thank-you gesture. She hadn't seen Lin this happy since Keith had passed away.

Hearing the salon door open, Stephanie poked her head around the booth and was thrilled to see both her children walk in. 'Look who's here,' she said to her mum and aunt.

'Wow, Lin. You look so elegant,' Dannielle gushed, hugging her aunt.

Tyler stood with his arms by his side when his nan gave him a cuddle. He was loyal, protective, and loved his family, but he had always found it difficult to show or receive affection of any kind.

'I've just opened a bottle of champagne. Would you like a little drop?' Stephanie asked her daughter.

'I want some too,' Tyler chirped up.

'No, you're too young,' Stephanie said, immediately.

Seeing her grandson's crestfallen expression, Pam ruffled his hair. 'Just give him a little drop, Steph. You and your sister used to have a little sip of wine at Christmas and on special occasions when you were his age.'

About to remind her mother it wasn't bloody Christmas, nor was it a special occasion, Stephanie opted to keep the atmosphere sweet by handing Tyler an extremely small drop of champagne in a glass. 'I took the initiative and booked the Bel-Sit in Woodford for seven. I know it's your and Ty's favourite and I know Nanny and Lin will love it there as well,' Steph said to Danni.

Dannielle immediately felt flushed. Neither her nor her brother were going out for the meal. That's why they had shown their faces in the salon to say hello to their nan and aunt. If they hadn't, their mum would have deemed them rude and gone apeshit. 'Please don't be angry with us, Mum, but I've promised Mimi that I'd stay with her tonight. Her mum and dad have gone to a do up town and they're not coming home till tomorrow. Tyler wants to stay with Brad because his grandad's just died and Brad's really upset about it. You don't mind, do you, Mum?'

'So, what you trying to say? Neither of you want to come out for a meal with us?' Stephanie asked, shirtily.

'It's not that, Mum. Mimi hates being alone in that house because she swears it's haunted and Brad's parents rang me at home earlier and asked if Ty could stay at theirs to cheer Brad up a bit,' Dannielle replied, awkwardly. The haunted house story was obviously total fiction, but she was telling the truth about Mimi's parents going out and Brad's grandfather dying, which made her feel slightly less guilty.

'They're all grown up now, Steph. You can't expect 'em to wanna spend their time with three old biddies like us,' Lin said, trying to defuse the situation.

Stephanie sighed, then smiled. She knew Dannielle would never lie to her about anything. If Tyler had told her Brad's grandad had died, she would have rung up and checked with Brad's parents before she let him stay out the night. 'Go on then, sod off the pair of ya, and make sure you both behave yourselves.'

Feeling her guilt increase, which then made her face redden, Dannielle grabbed her brother by the arm so they could make a quick getaway. 'Bye everybody, and I promise we'll both behave, won't we, Ty?'

As his sister dragged him out of the salon, as rapidly as if a bomb was about to go off inside, Tyler stared at her suspiciously. Danni had been acting weird all day and, as her clued-up little brother, he was absolutely positive that she was up to no good.

Barry Franklin parked up his Range Rover and went inside the pub to get a drink. He had no idea if Dannielle was going to turn up or not and he had already decided if she didn't show, he would go to the karaoke night again next weekend in search of her. Since meeting Dannielle last night, Barry had barely been able to focus on anything else. He liked her, really liked her, and that had nothing to do with wanting to heap more misery on Steph. Danni being her daughter just happened to be a bonus. Ordering himself a Scotch, Barry sat near the window, so he could partially see the car park. Martin, his pal, had joked with him in the Indian restaurant the previous evening by saying he was hell-bent on getting the ultimate revenge. 'What better way to ice the cake, eh? Can you imagine Steph's reaction when she finds out you've been shagging her daughter?' Martin had said, laughing.

Barry had chuckled rather than disclose his true feelings. He had always had an impulsive streak when it came to knowing what he wanted. Up until now, he had only ever been in love once properly in his life, and that had been when he had first met Stephanie. Barry had thought he had loved Jolene when they had first got together, but even though he had found her incredibly sweet and beautiful, he now knew what he had felt for her was not love. Clapping eyes on Dannielle last night had left Barry with feelings he thought he would never experience again. Barry wanted the girl, wanted her badly – and what Barry wanted, he usually got.

Tyler Jackman and his pal Brad put their hoods up as Mimi's front door opened. 'See, I was right. Look how dolled up Danni is. She said her and her mate were staying in to watch films and I knew she was bloody well lying,' Tyler said, angrily.

'I still don't think we should be spying on her, Ty. I mean, I know we like spying on people, but it ain't right to spy on your own sister. I bet she's just going to the pub or something.'

Ducking his head back behind the bush as his sister walked down the pathway, Tyler was furious as a minicab pulled up outside the house and the girls got inside. 'Oh, bollocks. Danni ain't just going to some pub, Brad. She knows I drink, I know she does, and she would tell me if she was going out on the lash. I know my sister and it's only today she's been acting weird. Something dodgy's going on and, seeing as we've got this week off school, me and you are gonna find out what.'

Dannielle was a bundle of nerves as the cab drove down Manor Road. She had no idea if the man she had met would be in a cab, his own car, or on foot. Nor was she even sure he would turn up. 'Say he was just winding me up? He might have thought I was some stupid kid or something and decided to play a prank on me,' she said to her friend.

Mimi glanced sideways at her pal. She and Danni had met at secondary school, had been best pals ever since, and Mimi had never known Dannielle to be as nervous and sickly over any boy or man before. Noting that her pal's hands were visibly shaking, Mimi squeezed them for comfort. 'Of course he'll turn up,' she said. Mimi then shut her eyes and silently prayed that Mr Whateverhisbloodynamewas didn't. He had already had a strange effect on her best friend and Mimi could sense that, whoever the bloke was, he was going to cause Danni nothing but bloody grief.

Unaware that her daughter was about to meet up with her very worst nightmare, Stephanie was surprisingly having a jolly time with her mum and Lin in the restaurant. She really hadn't felt like socializing at all earlier, but getting out and forgetting all her troubles had actually done her the world of good.

'Well, I have to say that was one of the nicest pizzas I have ever eaten in my life,' Lin said, polishing the last piece off.

'Yous pair aren't in a rush, are you? Shall I order us another bottle of wine?' Stephanie asked.

'Yes please! I thought I was in the Sahara desert,' Lin replied, cheekily.

Pam didn't see the funny side of her sister's humour. 'I don't think you should have any more, Lin. Don't forget we're going home by train and I can't carry you if you end up getting pissed.'

Stephanie chuckled. 'Mum, you are not going home by train. I've got an account now with a local cab firm. I set it up so I know that Danni's always safe when she's out gallivanting and it's handy for business purposes as well. You'll be getting a cab home tonight, and I'm sure if Lin collapses the driver will help you get her out the car.'

Pam relaxed. 'We're still paying for the meal and drinks though, aren't we, Lin?' she said, nudging her sister.

'Yep, of course we are! Now, can we have some more bleedin' wine before I die of dehydration?'

When the waiter brought the wine over, Pam decided that it was as good a time as any to bring Angela into the conversation. 'Your sister popped round at the weekend. I'm not just saying it, Steph, but since she came home from Greece and started being a proper mother to Aidan, she don't 'arf seem to have changed for the better. I think she wants to wipe the slate clean. She knows she was a horrible cow and she wants to make it up to you.'

Stephanie pulled a sarcastic face at Lin. In her heart, she would always love and miss Angie, but there was no way she was going to allow her sister or anybody else for that matter to ever hurt her again. Steph had endured enough humiliation to last her a lifetime, which had left her with a heart made of stone.

'Leopards don't change their spots, Mum,' she said coldly.

'I know what you're saying, love, and I can understand why you're saying it, but I truly believe that Angie wants to try and build some bridges now. She spoke to me in an honest way I've never heard her speak before. She said she realizes that she was an awful person in the past and a terrible mother. She also said that spending more time with Aidan has made her realize just how important her family is to her. Between me and you, I think she's loved-up. Aidan said something to me about she met this bloke out in Greece. He ain't moved over to England with her because he runs his father's business over there, but apparently he's bought her a beautiful apartment to live in in the Docklands and he gives her money every week so she don't have to go to work any more.'

'And has Aidan met this wonderful mystery man yet?' Lin sneered, with more than a hint of sarcasm in her voice.

'No, not yet,' Pam replied, wishing her sister would shut up.

Stephanie raised her eyebrows. 'What a surprise! The reason Angie hasn't introduced her lover to her son yet, is probably because the bloke she's hooked up with is some married old Greek sugar daddy.'

Lin spat her mouthful of wine back in the glass with glee. 'Or, worse still, Angie's mystery man might be your Wayne.'

When Stephanie fell silent, Pam glared at her younger sister. Lin had a terrible habit of saying the wrong thing once inebriated, but what she had just suggested to Steph was not only thoughtless, but well below the belt. Pam snatched Lin's glass of wine away from her and moved it over to the other side of the table.

'What did you do that for?' Lin asked, indignantly.

'Because I think you've bloody well had enough, that's why. You're bang out of order, Lin. I want you to apologize to Stephanie immediately.'

Steph pulled herself together and smiled. 'Don't have a go at her, Mum. Lin was only joking. Anyway, knowing my vindictive sister as well as I do, I wouldn't put anything past her. Wayne's dead, I know in my heart he is, but I bet Angie would have run away with him had she had the bloody chance. I will never forgive her for the way she showed me up in front of them police officers. She insinuated that my Wayne was a paedo, if you remember rightly, and the Old Bill were always funny with me after that. Looked at me like I was scum, they did, so please save your breath trying to organize a tearful reconciliation. I never want to see Angela again, Mum.'

Barry's heart skipped a beat as he spotted Dannielle through the pub window. She had a sleeveless, tight-fitting black dress on and looked even more sexy than she had the previous evening. Downing the rest of his drink, Barry stood up and went to greet her. 'You all right, sweetheart? I didn't know if you'd turn up or not. You look absolutely beautiful, may I say.'

Dannielle felt incredibly nervous as she looked around for Mimi. The cab had dropped them outside the car park, and when she hadn't spotted Barry waiting for her, Dannielle had allowed her friend to go inside the pub to say hello to her sister.

'There's no need to look so nervous. I'm not gonna bite you, babe,' Barry said, staring intently into Dannielle's eyes.

Dannielle felt nauseous through pure fear of the unknown. Barry was dressed immaculately in a dark grey suit and open-necked white shirt, and he was standing so close to her, Dannielle could almost taste his gorgeous aftershave. Whoever this guy was, he was sex on legs, and Danni had a feeling that she was way out of her depth. 'There you are. Where you been?' she asked with relief as Mimi reappeared.

'I'm sorry, Dan. My sister is upstairs looking after Callum. He's not well, bless him,' Mimi said. Callum was her two-year-old nephew. Mimi turned to Barry and glared at him. 'Hi, my name's Mimi and I'm Danni's best friend. There is no way I am letting her go out on a date with a strange man on her own, so either I come as well, or she don't go.'

Barry could immediately tell that Mimi hated him on sight, so decided to do what he did best, which was turn on the charm. 'I can fully understand your concern for your friend and of course you are welcome to join us, Mimi. Now, where would yous ladies like to dine? I know a couple of nice restaurants in Chigwell.'

'No, we can't go out round here. We're only sixteen, our parents will kill us if we're spotted in a restaurant with some old bloke,' Mimi said bluntly.

Barry couldn't help but chuckle. He had been called lots of things in his time by birds, but never 'some old bloke.' 'A pal of mine told me about a nice Chinese restaurant in Abridge. How about we go there?' he suggested.

Dannielle immediately shook her head. 'My mum has a beauty salon and quite a few of her clients live in Abridge, so we can't go there. Can we just go into Romford or somewhere? Me and Mimi don't want to get into trouble and we're less likely to bump into our parents' friends around there.'

Barry grinned and pressed the key to unlock his Range Rover. 'Your carriage awaits, ladies,' he said politely.

Suddenly feeling scared herself, Mimi grasped Dannielle's hand. 'We can't get in there with you. You're gonna have to tell us your name and your phone number first,' she said to Barry. Mimi had recently watched the movie *Essex Boys* with her mum and the way Barry was dressed, and the fact he owned a black Range Rover, reminded her of one of them gangster types in the film.

'If you want to take my phone number, I'll give it to you,' Barry said, grating his teeth. He had started to get very pissed off with Mimi already, but was desperate not to let it show.

'What's your name, then?' Mimi asked coldly, as she took a pen out of her handbag.

Looking into Dannielle's eyes, Barry decided it was either shit or bust. He would have to reveal his true identity soon, so rather than stand in the car park all night, he might as well do it now. 'My name is Barry and when Danni was very young she used to drive me mad to sing "Incy Wincy Spider" to her,' he said gently.

Dannielle put her hand over her mouth in shock. She knew she had recognized Barry when she had seen him last night. 'Oh my God! I can't believe it,' she exclaimed.

'Do you actually know him then?' Mimi asked, looking at her pal with a quizzical expression on her face.

'Yes! Yes, I do! He was once my Uncle Barry.'

When Dannielle threw her arms lovingly around his neck, Barry held her tightly and grinned. Stephanie had obviously kept her trap shut about what had happened between them, which thankfully left the pathway open for him and Dannielle.

CHAPTER THIRTY-EIGHT

Not wanting to spend her evening sitting in a restaurant like some gooseberry while Dannielle and Barry reminisced about the past, Mimi decided it was now OK for Danni to go out alone with Barry. 'Listen, I'm going to stay here with my sister if you don't mind? Me and her can get a takeaway and watch a film or something. I feel awful leaving her when I know she's so worried about Callum.'

'But, I'm meant to be staying at yours, Mimi. I don't want to have to go home,' Dannielle said anxiously.

'We can still stay at mine. Go for your meal, Barry can drop you off back here, then we'll get a cab home.'

'Is that OK with you?' Danni asked Barry.

Absolutely thrilled that the bitch of a friend wouldn't be joining them, Barry smiled. 'That's absolutely fine, and I promise I'll have you back here by eleven at the latest. Now, can we make a move? My stomach feels as though my throat has been cut.'

Giggling at Barry's funny comment, Dannielle kissed Mimi on the cheek. 'Have a nice evening with your sister and I'll fill you in on all the gossip later,' she whispered in her friend's ear.

About to get into his motor, Barry decided that now Mimi

wasn't coming with them, he'd better cover his arse. 'Ere, don't be saying nothing to your sister or anybody else about me taking Danni out tonight. If anyone asks you, she's out with a friend, OK?' he said as Mimi walked away.

Mimi turned around. 'What's the big secret, then?'

Telling Dannielle to get inside the motor, Barry walked towards Mimi. 'There is no big secret. The only reason I don't want anybody to know is because Dannielle's mother doesn't know I've moved back to England yet, and I would rather she be told by me or Danni than some local gossip. I take it you'll do as I ask?'

Knowing that Barry had just delivered a warning rather than a question, Mimi glanced at the coldness in his eyes and nodded.

'Thanks, and don't worry, I shall take good care of your friend,' Barry said as he walked away.

Watching the Range Rover pull out of the car park, Mimi felt a shiver travel down her spine. Uncle bloody Barry was trouble and she didn't trust or like him one little bit.

Over in Woodford, Pam was annoyed with herself for ordering a calorie-laden dessert. 'Well, I definitely ain't going to me weigh-in tomorrow. I must have put on half a stone this week, I ain't stopped bleedin' eating,' she said, pushing her empty dish away.

'Don't be beating yourself up. You've done so well and it doesn't hurt to have a little blowout once in a while,' Stephanie said.

'I've had more than a little blowout. I've eaten double me bleedin' points,' Pam replied, chuckling.

'How's Cathy, Mum? I haven't heard you mention her all day,' Steph asked.

'Yeah, Cath's fine. I told you her Michael has finally got his own flat at last, didn't I?'

Stephanie nodded. 'Where you going?' she asked her aunt as she stood up.

'For a slash,' Lin replied, as ladylike as ever.

'You've been guzzling that bleedin' wine like there's no tomorrow, so best I come with you in case you fall arse over tit,' Pam suggested.

Lin glared at her elder sister. 'I might be short, but I'm not a child and I am quite capable of going for a piss by myself.'

When Stephanie began to laugh, Pam raised her eyebrows. 'Ere, that Marlene's got herself a new bloke. Big black man he is. She caught me bogging at her out of the upstairs window the other day and gave me a right mouthful, the cheeky mare.'

'How funny. I hope you gave her a mouthful back?'

'Yeah, I did, and Angela turned up in the middle of the argument and gave her what for an' all.'

Seeing Stephanie's expression change when her sister was mentioned, Pam quickly changed the subject. 'Ere, I can't remember who it was now, but someone told me that they bumped into Tammy's sister in Hornchurch,' Pam lied. She knew Steph wouldn't want to listen to the story if she was aware it had come from her sister's mouth.

'How is Carla? Is she still a copper?' Stephanie asked.

'Oh, that was her name! I couldn't remember it. Well, she ain't a copper no more, but she works on the phones answering emergency calls, so I suppose that's still police-related, ain't it? Anyway, she said Tammy's still living in Spain with Richard and is pregnant with their first child.'

Stephanie felt extremely melancholy as she digested the information. She and Tammy had once been so close and it was such a shame Steph had never seen or heard from her friend since that stupid argument in the restaurant. Unlike her thick self, her clued-up pal had seen through

Barry's façade, and time and time again had warned her that Barry was a nasty piece of work. Steph could kick herself now for not taking heed of Tam's tip-off. Losing her dignity was one thing, but losing her best friend was something she would never forgive herself for. Steph let out a wistful sigh. 'Try and think who it was that saw Carla, Mum. I would love to get back in touch with Tammy again. I know it's been a long while and we've both got our own lives now, but I'm sure we could still be good friends again.'

'I've got a feeling it was Lairy Mary who told me that she bumped into Carla,' Pam said, blushing. She hated lying to Stephanie and wished now she had told her daughter the truth. 'Tammy's parents are only living in Romford, you know. Perhaps I could ask around to see if anyone knows their new address,' Pam added helpfully.

About to reply, Stephanie was shocked when her mother started to swear like a navvy. 'Whatever's the matter?'

'It's Lin. I saw her staggering towards us and now she's bastard well stacked it. I'm so embarrassed, Steph, there's all posh people in 'ere. Go and help her up for me, please. I knew she was fucking pissed.'

Trying not to laugh at her mother's obvious displeasure, Stephanie leapt out of her seat and went to her aunt's rescue.

Barry had learnt how to charm the birds out of the trees as a young lad, and as he reeled off tales about his life in Spain he would sense that Dannielle was mesmerized by him. 'Hark at me rambling on about meself. Tell me about your life, Dannielle. I want to know everything about you.'

Suddenly feeling nervous, Dannielle knocked back a large gulp of wine. Her life had been extremely dull compared to Barry's and she didn't want to start harping on about recently taking her exams or leaving school because it made her sound like a bloody child. 'My life's quite boring compared to yours. Tell me some more stories about your life in Spain,' she replied shyly.

Barry grinned. 'Why don't we talk about when you were young, then? Tell me what you remember about my visits?'

Dannielle paused, then smiled. 'I remember you coming to the house a lot and being there for us when my dad disappeared. I also remember you taking us on lots of fun days out, but apart from going to a farm once, I can't recall where else you took us. I was only young, so my memory isn't that clear, to be honest.'

'Well, you must have remembered me singing "Incy Wincy Spider" to you, else you wouldn't have known who I was when I said it in the car park earlier,' Barry said, chuckling.

'That is just soooo embarrassing,' Dannielle said, covering her face with her hands to hide her blushing cheeks.

Laughing loudly, Barry stood up. 'Have a look at the menu while I pay the Gentlemen's room a visit. I already know what I'm having, so when I return we'll order, babe.'

Seeing a couple of the other women in the restaurant glance at Barry as he sauntered to the toilets, Dannielle felt a warm glow inside. Because of their connection in the past, Danni had no idea if Barry was looking at her romantically or just being friendly, but the one thing she was sure of, even though she knew it was probably wrong because of the age gap, was that she fancied Barry something rotten.

Pam spent the entire cab journey back to Dagenham silently cursing Stephanie for having ordered an extra bottle of wine. Lin was incredibly drunk. Her eyes were rolling around in her head and she was driving the poor cabbie mad by asking him loads of questions, then constantly repeating herself. As the cab approached the Heathway and Lin asked the driver for the fourth time how many children he had, Pam finally lost her rag. 'For Christ sake, Lin, leave the poor man alone, will ya? He's trying to drive and you've got a case of verbal diarrhoea.'

Turning sideways, Lin's head wobbled as she tried to focus on her miserable sister. 'I'm only trying to be friendly to the cunt,' she slurred.

Pat hated the C-word. She thought it was disgusting when a man said it, let alone a woman. 'I am so sorry. My sister's had far too much to drink this evening and she has no idea what she's saying,' Pam said apologetically, as the driver thankfully turned into the road where she lived.

'Yes I do. I know exactly what I'm saying,' Lin mumbled, when Pam ordered her to get out of the cab.

When the driver pulled away, Lin turned to Pam and giggled. 'Didn't we have a laugh? Great night, weren't it?'

Pam stared at her sister with a look of pure disapproval. 'It was great until you performed and showed me up. Now, get up them stairs before I fucking brain ya.'

When Barry held her hand as they walked back to where he had parked the Range Rover, Dannielle honestly thought she had died and gone to heaven. Surely he must be looking at her through romantic eyes if he was holding her hand? Or was he just being a gentleman and escorting her to the motor? Having never had what you could call a proper boyfriend before, Dannielle wasn't sure. But the one thing she was sure of was that she loved the feel of Barry's skin touching hers. 'It's only quarter to ten and I told Mimi I wouldn't be back until eleven, so shall we have a quick drink in a pub or something?' Dannielle asked. She had enjoyed herself so much, she didn't want their date to end.

'I thought we'd go for a drive before I drop you back at the pub. I'm moving into a house in Chigwell tomorrow not far from where you used to live, so I thought I'd show you where it is, then you can pop round and see me, if you want? After I've shown you the house, I'll find somewhere quiet where we can park up and have a little chat,' Barry said.

'But we've been chatting all night. Is it something important you want to talk to me about?' Dannielle asked, nervously. She was terrified that Barry was going to tell her that he only wanted to be friends with her because she was too young for him.

Opening the passenger's side door for Dannielle, Barry shut it and then got in the driver's side. He then turned to her. 'I like you, Dannielle, and I mean *really* like you. For all I know, you might think I'm some old codger. Do you?'

'Of course I don't! I really like you too,' Dannielle said, tucking her hands underneath her legs. They were shaking with the excitement of it all, and she didn't want to make herself look a fool.

Barry smiled. Dannielle had been looking at him all evening like some lovesick puppy, but he thought it only polite to ask her how she felt anyway. 'Well, in that case there is only one thing, rather than two that we need to discuss.'

'What?'

Barry leant across his seat, held Dannielle's beautiful face in his hands and kissed her gently on the forehead. He then looked her in the eyes. 'Your mother.'

Arriving home, Stephanie felt so much chirpier than she had the past couple of days. Going out had done her the world of good and her mum hadn't mentioned seeing Barry any more, thankfully. Tyler was lying on the sofa watching a film, so Steph half leapt on him for a laugh. 'What's Mummy's little baby doing home, then? Behaving himself, is he?' she asked, planting kisses on his face.

'Urgh, get off me,' Tyler said, screwing up his face and closing his eyes.

Stephanie had known what her son's reaction would be, and couldn't help but giggle. She so enjoyed winding him up at times, especially if she'd had a couple of glasses of wine.

'I mean it, Mum, get off me,' Tyler yelled, as she tried to grab the cushion he had just placed over his face.

'OK, I promise I'll leave you alone, but only if you talk to me for five minutes.'

Tyler sat up and removed his cushion cautiously.

'So, why didn't you stay round Brad's house? I thought you were comforting him because his grandad had just died,' Stephanie enquired. She wasn't too concerned about Tyler being indoors on his own. She worked long hours in the salon and couldn't expect Dannielle to babysit her younger brother any more, so for the past six months or so, Tyler had been entrusted with his own key. Not once had Stephanie had a problem with Tyler when he was at home. The little sod only seemed to play up when he was outdoors.

'Me and Brad had a row so I came home,' Tyler replied.

'Well, you shouldn't have done that, boy, and you shouldn't have argued with Brad either. If the poor boy has just lost his grandfather, I shouldn't think he needs any more stress in his life at the moment.'

'But it was Brad's fault, Mum. I was only mucking about with him and he punched me, twice.'

'You didn't punch him back, did you?'

When her son sullenly shook his head, Stephanie smiled sadly. Tyler reminded her so much of Wayne at times, especially when he was upset or angry. 'Good lad, and when you wake up in the morning, I think you should give Brad a bell and make up with him, OK?'

'But why should I? He started it. He hit me and I never

did nothing back. He should ring me up and apologize,' Tyler replied adamantly.

Stephanie sighed. 'Grief does funny things to people, son. It makes them behave in a manner in which they wouldn't usually behave. Brad wouldn't have meant to lash out at you. He just did it because his grandad had died and he wanted to take his frustrations out on someone. Trust me on this one, because if anyone's an expert on the subject, I am.'

Tyler rarely mentioned his father or his disappearance, but guessing that was what his mother was referring to, he decided to ask some questions. 'Did you hit people when Dad went missing, Mum?'

'No, I didn't hit anyone, but I did some stupid things like anybody would if they were grieving,' Stephanie admitted, awkwardly. The shame of what she had actually done, Steph would take to her bloody grave with her.

'But how could you be grieving if you didn't know Dad was dead?' Tyler asked inquisitively.

'Because I was grieving the loss of your dad – you know, his disappearance. Now, shall I make you something to eat?' Steph asked. The sudden interrogation was making her feel as guilty as sin, and she was desperate to leave the room.

'Yeah, I'll have a chicken burger,' Tyler replied. 'Mum,' he shouted, as Stephanie walked out into the kitchen.

Praying that he wasn't about to ask her any more awkward questions, Stephanie poked her head back around the door. 'What, darling?'

'If I ask you something, will you promise to tell me the truth?'

Feeling her stomach churn at the thought of what her son might be about to ask, Stephanie nodded.

'Do you think someone murdered my dad?'

Walking towards Tyler, Stephanie crouched down in front of him. 'Yes, boy. I do.'

Dannielle could feel her heart beating rapidly when Barry parked the Range Rover in a dark, desolate country lane. He had already shown her the house he would be moving into, and even though Danni felt incredibly apprehensive, she really hoped that Barry was about to kiss her properly for the very first time.

'There's stuff I need to tell you, Danni, stuff which you may or may not already know about. When me and your mum were young, we were boyfriend and girlfriend for a very short time. Nothing sexual happened between us, I swear it didn't. We were only about fourteen years old.'

Dannielle felt the colour drain from her face. She'd had no idea that her mother and Barry had once dated and she did not know how to react to the confession. She tried to speak, but no words would come out of her mouth, and momentarily she thought she was about to regurgitate the Indian meal that she'd eaten.

Sensing the shock that had registered across Dannielle's face, Barry took his seatbelt off and leant towards her. 'Please don't be angry with me, babe, but I like you so much, I felt I had to be truthful with you from the beginning. Me and your mum were children, nothing more, and we were only together for a matter of weeks. The relationship ended when my mum moved to Spain and I went with her.'

Dannielle had had the perfect evening up until now and, unable to stop herself, she burst into tears. 'Why did you have to tell me that?' she cried.

'Because I think too much of you to bloody lie. Listen Danni, I know this is a lot for you to take in, but I didn't want there to be any secrets between us. If we are to have any future together, honesty is the only policy.'

Visualizing her mum and Barry kissing one another, Dannielle put her head in her hands. 'I want to go back to the pub. Can you take me there now, please?'

Barry put his seatbelt back on, started the ignition, then drove along in silence. He'd had no intention of telling Dannielle about his relationship with Steph on their very first date, but he was glad he had. He could have quite easily left it until he had reeled her in hook, line and sinker, but his conscience had told him not to do that. Shagging Dannielle was not his aim, nor was breaking her heart or having his own smashed to smithereens. He liked her, really liked her, and that's why he had to be truthful with her. Barry knew dropping a bombshell like he had could prove to be shit or bust, but it was better than loving her and losing her. 'We're nearly at the pub now, so please stop crying, babe. If you don't, your mate is gonna think I've attacked you or something and she might call the police,' Barry said, gently.

Realizing that Barry was right, Dannielle ordered him to pull over somewhere. She was acting like an idiot, and even though she was extremely confused, she didn't want him to think that she was some stupid kid. 'Thanks,' she said, as he handed her a hankerchief.

'Danni, I know this has been a shock for you, and if you never want to see me again, I understand, I really do. The ball's in your court, sweetheart. You've got my phone number and you know where I'm moving to, so I'll leave it entirely up to you. The only thing I do ask from you is to not say anything to your mother and make sure that mate of yours doesn't either. Mimi doesn't like me. I can sense she thinks I'm far too old for you, so when you get back to the pub, just tell her that you won't be seeing me again.'

'But she's gonna know I'm upset. She's my best friend,' Dannielle said.

Barry took a deep breath. 'The best thing you can do to protect the both of us is to say that I looked upon you only as a family friend or something. I know you're gonna feel a mug, but what else can you say?'

Dannielle looked into Barry's doleful eyes and forced herself to behave like an adult. She had no idea if she ever wanted to see him again, but one thing she did know was that she did not want to get him into any trouble. 'OK, I think I'll tell Mimi that I got a bit drunk, tried to snog you and you pushed me away. Does that sound all right?'

Barry smiled at her. 'That sounds perfect, darling. Now, I'd best be getting you back because it's nearly quarter past eleven.'

When Barry swung into the car park, Dannielle couldn't wait to get out of the Range Rover. 'Goodnight then, and thanks for the meal,' she mumbled uncomfortably, as she made a grab for the door handle.

Knowing that this could be the last time he ever saw Dannielle up close, Barry grabbed her by the hand. 'You are the kindest, prettiest, most wonderful girl I have ever taken out on a date in my life, Danni, and even if we never clap eyes on one another again, I just wanted you to know that.'

Desperate to get away from him, Dannielle snatched her hand away and ran inside the pub.

CHAPTER THIRTY-NINE

After a tearful, sleepless night, Dannielle had a quick shower, got changed into the fresh clothes she had brought with her, then woke Mimi up. 'I'm gonna make a move now, mate. You don't mind, do you?'

Mimi sat bolt upright. 'Why are you going home so early? I thought we were gonna go shopping in Romford and have a bit of lunch out.'

When Dannielle had got back to the pub last night, she had seen Mimi and had immediately burst into uncontrollable tears. Mimi had believed the yarn she had spun about her trying it on with Barry and him rejecting her, so Danni decided to play on that again. 'I can't face going shopping, not after what happened last night. I feel such an idiot, I really do. Promise me you'll never tell anyone I went out with Barry, or that I tried to kiss him? You won't, will ya?'

Seeing that her friend looked as though she was about to cry again, Mimi stood up and gave her a hug. 'I know you feel like a div at the moment, but in a couple of weeks' time we'll be laughing about this. I didn't like that Barry one little bit. He scared me, and I'm sure you'd have ended up getting your heart broken by him. He was far too old for you anyway, Dan. An age gap that big would have never worked out in the long run. You've had a lucky escape, mate, I know you have, and I swear I will never tell a soul about what happened, OK?'

Pulling away from her friend, Dannielle nodded. 'Thanks for being such a good mate. I'll bell you later when I've cheered up a bit.'

As Mimi watched Dannielle walk disconsolately down the pathway, Mimi pictured that horrible Barry's face and thanked God for small mercies.

Marlene and Marge hadn't had a girlie day out for weeks, so both women were really looking forward to their lunch date. It had been Marge's idea to go to the Harvester in Chadwell Heath and they had so much gossip to catch up on, Marlene hadn't cared where they ate.

'What we having to drink? Wine?' Marlene asked her pal.

'Yeah, order a bottle of white,' Marge replied.

Marlene gave their food and drink order to the waitress, then turned to her mate and grinned. 'Guess what?' she said.

'Dennis has the biggest cock you've ever seen?' Marge replied, crudely.

'Well yeah, but I've already told you that. Guess again?'

'You're up the spout?' Marge said, roaring with laughter.

'You're having a laugh, ain't ya? After the two monsters I gave birth to, I'd rather die than bang out any more. Now, you ready for this?' Marlene asked.

'Yep. Fire away.'

'Dennis spoke about us living together and I said yes! He's moving his stuff in mine at the weekend.'

'Good for you, girl. Blinding news! Fuck me, you don't hang about, do ya? Not even been with him a month, have you?' Marge asked.

'Hark who's talking! You met Frederick in Barbados and moved him in the day after we got back from holiday. Talk about pot calling kettle,' Marlene reminded her friend.

'All right, all right. I hold me hands up, I'm a fast worker an' all. I wonder if you and Dennis will end up getting married quick, like me and Fred did. Wouldn't it be fab if you did, Mar? I could be bridesmaid, that's if you can find a dress big enough to bleedin' fit me. If not you'll have to buy me a tent,' Marge said, chuckling at her own wit.

Thanking the waitress for bringing the wine over, Marlene took a large gulp of hers. 'I know I can trust you and I gotta tell someone. My Barry's been up to his old tricks again.'

'Tricks! What tricks?'

Looking around to make sure she was out of earshot of the other diners, Marlene leant forward. 'He's committed another murder.'

Unable to stop herself, Marge started to giggle.

'It ain't funny, Marge. That's why I got rid of him quickly out my bleedin' house. Been staying in a hotel since, he has. There's no way I could have slept with him there. He might have come in me bedroom and tried to strangle me again in the middle of the poxy night.'

Knowing if she continued to laugh, Marlene would get annoyed, Marge did her utmost to keep a straight face. 'So, who's he meant to have done in now?'

'That girl he's been with for years, Jolene.'

'Oh, don't be daft. Your Barry might be a lot of things, but he ain't silly enough to murder his own girlfriend. You're talking out of your arse, Mar.'

'No I'm not! Took the girl out on his boat to apparently end their relationship and the poor little cow ain't been seen since. I bet she threatened to grass him up over his dodgy fucking dealings or something and he lost his rag and slung her overboard.'

'I can't believe your Barry would do something like that, mate. Perhaps the girl was just devastated over him breaking up with her and she's disappeared to get her head together,' Marge said in earnest.

'Well, that's what Barry reckons, but I don't believe him. He swears Jolene's rung him a couple of times, but she ain't contacted her parents and her father's gunning for Barry, by all accounts. The old man's a scouse villain and he's already set fire to Barry's boat. You gotta remember, Marge, this ain't the first time that something like this has happened. Jake, Wayne, and don't forget he tried to kill me.'

Feeling a shiver run down her spine, Marge picked up the glass and downed her wine in one. Marge had always liked Barry, thought he was a son to be proud of, and she so wished Marlene hadn't told her that Jolene story. The reason being, for the first time ever, Marge believed that her pal might be right.

Unfortunately for Dannielle, who just wanted to be left alone, Tyler was indoors when she got home and her little brother was in one of his more irritating moods. 'Why do you keep asking me questions about last night?' Danni shouted at him.

'I'm interested, 'cause you're my sister. Just tell me what film you and Mimi watched? Then I'll shut up,' Tyler asked, watching Dannielle's expression for signs of guilt.

'We watched some shitty comedy on Sky and don't ask me the name of it because it was that bad, we turned it off and put some music on instead,' Dannielle lied.

'Why didn't you go out instead? You could have gone to the pub,' Tyler said.

'Because neither of us could be bothered getting ready.

Now, will you shut up, Ty? Because you are really doing my brain in.'

As Dannielle bolted up the stairs, Tyler picked the phone up and rang Brad. 'Are you OK, mate? Sorry I left you last night. My mum said I was out of order.'

When Brad then apologized for punching him and asked if he wanted to go out somewhere, Tyler grinned. 'Come round here asap. Danni's home and she was deffo lying about last night. I wanna know what she's up to, so today we're gonna be detectives and spy on her properly.'

Brad giggled. Both he and Tyler got a kick out of spying on people. Last year they'd found out where one of their schoolteachers, Mr Douglas, lived and had caught him snogging another man. They had told everybody at school and now the whole of their class referred to him as 'Gay Boy'. 'I'll be round in half hour,' Brad said.

Hearing her phone beep to notify her she had a text message, Dannielle fully expected it to be Mimi checking that she was OK and was stunned to see the name Bobbi flash up. She hadn't wanted to store Barry's real name in her phone in case her mum ever saw it, so had chosen the name Bobbi as it began with a B and she'd also had a girl in her class at school with that name. Her heart started to beat wildly as she read the message: *Hi, babe. I know I said I wouldn't contact you, but I just wanted to check you were OK? Bx.*

Aware of her hands shaking, Danni dropped the phone on the bed. She had lain awake all last night pondering what she should do and she still couldn't make a decision. Her heart told her that she had to see Barry again, and she would never forgive herself if she didn't get to hold him in her arms and see how things panned out. Yet, her head told her that if she did start dating him and her mum found out, it would cause absolute mayhem. Dannielle hated the thought of her mum being disappointed or disgusted with her. They had always been so close, and Danni would hate that bond to ever be broken. It also didn't help that her mum was a complete man-hater and she would probably have disliked any bloke that Danni had met, even if it wasn't Barry. Reading his text again, Dannielle decided she couldn't be rude. Barry had treated her to a lovely evening out and his only crime was to be truthful with her at the end of it. Her hands were trembling as she texted him back: *I'm fine thanks x.*

Dannielle was horrified as Tyler barged into her room, just as she pressed the send button. 'What do you want now, Ty?' she asked, angrily.

'Just a chat. I'm waiting for Brad to come round and I'm bored. We might hang out over the park today for a bit. What you doing? You going out?'

Dannielle eyed her brother suspiciously. He was never usually that interested in where she had been or what she was doing, so why the sudden curiosity? Surely he didn't know she had gone out for a meal with Barry. How could he?

'Who's that?' Ty asked, when Dannielle's phone beeped.

Petrified that the text was from Barry and Tyler might see it, Danni leapt up and physically escorted her brother from her room.

'What you doing?' Tyler asked, as Danni bundled him out the door.

'Getting rid of you, you annoying little shit. Now go away and leave me alone.' Locking her bedroom door, Dannielle felt the butterfly of all butterflies inside her stomach as she read the text message: *I've already moved into my new house. Please pop round and see me, sweetheart. We really need to talk. Bx.*

Dannielle sat on her bed and stared at the mobile phone

as though it were a new invention and she'd never seen one before. Barry wasn't some horny teenager like the boys she had met at school. He was classy, a gentleman, and Danni knew she could trust him not to try it on with her if she went to his house. Hands shaking, Danni picked the phone up and tapped in her reply.

Another person currently looking at her mobile phone as though she had never seen one before was Marlene. Five times Barry had rung her in the past hour and five times she had ignored his calls.

'Ring him back, mate. If you reckon he never constantly rings you, it must be bloody important, and if you ain't got your answerphone switched on, he can hardly leave you a message, can he?' Marge urged her friend.

Marlene poured the remnants out of her and Marge's second bottle of wine into her near-empty glass. 'I'm too fucking frightened to, mate. Say he's been caught and he's ringing me from the cop shop? I mean you've gotta look at this from my perspective, Marge. How are the people of Dagenham – never mind Dennis – gonna react when they find out I gave birth to a mass murderer of a son? I'm bound to get me windows smashed and hounded out of me home. And what if Wayne Jackman's father decides to get his revenge? Barry ain't got no bloody kids, has he? So it will probably be me who he comes after. Already murdered his old woman, Lenny has, so please don't tell me he ain't capable of slicing me up, 'cause he most certainly is.'

'Look, I understand why you have concerns over what Barry might and might not have done, but you can't ignore him, he's your son! Just ring him back, 'cause I'm dying to know what's happened.'

Marlene went into actress mode as she picked up the phone. 'Barry, it's Mummy. Now, whatever you've done, I want you to know I'm here for you. Between us, we can get through this, son.'

Marge stared intently at her friend as her expression went from the Marilyn Monroe pout to one of utter shock. 'Shit! I can see you're in a state, mate. If you need to go down to the Old Bill station, you know I'll come with you. Have they found his girlfriend's body? Is that what he rang you for?' she asked, when Marlene ended the call.

Pursing her lips, Marlene grimaced. 'No, he rang me to find out if he'd left his tan Gucci shoes round my house.'

Unable to stop herself, Marge burst out laughing.

Barry considered himself to be an extremely organized person and, seeing as he had only been back in England for what he would refer to as five minutes, he was certainly pleased with what he had achieved. A beautiful black leather three- and two-piece suite, a top-of-the-range widescreen TV, a stereo system, and a brand-new bed had all been delivered that morning. Not only that, on receiving Dannielle's text to say she would be round at two p.m., Barry had even managed to find the nearest supermarket and do his first shop.

'Right, your Sky's all set up to your TV, mate. We're off now,' the plump bald-headed man said to Barry.

Giving the man a score to have a drink with, Barry ran upstairs to get showered and changed. The gaff in Chigwell was three-bedroomed and, apart from the stuff he'd had delivered today, all he'd brought with him was his suitcase. He didn't care though. As long as he had gas to use his oven, electricity to use his appliances and, most importantly, the girl of his dreams on her way round, what else did he need?

Dannielle felt incredibly nervous as she knocked on Barry's front door. Part of her felt like running away as fast as she could before he had a chance to answer it, but she knew she would never forgive herself if she didn't listen to what he had to say. She owed him that much at least.

'Wow! You look amazing! Come in, babe. The house is a bit empty at the moment because obviously I haven't had time to furnish it properly yet, but I've got all the basics including a couple of bottles of bubbly and a pizza in the oven,' Barry said, winking at her.

'I like your sofas. Are they new?' Dannielle asked awkwardly as she sat down in the lounge.

Barry opened a bottle of champagne and handed Dannielle a glass. 'Yeah, I only had them delivered this morning. Please don't think I'm an alcoholic, will ya?' he added. 'I never usually drink so early in the day. I just thought it would be a nice touch, to toast me moving in and to settle our nerves. I dunno about you, but I didn't sleep well last night. I couldn't stop thinking about you, Dannielle.'

Feeling that massive butterfly fluttering away inside her once again, Dannielle avoided eye contact with Barry and gulped her drink back.

Barry sat down on the opposite sofa. 'So, how do you feel now about what I told you last night? I take it you don't hate me, else you wouldn't be here?'

Dannielle thought she had acted extremely childishly the previous evening and she was determined not to behave in the same manner again. Finding out that Barry had once dated her mother had come as a massive shock to her, but she had shared meaningless kisses with boys at school, so was that really any different? 'I'm OK now I've had time to think about things, and I would definitely like us to be friends.'

Barry chuckled. 'Friends! Is that it, then? Is that all you really want us to be?'

Dannielle shrugged. 'I don't know, Barry. I like you, I really do, but I'm so afraid of my mum finding out about us. Since my dad disappeared, my mum has been my world and she has worked so hard to provide a good life for me and Tyler. She has such high hopes for me, I know she has, and the fact she's a man-hater doesn't help the situation. Do you know, since my dad, my mum has never so much as looked at another man?'

Remembering the look of humiliation on Stephanie's face that night as she had lain naked and begging at his feet, pleading with him to stay, Barry couldn't help but smirk. The smirk was soon wiped off his face, though, as he realized that Dannielle had tears in her eyes. Moving over to the sofa where she was sitting, Barry put a comforting arm around her shoulders. 'Look, don't be upsetting yourself. You must stop worrying, babe. Perhaps you're looking too far into things and there's really no need, 'cause what will be will be. I ain't gonna put no pressure on you, Danni, I ain't like that, so why don't we just chill and take things slowly, eh?'

Annoyed with herself for nearly breaking down again, Danni ferociously wiped the lone tear from her cheek with the sleeve of her blouse. 'What do you mean exactly?'

Taking Danni's hands in his, Barry smiled at her. 'I mean, we've only just met really, haven't we? So, why don't we take things at a snail's pace and see how it goes? We should just enjoy one another's company for now, do fun things, and get to know one another a bit better. No one needs to know nothing that way, and if things do become serious between us in the future, we can worry about how we're gonna break the news to your mother then. Does that sound like a plan to you?'

Relieved that Barry wasn't going to pressurize her into making any rash decisions, Dannielle smiled. 'What sort of fun things are we gonna do? Can we go to the theatre? All my friends have been, but I haven't yet.'

Holding Dannielle's pretty face in his hands, Barry kissed her tenderly on the forehead. 'Your wish is my command, Princess.'

Stephanie was disappointed when she arrived home at teatime to find that Dannielle wasn't indoors. Tuesday nights was what they referred to as their 'girlie night'. It was the one evening a week where Steph would knock off work early and spend the whole evening cuddled up on the sofa with her daughter while they chatted about their lives and watched a film together.

Checking Dannielle's bedroom to make sure her daughter wasn't asleep, Stephanie marched into the living room where Tyler and Brad were totally engrossed in their PlayStation game. 'Where's your sister, Ty?'

Whooping with delight because he was currently caning Brad, Tyler didn't take kindly to his mother's interference. 'Can't you see we're busy?' he shouted, angrily.

'Do you know where your sister is or not, Ty? I've tried calling her, but she isn't answering her phone.'

Brad was the coolest friend that Tyler had ever had, and vice versa. Therefore, both boys always liked to show off to one another in front of their respective parents. 'Probably sucking her new boyfriend's willy,' Tyler said brazenly.

Stephanie was fuming as Brad and her son both burst out laughing. Tyler had a filthy mouth on him at times – where he got his foul expressions from, she did not know. Seething with temper, Steph walked towards her son and clouted him around the head. 'Don't you dare spout filth like that again in my house. Now, I asked you a sensible question, so answer me. Where is your sister?'

Furious that his mother had showed him up by smacking him like a child in front of his best buddy, Tyler leapt up to confront her. 'Don't be having a go at me. Danni's got herself a boyfriend. She's been acting well weird and she's been disappearing in cabs that she ain't booked from your firm. If you don't believe me, ask her yourself.'

When her mother rang for the fourth time, Dannielle knew it was time to go home. After the initial awkwardness when she had first arrived, she and Barry had had the most wonderful day together. They hadn't done much apart from listen to music, sip champagne and chat, but Danni was amazed by how well they got on. It didn't even feel as if there was a five-year age gap between them, let alone the nineteen-year difference that there actually was.

'I'm gonna have to go now, Barry. Tuesday night is the only night that me and my mum usually spend together, and she must be worried where I've got to. Can you drop me near home, so I don't have to wait for a taxi?'

Barry nodded, stood up, and handed Dannielle her jacket. 'Well, I dunno about you, but I've had such a good day, Danni. Why don't you come round tomorrow about twelve and let me take you out to a nice restaurant for lunch? Don't feel you have to say yes, though. If you've already made plans or you're worried about your mum getting suspicious, we can do it some other time.'

Dannielle grinned. Her college course didn't start until mid-September and, seeing as she had now left school, apart from Saturdays when she worked in her mum's salon, she had plenty of spare time on her hands. 'I would love to go out for lunch with you tomorrow, Barry, and thanks so much for today. I really have enjoyed myself.'

Barry took Dannielle by the hand. About to open the front door wider, he slammed it shut again.

'Have you forgotten something?' Dannielle asked him.

'Yeah, I've forgotten to kiss you, babe.'

Dannielle felt no guilt, no nerves, and no doubt whatsoever

as she dropped her handbag and flung her arms around Barry's neck. Their kiss was wonderful, extremely passionate, and when their lips finally parted, Dannielle felt a blissful happiness inside. Barry might be older than her, but nothing about their relationship felt wrong. From their conversation, to their humour and even their kiss, the whole package felt totally right.

CHAPTER FORTY

Stephanie decided not to mention Tyler's revelation to Dannielle, but over the next few days, Steph definitely noticed a change in her daughter's behaviour. Dannielle only usually went out three evenings a week, yet all of a sudden she was out all the time and wasn't returning home until at least midnight. Steph also noticed how Dannielle seemed to freeze when she asked her what she had been up to. It was as though Danni could barely look her in the eyes and Stephanie knew that was partly her fault for repeatedly warning her daughter about the dangers and pitfalls of dating lads. Steph could now kick herself for poisoning her daughter's mind with her own bigoted opinion, because she guessed it must be the only reason why Dannielle was keeping her boyfriend a secret from her.

The crunch for the mother-and-daughter chat to take place came late on Saturday afternoon. Dannielle had worked in the salon as she usually did on a Saturday and, as she was tidying up, informed Stephanie that she wouldn't be home at all that night because she was going to the pub and staying at a friend's house. Knowing that the inevitable birds and the bees talk needed to happen sooner rather than later, Steph looked her daughter in the eyes and gently squeezed both of her hands. 'I think me and you need to have a little chat, darling. Come out the back and I'll make us both a coffee.'

Dannielle felt incredibly anxious as her mother put the kettle on. Her and Barry had been getting along famously, and the thought of her mother ruining something so good filled Danni with dread.

Putting the two mugs of coffee on the little table, Stephanie sat down opposite her daughter. She hated her and Danni having any secrets between them and knew she had to tread carefully in case she pushed her daughter even further away. 'Look, darling, I'm not silly and I know there's a boy on the scene. Do you want to tell me a bit about him?' Steph asked, smiling.

Relieved that her mother had said the word boy rather than man, Danni relaxed slightly, but still decided to go on the defensive. 'I haven't got a boyfriend. I've just been going out more because I've left school now. I am sixteen, Mum. I'm not a child any more.'

'I know you're not a child any more, darling. Look at you, you're a stunning young woman and of course you are going to meet and attract boys. I'm surprised you haven't had them falling at your feet before now, so just because I'm some old stick-in-the-mud singleton, please don't feel you have to hide anything from me, will you? Me and you have always been so close, Danni, and if you've met a nice lad, I would love to meet him when you feel ready. Perhaps I'll book us a table in the Bel-Sit or somewhere and you can bring him out for lunch?'

Dannielle could hardly admit the truth, but she hated the thought of making up and describing an imaginary boyfriend, so she had no option but to stand her ground. 'Yes, I did meet a lad down the pub last weekend, but apart from swapping numbers and texting each other a couple of times, we haven't even met up yet. Whatever made you think I had some kind of serious boyfriend? You'd be the first to know if I did because I would tell you.'

Steph breathed a huge sigh of relief. Perhaps Danni had just been acting oddly because she liked this boy who was texting her. 'Sorry if you feel like I've just interrogated you. Your brother said something about you having a boyfriend the other day but, knowing Tyler, he was probably just winding me up. So, whose house are you staying around tonight, love?'

'Mimi's,' Danni said, blurting out the first name she could think of. She wasn't. Barry had booked them tickets to see a show in the West End and they were staying in a posh hotel afterwards. Being the gentleman that he was, Barry had booked them two separate rooms. 'I didn't want you to feel worried or pressurized that you had to take our relationship to the next level,' he had explained to Dannielle. Furious with her little brother for grassing her up, Danni tried not to show it as she grinned at her mother. 'What exactly did that lying little brother of mine say, then? I bet he was trying to wangle his way out of something he'd done wrong, wasn't he?' she joked.

Stephanie chuckled. 'Yeah, he was actually. He had given me some lip in front of Brad, and when I gave him a clout around the earhole, he turned the spotlight onto you.'

Finishing the last of her coffee, Dannielle stood up. 'I'd best be going now, Mum. I'm meeting the girls at seven and I have no idea what I'm going to wear yet.'

Stephanie stood up and hugged her daughter. 'You have fun, darling, and don't be having a go at your brother, will you? You know what a wind-up merchant he is.'

Danni promised she wouldn't, picked up her handbag and left the salon. After all she had done for Tyler over the years, he had chosen to betray her. When Danni got her hands on him, rather than have a go at him, she planned to find out exactly what he knew, then throttle the little shit with her bare hands.

Barry was just about to jump into the shower when his mobile phone rang. 'You all right, Phil? How's everything going?' he asked. Phil was Barry's pal over in Spain and Barry had entrusted him to run his property business out there when he had decided to return to England. Barry no longer owned the bar that Jake had left him in his will. He had sold it for good money a while back.

'Everything's OK on the property front, mate. I've sold two more of them apartments in Malaga this week, but it ain't that I'm ringing you about. Jolene's father came into the office yesterday. Going mental he was, and he threatened to blow my kneecaps off if I didn't tell him where you were living.'

'Oh, for fuck's sake. You didn't tell him nowt, did you?'

'Nah, course not. I just kept to the story that we discussed. He ain't giving up though, Bal. Reckons he's flying over to England next week to find you himself.'

'Well, he'll have a struggle finding me. Apart from me old pal Martin, me muvver, and one or two other people, no one really knows that I'm back. Anyway, he has no idea I own a house in Chigwell. I never told Jolene anything about my properties over here in England. I rue the day I ever got involved with that silly tart, I really do. Rang twice again the other night begging me to take her back, she did. Why can't she ring her fucking father, eh? I so don't need all this grief. All I wanna do is move on with me life.'

Phil said nothing. There were strong rumours sweeping Fuengirola that Barry had murdered Jolene and dumped her body in the sea, but he didn't want to get involved in all the tittle-tattle. Barry was his pal and, even though he had told Phil months before Jolene's disappearance that he needed to get rid of her, Phil would never tell a soul about that conversation. He was far too loyal, and if the rumours did turn out to be true and Jolene's body was washed up on a beach somewhere, Phil would still back his pal to the hilt.

'You still there, mate?' Barry asked.

'Yeah, sorry Bal, I was miles away.'

'Did you hear what I said about Jolene ringing me twice the other night?'

'Yeah, course I did. I take it she belled you on a withheld number again?' Phil asked.

'Course she did, the slippery fucker. She even threatened me, saying if I didn't agree to get back with her, she wouldn't contact her father until after he had done away with me.'

Phil wanted to believe what Barry was telling him, but somehow it didn't ring true. Jolene wasn't the type to say boo to a goose, let alone be dishing out threats of getting Barry 'done away with'.

'If the old man comes to the office again, Phil, just tell him to fuck off. Everybody thinks that Jolene is sweetness and light, but she ain't you know. When I took her out on the boat and ended it with her that day, she threatened me with all sorts, mate. She even threatened me with the Old Bill and the taxman, the psycho bitch.'

Realizing that Barry was probably trying to explain to him why he murdered Jolene, Phil decided to rapidly end the phone call. The less he knew about what Barry had or hadn't done, the better. 'I've gotta go, Bal, a client's just walked in. You take care and we'll catch up again soon, mate.'

Tyler and Brad were lying on the carpet in the living room, squawking like hawks over their stupid PlayStation game, when Dannielle rudely interrupted them by dragging her little brother out of the room by his head.

'What you doing? You gone loopy or what?' Tyler asked, fearfully.

'Get up them stairs now. Me and you need to have a little chat, Mr,' Dannielle hissed.

'What am I meant to have done wrong?' Tyler asked, innocently.

'Sit down you little shit,' Dannielle ordered, pointing to her bed.

Stunned that his usually mild-mannered sister had turned into a demented freak, Tyler did exactly as he was told.

'Why did you tell Mum that I had a bloody boyfriend?'

'Because she started asking questions about where you were and stuff. I didn't know what to say, did I? And you have been acting well weird recently.'

Walking towards Tyler, Dannielle pointed her right forefinger in his face. 'I am sixteen years old and what I choose to do is none of your business, Ty. As for blabbing to Mum, I think I'll do the same now. Does Mum know about your stash of porn, your lager, the crap you thieve, and the knife you never got rid of that you hide in the bushes, does she?'

'I am gonna chuck the knife away, I swear I am, I just ain't got round to it yet. How do you know where I hide things?' Tyler asked, shocked.

'Because I'm as bloody nosy as you are. Now, I'll do you a deal. You keep your trunk out of my business, Ty, and I'll keep mine out of yours.'

Tyler immediately held out his right hand. 'Deal,' he said meekly.

'Right, get out my room now, and if you breathe one word of this conversation to Mum, you're dead.'

Glancing at his sister as though she had turned into some

sort of alien, Tyler darted past her, then scuttled down the stairs as fast as his legs would carry him.

Dannielle glanced around anxiously as Barry's Range Rover ground to a halt. Loughton Station was where Barry always picked her up from now. It was much less suspicious than using a different minicab firm to the one that her mother had an account with, and seeing as Loughton wasn't the busiest station in the world, Danni could always have a good look around to make sure that there was nobody about who would recognize her. Satisfied that the coast was clear, Danni leapt into the passenger seat. 'Quick, drive,' she urged, ducking her head down as she always did as they drove away. She had once had an awful premonition about pulling up at a set of traffic lights, glancing to her left or right, and locking eyes with her mother.

'Well, I have to say, Danni, you always look stunning, but tonight you have taken my breath away. You look so, so beautiful. I love your hair up, it makes you look incredibly sexy, may I add.'

Dannielle giggled. She had chosen to wear a long red strapless dress and put her hair up as she had wanted to make herself look older. Barry was taking her to see the Abba musical, *Mamma Mia*, and seeing as they were staying at some posh hotel afterwards, Danni hadn't wanted the staff to think that she was only a kid.

When Barry put his foot on the accelerator, neither he nor Dannielle realized that they had two interested spectators spying on them from behind a nearby wall.

'Fucking hell! Did you see the geezer, Brad?' Tyler asked his pal.

'Sort of, but not that clearly. He looked quite old, did you think that?'

Tyler smirked. He had been seething earlier over the way Dannielle had mugged him off in front of his best mate, and she'd then had the cheek to blackmail him. 'Quite old is being polite, Brad. I got a good look at him when he first pulled up and I reckon he must be about forty or something. No wonder Danni ain't said nothing about him. My mum would fucking kill her if she knew what she was up to.'

'Are you gonna grass her up to your mum?'

'Dunno. Anyway, we gotta get more proof first,' Tyler replied.

'How we gonna get that, then?'

'We're gonna go to the shop and buy one of them cheap throwaway cameras. Then we will follow Danni again and take photos of her getting in that bloke's motor. If we're lucky we might even get one of them kissing or something.'

Brad giggled excitedly. He had a bit of a schoolboy crush on Tyler's older sister. 'Shall we go and get the camera now? You got enough money to buy it?'

'Yeah. I got a tenner on me. I can't wait to see Dannielle's face when I show her the photos. No one blackmails me and gets away with it, Brad. No one!'

Arriving home from work to an empty house once again, Stephanie decided there was little point in cooking if the kids were both out, so warmed herself up a microwave meal. The chilli con carne was tasteless, so she ate half of it and threw the rest in the bin. Feeling rather melancholy, Steph poured herself a glass of red wine, sat on the sofa, and glanced at the photograph of Wayne on the wall. She had only hung it there because she felt it was her duty never to let the children forget who their father was, but just lately looking at it made her feel very lonely. Dannielle was all grown up now, was out doing her own thing, and Tyler had never really needed her, even as a small child. Knowing that her mum was the best tonic in the world when she felt low, Stephanie picked up the phone and called her.

'You all right, love? Work been busy?' Pam asked her.

'Yeah, I'm knackered. The salon was mobbed today. I've only been home about half an hour or so.'

'I wish you'd cut down your hours, Steph, and go out and enjoy yourself a bit more. You're still a young woman and all work and no play is no fun for anyone. Why don't you get back in touch with them lovely girls you used to be friendly with in Collier Row? I bet they'd be up for a couple of good nights out,' Pam suggested.

Stephanie had loved her friends in Collier Row when she and Wayne had lived there, but after Angela had informed them all that Wayne had taken her virginity at thirteen, Steph had kept her distance from them. Unlike her big-mouthed sister, Stephanie was a very private person, and looking her friends in the eye again after what they had been told was something she just couldn't have stomached. 'I think most of my pals have moved away from Collier Row now, Mum,' Steph lied. 'What about Tammy? Did you ask Lairy Mary where her parents have moved to? I'd love to get back in touch with her.'

Now it was Pam's turn to lie. 'No, love. I haven't seen Mary yet, but when I do, I'll ask her. Where's the kids? Danni gone out tonight, has she?'

'They're both out, Mum. Since she's left bloody school, I've barely seen Danni at all. Tyler reckoned that she had some boyfriend, but I asked her today and she says she hasn't. She said she's staying round Mimi's house tonight and it does worry me. Say she has got a boyfriend and she's staying round at his?'

'You're worrying over nothing, Steph. Danni's such a good girl and I'm sure if she had met a boy she liked, she would tell you all about him. There is no way that girl would blatantly lie to you. If Danni said she's staying at her friend's house, then you can bet your bottom dollar she is, love.'

As usual when Stephanie listened to her mum's wise words, she immediately felt better and more relaxed. 'Thanks, Mum. I know I'm a worrier, but I also know you're right. My Danni would never lie to me like that.'

In a posh hotel in London's West End, Dannielle was having the best night of her life. *Mamma Mia* had been absolutely amazing; so had the restaurant that Barry had taken her to afterwards. They were now having a nightcap back at the hotel bar.

'What's this in aid of?' Dannielle asked, as the waiter popped a cork and then poured her a glass of champagne.

'The gentleman insist on champagne for the lady,' the Spanish-looking waiter said, smiling.

Barry put a casual arm around Dannielle's toned young shoulders. 'I thought a bottle of bubbly would be the perfect end to a perfect evening, babe. I'll be honest with you, when I booked them theatre tickets, I thought I would be bored shitless watching that show, but I weren't. I enjoyed it just as much as you, I think,' Barry admitted, chuckling.

Leaning towards Barry, Dannielle gave him a tender kiss on the lips. Barry was everything she had ever dreamed of in a man. He was handsome, funny, rich, a gentleman, but a man who was still grounded – and that was important to Dannielle. She adored his cockney accent and some of the rough expressions he sometimes used. She would have hated to have ended up with some posh bloke who was up himself. In her eyes, Barry was perfect.

'What you thinking, babe?' Barry asked, aware that Dannielle was studying him.

'I was thinking that you should cancel my room and let me stay in yours,' Dannielle replied, boldly.

Barry looked into his beautiful girlfriend's eyes and suddenly felt quite nervous himself. He already knew that he was besotted by Dannielle and, once they had made love, he knew there was no turning back. 'Are you sure?' he asked, his heart beating like a drum.

Dannielle nodded. 'I'm positive, Barry.'

CHAPTER FORTY-ONE

Dannielle had always imagined that losing her virginity would be the most terrifying experience in her life, but as Barry took her in his arms and their naked bodies writhed together for the very first time, everything felt so right.

'You're so beautiful, Danni,' Barry groaned, as he gently thrust himself backwards and forwards against her soft young skin. It had been his idea to use a condom. Danni had admitted that she was still a virgin and wasn't taking contraception on the way up in the lift, so Barry had headed straight back down to the ground floor to purchase a packet of three in the Gentlemen's toilets. Barry had already guessed that Dannielle was a virgin but, even so, hearing it from her lips was still music to his ears. They might have only been seeing one another for a short period of time, but Barry already knew that he loved her more than he had ever loved any girl or woman in the past, and the thought of another bloke mauling her beautiful body before he had would have really played on his mind. 'Are you OK, sweetheart? I'm not hurting you, am I?' Barry panted, as he began to thrust harder and faster.

'No, I'm fine,' Dannielle whispered, staring at his handsome face. He was making some wonderful expressions and weird noises, and even though Danni had had no sexual experience, she could still sense that Barry was really enjoying himself. She had watched similar scenes in films in the past.

'Oh, Danni, Danni, Danni,' Barry shouted out, as his body suddenly went rigid.

'Are you all right?' Dannielle asked anxiously, when Barry rolled off her and lay flat on his back.

Propping himself up on his elbow, Barry looked at Dannielle and chuckled. 'I'm better than all right, babe. That was absolutely amazing. You are the most gorgeous creature I have ever had the pleasure of making love to in my life.'

Dannielle giggled. 'What shall we do now? Shall we put the TV on?'

Barry kissed Dannielle tenderly on the lips, then grinned as he laid his head gently on her breasts. 'You don't need TV when you've got me, girl. I've got a plan. I'm gonna order us another bottle of bubbly and a plate of sandwiches. Then I'm gonna ravish you all over again, but this time I shall make sure the pleasure is all yours.'

When Barry rubbed his finger against her vagina, Dannielle sighed with pleasure. 'That's just one of the things you've got to look forward to, Princess,' Barry said, as he snatched his hand away and leapt out of bed. He rang room service, then went to use the bathroom.

Watching Barry's firm buttocks walk away from her, Dannielle lay back against her pillow and thought about him. Two of her friends had already lost their virginity and both had described the first time as a bit of a let-down. Danni let out a happy sigh. Apart from one short stab of pain when Barry had first entered her, she had found the whole experience exhilarating – so much so, she could hardly wait to do it again.

Barry grinned as he leapt back into bed. He then teasingly

began kissing Dannielle, starting from her lips, then heading downwards.

'Oh my God!' Dannielle gasped, as Barry's tongue made contact with her clitoris. She had no idea if what Barry was doing to her was morally acceptable, but for once she didn't give a damn about what was right and what was wrong. How could anything that felt this good be bad?

Sunday was Stephanie's only day of rest, so she wasn't best pleased when she was awoken by the phone next to her bed ringing at eight a.m.

'Hi Stephanie, it's Mimi. Sorry, did I wake you?'

Knowing that Dannielle had said she was staying around Mimi's the night before, Stephanie immediately sat bolt upright. 'Is something the matter?'

'No, nothing's wrong. I rang because I thought Dannielle might want to come to Lakeside with us. My mum's driving, but she wants to leave before ten to avoid the traffic. I've tried Danni's mobile, but it's switched off, so I guessed she's still in bed?'

Stephanie immediately felt physically sick. 'Danni's not here, love. Didn't she stay at yours last night?'

'Err, no. She was going to, but I think she then decided to stay at Carly's house,' Mimi stammered nervously. She had barely seen Dannielle this past week or so, and now guessed the reason why. Her friend had obviously deserted her and lied to her own mother because that awful Barry Franklin was still on the scene.

Mimi's pause and lame excuse told Stephanie all she needed to know. 'Don't take me for a fool, Mimi. I know you're lying and I also know that Danni's got a boyfriend, so who is he?'

'I don't know about any boyfriend, honest I don't,' Mimi replied, near to tears. She was now desperately worried about her friend herself, but under no circumstances would she ever grass Dannielle up to her mother.

Stephanie sighed. She wanted to shout and scream at Mimi, but knew that was the wrong thing to do. When she and Tammy were Dannielle's age, they had always covered one another's arses to their respective parents, so she could hardly tear Mimi off a strip for doing the same. 'Do me a favour, Mimi, if Danni rings you before she contacts me, can you tell her to come straight home, please?'

'Yes, of course I will.'

Stephanie ended the call and immediately rang her daughter's mobile. The phone was switched off. About to leave Dannielle a threatening message, she somehow stopped herself from doing so. When she had first met Barry all them years ago, her mum had been dead against their relationship, which had forced her to sneak around and meet up with Barry behind her mother's back. Suddenly feeling tearful, Stephanie put her head in her hands. Dannielle had such a bright future ahead of her and all Steph could do was hope and pray that she didn't ruin it all by getting up the spout at a young age, like she had with Wayne. Whoever this lad was, Dannielle obviously really liked him, so all Stephanie could really do was try to like him also and hope the relationship soon fizzled out. If it didn't, or worse still, she hated her daughter's choice of boyfriend, Steph knew without a doubt she would go absolutely mental.

Having breakfast in bed was Barry's idea, but even though the food was delicious, Dannielle could only pick at hers. She and Barry had made love three times last night before they had finally fallen asleep in one another's arms, and once again this morning, and Danni couldn't get their lovemaking out of her mind. It had been absolutely thrilling, especially when Barry used his tongue on her down below.

That was the part when Danni would groan with pleasure until her body came to one final shuddering halt.

'You ain't eaten much, babe. Aren't you hungry?' Barry asked.

Not wanting to admit that the real reason she couldn't eat was because her stomach was in knots thinking about him, Danni picked at her scrambled egg. 'I've never been a big breakfast eater, to be honest. I prefer lunch.'

'Well, in that case, why don't we go for lunch somewhere before I drop you home? You're not in a mad rush to get back, are you? Where did you tell your mum you was staying?'

'I told my mum I was staying at Mimi's, but I'd better get home sooner rather than later in case my mum rings her house.'

'Surely your mate will cover for you, won't she?' Barry asked.

'Yeah, Mimi would never dob me in it, but I never asked her to cover for me, so if my mum rings her, chances are she'll put her foot in it,' Dannielle explained.

Putting his and Dannielle's breakfast trays on the carpet, Barry took his young girlfriend in his arms. 'You don't think I'm too old for you, do you, sweetheart?'

'Of course I don't! I wouldn't be here if I did.'

Barry kissed Danni passionately, then tilted her chin so that he could look her in the eyes. 'I think the world of you, Dannielle, you know that, don't you?' he whispered.

Feeling as though she was about to burst with happiness, Dannielle grinned and clung to Barry like a leech.

Back in Loughton, Stephanie had just dished her son's breakfast up and plonked it on the table in front of him.

'What's a matter with you today? You look well miserable. You got your period again?' Tyler asked, cheekily.

Stephanie felt like picking the plate back up and smashing it over Tyler's head, but instead chose to berate him. 'I am not in the mood this morning for your obnoxious little comments, Ty, so shut your trap and eat your breakfast.'

'I was only asking a question, Mum.'

Remembering that her son was the first one to inform her that Dannielle had a boyfriend, Stephanie sat down opposite him. 'Did you speak to your sister at all and ask her if she had a boyfriend?'

'I thought you wanted me to shut me trap,' Tyler replied cockily.

'Don't mess me about, boy. I've just asked you a serious question, so answer it.'

'Nah, she ain't said nothing to me, but I can find out for you if you want me to? I'll follow her when she goes out.'

'No, Ty! You can't spy on your own sister. Not to worry, I'll speak to her myself when she gets home. Once she knows she's been caught out she's going to have to tell me who the bloody boy is.'

'How has she been caught out?'

Stephanie stood up. 'None of your business. Now eat your bloody breakfast.'

Dannielle was mortified as she listened to her answerphone messages. She had five in total and they were all from Mimi telling her to ring her urgently. The fifth and last message confirmed Dannielle's worst fears. 'Danni, it's me again. Your mum knows you didn't stay at mine last night, so you must call me before you speak to her. I'm in Lakeside with my mum, so ring me on my mobile.'

'What's up, babe?' Barry asked, as he noticed the colour drain out of Dannielle's face.

'My mum knows I never stayed at Mimi's house. What am I gonna say to her, Bal? What am I gonna do?'

'Was it your mum who left you the message?' Barry asked.

'No, it was Mimi. She's left five asking me to call her back.'

Seeing that Danni looked near to tears, Barry bumped the Range Rover onto a nearby kerb. 'Don't get upset, darling. Ring your pal back, find out exactly what's been said and then we'll think of a plan, OK?'

Dannielle's hand shook as she held the mobile phone to her ear.

'Danni, I've been so worried about you. Where the bloody hell are you?' Mimi asked.

Dannielle ignored her friend's question. 'Tell me what's happened?'

Mimi repeated the conversation she'd had with Stephanie virtually word for word. 'So, are you gonna tell me where you've been? I take it you're with him?'

'Yes, Barry's with me. You didn't mention him to my mum, did you?'

'No, but you seriously need to get your eyes and brain tested, Danni. Your mum will kill you if she finds out.'

'I can't really talk now, but will you be in this afternoon? If so, I'll pop round after dinner.'

'You ain't bringing him with you, are you?' Mimi asked, defensively.

'No. Listen, I'd best ring my mum now. She must be going out of her mind with worry.'

Mimi wasn't usually a sarcastic person, but for once she couldn't help herself. 'Ain't we all, Danni? Ain't we all?'

When the phone rang, Stephanie took a deep breath as she realized it was her daughter's number flashing up on the screen. 'Be calm, be calm,' she mumbled to herself.

'All right Mum? I'll be home in a little while. I didn't stay around Mimi's in the end last night. Me and Carly found a new pub that don't ask for ID, so we had a couple of drinks in there and then I stayed round hers instead,' Dannielle lied. She had just spoken to Carly, and Carly had agreed to back her story up if her mum didn't believe her.

Stephanie wanted to scream abuse at her lying little minx of a daughter, but knew that would get her nowhere, so she took another deep breath instead. 'Just come home now, love, and we'll chat when you get here,' she replied as calmly as she could.

'Are you OK, Mum? You sound a bit out of breath.'

'Yes, I'm fine. I'm trying to talk to you and mop the kitchen floor at the same time, which is why I'm breathless. How long will you be?'

'About an hour.'

'OK, I'll see you then,' Steph said chirpily. Seconds later, she burst into tears.

Because he wanted to chat to his pretty young girlfriend for a few minutes and give her a kiss goodbye, rather than drop her at Loughton Station, Barry parked up in a nearby side road. 'Now, are you sure you're gonna be OK? Because if you ever want me to speak to your mum on your behalf, I will. She is gonna have to find out about our relationship sooner or later, Danni. We can't keep it a secret forever.'

Dannielle sighed worriedly. She knew her mother was going to go ballistic when she found out about her secret love and she wasn't quite ready to deal with that yet. 'I'll tell her at some point, Barry, I promise. Not yet though, eh?'

'It's entirely up to you, babe. I won't pressurize you to do anything you're not ready to do, but your mum and mates are bound to get suspicious if we are spending lots of time together. When am I gonna see you next? You gonna pop round tonight for a couple of hours?'

'No, I'd best not tonight, but I'll come round tomorrow when my mum's gone to work. As soon as she leaves, I'll call you and you can pick me up from the station. It will probably be about midday.'

'OK, and would madam like to be taken out for lunch tomorrow? Or shall we have a bottle of bubbly and christen that new bed of mine instead?' Barry asked, cheekily.

'Let's go for plan B,' Dannielle said, giggling.

Cupping Dannielle's face with his hands, Barry kissed her passionately. 'Go on then, you'd better get yourself home.'

'Bye Barry, and thanks for a wonderful time yesterday. I loved *Mamma Mia* and staying in that hotel. It was brilliant.'

When Dannielle shut the passenger door, Barry opened the window. 'Oh, I forgot to tell you something.'

'What?' Danni asked.

'That I love you.'

When Barry winked at her then drove away, a gobsmacked Dannielle stood rooted to the spot. She knew exactly how important the L word was. She and her friends had discussed the subject many times and she hadn't expected Barry to tell her he loved her so early in their relationship. Absolutely thrilled by her boyfriend's surprise declaration, Danni headed happily towards home.

To calm herself down a bit, Stephanie had opened a bottle of wine and was currently on her second glass. She had been desperate to talk to her mother about the Danni situation, but her mum had gone to the Dagenham Sunday Market with Lin and David and wasn't home yet. Stephanie silently cursed her mother. She had recently begged her to let her buy her a mobile phone, so she could always contact her in case of emergencies, but Pam had been dead against the idea. 'What do I want one of them bleedin' things for?

Apart from popping into Romford or up the Heathway, I'm always in-bloody-doors anyway,' she'd insisted. Downing the rest of her drink in one fell swoop, Stephanie went into the kitchen to put the chicken in the oven. She had never felt less like cooking a Sunday roast in her life, but she knew she had to try and carry on as normal. Hearing the front door open and shut, Stephanie felt her heart beating faster. She knew it wasn't Tyler as he had gone out for lunch with Brad and his parents. 'Is that you, Danni?' she shouted, trying to keep her voice sounding cheery.

Dannielle felt sick with nerves when she walked into the kitchen. She loved her mum, hated lying to her, but what choice did she have? 'Mmm, dinner smells nice. What have we got?' she asked, not knowing what else to say.

Wanting to scream that she had only just that second put the chicken in the fucking oven, Steph somehow stopped herself. She turned to her daughter and falsely smiled. 'Chicken. Would you like a glass of wine with me, darling? Then we can sit in the lounge and have a chat.'

Dannielle eyed her mother suspiciously. She was acting really strangely. Apart from on special occasions, she had never encouraged her to drink alcohol before. 'I will if I'm allowed to have a glass.'

'Well, you're not a child any more, are you? Me and Tammy were having a tipple when we were your age, so now you've left school, why shouldn't you?'

Dannielle took a large gulp of the wine just to calm her nerves. She then walked into the lounge and sat on the sofa. She knew she was about to be grilled, she could feel it in her bones.

Stephanie sat down on the sofa opposite her daughter. She felt she had done enough beating around the bush and she now wanted some bloody answers. 'Look Danni, I know you never stayed around Carly's house last night and I also know that you have a boyfriend.' As her daughter went to interrupt her, Steph raised her hand to stop her from doing so. 'Let me finish before you speak, Danni. I can understand why you've been wary of telling me that you've got a boyfriend. It's my fault for coming across as a man-hater and pushing you to concentrate on your studies and career. But, please don't ever feel as though you have to lie to me again, darling. I am not a fool and I have noticed a massive change in you these past few weeks. I am only thirty-five, remember? I'm not ninety. I do remember what it feels like to fall in love for the very first time. So, who is this lad?'

Dannielle knew she had no choice other than to stick to her original story. 'I don't know what you're talking about, Mum. I swear I stayed at Carly's last night. If you don't believe me, you can ring her yourself.'

'So, what pub did you and Carly supposedly go to, then?' Steph asked, her hackles beginning to rise.

'I can't remember the name of the pub, but I know it was somewhere in Hainault,' Dannielle stammered.

'Well, if you can't remember the name of the pub, perhaps you can show me where it is?' Stephanie said, leaping off the sofa and snatching her car keys off the table.

Wishing she had never mentioned going to a bloody pub, Dannielle immediately went on the offensive. 'Why don't you ever believe anything I say? Even if I did have a boyfriend, which I haven't, I could never let you meet him. You would question him like a police officer and he would think you was mental.'

The sheer annoyance that Dannielle thought she could pull the wool over her eyes – and at the same time call her mental – forced Steph to grab her daughter roughly by the arm. 'Right, me and you are gonna drive to this pub and I shall ask the guv'nor and all the staff if they have ever seen you before.'

'I don't know how to get to the pub from here. Please let go of me, you're hurting me,' Dannielle cried.

'No, of course you don't know where it is, you lying little mare. Now, who is this fucking boy?' Steph yelled, with a neurotic tinge to her voice.

Dannielle looked at her right arm and saw blood where her mother had dug her false nails in so hard. 'Look what you've done to my arm. Leave me alone. You're mad, you are.'

Seeing the marks she had caused, Stephanie immediately let go of her daughter's arm. 'Danni, I'm sorry. Where you going?' she shouted, as Dannielle bolted out of the room.

Ignoring her mother's question, Dannielle picked up her handbag and ran sobbing from the house.

Pam had really enjoyed her day out with Cathy, Lin and David. Firstly, they had gone to the Dagenham Sunday Market and had a good old mooch around, and then they'd had a few drinks and lunch in a local Wetherspoon's, which had made a nice change from cooking herself. 'Didn't we have a good day?' Pam said, plonking herself on the armchair opposite Lin and Cathy.

'Yeah, we did, sis. I didn't like that bleedin' roast in that Wetherspoon's, though. Weren't a patch on what you cook,' Lin said critically.

Cathy chuckled. 'Back to the oven for you next Sunday, Mrs Crouch,' she said to Pam.

Pam raised her eyebrows in pretend annoyance. 'I can't believe I got a top to fit me off the market. I'm shrinking that fast I'll be able to fit down the drainholes soon,' she joked. Her diet had gone up the swanny somewhat recently, and on her last three weigh-ins she had put on a total of seven pounds.

Lin and Cath both roared with laughter, and when the

phone suddenly burst into life, it was Lin who stood up first. 'I'll get it. I wanna get meself another beer anyway.'

'She seems so much happier since she's moved in with you, you know,' Cathy said in a hushed voice.

Lin returned holding the handset. 'It's Stephanie. She sounds really upset,' she mouthed, handing her sister the phone.

'Whatever's the matter, love?' Pam asked, when she heard her daughter's racking sobs.

'I've got big problems with Danni, Mum, and I can't handle it.'

Pam took the phone into the kitchen. 'Of course you can handle it, darling. Now stop all them tears, tell me exactly what's happened and we'll sort it out between us.'

Mimi sat down on the bed next to her friend. Dannielle had just admitted to her that she had lost her virginity to Barry the previous evening, and even though Mimi wanted to hide her disgust, she was struggling to do so.

'Oh, it was wonderful, Mimi, and you know them orgasms that everyone talks about, well I had three of them. It didn't happen during actual intercourse, though, it happened when Barry kissed me down below,' Danni said, dreamily.

The thought of an old man kissing her best friend around her nether regions was all too much for Mimi to take in. Not only did the visualization of what had happened make Mimi want to vomit, but she knew it was her duty as a best friend to try and make Danni see sense. 'Please don't describe anything else to me, Dan, because you're making me feel ill, mate. I cannot believe that you have done all this stuff with some old man that you used to call your uncle. He used to sing "Incy Wincy Spider" to you, for fuck's sake!'

Wishing she had kept her mouth shut about certain things,

Dannielle tried to change the direction of the conversation. 'Barry isn't my bloody real uncle, is he, Mimi? I only used to call him that because my dad went missing and at the time he was sort of a replacement relation.'

Feeling a bit guilty, Mimi held her friend's hand. 'Look, I'm just worried about you, that's all, and I think you might have hit the nail on the head by what you just said. Perhaps you are with Barry because you crave a father figure in your life, Dan. I mean, I love my dad, and it must have been so difficult for you growing up without one.'

Snatching her hand away, Dannielle glared at her friend. 'I barely remember my dad, so how can you say that? It's not as though he disappeared when I was twelve, is it?'

Mimi shrugged. 'I just can't get my head around you being with someone that old. It's not your fault. It's Barry who should know better.'

'And what exactly do you mean by "know better"?' Dannielle asked angrily. She had wanted to tell Mimi that Barry had told her he loved her for the first time this morning, but she wasn't going to bother now.

'I mean, Barry's only two years younger than my dad, Danni. It's not right, mate, and if you want my honest opinion I think that your wonderful boyfriend is one of them paedophiles.'

Absolutely furious by her friend's horrendous comment, Dannielle leapt off the bed and pointed a finger in Mimi's face. 'Don't you dare call my Barry a paedophile. He is a wonderful person and I love him. As for you, if you can't accept my choice of boyfriend, then you're not the good friend I thought you was.'

'Where you going?' Mimi asked, when Dannielle picked up her handbag.

Ignoring her pal's question, Dannielle ran down the stairs and slammed the front door.

CHAPTER FORTY-TWO

Tyler got up and reluctantly took his school uniform out of the wardrobe. He hated school at the best of times, it bored the pants off him, and he especially hated going back after any school holidays. Opening his bedroom door, Tyler trudged dejectedly towards the bathroom. It was then he heard sobbing coming from the direction of his mother's bedroom.

'What's wrong, Mum?' he asked, opening the door slightly.

Stephanie was seated on the edge of her bed with her head in her hands. Her eyes were red raw, and Tyler couldn't help but think how tired and ill his mother looked. He was so used to seeing her all glammed up, but this morning she somehow looked haggard. 'Your sister never came home again last night. I asked her if she had a boyfriend, but she denied it and then we had a big row. I'm so worried about her, Ty. I mean, she must be staying at this boy's house, and it makes me wonder what type of family he comes from. Surely if his parents were decent people they would check with me first to see if it's OK for Danni to stay there? And say they are letting them share a bedroom with each other? If your sister gets herself pregnant, she will ruin her life. I just wish I knew who this boy was.'

Tyler felt torn between the devil and the deep blue sea. Even though Dannielle had made a mug out of him in front of Brad and he wanted to pay her back, he had only been spying on her because he had planned on confronting her himself. Grassing his sister up to his mum wasn't something he would relish doing. He might blurt out the odd insult and cocky comment from time to time, but that was about it. On the other hand, Tyler hated seeing his mum in such a state, and he was also now worried about Dannielle himself. The man whose Range Rover she had got into had looked really old, and when he'd had time to properly think about it, that had disturbed him greatly. Tyler was not a touchy-feely kind of boy, but for once he put his arms around his mother and awkwardly hugged her. It wasn't just the fact his sister had got into an old man's motor that was worrying him, it was also the quality of the motor. Tyler might not be academically bright, but he was extremely streetwise, and he knew that black Range Rovers with dark tinted windows were usually owned by gangsters or footballers. Danni's boyfriend had looked too old to be a footballer, therefore Tyler was sure he must be a gangster.

'What am I going to do, Ty? I mean, how am I going to find out who this boy is if Dannielle doesn't want to tell me?' Stephanie wept, clinging to her son.

'If you don't make me go to school this week, then I can find out who he is for you. Brad's got the week off 'cause his mum said he don't have to go back till after his grandad's funeral. He'll help me.'

Pulling away from Tyler, Stephanie looked him in the eyes. 'How are you going to find out who he is though, Ty? And I don't think you should really be skipping off school, boy.'

Tyler thought about his answer before he blurted anything stupid out. 'Danni's bound to come back today when she thinks you're at work for a change of clothes, Mum. I can then follow her and see where she goes.'

'Oh, I don't know, Ty. Say the boy don't live locally and she gets a bus or train to meet him or something. She's not been using my cab firm, I've already checked.'

Desperate to have another week off school, Tyler decided to disclose a bit of inside information. 'She don't get a bus or train to meet him. He picks her up in his motor.'

The word motor immediately sent chills down Stephanie's spine. One of her best clients at the salon, Sherri, had lost her youngest daughter in a car crash last year. The girl had met a lad who had just passed his driving test and Sherri's daughter had been killed because the silly little sod of a boyfriend had been racing with another car. The lad had survived with nothing more than a few cuts and bruises, and a slap on the wrist from the courts, but for Sherri's poor daughter it had been curtains. 'Where does he pick her up from, Ty? Have you actually seen him? What does he look like? How old do you think he is?' Steph asked, frantically. She knew she was bombarding her son with too many questions, but such was her anxiety, she couldn't help herself.

Tyler didn't want to reveal everything he knew, as he felt that his mum would not only go off her head, but also take matters into her own hands and follow Dannielle herself. 'Let me have the week off school and I promise you I'll get you photos of the geezer and his motor.'

Desperate to know how old her daughter's boyfriend might be, what he looked like, and what car he drove, Stephanie nodded her head. 'OK, you can have this week off, but if you don't get me any evidence, Ty, and I find out you've said all this just because you don't want to go to school, I swear I will kill you.'

Tyler stood up. 'I won't let you down, Mum, I promise.'

* * *

Dannielle groaned with delight as Barry flicked his tongue against her clitoris and gave her another wonderful orgasm. Twice last night they had made love, and twice again this morning, and each time they did so, the sex between them just seemed to get better and better. The only bit that Dannielle hadn't really enjoyed so far was when Barry had encouraged her to put his penis in her mouth. She hadn't really known what to do. However, it didn't taste that bad, and she was sure that in time she would get used to it. Dannielle sighed and laid her head on Barry's chest. 'I think I'll pop home and get changed soon; then if you want we can go out for lunch somewhere.'

Barry kissed her on the forehead. 'Your wish is my command, Princess. What you gonna do tonight? You gonna stay here again or face the wrath of your mother?'

'I'd best go home tonight and see how the land lies, Barry. If Mum kicks off badly, I can always come back.'

Lifting up the arm that Stephanie had dug her nails into, Barry planted gentle kisses on the small grazes. 'If your mother attacks you again, she'll have me to deal with next time,' he said protectively.

'My mum didn't mean to hurt me, Bal. She was just angry and it was her nails' fault, not hers. If my mum didn't wear false nails she wouldn't have hurt me at all.'

'OK, you believe what you want,' Barry replied rather abruptly.

Desperate for them not to have their first lovers' tiff, Dannielle decided the best way to avert it was by pleasing her man. She knew Barry had been quite disappointed when she had only put his penis into her mouth briefly last night, so she decided to try again.

'Ahh, Danni,' Barry whispered, as he felt her sweet young lips connect with his prize asset.

As Dannielle forced herself to give her first-ever proper

blow job, Barry Franklin couldn't help but smirk. He loved Danni dearly, but he still got a kick out of wishing Stephanie could see her daughter right now.

Tyler was playing a game of Virtua Fighter on his PlayStation with Brad when his hussy of a sister arrived home. 'Where you been?' he shouted out, casually.

'Out,' Dannielle yelled as she ran up the stairs.

'Right, let's go. We can play this again later,' Tyler said to Brad. They had already concocted a plan between them. Tyler was going to wait at Loughton Station and Brad was going to be the one to follow Dannielle in case she took a detour. Both lads now had disposable cameras. Tyler had made his mother leave him a score this morning, in case he needed the money to complete his task successfully.

'We are still gonna buy some fags and lager later with all that money you got left over, ain't we?' Brad asked his pal.

'Yeah, of course we are. Now, I'm gonna shoot off to the station and you hide where I told you to. Keep your hood up at all times and keep in touch with me by phone. If Danni sees you, just walk the other way, then ring me.'

Brad jokingly saluted Tyler. 'Sorted, boss.'

Unable to concentrate on work, Stephanie asked Maria to see to her latest client for her.

'Are you OK? You look a bit peaky today, Steph,' Maria asked, concerned.

Stephanie was not one to discuss her personal life with her staff, so chose to tell a small white lie. 'I've got a feeling I've got the start of a bug or something. I'm going to sit out the back for a while as I need to make a few phone calls. Give me a shout if you have any problems, Maria.' Steph shut the door and sat in the room she had converted into her little office. She hadn't wanted to speak to her mother when she had rung her at home this morning, so she had made Tyler take the call and tell his gran that Steph was busy and she would call her back later.

'You all right, Mum?' Steph asked, as Pam answered the phone.

'I'm fine, love. Me, Cath and Lin have been rolling up. The old slapper and the black man have just had a full-scale argument in the street. "Fuck off to your precious family of racists then," Marlene screamed out. Then, as her boyfriend walked off she shouted, "And don't bother coming back 'ere, you black bastard." Talk about airing your dirty washing in public, and how has she got the front to call him racist names if they're living together? I know I don't like the woman, Steph, but she is pure entertainment and I'd hate her to move. I enjoy watching her more than I do *EastEnders*. So, how are you today, darling? Did Danni come home after I spoke to you late last night?'

'Nope, not seen hide nor hair of her still,' Stephanie replied miserably.

'Oh dear! Shall me and Lin come over to the salon?'

'No, don't worry. I'm gonna shoot off home in a minute and leave Maria in charge. I'm not in the mood for work today.'

'So, have you rung Danni to see where she is?' Pam asked anxiously. Stephanie had never had a moment's worry with Dannielle in the past, and it was so out of character for her granddaughter to behave in such a rebellious way.

'No, there's no point me ringing her because if she answers, she's only going to lie to me, and then I'll go off me head at her again.'

Pam sighed. She knew exactly how her daughter was feeling. 'Look, the best thing you can do is try and calm down a bit, love. I know it's difficult because when you and your sister were Danni's age, many a time I felt sick and out of me mind with worry. The more you lose your temper with her though, Steph, the more you're gonna push her into this boy's arms – and you don't want that to happen, do you now? Take my advice and don't lose your rag no more, and I bet within the next few weeks, Danni will introduce you to this lad of her own accord. Better still, the relationship might have even fizzled out by then.'

'Let's hope so, Mum. The thing that has worried me more than anything is this morning Tyler informed me that this lad has a car.'

'How does Tyler know that? Did Danni tell him?' Pam asked, suspiciously. She knew what a wind-up her grandson could be at times.

'He wouldn't tell me how he knew, but he swears he can find out who this lad is for me, so I've let him have the week off school.'

Pam couldn't help but chuckle. 'He's a thirteen-year-old boy, Steph, he ain't bleedin' Inspector Morse. What's the betting the little sod's pulling a fast one just so he can have another week off?'

'I thought that at first, but I've got a feeling Ty already knows more than he's letting on, Mum. We shall see if he comes up with any evidence. He asked me for twenty quid to buy some of them throwaway cameras and he swore to me that he would get pictures of the boy and his bloody car. I'm petrified this lad has just passed his test and is racing about like some loony, Mum. He might drink and drive or anything. Worried sick, I am. So much so that, apart from half a chicken sandwich yesterday, I've not eaten anything since Saturday evening.'

Pam sighed. 'You must start eating, love, else you're gonna make yourself ill. You sure you don't want me to come over?'

'I'm fine, Mum, honest. I'm not much company at the

moment and I promise I'll get myself something to eat in a minute. Are you in all day?'

'Yep, not going anywhere.'

'Well, as soon as I hear from Tyler or Danni comes home, I'll ring you,' Stephanie said.

'OK darling, and try and keep your chin up. Things will sort themselves out in the end – they always do.'

Tyler was standing in view of the station when he saw the black Range Rover pull up. He immediately put the hood of his sweatshirt up and rang Brad. 'He's here, Brad. Danni ain't seen you following her, has she?'

'No, she ain't even left the house yet.'

'Blinding! Right, get your arse down 'ere and then I'll start clicking away with the camera. I want you to ask the man if you can have a photo taken with his motor. That way I can take a few and get him in the picture an' all,' Tyler told him.

'I don't really want to ask him. Can't you ask him and I'll take the pictures?' Brad asked, nervously. He didn't like the look of the man they'd seen in the Range Rover one little bit.

'No, because if he lives local he might know what I look like. For all I know, Danni might have shown him some family photos or something. Just bowl up to him and say nice car, mate. Then ask, is it OK if my pal takes a photo of me standing next to it? I doubt the old codger will say no, then I can make sure I get him in the photo an' all. Once we're done we can go get some beer and fags.'

'Danni's just opened the front door, Ty,' Brad replied.

'Well fucking hurry up then. Quick, run.'

While waiting for Dannielle to arrive, Barry decided to give his mate Martin a call at work. 'How's it going, big man? When you gonna pop round and see me new gaff?'

'When I get a proper invitation,' Martin replied, chuckling. 'So what's been occurring? How's it going with the new girlfriend?'

'Yep, all good.'

'What about Jolene's father? You received any more threats?' Martin asked.

'No, but I've heard through the grapevine that he's flying over to England today to try and track me down. Been running around Fuengirola telling everyone I'm a murderer, the mug has, and it sounds like people have started to believe him.'

'Well, I suppose it don't look good on your behalf if Jolene ain't been since you took her out on the boat, does it? What you gonna do if he turns up at your gaff?'

'I truly hope the cock does find me now, 'cause I've got a nice little surprise waiting for him if he does.'

'Enlighten me?' Martin asked, intrigued.

'I'll fill you in properly tomorrow, Mart. I've got some nuisance of a kid banging on me window and Danni will be 'ere any sec. Laters, yeah,' Barry said, opening his window. 'What do you want, boy?' he asked.

'I love your car, mister, it's well cool. Is it OK if my mate takes a picture of me standing next to it, please?' Brad asked politely.

Barry grinned. The kid had a right cockney accent and reminded him of himself as a lad. 'I'll go one better than that. You jump in the driver's seat, get your mate to stand next to you and I'll take a picture of the pair of you,' Barry said, leaping out of the motor.

'He wants to take a picture of both of us,' Brad shouted to Tyler.

Academic Tyler wasn't, but quick-thinking he most certainly was. 'I need to take it because it's for a school project. We're doing a photography lesson and our teacher said we have to take all the photos ourselves,' he said, walking towards Barry.

'Why you got your hood up on a hot day like this?' Barry asked, chuckling.

'Because it's the fashion. So, can I take the photos please?' Tyler replied. He was worried that Dannielle might appear at any second.

When Barry nodded, Tyler quickly started clicking away. He then held out his right hand to Barry. 'Thank you, and what's your name, mister, in case my teacher asks whose motor it is?'

Barry laughed. 'Me name's Barry, lads, but me pals call me Bazza.'

'Cheers, Bazza. Come on, we gotta go now,' Tyler said, grabbing Brad's arm and half dragging him away.

As the boys ran down a nearby street, Tyler burst out laughing. 'That was well wicked. I got about three close-up pictures of him.'

'Getting his name was well cool. Me and you make a great team, Ty. We should be private detectives when we're older and start our own business,' Brad suggested excitedly. 'Shall we get the lagers and fags now? David Smith's brother said he'll go to the offie for us. I asked him this morning.'

Out of breath through excitement, Tyler leant on a nearby wall. 'We need to get the photos developed first. That shop I showed you had a sign saying that they're ready in one hour. We can get the beer and fags after.'

Brad grinned. 'Come on then, let's go.'

Stephanie was forcing herself to eat a prawn mayonnaise sandwich when her mobile phone rang. Her heart lurched when she spotted the caller was her son. 'What's happened? Has she come home?' she asked, on tenterhooks.

'Yep, she came home, got changed, went out again, and I've got the photos I promised you.'

'Go and get them developed, Ty. I'll give you some more money, boy,' Steph said, her heart beating nineteen to the dozen.

'I've already got 'em developed, Mum. I'm looking at 'em as I speak.'

'Oh my God! Well done you! Where are you now, Ty?'

'I'm heading back towards home.'

'Well, stay where you are and I'll pick you up to save you walking.'

'Nah, don't do that, Mum. I think it's best that I meet you at home.'

'Why? What's the matter?'

Tyler screwed his face up. He was dreading telling his mother this piece of information, but she was going to find out soon enough anyway. 'You ain't gonna like this, but Danni's boyfriend is really old.'

'Really old! How old? Does he look about twenty? Twenty-five, or what?'

'He actually looks older than you, Mum,' Tyler said bluntly.

Stunned and horrified, Stephanie dropped the phone in shock.

CHAPTER FORTY-THREE

Unaware that her distraught sister had just gone zooming past her in her BMW, Angela Crouch pulled into the car park of Ye Old Kings Head in Chigwell. Angela was with her old school pal, Chloe Martin, who had recently moved into a house nearby on the Limes Farm Estate, and after lunching in Buckhurst Hill, the girls had decided to stop at a pub on the way back to Chloe's house.

'Oh, I don't like the look of this, Ange. There ain't many cars here and it looks a bit old-fashioned. Shall we find somewhere a bit more modern and lively?' Chloe suggested.

'Anywhere particular you fancy trying?' Angie asked. She didn't care where they went.

'I don't really know anywhere round here yet, mate. Have a look on that list you bought with you,' Chloe replied.

Angela was no expert on the area, so had printed out a list of nearby pubs and restaurants that she had found via the internet. 'Where did I put that list, Chloe?' she asked, as she searched through her handbag.

Chloe was too busy watching the handsome gangster-looking bloke and the young girl who had just walked out of the pub grope one another to answer her friend's question. 'Ere, look at them two, Ange. He's well old for her and I bet he's a drug dealer or something. Look at his flashy motor and his expensive-looking black suit and sunglasses.'

Angela looked up just in time to see the dark-haired bloke get into a spruced-up black Range Rover. The girl was also about to get in, but suddenly turned on her heel and went back inside the pub. 'Oh my God!' Angela exclaimed, her eyes fixed on the girl.

'What's up? Do you know them or something?'

'I didn't really see the bloke, but that girl is my niece. That's Dannielle, Stephanie's daughter.'

Chloe couldn't help but burst out laughing. She had never liked Angela's sister when they were kids. Steph was too up herself for Chloe's liking. 'Are you sure it's Steph's daughter? I didn't think you'd had nowt to do with her or her children for years?'

'I haven't, but Jason threw a birthday party for Aidan recently and Danni was there. I didn't want to go, but Aidan begged me to, so I went and stayed for about an hour. That is definitely her,' Angela said, as Dannielle walked out of the pub towards the black Range Rover once again.

'Well, well, well. I wonder what Miss Prim and Proper thinks about her daughter dating some middle-aged gangster then?'

'I've got to follow them, see where they go,' Angela said, turning on the ignition. 'I never saw the bloke's face, I only saw the back of him as he got in his motor. How old would you say he was, Chloe?'

'I reckon he looked older than us, mate, but I must say he was quite a sort. I'd definitely swap him for my Paul, if I could.'

Angela chuckled. Chloe's husband, Paul, was a pleasant

bloke and a good dad, but he'd put on a lot of weight recently and was certainly no oil painting. 'I hope the bloke don't clock we're following him,' Angela said, indicating left to follow the Range Rover.

'Would your niece recognize you, do you think?'

'I doubt it. She was at Aidan's party with three of her friends and I never spoke to her or anything. I've got a feeling Aidan never told her I was there, and as I said, I didn't stay long anyway.'

'He's indicating to turn into a driveway. If you pull up just past it, I'll walk back and clock the gaff if you want?' Chloe offered a few minutes later.

'No, let's drive up the road, wait five minutes, then drive back again. You never know, he could have clocked us following him and he might just be turning around or something.'

Angela sat in silence as Chloe waffled on about her two children. Aidan had always told her what a lovely girl Dannielle was, and even though Angie didn't see eye to eye with her sister, she didn't want her niece to end up going down the wrong road. If something like this had happened a couple of years back, Angela knew she would have gloated over it, but meeting Theo and finally bonding with Aidan had somehow changed her views on life. She could still behave in an inappropriate manner at times, she knew that, but because she was now happy in her own life, her evil streak rarely raised its ugly head any more. 'Right, let's drive back now. What I'll do is drop you off, then I'll park up on the corner and you can meet me there. Just clock what the house is like, and check if there are any other motors on the drive. I would walk past there myself, but I'd rather not, just in case Danni does see me and recognize me.'

'Come on then, what we waiting for? I'm dying for

another glass of wine, so the quicker we do this, the faster we get to a pub,' Chloe said, grinning.

Angela did as she was told and stopped near the driveway. 'It's the one opposite that red jeep,' she told her pal.

When Chloe got out, Angela drove to the end of the road and waited patiently on the corner. 'Well?' she asked, as her friend reappeared a few minutes later.

'The house looks quite big. If I had to guess, I would say it was a four-bedroomed, and the black Range Rover was the only motor on the drive. It must be that bloke's house, I reckon. It has to be.'

'Oh dear,' Angela said, starting the ignition.

'So, what you gonna do now? Will you tell Steph?' Chloe asked.

'I don't even know my sister's address, let alone have her phone number. If I was gonna do anything about it, I'd tell me Mum, but I know she won't believe me, so what's the point?'

'But, why would she not believe you? I'll back you up if you need me to. I mean we're mothers ourselves, so surely your mum will realize we wouldn't muck about if it was something to do with Steph's daughter?'

Keeping her eyes firmly on the road, Angela shook her head knowingly. 'Actually, I think I will tell her, because if something bad happened to Dannielle, I could never forgive myself. I doubt it will do much good, though. My mum is so blinkered when it comes to Steph, she thinks the sun shines out of her and her kids' arses. I know my own mother, and she would rather eat dog shit than believe that Steph's precious little girl is up to no good.'

Chloe chuckled at her pal's turn of phrase. 'Well, best she start eating dog shit then.'

* * *

Tyler was sitting in the lounge with Brad when his mother came running in like a bat out of hell. 'Where are they?' she asked in an anxious, breathless voice.

Guessing his mum was referring to the photographs, Tyler handed her the envelope and shut his eyes. He was dreading hearing her reaction, let alone watching it.

Stephanie thought her mind was playing tricks on her as she stared at the first photograph. The guy was looking to his left and, at an angle, he reminded Steph of Barry bloody Franklin. Hoping there was a clearer shot, so she could get a better idea of his age, Steph moved onto photo number two. That was blurred, so she immediately skipped to the third. Gasping with shock at what she saw, Stephanie collapsed to her knees with the photo still in her hand. She stared at it again just to be sure. There was no doubt about it. It was definitely him.

Tyler and Brad both nigh on jumped out of their skin as Stephanie let out the most deranged-sounding scream that either boy had ever heard.

'I think I'd best wait in your bedroom,' Brad whispered, when Stephanie began to make a strange howling noise, which reminded him of a badly injured dog.

Tyler gestured that it was OK for his pal to escape the madness, then crouched down next to his mother. He felt quite scared himself. He had rarely ever seen his mother cry, let alone howl and scream like a loony. 'Everything will be OK, Mum. I know the man looks old, but perhaps he's younger than he looks. Please stop crying. I even found out his name for you. It's Barry,' he said, awkwardly trying to hug her.

Pushing her son away from her, Stephanie grabbed the onyx ashtray that she kept on the coffee table.

'What you doing, Mum? Please stop it, you're frightening me now,' Tyler begged, as Steph began repeatedly smashing the ashtray against the photos that were now scattered over the carpet.

Steph ignored her son's plea and carried on with her frenzied attack. 'I will kill you, you fucking cunt. I swear to God, I will fucking kill you,' she screamed.

Pam was in the kitchen dishing up her beef stew when the phone rang.

'It's Tyler. He sounds like he's crying,' Lin whispered, handing the phone to her sister.

'You all right, boy? What's the matter?' Pam asked anxiously.

'You're gonna have to come over, Nan. Mum's gone off her head and I don't know what to do. She's just smashed the glass coffee table with the ashtray,' Tyler said, his voice trembling with fright.

'Oh my gawd! Why did she do that?' Pam asked, horrified. The coffee table was brand new and had cost Steph a bloody fortune.

'Because I took some pictures of Danni's boyfriend and he's really old.'

Pam felt the colour drain out of her face as she heard the words 'really old'. 'I'll ring a cab right now. I won't be long. You be a good boy and look after your mum for me till I get there, OK?'

'OK,' Tyler said, wiping his eyes with his sweatshirt. He was angry with himself for crying because in his eyes only nancy boys cried. Tyler ran back into the lounge and was relieved to see his mother had now calmed down and was sitting on the sofa with her head in her hands. Tyler sat next to her and put both his arms around her. 'I've rang Nanny and she's on her way over. She'll know what to do, Mum. Let her speak to Danni instead of you doing it, eh?'

Steph lifted her dejected head and stared into her son's

sincere blue eyes. 'You don't understand, Ty. I know who the man is in them pictures, and he is pure evil. He isn't wooing your sister because he likes her. He is only wooing her because he holds a grudge against me.'

Tyler was confused. 'But why would he do that?'

Bursting into tears again, Stephanie held her son tightly. 'Believe me, Ty, Barry Franklin is the devil in disguise.'

Unaware that her mother now knew the truth, Dannielle was lying in Barry's bed with her head on his chest. They had just finished making love and Danni adored the manly smell of her man when he was all hot and sweaty. 'What do you think happened to my dad, Barry?' she asked out of the blue.

Surprised at such a question being thrown his way, Barry propped himself up on the pillow. He needed to be careful how he answered this, so chose his words cautiously. 'Why have you asked me that, darling?' he replied, stroking Danni's hair at the same time.

'I dunno really. I was just thinking it would be much easier for us to tell my mum we was a couple if my dad was still around. I think she gets lonely and I think Dad going missing broke her heart. Perhaps that's why she always wanted me to concentrate on my career. She has often warned me against having boyfriends, you know.'

'Look, it's obvious your mum is gonna find out about us one day, sweetheart. But, when you tell her is up to you. I love you and it's your call, babe.'

Dannielle lifted her head and grinned at him. She adored it when Barry told her he loved her. It made her feel happy, secure, and gave her a warm tingle inside. 'So, what do you think did happen to my dad? My mum always told me you were with him on his stag night when he disappeared. Was he really drunk or acting weird or anything?' Danni asked, genuinely interested.

'It weren't just me there with him; there was a few of his other mates there as well. Your dad left the club before me and what happened to him afterwards is one of life's mysteries, I'm afraid . . . Now, I dunno about you, but because we never ended up having lunch out, I am now bloody starving. How about a nice Chinese takeaway? You up for that before you go home?'

Dannielle nodded. It had been her suggestion that they just went out for a quiet drink earlier instead of going to a busy restaurant, and she was now ravenous herself. 'Can we have crispy duck? And I'd really like some prawn crackers as well.'

'Go downstairs and get the menu then, babe. It's on the side by the phone. Your legs are younger than mine.'

When Dannielle skipped happily out of the bedroom, Barry flopped back on the pillow and smirked. He knew exactly where Dannielle's father's six-foot frame was currently residing, but he couldn't tell the poor unsuspecting girl the truth. It would break her fucking heart.

Tyler was relieved when he saw his nan pull up in a cab outside. For the past half an hour or so, his mum had been curled up on the sofa in a foetal position, weeping, and although Tyler had tried his best to comfort her, he hadn't really known what to say or do. What he did know was that there was stuff about this Barry Franklin that his mother wasn't telling him. Like, why did he hold a grudge against her, for instance?

'Where is she? You been looking after her for me?' Pam asked Tyler as she walked into the hallway, followed by Lin.

'Yeah. I'm gonna go upstairs with Brad now,' Tyler said, thankful to make his escape. Seeing his mother in such a state had made him feel extremely uncomfortable. He was livid with his stupid sister for causing all this upset in the first place.

'Put that beef stew in the kitchen, Lin,' Pam ordered her sister. She had brought a container full with her because she was worried about her daughter not eating again. She walked into the front room. 'Sit up, darling. Mummy's here now,' she said, sitting on the edge of the sofa that Steph was curled up on.

'Mum, it's Barry Franklin. It's him who's got his claws in my baby,' Steph sobbed, clinging to her mother like a child.

'What you talking about? What's Barry Franklin got to do with Dannielle?' Pam asked, bemused, as Lin walked in the room.

'Barry's her secret boyfriend, Mum. Look at the photos. They're a bit screwed up now, but you can still see it's him.'

Pam and Lin were both astounded as they recognized Barry immediately.

'The dirty fucking pervert,' Lin spat.

Pam shook her head in disbelief. 'I'm sorry, Steph, but I cannot believe our Danni would fancy a man of Barry's age. She's only a baby, and a wet-behind-the-ears one at that. What's the betting they're just good friends and Danni's frightened to tell you in case you disapprove? She's never really had a father figure in her life, has she? And I bet Barry has filled that gap.'

'Don't be so ridiculous! Danni doesn't even come home of a night any more. If he was just her friend, or a bloody father figure, she would hardly be sleeping in the noncy cunt's bed, would she?' Steph screamed hysterically.

'I agree with Steph. It's sick. I think we should ring the Old Bill and get the pervert locked up. Either that, or pay a hitman to shoot the bastard,' Lin suggested.

Pam glared at her younger sister. 'Let's not start with the silly talk now. For a start the Old Bill ain't gonna do sod all. Danni ain't twelve, she's sixteen, for Christ's sake.

Anyway, before we do anything, we need some proof that they are actually an item. I know for some strange reason you don't like Barry Franklin, Steph, but you can't go around accusing the man of stuff like this without any evidence. For all you know, Dannielle might have a little boyfriend of her own age and Barry's just giving her parental type of advice or something.'

Her mother's stupid comments were like a red rag to a bull to Stephanie. 'You really don't know what you're fucking talking about, do you? Barry has enticed my baby girl into his bed for one reason and one reason only – for revenge. He has no feelings for Danni; he has done this because he hates me,' she yelled.

'Oh, don't be so bleedin' daft and dramatic. That man was so kind to you and the kids after Wayne went missing, you're forgetting all that, Steph,' Pam reminded her daughter.

Stephanie leapt off the sofa and glared at her mum. Her eyes were blazing, such was her anger. 'Oh, I'll never forget Barry cunting Franklin's kindness, Mother. He was there for me all right. He played on my heartbreak and loneliness by making sure I fell for him. Then he slept with me, dumped me, and laughed in my face when I begged him to stay. Now, do you understand why I hate him so much? Apparently, he never got over me leaving him for Wayne, which is why he is now trying to ruin my life again by dating my daughter.'

Pam stood open-mouthed. 'Oh, Steph. I'm so sorry. Why didn't you tell me all this before, love?' It all made sense now. Stephanie refusing ever to talk about Barry, not to mention her hatred towards men in general.

'Because I felt so ashamed that I was so stupid as to be led up the garden path like I was. I also thought everybody would think I was a right slapper if they knew I'd slept with

Barry. My poor Wayne, God rest his soul, had only been missing a matter of months.'

Lin walked towards Stephanie and put her little arms around her niece's waist. 'Don't beat yourself up, Steph. Grief does funny things to people. You were just lonely and gullible. We've all been there. We've all done stupid things in the past, me included.'

The act of kindness from Lin evaporated Stephanie's anger, and as she sat back down on the sofa, she started to cry again. 'Now I've told you that, I might as well tell you the worst bit,' Steph mumbled, her voice trembling.

'Get it all off your chest, love. You'll feel much better for it,' Pam said, gently rubbing her daughter's arm.

With a fearful expression on her face, Stephanie turned to her mother. 'Barry's a murderer. It was him that killed Wayne.'

When her ashen-faced mother held Steph's shaking body in her arms, Stephanie felt relieved that she had finally told the truth. What she didn't realize was that her thirteen-year-old son had been earwigging outside the door and had heard every single word that she had said.

Dannielle ate her Chinese and then glanced at her watch. She was dreading going home to face the music, but she knew she couldn't avoid it any longer.

'I thought you was hungry, darling? You haven't eaten much,' Barry said, picking up a big lump of crispy duck and swallowing it whole.

'I had two pancakes. I just keep thinking about going home, Bal. I'm really not looking forward to it, in case me mum kicks off again. I think I'll switch my phone on now in case she has already contacted me. At least if she has, I'll know by her tone what I've got in store for me.'

'As I said to you earlier, babe, if it all kicks off, just ring me and I'll come straight back and get you.'

Dannielle smiled, and then jumped as her phone alerted her that she had received an answerphone message. Danni put the phone to her ear and felt physically sick when she heard what her brother had to say. 'Oh my God! I can't go home, Barry, I can't! My mum knows everything,' Danni said, bursting into tears.

'It's OK, sweetheart. Please don't worry because I promise I will sort it,' Barry said, reassuringly. 'She had to find out sometime, Dan, it's just sooner than we anticipated. What did she actually say in the message?'

'It wasn't her, it was Tyler. He was really nasty to me. He said that I'd better get my arse home now because Mum knows all about you and he said she's going mental. He even said your full name, so he can't be lying, and he called me a stupid slag and said he's never gonna forgive me for this.'

'Sssh, it will all be fine,' Barry said, kissing Dannielle on the top of her head. 'Tomorrow, I will go and talk to your mum for you, OK? You're sixteen, Danni, she can't tell you what to do any more. Anyway, we love one another, and I will never let anyone take what we have away from us. Your mum's just going to have to accept it, I'm afraid. You do really love me, don't you?'

'Yes, of course I do, but say she don't accept it? I know she's gonna think you're too old for me.'

Wiping the mascara that had run down Dannielle's cheeks with a tissue, Barry hugged her again and rested his chin on top of her head. 'Your mum will get used to the idea in time, I promise you that,' he said softly.

Unable to stop himself, Barry grinned broadly. His feelings for Danni were genuine but, even so, he was still looking forward to seeing the expression on that bitch Stephanie's face when he knocked on the door tomorrow. In fact, he couldn't bloody wait.

* * *

Once Steph had got the burden she had carried around for years off her chest, the anger started to kick in once again. She had to do something and she had to do something fast. The thought of her beautiful daughter spending another night in that murdering monster's bed was far too much for her to bear, so it had been her idea to drive over to Mimi's house. Mimi and Danni had been best friends for years and if anyone could tell her where that bastard Barry Franklin lived or what exactly was going on, then Mimi was that person. Stephanie had wanted to pay Mimi a visit on her own, but Pam had insisted that she and Lin should accompany her. 'We're just as worried about Danni as you are, and I don't want you sounding off at poor Mimi. If you do, you might lose the only link we have to finding her at this moment in time. I think you should let me talk to the girl,' Pam had urged her daughter.

'Right, this is Mimi's house and, honest Mum, I've calmed down a bit now. I would rather do the talking myself, if you don't mind? I'm hoping Mimi's mum, Carol, is in, because even though I've only met her a couple of times, I got on quite well with her.'

'OK, but don't start shouting your mouth off, whatever you do. Me and Lin will wait in the car for you,' Pam warned her daughter.

Stephanie walked up the driveway and knocked on the front door. 'Is Mimi there please, Carol? I'm sorry to bother you, but something terrible has happened.'

Carol called her daughter and Stephanie immediately clocked the terrified expression on Mimi's face as she walked down the stairs. 'Mimi, Danni's in real danger and I need to ask you some questions. Please don't be worried that you'll be grassing her up, as I'm already well aware of her relationship with Barry Franklin.'

'Why don't you come inside? Terry's not home from work yet; probably in some wine bar up town with the lads,' Carol said to Steph.

Stephanie walked into the lounge and explained to Carol the crux of what had happened. 'Honestly, this Barry Franklin is a real nasty piece of work and that's why I'm so worried about my Danni. She didn't come home last night and I very much doubt she will tonight either. Barry is thirty-five, the same age as me, and I don't know about you, Carol, but I find his behaviour towards my daughter bordering on paedophilia.'

Carol was absolutely horrified. She insisted Mimi tell Steph every little bit of information she knew.

Mimi was more worried about Danni's safety than whether her friend would ever speak to her again, so immediately spilt her guts. She told Steph where Danni had met Barry, how he had asked to meet her the following evening, and how she had accompanied her pal to that date, but then never ended up going on it. 'Once I knew that Danni knew Barry and she used to call him her uncle and stuff, I just surmised she'd be safe. I thought they were old friends,' Mimi explained nervously.

Stephanie squeezed Mimi's hand. 'Please don't be blaming yourself for not going with Danni that night. It's really not your fault. Did Danni tell you where Barry lives, Mimi? If she did, you must tell me.'

'Since Danni met Barry that night at the pub, I've hardly seen her at all. She popped round yesterday and we ended up having a big row over something. She stormed off, but before we fell out she did tell me that he'd just moved into a house in Chigwell. I don't know the address though, I swear I don't.'

Stephanie believed Mimi, but needed to know one more thing. 'What did you fall out over, love?'

'Barry, of course,' Mimi replied, honestly.

Stephanie crouched down and squeezed Mimi's hand. The girl looked very near to tears and Steph did realize what a difficult situation Mimi was in. She and Tammy had never grassed one another up over anything when they were young, but nothing this serious had ever happened to test that resolve. 'I need to ask you one more question, Mimi, then I will leave you alone. I swear to you on both Danni and Tyler's lives that I will never repeat this conversation to anyone, OK? So whatever your answer is, nobody else will ever know.'

'You tell Stephanie the truth, Mimi,' Carol said sternly. She was absolutely appalled by the whole thing, but even though she felt terribly sorry for Steph, she was so thankful that it wasn't her Mimi that monster of a man had got his dirty hands on.

Stephanie looked Mimi straight in the eyes. 'I need to know if Danni has had sex with Barry yet?' she asked bluntly.

Looking fearfully at her mother, then back to Steph, Mimi nodded.

Not being able to stomach the thought, Stephanie immediately stood up. She felt drained, disgusted and physically ill. 'Thanks, Mimi, and thank you, Carol. You've both been a great help,' she said as she bolted out of the room.

Steph could barely breathe as she ran down the driveway. The thoughts racing through her mind were despicable. That disgusting shitbag had not only tricked Stephanie herself into bed, he had now taken her beautiful young daughter's virginity. Leaning against a nearby wall, gasping for breath, Steph began to retch. The thought of her baby, who she'd had such high hopes for, lying naked in Barry's arms, made her want to curl up and die. But she would never contemplate suicide again. Prison perhaps? Because as soon as she laid eyes on Barry Franklin, Stephanie knew without a doubt she would be capable of sticking a knife straight through him. Life in prison didn't frighten her at all. As long as her daughter was free of that monster, Steph knew she would be willing to pay for her crime.

CHAPTER FORTY-FOUR

Unable to sleep, Marlene got up early and shuffled downstairs in her bright red nightdress and fluffy slippers. Arguing with Dennis had really upset her. It had also made her realize how much she had enjoyed living with a man again. Since Marge had married Frederick, Marlene had felt like an old spare part, but Dennis appearing in her life had changed all that. He made her feel wanted, sexy, and had definitely put the smile back on her face again. Taking her coffee into the lounge, Marlene put it on the table and picked up the phone. 'Marge, it's me. I didn't wake you, did I?'

'No, I was just about to suck Frederick's cock,' Marge replied, chuckling. 'What's up, mate? You sound miserable.'

'I am. I had a big row with Dennis yesterday and I think I might have ballsed everything up. I was so angry, and you know how acid-tongued I can be when I go into one?'

'What happened? What was the row over? I thought yous two were love's young dream.'

'It was over his bloody family. It was his sister's fortieth yesterday and the whole family, including Dennis's two daughters, were celebrating it in some restaurant in Clapham. I wanted to go with him, but he said I couldn't. Apparently, his mum and sister are quite racist and he hasn't told them I'm white yet.'

'Oh dear!' Marge said. She'd had no such problems with Frederick's family; they had accepted her with open arms.

'As Dennis left, I called him everything, Marge. "I'll give you racist, you fucking black bastard," I screamed, as he walked up the road.'

Unable to stop herself, Marge burst out laughing and repeated to Frederick what Marlene had called Dennis.

'You should have called him Batty boy. He like Batty boy better,' Frederick shouted out.

About to ask Marge if Frederick would ring Dennis up and try to smooth things out, Marlene heard a knock at the door. 'Stay on the phone, Marge. Let me see who the fuck this is at the door and I'll get rid of 'em. It's probably the bastard God squad again.'

Marlene walked to the front door and flung it open with frustration. The man who was stood in front of her was quite tall, stocky, with a shaven head and a boxer's nose. He looked rather like the doorman Marlene had had a brief fling with many years ago. 'I know you from somewhere, don't I?' she asked, wondering if it was him.

'You should do! I'm Jolene's father. Now, where's that murdering fucking son of yours?' Mickey Jeffers spat, barging his way past Marlene and kicking the door shut.

'Get out my house. I don't know where Barry is. I have very little to do with him these days,' Marlene yelled, hoping that Marge hadn't hung up on her and would overhear the conversation.

When Mickey Jeffers put his hand around Marlene's throat and pushed her into the lounge and onto the sofa, Marlene's eyes bulged with terror. She always knew that her son would one day get his comeuppance, but she hadn't expected to be quite so involved herself. 'Get off me,' she screamed, trying to claw Mickey Jeffers' face with her false nails.

Mickey took a dagger out of his sports bag and shoved it against the side of Marlene's neck. 'I'll give you two minutes to give me your Barry's address, and if you don't, I'll kill you.'

'OK. I'll give it to you. It's in my address book,' Marlene admitted tearfully.

'Where's your address book?' Mickey hissed. He didn't really enjoy terrorizing women as a rule but, seeing as this bitch was responsible for giving birth to the bastard who had wiped out his baby girl's life, Mickey was willing to make an exception.

'It's in my handbag,' Marlene said, her voice trembling with fright.

Mickey tipped the bag upside down with one hand. He was still holding the dagger in the other. He picked the address book up and threw it at Marlene.

Hands shaking uncontrollably, Marlene flicked through the pages until she came to the one she was looking for. 'That's it there,' she stammered.

Mickey snatched the book out of Marlene's hands and stared at it. He tore the whole page out, threw the book on the floor and pointed the dagger at her once more.

'Please don't kill me, I beg you. Whatever my son has done isn't my fault,' Marlene wept, covering her face with her hands in trepidation about what was to come.

'I'm gonna let you live, but if I find out that you've warned your son, or you tell the Bizzies about my visit, I swear I will come back and fucking kill you. Now, do you understand?'

Relieved that her life was about to be spared, Marlene's head movements reminded Mickey of one of them nodding dogs he'd owned as a child. 'I promise I won't say a word to anyone,' Marlene wept.

Approximately two minutes after Mickey left her house, Marge and Frederick turned up. Marge had a spare key that Marlene had asked her to keep hold of in case of emergencies. 'Are you OK, mate? I knew something was wrong when I heard you yell, "Get out of my house." So me and Fred quickly got dressed and came straight round. What happened? You look awful.'

Ever the actress, Marlene laid it on good and proper as she relived the story. She even added bits on and told Marge that she had thought her unwanted guest was going to rape her. When she got to the bit where Mickey had pointed the dagger at her, to dramatize the effect, Marlene said he had a gun.

Marge was stunned. If Jolene's father had turned up gunning for Barry, it proved that Marlene's theory about her son murdering Jolene had been right all along. 'Go and get a bottle of brandy from the shop round the corner, Fred. She's in shock, bless her,' Marge said to her husband.

When Frederick left the house, Marge held her traumatized friend in her arms. 'I'm sorry I ever doubted you about Barry, mate. I just never wanted to believe he was capable of murder, I suppose.'

'Oh, I always knew he was. I want no more to do with him after this little turnout, Marge. I never want to set eyes on him again.'

'I don't blame you, mate, but don't you think you should just warn Barry that Jolene's father is on his tail? I know what Barry's done is bang out of order, but he is still your son, mate. I'll ring him for you if you like?'

'No, you fucking won't! After what that little bastard has just put his poor mother through, he can rot in hell as far as I'm concerned,' Marlene said callously.

Marge eyed Marlene suspiciously, but said nothing. Knowing her pal as well as she did, she couldn't help but wonder if Marlene was hoping to get her hands on her son's fortune. Barry had no children, neither was he married, and if the lad popped his clogs, Marlene would more than likely cop the lot.

Stephanie was awoken by her mother coming into her room with a breakfast tray. On it was a mug of steaming hot tea and a boiled egg with toast. The toast was cut into what she used to call soldiers as a kid, and the fact that she had carried on the same theme with Dannielle immediately made her feel very sad. 'Thanks, Mum, but I'm really not hungry. I'll drink the tea though,' Steph said, lifting it off the tray.

Pam put the tray down on the carpet and sat on the edge of Steph's bed. 'Probably a silly question, but how did you sleep?'

'Bloody awful! Every time I closed my eyes, I had the most terrible thoughts going through my mind, so I tried to keep them open. I was still awake at six, so I must have dozed off just after that. I checked on Tyler about four times in the night just in case he'd been sick. I was worried about him choking on his own vomit.'

Pam squeezed her daughter's hand. Tyler had arrived home about ten o'clock the previous night and had been so drunk he could barely stand up. 'Ty's fine now. He's just gobbled up a big plate of egg and bacon I cooked him, so he certainly ain't suffering from any after-effects. I was gonna give him a bollocking, but I'd thought I'd best leave that to you.'

'Ty getting pissed is the last of my worries at the moment, Mum. I think I'm gonna take a drive around Chigwell, see if I can spot that Range Rover. We've got most of the registration in the photograph, so it's either that or ring the police and report Danni missing. I cannot spend another day worrying. I need to find Danni and tell her the truth about everything.'

About to reply, Steph's landline rang. 'You answer it, Mum. Unless it's Danni, I don't want to talk to anyone. Just say I'm ill.'

'Hello,' Pam said.

'Oh, I'm glad it's you, Pam. It's Cath.'

'Everything all right?' Pam asked, guessing that Cathy had just rung up to check if things were OK her end.

'Well yeah, but I had to ring you in case this might be important. Your Angie turned up at yours late afternoon yesterday. Anyway, I heard knocking, so went outside to investigate. I just said you were out 'cause I know you don't like her knowing any of Steph's business. Anyway, she turned up again this morning and knocked on my door. I never said anything to her, I swear I didn't, but she asked if you had stayed at Steph's and then said she had some information about Dannielle for you. She said it's really important and she asked if I could ring you. She's sitting outside in the car as we speak. Do you wanna talk to her?'

'Go get her and put her on the phone, Cath,' Pam said immediately.

'Who is it?' Steph whispered.

'It's Cath. Angie has turned up round there. She reckons she has some important information about Danni.'

Stephanie jumped up as swiftly as a jack-in-the-box. 'I don't want that bitch knowing anything. She'll fucking love it, she will,' she spat.

'Let's just see what she has to say. Surely finding Danni and getting her home safely is more important than yours and your sister's bloody feud?' Pam replied, sensibly.

When Steph stomped out of the room in a huff, Angela came to the phone seconds later. 'Hello, love. Cath said you had something urgent you wanted to speak to me about.'

'Yeah, I do. I was unsure whether to tell you at first as I didn't think you'd believe me, but the more I've thought about it, the more I knew I couldn't live with myself if I didn't say something.'

'Get to the point then, love,' Pam said bluntly.

'I went out for lunch yesterday with my old school pal Chloe. Anyway, we happened to stop at a pub in Chigwell. We were gonna have a quick drink, until I saw Dannielle come out the pub with some bloke. I only saw the back of the man, but Chloe said he was definitely older than me and her. She also said that he looked like a villain. Well, obviously, I was extremely worried about Danni, so I followed the Range Rover they got in.'

'Did you get an address?'

'Well, I followed them to the house, but I didn't see the name of the road or anything,' Angela replied, a bit taken aback. It was obvious by her mother's reaction that Danni's sordid little secret was already out in the open.

'Would you know how to get there again?'

'I think I would if I drove from the pub where I first spotted Danni.'

Pam breathed a sigh of relief. 'Will you come over to Steph's straight away? I'll give you her address.'

Glad to be a help to her family rather than a hindrance for once, Angela immediately agreed.

Unaware that his life was currently in danger, Barry rubbed his erection against Dannielle's thigh. 'No woman I've met in my life has ever made me feel the way you do,' he whispered in her ear.

Instead of responding to his sexual advances like she usually did, Dannielle got out of bed.

'What's the matter?' Barry asked, worried. Surely she hadn't had second thoughts about their relationship?

'We need to sort this out with my mum asap, Barry. It's really worrying me now.'

Erection deflated, Barry leapt out of bed and hugged his young girlfriend. 'It will only take me half an hour to shower and stuff me face, then I will go and speak to your mum.'

'I'm coming with you. I think it will be better if we speak to her together,' Dannielle insisted.

About to argue the point, Barry heard a noise downstairs.

'What was that?' Dannielle asked.

'I dunno. Get yourself dressed and wait here, OK? Do not say a word and do not come downstairs,' Barry whispered, putting on a pair of tracksuit bottoms to cover his prize asset. Over in Spain, Barry had kept all sorts of weapons indoors, but for obvious reasons he hadn't been able to bring them to England with him. He would never have got through customs.

Barry crept downstairs and checked the front door first. It was still locked, so he then decided to check the other rooms. Stepping cautiously into the lounge, Barry gasped as a big hand grabbed him and covered his mouth.

'One word and you're dead,' a voice said, as a gun was placed at Barry's temple.

Jolene's father was a scouser and there was no mistaking his voice. 'I can explain,' Barry tried to say, as thick black tape was put over his mouth.

Ordering Barry to lie face down on the carpet, Mickey tied his legs and arms together with the thick tape as well. Satisfied that there was no way Barry could move, Mickey crept upstairs to find the unwanted house guest. He'd heard a woman's voice, and it had made his blood reach boiling point to think that his daughter was barely cold and the scumbag who had killed her had already moved on. Perhaps that was the reason why Barry had chosen to kill Jolene in the first place?

'There you are. I was getting worried,' Dannielle said, as

the bedroom door slowly opened. Seconds later, she let out a blood curdling scream.

Stephanie glared at her younger sister as she followed their mother into her lounge. 'I bet you're loving all this, aren't you? Must have made your year?' Steph asked, sarcastically.

'Actually, I'm not loving it. I might not know Dannielle particularly well, but my Aidan reckons she's a lovely girl. I don't want to see her come to any harm, hence why I went round Mum's,' Angela explained.

'Now, no silliness, please. Come on, let's go. What we waiting for?' Pam said, standing up and motioning to Lin to do the same.

Stephanie stood up. 'Actually, I would rather go with Angie on my own. I don't want a big entourage with me. I need to sort this myself.'

A bit put out, Pam and Lin sat back down on the sofa. Both women had wanted to give Barry Franklin a piece of their minds, and now the opportunity to do so had been taken away from them. 'I really don't like the idea of yous two going alone. Say that pervert attacks you or something?' Pam said.

'I agree. That man is obviously a fucking animal and could be capable of anything,' Lin added.

'Don't worry. I won't leave Steph alone with this bloke,' Angela promised. She was a bit confused as to why her mum and aunt were talking as though they knew Danni's boyfriend. Perhaps he was a family friend or something? Angela wondered.

With an icy expression on her face, Stephanie turned to her younger sister. 'Come on then, let's go.'

Dannielle was petrified as the man put thick tape over her mouth and then around her hands and feet. Who was this man? What did he want? Worse still, had he hurt Barry?

Mickey picked up a mobile phone off the bedside cabinet and waved it in Dannielle's face. 'Is this yours?'

Trembling as though she had a bad case of Parkinson's disease, Dannielle shook her head from side to side.

Guessing it must be Barry's, Mickey spotted a handbag on the carpet next to the wardrobe. 'Bingo,' he mumbled, as he tipped it upside down and picked up what was obviously the girl's mobile phone. Mickey very much doubted that Barry or the young girl would be able to escape because he had bound them up so well, but you could never be too careful. He had already checked downstairs for a landline when he had entered the house via the unlocked back door, and cut the phone wire. Clocking the 'scared rabbit caught in headlights' look in Dannielle's eyes, Mickey felt a pang of guilt. The poor girl was only young – didn't look much older than a schoolkid – and that made him hate Barry even more, if that were possible. 'I'm not going to hurt you, I promise. Just lie down on the bed and I'll untie you soon,' he said, softly.

Mickey shut the bedroom door, took a deep breath, and leant against it. The petrified look in the girl's eyes had thrown him a bit. The quicker he got on with the job he'd come here to do, the better. The girl might not thank him now, but little did she know by ridding the earth of her evil bastard of a boyfriend, he was actually doing her a massive favour in the long run.

Mickey walked back down the stairs. He already knew the exact story he was going to tell the Old Bill. The gun his pal had lent him was just a replica. He daren't have carried a real one, as he knew as soon as he'd set eyes on Barry's cocky face, he would have shot him to pieces. Serving a life sentence over that piece of shit was something Mickey wasn't willing to do. Stabbing Barry to death with the dagger that his pal had also given him was a much better option. It enabled him to tell the courts he had acted in self-defence. The plan was, he was going to force Barry to hold the dagger in his grubby little hands, so it had plenty of his fingerprints on it. The dagger was fingerprint free at the moment. Mickey's pal had worn gloves to handle it and so had he. Mickey wasn't stupid; he knew he had to look like he had fought Barry hard, so he was going to head-butt a door and stab himself in the arm a couple of times to make the situation look realistic. His story to the Old Bill was going to be: he had taped Barry up to find out the truth about what had happened to his daughter, Barry had managed to break free, then had attacked him and tried to kill him. Mickey had been pissed off when he had first heard the female voice upstairs and realized Barry had company. Now, though, he had a feeling it might work in his favour, as he could tell the Old Bill that Barry had escaped when he had taped the girl up.

Walking back into the lounge, Mickey smirked as he caught sight of Barry Franklin. With his bare chest and arms tied behind his back, he reminded Mickey of a Christmas turkey waiting to be put in the oven. Taking the replica gun out of his pocket, Mickey walked towards his victim. Before calling the police, he needed to hide the gun in a bush somewhere nearby, so his pal could collect it later. Neither Marlene nor Dannielle had seen the gun and, seeing as Barry would be dead before he called the police, the Old Bill had no need to search for it. Barry put the handle of the dagger in between Barry's hands. 'Hold it,' he ordered.

Guessing that Mickey was planning to kill him and then cry self-defence, Barry let the dagger slip through his fingers and shook his head vehemently. He desperately wanted to speak, but couldn't because of the tape over his mouth. All

Barry could do now was hope and pray that Mickey Jeffers removed the tape before killing him. Barry could then tell the stupid scouse bastard the truth.

Stephanie sat in silence as her sister tried to make polite conversation with her. Angela had just asked her if she knew who the bloke was who Dannielle was dating. And Steph had completely blanked the question. Knowing what a bitch her sister could be, it would not surprise Steph if Angie had recognized Barry Franklin herself and turned up today just to milk the horrendous situation.

'I'm sure this is the right way now. I recognize that big house on the corner,' Angela said. She had got lost and had to turn around a couple of minutes ago, and had clocked the look of displeasure on her sister's sour face.

'I bet you don't even know where the fucking house is. You probably only turned up to stick your beak in and gloat,' Steph said nastily.

Sick of her sister's pissy attitude, Angela chose to stick up for herself. 'You are so bloody wrong about me, Steph. I know I was a bitch in the past and I'm sorry for that, but since moving back from Greece and building a relationship with Aidan, I really have changed. I'm a much nicer person now than I used to be.'

'Yeah, and pigs might fly,' Stephanie mumbled under her breath.

'This is it! This is the road where I followed Danni to,' Angela exclaimed.

'Which house is it?' Steph spat, undoing her seatbelt. She had the meat knife she had sharpened the previous day in her handbag, and if Barry Franklin refused to let Danni go, she would shove it right through his heart.

Angela pulled over on the corner of the road and put the handbrake on. 'It's the house opposite the red jeep. Providing this bloke's at home, you will see the black Range Rover on the drive. I'm coming with you, Steph. I can't let you do this alone,' she insisted, putting her car keys in her handbag.

Stephanie stared at her sister's perfectly made-up face and shook her head. Angie might have been a cow over the years, but she was still her sister and there was no way Steph could involve her in a murder charge. 'Go back to mine, Ange. Mum and Lin are gonna need you more than I do.'

As Steph slammed the car door, Angela felt the hairs on the back of her neck stand up. She had clocked the unhinged look in Stephanie's eyes and guessed she might be planning to do something stupid. Grabbing her handbag, Angie leapt out the car. She had to stop Steph from ruining her life. She owed her that much at least.

Mickey Jeffers crouched down next to Barry and ripped the tape off his mouth. 'Did she suffer?' he asked, his face contorted with grief.

Barry took deep breaths. He had truly thought he was going to die momentarily, and the thought of never seeing Dannielle again was far worse than the thought of death itself. 'Jolene's still alive! I swear I can prove it if you give me my phone. I've got a number for her now. She's staying in Marbella with a girl called Ellie.'

'Don't fucking lie to me, you slimy little cunt. My Jolene would never put me and her mother through the hell we've been through the past month or so if she were still alive. She would have contacted us, I know she would,' Mickey yelled.

'She didn't contact you because if I didn't get back with her, she wanted me dead. She said if she couldn't marry me and have my kids, then she'd make sure that no other woman would. Just take the tape off my hands and I'll ring her and prove it to you, Mickey. Hell hath no fury like a woman scorned, and Jo's lost the plot, I'm telling you. She only gave me her fucking number because she thinks I'm gonna get back with her now. I've even booked a ticket to fly out to see her on Friday because I wanted to sort this shit out. I don't want all my old pals in Spain to think I've bastard well killed her, do I? As soon as I got there, I was gonna make her ring you,' Barry insisted.

'I'll ring the fucking make-believe number,' Mickey said, snarling as he took Barry's mobile out of his own pocket. The young girl's phone was pink, so there was no getting them mixed up.

'No! Please! Just let me ring her. If she hears your voice, she'll end the call. Give me the phone and I'll put it on loudspeaker so you can hear every word she says. Honest to God, I am not lying to you, Mickey. Why would I make all this stuff up when I know if I couldn't prove Jo was alive, you would shoot me anyway?' Barry said. If Mickey didn't let him make this phone call, he was as good as a dead man.

'If she don't answer, you're dead,' Mickey growled, cutting the tape in between Barry's hands.

Barry said a silent prayer as his shaking hands scrolled through his phone. He had been ringing her four times a day just to keep her sweet, and every single time, she had answered within seconds. Breathing a massive sigh of relief as he heard the familiar sound of her voice, Barry pressed the loudspeaker button.

'Why didn't you ring me earlier at the time you said you was going to?' Jolene asked accusingly.

Absolutely gobsmacked, Mickey Jeffers sat on his haunches and put his head in his hands. Half of him was so happy that his beautiful daughter was still alive, yet the other half of him wanted to kill her himself for making such a fool out of him and putting him and her mother through such heartbreak.

Hearing his daughter start to interrogate Barry again, Mickey snatched the phone out of Barry's hand. 'Jo, it's your dad. You've got some fucking explaining to do, girl, I know that much. Ring your mother immediately and let her know you're OK. Then I expect you to go straight home and apologize in fucking person to her. Broken our hearts, you have.'

When Jolene began sobbing like a baby, Mickey heard a frantic banging on the front door.

'Danni, Danni, open this door now. I know you're in there. I know everything,' a woman's voice screamed.

Recognizing Stephanie's dulcet tones, Barry snatched the phone off Mickey and ended the call. 'Quick, get this tape off me legs. Where's Danni?'

'Upstairs, I taped her up as well. I'll go and set her free,' Mickey said, cutting the tape around Barry's ankles.

'I'll free her meself. You just put that dagger and gun away and get rid of all the tape. The woman knocking on the door is Dannielle's mother, and I don't wanna give her any more reason to kick off than she already has,' Barry spat, darting up the stairs.

'I know you're in there, Barry. I've just heard your voice, you paeodophiliac murdering bastard. I know what you did to my Wayne. I know it was you who killed him,' Stephanie screamed hysterically.

'Stop, Steph. Please stop it, or you'll hurt yourself,' Angela said, as her sister picked up a brick and smashed it against one of the bay windows.

Stephanie turned to Angela. 'I thought I told you to go back to mine and look after Mum and Lin for me. Fuck off. Go on, fuck off,' she yelled.

'I'm not leaving you like this, I can't,' Angela said. Stephanie looked and was acting like a mad woman, and for the first time ever, Angela was truly concerned for her welfare. Why was she rambling on about Wayne being murdered? It didn't make any sense.

'Where is he? Where's Barry?' Stephanie yelled, when a shaven-headed man opened the front door.

Angela was stunned as she followed her sister into the lounge and recognized Barry Franklin. No wonder Stephanie had been so upset.

Stephanie felt physically sick as she saw that her daughter was sitting on the sofa, holding hands with Barry. She wanted to take the knife out of her bag and repeatedly stab Barry with it, but she couldn't do that in front of Dannielle. It would scar her daughter for life. 'Get away from him, Danni. You don't know him, he's evil,' she screamed.

'No, he's not! Look, Mum, I'm sorry I lied to you, but I love Barry and we just wanna be together. I need you to accept our relationship. Can you do that? Please, for me?' Dannielle asked, in an adult manner. She was showing no signs of the frightening ordeal she had just been through. When Barry had untied her, he'd told her that the shaven-haired man was his ex-girlfriend's father, and him turning up today was just a silly misunderstanding. He said he would explain properly later. He had also said that she needed to be and act strong when facing her mother.

Stephanie shook her head. 'I will never accept you being with him, Danni, and I mean never. Has he told you that he killed your father, has he?' she yelled. She wanted to add 'and slept with your mother', but was far too ashamed to do so.

Seeing her daughter's eyes well up with tears, Steph was relieved to see her daughter snatch her hand away from Barry's. 'Barry is a wrong 'un, darling, a murderer. You can't date a man who is responsible for killing your own father, can you now? Just get your stuff together, Danni, and come home with me.'

'You didn't kill my dad, did you?' Dannielle asked Barry. To say she was astounded over the awful accusation was an understatement.

Angela, Stephanie and Mickey all glanced at one another as Barry began to laugh. Wondering if he was about to lose the plot, Mickey decided to make his escape. 'I'm gonna go now, Barry. I'm sorry about the silly misunderstanding. I can't apologize enough. Are we OK?'

Still laughing, Barry stood up and turned to Mickey. He was enjoying himself now, really enjoying himself, and the best bit was yet to come. 'Yeah, we're best buddies, you muggy cunt. Go on, fuck off, and do me a favour, keep that loony of a daughter of yours away from me in future. If I have any more grief from her, I shall have to hold you entirely responsible, *comprende*?'

Mickey Jeffers was no man's fool. 'Who you calling a muggy cunt? You cockney twat,' he said, lunging at Barry.

'Leave him alone or I'm calling the police. I'll tell them everything,' Dannielle screamed, as both men fell to the floor, brawling.

The word police was enough to make Mickey see sense. He'd just tied two people up, had a dagger and a fake gun on him, and had also terrorized Marlene. He stood up, picked up his bag and bolted out of the front door. His old woman would kill him if he got banged up. The quicker he jumped on the first available flight back to Spain, the better.

Barry decided to let Mickey go rather than chase after the cheeky bastard. 'Me and you ain't finished, Jeffers,' he shouted. Turning back to Stephanie, Barry grinned. 'Where was we before I was so rudely interrupted? Oh yes, we were talking about your wonderful doting fiancé, wasn't we?'

'Don't you dare take the piss out of my Wayne. He was a lovely man and a good partner. We would have still been extremely happy now, if you hadn't fucking done away with him. It was all about revenge for you, wasn't it, Barry? Revenge, because I chose Wayne over you at fifteen years old. You're sick, do you know that? And I know that is why you've now got your claws into my daughter. You don't want her, nor do you love her; you just want to get back at me once again for what happened when we were kids,' Stephanie said, walking over to Barry and smacking him around his cocky face.

'Leave him, Steph. He ain't worth it, sis,' Angela said, pulling Stephanie away.

'For your information, I love your daughter more than I've ever loved any other woman in my life,' Barry said, truthfully.

'She ain't a woman. She's a child, you perverted piece of fucking shit,' Steph said, lunging at Barry, fists flailing.

'Stop it, Mum. Stop it,' Dannielle screamed.

Grabbing Stephanie's wrists, Barry glared at her. 'If anyone's a piece of shit here, darling, that's you.'

'Stop it, the pair of you. You're upsetting Danni. Look at the state of her,' Angela said, cuddling her niece.

Dannielle's thoughts were all over the place. Barry was so kind and loving towards her, she could never imagine him hurting a fly. But if what her mum was saying was true, then she would have to finish with him. She didn't really remember her dad that well, but sharing a bed with the man that murdered him made her feel sick to the stomach. 'I need to know what happened with my dad, Barry. What is Mum talking about?' Dannielle asked, dreading the answer.

'He killed your father, Dannielle. Murdered him on his stag night, the wicked fucking schemer,' Stephanie said, thankful that the penny had finally started to drop.

Barry started to laugh again. He hated Stephanie so much, he wanted to milk this situation for all it was worth before he delivered the final blow.

Annoyed that her boyfriend was finding her dad's death so funny, Dannielle walked over to her mum and gave her a big hug.

'It's OK, Danni. I knew you'd see sense in the end. We're going home soon, darling,' Stephanie said, soothingly.

Barry leapt off the sofa. It was time to shove Stephanie's words and dumb accusations right down her bitter, twisted throat. Barry walked over to the other sofa, put his hand underneath one of the cushions and produced an envelope. ''Ere you go, sweetheart. All the answers about what happened to your loving, doting fiancé are in there. As for calling me wicked and a schemer, I think you'll find that good old Wayne wins that contest hands down. He's the schemer, Steph, not me, girl. Have a butcher's inside the envelope, go on,' Barry urged her.

The envelope had Spanish writing on the outside, and when Stephanie put her hand inside, she pulled out another envelope which she knew contained photographs. Her heart was beating like a drum. She didn't know what to expect.

'I'd sit down if I was you,' Barry said cockily, as he put an arm around Dannielle's shoulders and kissed her on the top of the head.

'No! It can't be him. It must be somebody who looks like him,' Stephanie stammered in disbelief when she looked at the first photograph.

Angela stared over her sister's shoulder. 'Fucking hell, Steph. It is him!'

'It is who?' Danni asked anxiously.

'Your dad,' Barry replied bluntly.

When Stephanie looked at the next photo, she sank to her knees in shock. Wayne was standing next to a big boat, looking as happy as Larry. He looked tanned and much older than when she had last seen him, but there was no mistaking it was him.

Stephanie could barely breathe. 'How could he do it to me? How could he?' she croaked.

'Unfuckingbelievable! What a no-good, evil bastard,' Angela spat, as she snatched the photo out of her sister's hand to take a closer look. There was no mistaking it was Wayne in the photo. His smarmy grin stood out like a beacon.

Barry couldn't help but smirk as the stunned, open-mouthed Stephanie started to sift through the rest of the photographs. While living in Fuengirola, he had heard through the Spanish grapevine that Wayne was alive and well and larging it in Alicante, so he had hired a private investigator to find out the truth. He had been well chuffed to find out that the rumours were true, as he'd had a strong hunch that he might one day use the evidence to his advantage. Falling in love with Dannielle hadn't been planned, it was coincidence, but even if he had never met the love of his life, Barry would still have made sure that Steph found out about her beloved Wayne one day. After the way she had treated him, she deserved to not only be hurt, but to also know the truth. Now, as he watched Stephanie's tearful face flicking through the thirty or so photographs, Barry knew she had finally got her just deserts. One day, he would also make sure that Wayne Jackman got his as well.

When Steph threw the photos onto the sofa, Dannielle grabbed them. 'I can't believe my dad did this to us. Why would he pretend to go missing? And why would he abandon me and Tyler?' she sobbed.

'Because he was a no-good fucking arsehole,' Angela replied, holding Stephanie in her arms.

'If your mother would like to look through the rest of

the photos, she will learn exactly why your dad decided to do a runner,' Barry said to Dannielle. He knew he was being a bit callous, but he just couldn't help himself.

'You're really fucking enjoying this, aren't you?' Angela asked Barry, as Stephanie snatched the photos back off Dannielle.

'No, I'm not actually. But I do want to spend the rest of my life with Dannielle, so the quicker all this shit is out the way, the better,' Barry replied. He knew what was coming next, and he couldn't wait to see the look of utter disbelief on Stephanie's sour face when she finally learned why Wayne had left her.

'Fucking paedo,' Angela mumbled.

'No, no, no, no, noooo,' Stephanie screamed, collapsing to her knees again.

'What is it, Mum? Who is that woman?' Dannielle asked, picking up the photo her mum had been holding.

Angela leant over her niece's shoulder and couldn't believe her eyes. There was no mistaking that auburn hair and mysterious grin. The woman and Wayne were sitting together like love's young dream, sipping cocktails on a boat. 'Oh my God, Steph! I'm so, so sorry for you,' Angela said, crouching down next to her devastated sister.

Howling like a severely wounded animal, Stephanie clung to Angela like a leech.

'Everything will be OK, Steph. I know I've never been there for you in the past, but I'm here for you now. I'm your sister, I love you, and together we'll get through this, I promise.'

Suddenly aware of the devastation his bombshell had caused, Barry hung his head in shame. He wasn't a bad person, yet for years he had harboured a hatred and grudge against Steph for something that had happened when they were no more than kids. 'I'm sorry, Steph. I'm sorry about

Wayne and about the way you've found out,' he mumbled, trying to make amends.

'Drop dead, you evil bastard,' Angela spat, as she tried to help her crestfallen sister stand up.

'Who is the woman in the photo? Will someone fucking tell me who she is?' Dannielle screamed.

Knowing that he could now finally forget the past, Barry grabbed hold of his future and held her close to his chest. 'The woman in those photos was your mum's best friend at school and for many years afterwards. Her name is Tammy.'

Epilogue

Tammy Andrews swam up to the boat and screamed as loudly as she could as the engine started up. 'Wayne, please don't leave me here. I'm pregnant,' she yelled in vain. She desperately tried to claw her way up the side of the boat, but it was a fruitless idea. She was wet, the boat was slippery, and there was nothing to grab hold of to yank herself back onboard.

What had she done to deserve this? she thought to herself as the boat started to pull away from her. Then she remembered exactly what she had done to deserve it. She had betrayed her best friend in the worst possible way known to womankind. Perhaps this was God's way of paying her back.

Tammy had never intended on falling in love with Wayne Jackman. It had just happened, and their six-month affair had been extremely intense before they had finally run away together. There never had been any boyfriend called Richard. It had all been Wayne's idea for her to make up that story; the 'Richard' who Tammy had introduced to her family and friends had actually been a chap from a London escort agency whose real name was Toby. Toby hadn't been aware of the whole set-up. On Wayne's advice, Tammy had told him that she needed to pretend to her family and friends that she was moving to Spain with him, because she was actually a lesbian and was moving there with her girlfriend, Susan. Tammy had explained to Toby that she was desperate to keep her sexuality a secret, which is why she had hired him to play the role of Richard. Tammy had hated not being able to tell her mum, dad and sister the truth. She had loved Wayne so much that she had wanted to scream it from the rooftops. But how could she when she had stolen her man from her best friend and he was on the missing list, presumed dead?

Tammy began to sob as the boat began to disappear out of sight. All she had ever wanted was for Wayne to love her, and to have his baby, and after two miscarriages, she finally thought her dream of being a mother was about to come true. Losing two babies had made Tammy feel like a failure at the time, which is why she had decided not to tell Wayne about this pregnancy until she had got past the dreaded twelve-week mark. She had told her mum and sister the news over the phone, just because she'd had to tell someone. They obviously thought that Richard was the proud father-to-be. The same imaginary Richard, who never came with her when she visited them in England because he was too busy working. Many a time, her parents and sister had asked to visit her in Spain, and Tammy had had to fob them off with lie after lie. She'd hated doing that, but what choice did she have?

Tammy had never felt so scared in all her life as she stared at the loneliness of the ocean. She was an extremely strong swimmer, had won numerous awards in the sport as a child, but Wayne had obviously chosen his moment to literally dump her. She was miles and miles away from the shore and there were no other vessels in sight. About to give up, Tammy thought about the life growing inside her. She couldn't just admit defeat; she had to fight for the sake of her baby. Absolutely petrified, Tammy saw a dot in the distance and guessed it was probably a boat of some kind. Hope renewed, she started to swim towards it as though her life depended on it. And for the first time ever, it actually did.

Wayne Jackman felt a mixture of guilt and relief as he headed back towards the coastline. He hadn't been in love with Tammy for some time now, but he certainly hadn't hated her either. Ending her life hadn't been Wayne's preferred method of ending their relationship, but due to their unusual circumstances, it was the only answer.

Deciding to have one last reminisce before he blocked Tammy out of his mind forever, Wayne thought back to when they had first got together. He had loved Tammy back then. He must have really loved her to abandon Stephanie and his two young children in the callous way that he had. Like many relationships that begin at such a young age, Wayne had begun to get itchy feet with Steph by the time he was twenty-one. Being tied down with one kid at such a young age was bad enough, but then Steph fell pregnant with Tyler. That was roughly the time when Wayne's wandering eye went into overdrive. First he had a few one-night stands, and then a three-month affair with an older woman who trained at his gym, but it was all just a bit of meaningless fun. Wayne's feelings for Tammy were different, though. He had loved her company and had watched her change over the years from a plain schoolgirl into a ravishing beauty. Wayne had always looked forward to the nights that Tammy visited Steph. He loved hearing about her high-flying career and her social life up town, and he and Tammy would sit up for hours drinking champagne after Stephanie had gone to bed. It was on one of these evenings that they shared their very first kiss and from that moment it was all systems go. The sexual tension between them had been simmering for quite a long time, and when they finally made love in a hotel room up town, the magical experience almost blew Wayne's mind.

From that day onwards, Wayne couldn't get enough of Tammy. As their affair deepened, so did Tammy's guilt. She hated betraying her best friend, so told Wayne he had to make his choice. Wayne chose Tammy and with the help of his father, dreamed up the plan for his disappearance. Everything from that moment on was organized meticulously. Firstly, there was the massive fall-out with his dad. That had been staged just before his father had left for Spain to find them all somewhere to live. Then, there was the build-up to the wedding. Wayne had felt extremely guilty watching Stephanie's excitement as their wedding day neared, but his feelings for Tammy somehow outweighed his guilt. Wayne also felt incredibly bad about leaving his children, especially Dannielle. Tyler had only been a toddler at the time and, even though Wayne didn't like to admit it, the boy's temper tantrums and overall behaviour had driven him to the edge of destruction.

Apart from his father and his grandparents, the only other person in the know was his cousin, Billy Jackman. Wayne hadn't known how his cousin Billy would react, as he was a father himself, but Wayne had needed to receive regular updates on his kids, so he had taken the chance and explained the situation. Billy had understood and had been brilliant over the years. He had sent photos and relayed any snippets of information he heard, and that's how Wayne had watched and heard about his children growing up. In return for his cousin's loyalty, Billy and his family had loads of free holidays at Wayne's expense. They never stayed with him and Tammy, though, as Billy's wife was kept in the dark about the set-up.

Obviously, Wayne could not use his real name when he moved abroad and it had been Wayne's dad who had sorted out his false indentity. His dad had met a fraudster in prison who had a contact inside the passport office, and Wayne was given new documentation in the name of Warren Fisher. Tammy had hated his new surname and Wayne could remember her joking that she could never marry him now as she would hate being called Mrs Fisher. The hardest part of the actual plot itself was the build-up to his stag night. Wayne had already sold his business and transferred the money abroad; then he'd had to play the destitute pauper role, which he had hated. He'd even got sick of hearing himself ramble on to the lads at the gym and then Barry, Danno, Potter and Cooksie about how bloody skint he was. But it had had to be done; it was part of the plan. The idea was that the Old Bill would think that Wayne was so up to his eyeballs in debt that, rather than tell his beautiful bride about his financial dilemma, he had decided to end his own life instead. That had been why he had gone to see his GP. He'd even discussed his make-believe black thoughts with his doctor and got given antidepressants.

Barry turning up out of the blue was not part of the plan, but once Wayne learned that his old pal was back in England, he thought he would use him as another pawn in his game. That's when Tammy had played her part. Wayne ordered her to try and convince Steph that Barry Franklin was responsible for his disappearance. Even though he was leaving, Wayne didn't want Barry getting his feet under the table; he had hoped Steph would become suspicious of him and banish him from her life. It hadn't quite worked out that way, though, as Barry and Steph were still as thick as thieves when Tammy followed him out to Spain six weeks later. Wayne hated that thought, but never admitted it to Tammy.

The night of his actual disappearance went without a hitch. Wayne had taken his sports bag with him to the hotel and had left it packed with vital pieces of information. The antidepressants, brochures of beauty salons, and the pawnbroker's receipt were all left for the Old Bill to find, along with some clothes. Wayne had also gone to the club where Angela worked on purpose, as he wanted to spin her the tale about how awful he felt because he couldn't afford to buy Steph the beauty salon he had promised her as a wedding present. He'd then left the club alone at midnight and met Tammy, who had driven him straight to the airport. From that moment on, he was no longer Wayne Jackman, he was Warren Fisher.

Wondering if Tammy was dead yet, Wayne turned the engine off and lit up a cigarette. It was time to stop thinking about the past now and concentrate on the future. Holding the cigarette between his recently bleached teeth, Wayne took his beloved photographs out of his pocket and stared at them. Stephanie looked absolutely stunning in them, and Wayne was really impressed she was now a successful businesswoman. Flicking through the photos, Wayne stared at Tyler and grinned. His son looked uncannily like he had at the same age; just the way he was standing with his hands in his pockets in his trendy Adidas tracksuit told Wayne that he was not the backward boy he'd once thought his son would turn out to be. Putting the photo to the bottom of the pile, Wayne stared at his beautiful daughter. Dannielle was a young woman now and that worried Wayne immensely. She reminded him so much of Steph when she was younger, but Danni was much more glamorous in appearance and looked striking enough to be a top model. Wayne sighed. His daughter was ripe pickings for some flash Harry, but instead of being there to protect her, like most dads would be, he'd wasted ten years of watching her grow up by sunning himself in poxy Spain. He had heard recently that Danni had been spotted out and about with some old geezer – over his dead body was he going to continue larging it in Spain while his daughter chucked her life away. The thought of some old bloke mauling his little girl made Wayne feel physically sick and he couldn't expect Steph to deal with shit like that. It was his duty as a father to sort it.

Restarting the engine of his boat, Wayne made a pact to himself. As soon as he moored and got back to his apartment, he was going to book a flight to England. Now Tammy was out of the picture, there was nothing stopping him from sorting the mess out he'd created for himself and his family. Reuniting with them was not going to be an easy task, but he had his story well prepared. Wayne smirked. If anyone could pull such a story off, then he could. After all, he was the schemer of all schemers.

Read on for an extract from
Kimberley's next book
The Trap

Coming January 2013

If you trap the moment before it's ripe,
The tears of repentance you certainly wipe;
But if once you let the ripe moment go,
You can never wipe off the tears of woe.

William Blake

Prologue

1965

Unable to make himself heard above Sandie Shaw belting out 'Long Live Love', Donald Walker made his way over to the Wurlitzer jukebox and turned the volume down.

'Don't do that! You know I like Sandie,' Mary Walker said, as though she knew the singer personally.

'There's somebody knocking at the door,' Donald informed his wife.

Mary walked over to the door and unbolted it. She was greeted by a sturdy-looking woman in a dark grey overcoat. Mary guessed she was probably in her mid-fifties, but it was hard to be sure because of the curlers and hairnet on her head. 'Hello. Can I help you?' Mary asked, politely.

'No, but I can help you,' the woman replied, barging her way past Mary and into the premises.

Donald and Mary knew very little about the East End or its natives. They were North Londoners and had lived in Stoke Newington for many years, but this café in Whitechapel had been far too cheap to turn down, which is why they had decided to up sticks and move.

'Hello, I'm Donald and this is my wife, Mary. As you

have probably already realized, we are the new owners of the café. We officially open for business tomorrow but, would you like a cup of tea or coffee?' Donald asked, politely.

Shaking her head, the woman held out her right hand. 'I'm Freda. Freda Smith. I live just around the corner.'

'And how can you help us?' Mary enquired. She had a feeling that Freda was about to ask for a job, but there was no chance of that, as her and Donald had spent every penny they had refurbishing the rundown café and were in no position to employ staff just yet.

'I can help you by telling you why this café has been empty for eighteen long months before you bought it, and why you probably got it for peanuts,' Freda spat.

Mary gave her husband a worried glance. This café had been half the price of any others they had looked at, and the only one within their meagre price range. But this woman seemed unhinged, somehow, and Mary wondered if she held a grudge against the previous owner.

'Would you like a glass of water?' Donald asked. He had noticed that beads of sweat were forming on the woman's forehead and had now started to drip onto one of his brand new melamine tables.

'No, don't want nuffink. Just come to let you know the score. No one else round 'ere will tell you. They're all too bleedin' well frightened of 'em, but I ain't.'

'Frightened of who?' Mary asked, perplexed.

'Frightened of the Butlers. They own that snooker club just around the corner. Old Jack who used to own this café, they killed his son, Peter. Broke his wife Ethel's heart it did, and if you don't abide by their rules, they'll rip the heart out of your family too. I saw you move in. You got two little kids, ain't ya? Well, if you just do as I say, you'll be okay. Albie's the dad. He's a pisshead, a proper waster. The mother is the brains of the family. Hard-looking old cow called Queenie. Her sister is Vivvy, she has a mongol son, and Queenie's kids are Vinny, who is the worst out the bunch, Roy, Michael and young Brenda. When they come in here, look after 'em. Serve 'em before any other customers and don't charge 'em for food or drinks, you get me?'

Seeing the distressed look on his wife's face, Donald was extremely annoyed. Opening their café tomorrow was meant to be one of the best days of their lives, and yet this mad woman was here, upsetting his Mary and threatening to spoil such a joyous occasion. 'I can assure you, Freda, that Mary and I will not be giving free drinks or food to anybody and our customers will be served in the order they arrive in. Now, if you don't mind, could I please ask you to leave? Mary and I still have lots of work to do before we open tomorrow and we have very little time left to accomplish that task.'

Absolutely furious that her sound advice hadn't been listened to, Freda stood up, stomped towards Donald and poked him in the chest. 'Dig your own grave, what do I care? But, don't say I didn't warn you. The Butlers, remember the name,' she yelled, as Donald escorted her out of the cafe.

'Oh my God! What have we done, Donald? And who the hell are the Butlers?' Mary said, when her husband locked the door.

Donald took his wife in his arms. At six foot, he towered over Mary's five-foot frame. He was the man of the family and protect her he would. 'Do not worry yourself, my darling. Freda is obviously the mad local scaremonger. And even if that Butler family do come in here, we won't have any problems with them, I can absolutely assure you of that.'

Nestling herself against Donald's broad chest, Mary

breathed a sigh of relief. Her husband's instincts were never wrong.

Five minutes later the jukebox was back on and Mary and Donald were working happily side by side, singing in unison to the Beatles' 'Help!'. What they didn't realize was that, in the not too distant future, they would be needing help themselves. Every word that Freda Smart had spoken happened to be the truth. She wasn't mad, nor was she a scaremonger. She was just a realist who had done her utmost to warn a decent family of the perils of moving to Whitechapel.